THIS
CHARMING
MAN

By Ajax Bell

Queen City Boys Books:
Bad Reputation
This Charming Man

Novellas:
Star Quality

www.flickerjax.com

THIS
CHARMING
MAN

A QUEEN CITY BOYS BOOK

AJAX BELL

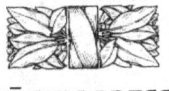

JŪGUM PRESS

First print edition: November 2014
ISBN-10: 1939423252
ISBN-13: 978-1-939423-25-2

Cover by Lisa Tilton Design
Cover copyright by Ajax Bell
Book design by Annie Pearson

Published by Jugum Press
505 Broadway East #237
Seattle, Washington
Find ebook editions at
www.jugumpress.net/ajaxbell
Contact:
JugumPress@outlook.com

For Michael W. Frazier

1964–2004

The world has not been as bright since your light went out,
but my love for you has never dimmed.

QUEEN CITY is often used to describe the largest city in a country, state, province, or territory that is not the capital. In 1869, Seattle was given the epithet "The Queen City of the Pacific." This lasted until 1982, when the Seattle–King County Convention and Visitors Bureau adopted "The Emerald City" as the new moniker. Seattle has many names: Jet City, Rain City, the City of Flowers, the City of Goodwill, the Emerald City. Still, some residents find the old name better recognizes the culture they live in and speaks to the hidden history of their city.

Contents

THIS
CHARMING
MAN

Part One

Summer 1991

1.
Unadulterated

"Bump?"

At the sink next to Steven, a man with jet-black hair and pale, unsettling eyes offered his hand. A tiny mountain of cocaine rested on the curve between his thumb and forefinger. The steady pulse of Moby's "Go" was audible through the club's bathroom walls, the pounding beat subdued just enough to make normal conversation possible.

"Oh, sure, thanks," Steven said.

The burn made his eyes water. Still sniffing, Steven tipped his head back so as not to smear his eyeliner. The man, smiling warmly, proffered a second bump. Steven took it, glad for the balance of the burn on both sides. He blinked in the mirror as reality slammed home: he'd swallowed a tab of ecstasy before he walked into the club, forgotten in the surprise of the cocaine offer.

Steven was about to be really fucking high.

"Thanks," he murmured again when the burn passed. He swallowed the bitter drip at the back of his throat, its taste comforting. A Pavlovian response, in anticipation of how he'd feel in a minute.

His cocaine benefactor leaned against the counter and watched as Steven ran a hand through his hair. Pleased with the attention, Steven straightened to show how his tight t-shirt fit his body. A lightness rolled through him, faint waves of pleasure not yet cresting. Either the cocaine was exceptionally good or it had pushed the ecstasy to come on quickly. He closed his eyes, every nerve vibrating with the music.

"I've seen you around. You're hot. Want to dance?"

"Oh." Steven snapped awake; he'd forgotten where he was. "Yeah, sure." A dance wasn't a bad trade for a couple of bumps. Despite his unnerving eyes, the guy was good looking. And Steven wasn't in a gay bar, all dressed up and high, just to stand around. Even if it was a fuck the guy wanted, Steven might be up for that.

"There you are."

Adrian banged into the bathroom, his silvery voice bouncing off the mirrors and tile, breaking through Steven's haze.

"I'll be out in a minute," Steven said to the black-haired man, who gave Adrian an appraising glance and then nodded pleasantly to Steven as he left.

There you are. The same words Adrian said the first time they met six years ago when, naïve for nineteen, Steven ventured out alone to Club Broadway. Adrian had grabbed him and declared, *There you are!* Unsure, Steven quietly asked, *Do I know you?* Adrian pressed his face into Steven's neck and whispered, *Just pretend, okay? I need you to rescue me from this guy who won't leave me alone.*

Years later, Adrian still greeted him with *There you are* in a way that sounded like *I need you.* And Steven was always there, whatever Adrian needed.

Now Adrian stood close behind, his hands on Steven's hips. The same height and similar builds, but their heads side by side in the mirror emphasized their differences: Steven, tawny with freckles and red hair; Adrian, angelic white, translucent skin glittering metallic with makeup, hair bleached to a platinum shock, and ice-blue eyes that froze you in place when he glanced your way. In darker moments, seeing his freckles as smudges that couldn't be rubbed away, Steven felt like an imperfect copy beside Adrian. Tonight, though, they were both perfect, not mirror images but rather a beautiful positive/negative pair.

Adrian shimmered in the reflection.

"Just you and me against the world," Adrian said to their reflections, his voice pitched for Steven's ear and no one else. "Look at us; we have what no one else has."

The ecstasy had come on and now both drugs pounded through Steven's veins. His heart raced to match the DJ's house beat throbbing up through the floor. Cocaine hadn't been the best idea.

Adrian moved from behind Steven. Even their clothes were opposites, coming from both ends of the color spectrum. Steven wore a tight black t-shirt with four narrow pink stripes around the chest, and fitted, suggestive black Levi's, black boots, black eyeliner, pink Swatch on his right wrist. Adrian, ethereal in tight white leather pants and a white fishnet t-shirt, wore bright turquoise boots that matched his belt and thin leather collar. A shadow across his back, under his shirt, seemed to move with him.

"Did you hear me?"

"What?" Steven dragged his attention from Adrian's body and that mysterious shadow.

"I *said* get a condom if you don't have one, and come here."

Adrian pointed to the last stall. Obedient, Steven dug in his pocket for the condom he'd grabbed (just in case) when he left the house. He followed Adrian into the stall. The drugs drove his body to action way ahead of his brain: flushed, warm, and ready to fuck, not caring about the predictable aftermath of Hurricane Adrian.

"What do you—"

Before Steven could ask, Adrian slammed him back against the door, his hand closed tightly under Steven's jaw and his mouth on Steven's in a brutal kiss.

"Oh, Ade, I never knew you cared," Steven teased, breaking the kiss.

"I care about getting fucked," Adrian breathed, his voice low and soft, his forehead pressed against Steven's, "and you're the easiest option right now."

"You say the most romantic things."

Their teeth clicked when Adrian kissed Steven again, forcing his tongue into Steven's mouth, his hand pressed against the placket of Steven's jeans, making him rise. The cocaine and ecstasy helped as much as Adrian's fingers.

"You're beautiful," Adrian said. "The best friend I've ever had. And the only person in this entire place good enough to fuck me. Happy now?"

Steven laughed. Adrian's idea of *amour* was as blown as his pupils, but it didn't stop the rush of pleasure Steven felt at being chosen, the one Adrian needed in this moment. Steven gazed into those black eyes, the irises only a tiny ring of pale blue.

"What did you take?" Steven asked, turning away as Adrian tried to kiss him again.

"Really good MDA, and couple hits of speed. Because MDA is always too mellow, you know?" He kissed Steven, deeper and gentler this time. Steven tasted vodka and cranberry.

Adrian held Steven against the door with one hand while he reached in his pocket and pulled out a one-inch square of pink plastic. Confused, Steven leaned down to see what it was. Adrian laughed.

"It's lube, dollbaby. Single sized. I only have two so you better make this one worth it." He reached for Steven's zipper. "God, I can't remember the last time I wanted to get fucked like this."

Steven's cock twitched in the heat of Adrian's hand, making Steven harder, but it was Adrian's impatience for satisfaction that spurred Steven on. In this grim cubicle with raunchy graffiti scrawled across all its surfaces, only Steven could please him. A rare and perfect bubble enclosed them, Steven willing to give Adrian what he most wanted, the two of them taking and giving pleasure.

They struggled to find room for arms and elbows in the small space, though Adrian pushed down his white leather pants and bent over with grace. Steven rolled on the condom and filled his hand with cherry-scented lube from the pink packet, its sweet chemical fragrance filling the cubicle. Steven slicked it over his hard dick and rubbed the rest of it over Adrian's ass.

Steven pressed a finger inside the tight heat of Adrian's body. Adrian moved back against him. Since the beginning, Steven had never been able to resist Adrian's flame. But they were only friends. Fucking was a new blip in their long history together. In these rare, close moments, Steven was merely the wire, lit by Adrian's electrifying charge. This close to Adrian, smelling his fine sweat and tasting the soft, tantalizing skin of his neck, the switch deep inside Steven jolted to *on*. The rushing current of their connection coursed through Steven harder than any drug, reminding him of why he put up with Adrian's bullshit and confounding bouts of cruelty.

As he fingered Adrian's ass, he shivered with the sensation of being elevated above his everyday life just by touching Adrian, just by being the one Adrian needed right now. Ready to be inside the voracious heat of Adrian's ass, Steven pushed in a second finger.

"Just fuck me," Adrian said. "Don't worry. I want it hard."

Equally eager to skip the usual prep, running on instinct, Steven pulled Adrian's hips into place as Adrian braced his hands on the wall. Steven entered slowly, letting Adrian get used to the breach. Adrian's tight heat sent waves of pleasure over Steven.

Steven tugged up the thin fishnet t-shirt and ran his hand down Adrian's spine. The shadow proved to be a new tattoo: angel wings across the plane of Adrian's back. A delicate, complex tattoo that perfectly suited Adrian—and that Adrian hadn't mentioned. Steven suppressed a spark of jealousy at being left out. One more secret not shared between them, one more piece of the mystery that was Adrian.

"When did you get this?" Steven asked, staring at the lacy lines of the feathers, tracing the pattern to feel the faint line where it wasn't quite healed, hadn't fully melded into Adrian's pale skin.

"Oh god, not now, please," Adrian huffed. "Move."

Steven grabbed Adrian's hips and began to thrust, hard and insistent. He burned, a white-hot ember, as Adrian thrust back against him and claimed his pleasure. Steven dropped his free hand from the wall and traced the line of those wings with his thumb. Swept into the strength of their physical connection, Steven felt like he was part of Adrian, a creature so inexplicable he might as well be an angel. Or devil, in a different mood. Adrian either seared you or froze you out. Never a middle ground.

"Oh god, Steven. Fuck. Yes. Fuck me. Want you. Want you like this in me."

The low, rough growl of Adrian's voice drove Steven on, drawing their connection deeper, so much more than just the heat of Adrian's body gripping Steven's cock, more than his own gratification. Adrian laid bare, open to pleasure only Steven could provide. "So good, dollbaby. Oh yes. Just fuck me. Please. Please."

Determined to keep Adrian begging for him, Steven twisted to push deeper, pounding him, their bodies carried forward in syncopated rhythm. Steven braced his hand on the wall to keep from crushing Adrian against it, feeling his body to be a finely-tuned machine made to move like this, to be connected to the steady, searing engine that was Adrian. Steven kept thrusting, varying speed and building intensity, desire pounding through him like the house beat vibrating in the wall under his hand.

The unadulterated high of having Adrian want him surpassed the drugs in Steven's bloodstream. Adrian met him, perfectly in sync, their rhythm now everything. Time slipped away in their steady thrusts. The house music drummed, setting a pace that matched Steven's heartbeat. Only Adrian's low patter broke through into Steven's thoughts.

"Steven, baby. Please. Oh god. I didn't think I was gonna be able to come. But you're gonna make me."

Steven's cock was rigid as steel in the hot, slick press of Adrian's ass. The exquisite sense of winning a rare prize shivered through Steven, having realized his duty: bringing Adrian to the brink.

"Make me come. Fuck me until I come. Jesus Christ, Steven. Fuck yes. Yes yes yes." Adrian's patter drove Steven on, ready to fulfill Adrian's demands.

Yet Steven wouldn't come, not even with Adrian praying his dirty litany below him. It hadn't been that much cocaine. Just enough to make him hard and keep him that way, without coming. He closed his hand around Adrian's cock, ready to bring him off.

"Steven, please. Talk to me."

From the half dozen times they'd fucked, Steven knew the script, hated that he thought of it that way, but it was only a role Adrian assigned. Steven talked dirty only to please Adrian. The words came out in mixed French and English, allowing Steven to keep his secrets, to say what he wanted to say, though surely Adrian guessed.

"Oh yeah, you like that? *J'te veux! Toi, tu m'excites!* Want to make you come so hard."

"Yesss," Adrian hissed. Steven stepped up his pace. His hips ached, bruising with each hard slap against Adrian's ass. The stall's metal wall rattled with each thrust as Adrian's shoulders banged against it, his face shoved hard against the graffitied panel.

"This what you want?" Steven clenched his teeth. *Tell me you need me.* "*Tu veux que je te prenne? Dis-moi que tu me veux.*" A fiery mess of needy desire, he burned hotter with the potency of his own words, another shared force that joined them, even if Adrian didn't understand. Steven thrust, determined to keep the physical and mental connection between them.

"Love you in my fucking hole. God, I want that cock." Adrian ground back against Steven as he spoke.

Shuddering, Steven rapidly stroked Adrian's dick. He moved his other hand up to Adrian's shoulders, over the rippling muscles that made the new tattoo flex and move. Steven gripped hard, digging into the skin there, owning Adrian's power to fly, keeping them locked together. Steven's soaring lust burst forth in his muddled languages, words blurring together.

"*Que c'est bon!* Need you like this, *mon Amour. Saute-moi!* Fucking take me!" Steven said, playing a game where he was never sure of the rules.

"Your fucking French is hot. Like I broke you down."

Steven bristled at that and thrust into Adrian with punishing intensity, jerking him off harder.

"Oh god. You feel so good. Don't stop," Adrian demanded.

"Come for me, *like you never come for anyone else, just for me.*" French overtook English in the rush of Steven's lust.

"Just fuck me. Fuck me."

Steven obliged. He felt Adrian shudder and hoped he was close. Adrian pushed Steven's hand away and grabbed his own cock.

"You never do it hard enough," Adrian grumbled. Adrian brought himself off rough and fast, his ass clenching around Steven. He sagged when he was done. Steven pulled Adrian's back to his chest, holding him up, pressing his nose against the soft hair at the back of Adrian's neck, their huffing breaths melting together with the blistering heat of their bodies.

"Get off," Adrian complained.

Steven pulled out, still hard. He tossed the condom away while Adrian cleaned off lube and come, and then fixed his clothes. When they were both righted, Adrian grabbed Steven's face and kissed him again, sweetly this time.

"Thank you," he said against Steven's lips. "Always there when I need you and your cute French mumbling. So reliable."

"Always."

Contentment fluttered and broke through the surface of the sparkling high shimmering through his blood. His own release didn't matter now, when he'd made Adrian come like that, like he'd given up his own orgasm for Adrian's.

"Do you need a hand?" Adrian pressed Steven's cock through his zipped jeans.

"It's okay," Steven said. "I couldn't get off right now anyway."

A couple of guys were talking at the sink when Steven and Adrian came out of the stall. Looking them both up and down, the taller one caught Steven's eye and said, "Nice trick." Steven grinned back at them, perversely pleased that they had the wrong impression.

Adrian washed his hands and checked himself in the mirror. Steven hovered behind him, untethered as their connection flickered and dimmed. The face in the mirror was his own and yet altered. More than just the flush of the recent fuck. The cocaine and ecstasy turned him into someone else, someone bold and daring—no, that was bullshit. Steven's lip turned up in a disdainful snarl. Drugs and Adrian made him into someone willing to do whatever it took to have a share of Adrian's glimmering power. For one moment, bound to Adrian by sex, he'd been invincible, hovering in a magic doorway that he hoped to step through one day, permanently coupled with Adrian.

"See you out there," Adrian called, sashaying out the door.

The sound of the slamming door severed the tether that sex had tied between them. The other men followed, still talking. And just like that, Steven was alone, the glow of invulnerability slipping away, only his true face reflected in the mirror. The flickering, faintly green fluorescent lights washed him out. He fixed his eyeliner with a paper towel, pressing lightly in case his exterior fractured and chipped, like his heart. The grimy bathroom shuddered with the beat of music. Steven let it roll through him, pulsing into the space he'd opened for Adrian, who carried away pieces, leaving a raw, jagged hollow cavity in Steven.

He washed his hands, focusing on that small task, and then turned his attention to his body, to the hard-on still aching in his jeans and the cocaine roaring in his system while the music did its job, driving back the ache of Adrian's absence. He took a deep breath, letting the drugs buoy him up until his body shimmered with the ecstasy, pleasure flowering under his skin. He needed to move.

And he really needed a drink of water.

2.
Ecstasy Zen

STEVEN CRUSHED HIS FEELINGS FOR Adrian into a small box at the back of his mind, best left unobserved until the next crashing hook-up smashed the box open again. He stepped out of the bathroom a new man, with only the blooming rush of ecstasy, wanting to dance under colored lights until nothing but music existed in his head.

Ecstasy Zen: shake your ass and your mind will empty.

At the bar, Steven ordered water, drinking it and watching the dancers. His dick pressed at his jeans, but not uncomfortably so. The beats from the dance floor throbbed through his bones. The slow promise of a new song came on like a rising tide, new beats filtering through the old. As he finished his water, his black-haired drug patron from what seemed like hours ago beckoned to him from the dance floor. Steven went to join him.

Steven moved deep inside the song, perfectly in sync with his partner, with everyone in the bar, with the universe. Each bass thump was a heartbeat, the melody jangled in his muscles, and the steady rhythm swept away his thoughts until nothing bad was left.

The man, Don maybe, it had been hard to hear over the music, was much more beautiful with the lights swirling rainbows over him than Steven remembered from the bathroom. Every time Don smiled, Steven was charged with a burst of his positive energy.

Don's body was a thick, tight wall of muscle that shielded Steven from thinking about anything else. His breath was hot across Steven's cheek when they moved close, their lips nearly touching before Don pulled back with a teasing smile.

Suffused with the warm glow of Don's obvious interest and apparent goodness, Steven felt as bright as the light he saw in Adrian. When Don's hand pressed on Steven's hip,

Steven's gaze met those unnaturally pale eyes and moved closer until they ground together. The songs played on, each one better than the last, bringing them closer, dancing toward the possibility of a dirtier grind later.

Then all the heavy bass dropped away and the rising intro melody of Madonna's "Vogue" hummed through the room. As the beats kicked in, Steven was twisted around by firm hands on his shoulders. Steven's heartbeat skipped, losing the tempo of the music, seeing Adrian glowing like an angel in the lights. He leaned close to Steven and yelled past him to Don.

"What?" Steven yelled into Adrian's ear.

"I told him you were mine for this one." Adrian ground his hips against Steven, raising his arms to catch the song's rhythm. "It's our song, dollbaby."

Joyful, Steven brightened. Together Steven and Adrian radiated enough to light the early summer Northern sky. A perfect union on the dance floor, their movements were timed flawlessly. Steven wanted to taste the glitter that accented Adrian's cheekbones. He wanted to touch Adrian again, feel the heat of his skin, learn how gentle his kiss could be. No one else was ever this beautiful. Adrian smiled like a sun that shone only for Steven, who for a moment was the most valuable, precious thing ever.

But that light went out, as it always did.

By the third song, dark-haired Don wandered away, eclipsed by the glow of Adrian, though Adrian's search for his next partner was already under way. The warm exhilaration of their dance-floor fusion faded. Adrian asked Steven to help him choose his next target. Then Adrian was gone.

Frozen out again, Steven used the drugs to cushion the letdown as Adrian walked away with a broad-chested brunet dressed in a perfect black leather accompaniment to Adrian's ethereal white outfit.

Shoving aside disappointment so he could float the good ecstasy high over it, Steven went to find more water. He leaned against the bar and surveyed the room. Don had a new partner, and Adrian had disappeared with his new companion. Steven surrendered to loss.

Just good friends. Who had sex when no one else was available. No jealousy when either of them found someone else. It wasn't like Steven was in love with Adrian, who was impossible: flighty, unreliable, sometimes outright mean, though never to Steven. Yet Steven hadn't found any other man engaging enough to pull him from the gravity that kept him in Adrian's orbit.

Steven's body pulsed with lesser waves of pleasure, the hard rush of the cocaine gone, sweated out on the dance floor. He wanted to be elsewhere, somewhere quieter, but if he left now he'd be alone in his apartment peaking on ecstasy. Which could be okay, but there had to be better options out there. He saw Don heading out the door hand-in-hand with a butch blond. He watched the writhing crowd of half-dressed men, glittering under the lights, to see if there was anyone he should try for. The dance floor was still crowded, so Steven could probably find a partner just by going out there alone. But then he wouldn't get to choose.

At the end of the bar, blond hair verging on white caught his eye. Streaked with dusty gold, but real, not like Adrian's platinum shock. The guy looked like an actor in an old movie. Solid, classic man: chiseled jaw, sharp cheekbones, broad brow. And a wide, full mouth made for kissing. His fitted black shirt was buttoned low, showing a light patch of hair on his chest, and the short sleeves gripped the curve of his biceps. His faded, well-worn jeans looked custom made, displaying his narrow hips and the solid curve of his ass.

The man turned, seemingly aware of Steven's regard. Their eyes locked for a second and Steven gasped, unprepared for the intense, appraising gaze. Heart hammering, Steven stepped forward, ready to speak, right at the moment another man approached, handing the pale blond a drink and leaning next to him, blocking Steven's view.

Chest tight, unable to tear his eyes away, Steven moved down the bar to get a better view. When a spotlight drifted over the man's aristocratic face, Steven's breath huffed as if he'd taken a blow. The guy was at least ten, maybe fifteen years older than Steven, with a confidence in the way he moved, as if he always knew exactly what to do.

Butterflies fluttered softly in Steven's belly, rushing up higher until they thumped in his chest. He'd never sought out older guys, but when the man laughed at his friend's joke, Steven longed to be the cause of that gorgeous smile. This guy's face told a story about open, sincere kindness.

Steven moved across the room, knowing it was creepy, but not letting the guy out of his sight as he watched the two men talk. A glorious feeling crackled through him, filling his hollow emotional spaces. Steven laughed, giddy with this beautiful discovery.

Another guy arrived, tall with black hair and a stern expression. He dragged the first interloper on to the dance floor when New Order's "Temptation" pulsed through the bar.

The ecstasy rolled through Steven in a cresting wave, making him aware of how brilliantly, crisply beautiful everything was. Not just this exceptional man, but the colored lights of the dance floor and the men dancing under them, the shimmering sparkle of the racked bottles behind the bar, the gloriously uniform pattern of the black-and-white floor tiles. So much exquisite beauty in this room.

Fighting the newly blossoming high, Steven focused on the man again. No, it wasn't just the drugs. This guy had presence. He didn't belong in this room—even relaxed and dressed like everyone else, the man was too classy for it. Steven finished his water and walked back to the bar, headed for the opening next to this guy, his natural rhythm carrying him smoothly through the dancers to the bar edge.

In this moment, Steven did the hardest thing he remembered ever doing: acting casual while he ordered water and leaned on the bar beside this man, so close that he could feel body heat at his shoulder. Tempted by the proximity, Steven closed his eyes and inhaled, smelling cedar, the bright green of cut summer grass, and the scent of clean skin. Vibrating with the effort to appear calm, Steven leaned over, his face tantalizingly near this guy, mouth by his ear.

"Are you here with someone?"

Steven's body resonated with the force of the man's commanding presence and discerning glance.

Breath hot on Steven's ear, his voice rich and deep, the man said, "Some friends. They're dancing." Even over the music Steven heard a huskiness that shot straight to his groin. Fuck, he was half hard again.

"Do you want to dance?" Steven asked, surprised how much he wanted to hear the word *yes*. He rarely pursued anyone, while never lacking for someone vying for his attention. Standing on the other side, pursuing instead of being pursued, was disorienting.

The man smiled gorgeously. Steven's heart would break if rejection accompanied that smile. He knew even less about accepting rejection than he did about conducting an active pursuit.

"Thank you," the man said gruffly. "I'm happy you asked me. But I'm not much for dancing tonight."

The lilt of the man's phrasing and the loud music caused Steven to mishear. Dazzled, his mind put nonsensical French translations to the sounds before he shook off the aural hallucinations of the ecstasy and grasped that he was being rejected.

"Oh. Sure. *J'étais juste—*" Steven's slack response and lapse into unintentional French was cut short by the return of the man's friends. One smiled, a handsome bear of a man, his eyes sparkling. The tall, dark, severe one raked his eyes over Steven, judging him unworthy before he turned his attention to the blond man. Steven looked away, hoping his face didn't reveal the sharp jolt of disappointment that coursed through him. He faded back discretely, headed for the bathroom.

Inside, he washed and dried his face. His eyeliner was mostly gone, but he was grateful he hadn't appeared disheveled in front of the most provocatively handsome guy he'd ever seen. He tried to brush it off, attributing his feelings to the drugs. But something had happened when that man looked into his eyes. The inner flutter of butterflies was different from all other real and chemical emotions he'd experienced that night. Surely it was more than just a response to an exceptionally attractive face, graceful ease, and the low burr of the man's voice.

Steven knew that love at first sight didn't exist, but this immediate magnetic attraction had never happened to him before. With Adrian it took weeks for Steven's longing to fill him with urgency, yet he felt this way after scant minutes near this guy. Shaking off ridiculous notions, Steven relieved himself, washed again, and arranged his hair.

The face in the mirror scolded him for giving up when the man's friends arrived. Annoyed, Steven grinned maniacally at his reflection, until it forced him to laugh. His real smile returned, together with his determination. He was going back to the bar: he needed a name, something to hold on to until he could see this guy again and talk to him.

Steven stepped out of the bathroom. A hand closed over the back of his neck.

"Hey you," Adrian said, smelling of sweat and sex and someone else's cigarettes, his black-leather clad friend standing nearby. "We're going to The Dog House. Want to come? Or did you finally find someone to hook up with?"

"Maybe, I don't know. I didn't talk to him."

Adrian rolled his eyes. "Let's go. Grab him if you see him on the way out and bring him along."

Senses heightened as he walked through the bar, Steven turned at every movement in the corner of his eye, hoping that man was just around the next corner. But he was either hidden by the crowd of dancing men or he'd left while Steven was pulling it together in the bathroom. The lost chance crumpled the last good feelings from the ecstasy.

As they walked up the street in the early June night, air still chilly, Steven wished he had a jacket. It was the beginning of summer, but Seattle wasn't warm yet. And he felt so raw from the night's events that a jacket could offer the armor Steven wished for.

That man's face lodged in Steven's mind, that smile unfolding over and over again. *It's just the ecstasy. No one is that handsome in real life, in the light of day. You merely hallucinated him.*

3.
Computational Linguistics

Steven shrugged his backpack higher up his shoulder as he walked into B&O Espresso. The room was packed with people in close groups at tables along each side of the narrow room. The vintage floral table coverings, colorful wall prints, and cluttered shelves of *objets d'Art* called up images of a Parisian cafe decorated with castoffs from an aristocratic grandmother's house.

Glad of the busy noise, Steven headed to the counter at the far end of the room, seeking coffee and cake to help him study. Halfway down the room, a quick movement caught his eye: his friend Lisa, the most beautiful woman he knew, waved at him. She was seated under a vibrant Art Nouveau mural that contrasted sharply with her mahogany skin and bright-white dress shirt. Her newly shorn hair highlighted the strong bones of her face and enhanced her smile.

Three paces away, arms out to greet her, Steven stopped, his heart hammering. Lisa's companion was that gorgeous blond man from the club a couple of weeks ago.

"Leese! Oh my God, your hair!" Steven forced the words out, his throat tight with giddy anticipation while he tried to keep his attention on Lisa.

"What?" Her silver watch and rings flashed as she patted the close-cropped curls. She cut her onyx eyes at Steven, her jaw set.

Although eager to know how they came to be sitting together in Steven's favorite coffee shop, he narrowed his focus, speaking only to Lisa. "I'm worried. You were beautiful before, but this cut is so stunning, I'll have to fight off your admirers to get your attention. You barely have time for me as it is." Feeling fluttery and flirtatious, he leaned down to kiss her forehead, then caught her hand and kissed that, too. "You look amazing."

"Thanks, sweetie. You don't look so bad either." Lisa squeezed his hand. Steven scowled at her—comically, he hoped. She grinned. "Steven, have you met my friend John?"

Faced with the bluest eyes ever known, eyes the color of Montana skies, piercing and strong, eyes like the ocean, like sparkling sapphires, Steven was writing a poem, lost in those eyes, when the man stuck out his hand.

"Steven," he said, his voice gruff in the way Steven remembered. "John Pieters. We've met, haven't we?" His accent had been too faint to pick up in the club noise, but now Steven was guessing: not German; maybe a Scandinavian country? No, it was more familiar than that.

Mind whirling with this proof that good things happened if you wished hard enough for them, Steven shook John's hand. "Steven Frazier," he said, limiting his words to avoid spilling the dirty thoughts he had about John's mouth and hands.

The work-roughness of John's palms matched his gruff voice. Steven clasped his left hand around John's as if giving him a great honor. John smiled at the gesture. In fact, after their first too-brief meeting, Steven was reluctant to release John's hand, lest the man disappear again. Heart pounding, afraid John might read his thoughts, Steven released John's grip and answered the question.

"Well, not exactly. I think we spoke once."

"Yes, at Neighbours, two weeks ago," John said. "I don't forget a face."

John remembered him. The rush of blood from his pounding heart went straight to Steven's head, leaving him dizzy. Something *had* happened when their eyes first met. That same notion flared again, a flashback hovering in the back of his brain.

"Oh?" Lisa said, her head cocked, her smile softening the question. "What were you doing at Neighbours, John?"

John's smile was faintly crooked around his straight, white teeth, as if repeated use had pulled it askew. Even though that smile was for Lisa, Steven's heart clenched at the sight of it. The man was even more appealing than Steven remembered.

"Oh, you know Bash and Shane," John said. "Friends believe they know best when you need to get back out and meet people. So of course they dragged me there." John's fond tone led Steven to reassess his judgment of the interlopers from that night, yet he focused on the significant words. *Back out:* he's single!

"It's nice to truly meet you, John." Steven's eyes cruised John in a quick once over, a subtle hint at his interest.

Catching Steven's attention, Lisa said, "Do you want to join us, sweetie? It's so crowded here, you won't find a table. I bet we can get a chair to squeeze you in." Lisa nodded to a four-top table with only three people seated at it.

Homework forgotten, there was nothing Steven wanted more. However, politeness overruled. "Oh no, I don't want to interrupt you guys. Just came to say how pretty you are."

Lisa laughed at Steven's flattery, patting her hair again.

"Please join us," John said, his voice like walking barefoot through warm sand, scratchy and smooth all at once. "We finished talking business. I have to go in a minute, but join us, please."

John stood to ask the nearby table for their extra chair, carrying it back and setting it next to his own. "Have a seat," he said, hand out in a gesture of offering. Steven sank onto it, knees weak.

Settled back in his own chair, alert eyes fixed on Steven, John asked, "What are you doing tonight, Steven? Coffee before clubbing?" John raised his espresso cup in a toast.

"No, not tonight." Steven considered John's lavender shirt, shot through with grey stripes, tucked neatly into fitted, well-faded jeans. A darker grey blazer hung on the back of his chair. When John moved, the light hair on his chest flashed between the open top two buttons on his shirt. Mouth dry, Steven licked his lips, trying to remember what he was saying, why he was here. "I have to study for finals. You might think it's weird, but I find it easier to study here than in my apartment."

John nodded, chin settling on his fist, eyebrows lifted in curiosity at the mention of homework.

"Yes, Steven is back in school. I'm crazy proud of him."
Lisa laid her hand fondly on Steven's shoulder for a second.
"We met at Seattle Central years ago, but he didn't come back
to finish until now."

Steven smiled awkwardly at the praise, hating the dig at
how long he'd been out of school. He'd take responsibility for
it, but there had been extenuating circumstances. He'd
moved in when Adrian's former roommate moved out, just as
school started six years ago. Through the endless party that
was Adrian's life, Steven had managed to attend classes at
Seattle Central Community College while working at the Fred
Meyer store on Broadway.

Despite the time he spent partying with Adrian, Steven
passed his classes, doing well in all of them those first two
years. His beautiful Pakistani anthropology professor said
that Steven had an exceptional grasp of the nuances of lin-
guistic anthropology. So Steven took more language classes,
branching out from his mother's French and his own high
school Spanish into Japanese and German. He'd brought
home extra books to study and visited the University of Washington's Anthropology department, ready to apply when he
finished his two-year degree. But academic passion wasn't
enough to combat the allure of Adrian's sparkling life. Under
the guise of saving money for tuition, Steven took a year off,
which became three years, before finally entering the University of Washington.

"What are you majoring in?" John asked. Usually that
question seemed patronizing, as if Steven were a child expected
to give a prepared answer. But John's attention left Steven
wanting to please him so badly that his heart raced.

"I went back for anthropological linguistics. But after
taking a few computer classes, I'm switching my major at the
end of this quarter."

"Turns out this boy is great with computers," Lisa said.

"Interesting." John's head tipped as he smiled, considering that idea. Steven resisted shifting under the weight
of John's regard. Heat bloomed in his belly: John's smile was

for him only. "How do you get from, what did you say—anthropological linguistics—to computers?"

"It's not that crazy. I loved Anthropology when I was at SCCC with Lisa, but I was young then—"

"As opposed to now." The lilt in John's tone revealed less than his eyes, which crinkled at the corners in amusement.

Lit up by that intimacy, though the joke was at his expense, Steven laughed. "Yes, as opposed to now, when I'm clearly aged and full of wisdom and experience."

Both Lisa and John laughed with him. Steven went on, boosted by John's interest and Lisa's fondness.

"Everyone loves Sociology or Anthropology when they start college, but only a few people are cut out for academic careers. Which you figure out is your only option if you study that stuff. I've always been good with math and languages, so when there was a computer language class, I signed up just to see."

Steven, excited to find willing listeners, couldn't stop talking about his obsessions once he started. "So far, I love it. It's like linguistics and math had a beautiful baby. The rules are hard and fast. It's satisfying to study a puzzle until it's solved, and yet it's like magic, how a computer language generates into code that runs programs." Steven fidgeted with the seam on his jeans. He wished he'd gotten coffee. His rambling could maybe be stopped if he had a cup to sip to slow him down. "Sorry, I get carried away. I should sign up for a class on how to stop giving impassioned speeches to the uninitiated." He swallowed and sat up straighter in his chair. Discomfited, Steven glanced back to the counter. "I should get coffee."

"I'll come with you. I could use refill myself," John said.

Walking to the counter, Steven was too aware of John's body close behind him. John wasn't much taller than Steven, but he stayed close enough that Steven was able to gauge his height, at least two inches more than Steven's five-eleven. Their shoulders touched lightly as they stopped at the counter. Feeling John's body heat so near was such a distraction that the barista's greeting startled him. Unintentionally, he stepped just a bit away from John.

"Hey," the barista said, smiling when she recognized Steven. "How goes it?"

"Great! I'll be better if I have coffee though." Steven wondered if she thought he and John were together. He warmed at the idea of introducing John to people in a way that indicated John was definitely with him.

She made a serious face. "Luckily I can help you with that. Usual?"

"Yeah. Please."

"And you?" She smiled at John.

"Double espresso." John tapped his fingers on the counter, drawing Steven's attention to how graceful they were: long and neatly manicured, in opposition to the calluses Steven felt when they shook hands earlier. Steven shivered, imagining that roughness across his bare skin.

"Anything else?"

Jarred back to the present, Steven looked into the pastry case. The barista said, "Oh, we have that one you really liked again. The strawberry gateau."

Steven happily abandoned his perusal of the case. "*Le fraisier?* I'll have that, for sure," he said, catching John's expression from the corner of his eye but unable to interpret the question in John's eyes or the slight smile curling his lips.

Steven felt he was being unusually performative. He was just ordering coffee and a sweet, yet he wanted John to pay attention to the kinds of things Steven liked, in the same way that Steven would be deeply interested in everything his crush chose.

"*Le fraisier.*" John mused as they watched the girl pull it from the case and plate it for Steven.

"Have you ever had it? It's amazing. Of course, they do it great here. Though I like almost anything strawberry."

John said something too softly for Steven to hear, but he imagined it was, "Of course you do, *mon petit fraisier.*" Steven wondered if he was flashing back again, like the night he first saw John, when his languages got confused in aural hallucinations of what he hoped to hear.

Before Steven could ask what John had said, the girl slid the plate across the counter. The second barista set down Steven's coffee and John's espresso.

"What's that?" John asked, looking into Steven's cup.

"Café au lait," Steven said, once again offering information and hoping John was cataloging it.

"Very European." John's eyes twinkled with amusement and that curiously knowing smile again. He reached across Steven to hand cash to the girl, close enough that Steven again smelled the cedar and cut-grass of John's cologne. Distracted by the heady memory of that scent from their first meeting, Steven didn't reply quickly enough to the barista.

"All together?" she asked John.

"Yes, please."

"Oh no," Steven protested, "I can't let you do that."

"Of course you can. Here I am, keeping you from your studies. The least I can do is make sure you're awake enough to finish them this evening."

John folded his change and tucked it into the pocket of his jeans before picking up the tiny espresso cup and saucer and Steven's cake, and heading back to join Lisa.

At the table, John set the cake at Steven's place and pulled out Steven's chair. Before Steven could truly appreciate that thoughtful action, Lisa's eyebrows shot up and her lips pursed in a scarcely suppressed smile. Steven could see that she was getting ready to comment, so he kicked her lightly under the table.

"Ow!"

"Sorry, did I get you as I sat down?" Steven gave Lisa a falsely sympathetic look and then a quick warning glare.

"Sweetie," she grinned, "I think maybe you're looking to get something. Oh, but I see you got cake. Maybe that's enough for now."

John, inquisitive, glanced between them.

Steven felt the back of his neck heating. As a diversion, he said, "You know, I'm usually good with accents—it's part of the languages thing. But I can't place yours. It's so faint."

"Ah, you have a good ear. I hope hardly anyone notices anymore." John settled back against his chair, which again drew attention to the open shirt buttons, where Steven imagined pressing his tongue into the hollow of John's throat and feeling the pulse that visibly throbbed there. Stomach fluttering, Steven sipped his coffee and tried to focus on John's words. "I grew up in Belgium and Switzerland, speaking French and Flemish at home. And, of course, English."

"Why wouldn't you want anyone to notice?" Steven asked, processing the delightful knowledge that John spoke French as a native language: one impossible thing Steven would never dare hope for.

"I like to think that I can master anything," John said, his eyes on Steven. "So I despair that after twenty-five years in America I haven't mastered English well enough to pass unnoticed."

Steven was fairly certain that John could master anything just by looking at it with those piercing eyes. He shifted in his seat, thinking again of John's calloused fingers rasping across his bare skin.

"I assume that, after twenty-five years, you figured out that most people think it's attractive," Lisa said. Steven nodded.

"Yes, I've heard that." John smiled.

"*Oh, ça alors! C'est toujours un plaisir pour moi de trouver quelqu'un avec qui parler français.*" Steven pushed aside his lascivious thoughts and expressed happiness at their shared second language.

"*Oui, pour moi aussi.*"

Warmth flared in Steven's core. John's *Français de Belgique* accent differed enough from the Québécois, Algerian, and Parisian accents Steven typically encountered that he didn't catch it until he heard John speak *en Français*.

Steven sat forward, not caring how eager he seemed. "*C'est super le fun, ça! En connais-tu d'autres ici avec qui tu parles français?*"

Steven asked who else John spoke French with. Outside his family, Steven spoke mostly with older people from his parents' social group and the African émigrés he encountered and made friends with at the grocery store.

"*Some friends, my brother. I've been lucky to meet people through work I can talk to.*"

Steven felt a pang of jealousy at not yet being counted among that special group.

John sat forward, his elbow brushing Steven's, obviously impressed in a way that sent Steven soaring, because he'd done something right. "Your French is exceptionally good. Part of your study in linguistics?" John asked in English.

"Steven's mother is French-Canadian," Lisa said.

Steven nodded. "When she married an American, her father begged that her kids be raised bilingual. They sent me to a French-immersion elementary school near Lake Sammamish. Lucky for me. I might not have gotten started with languages like I did if my *Papi* hadn't insisted."

"Do you know many other speakers outside your family?"

"Not enough, though there's a surprising number of Algerians I run across, mostly at stores. But not many of my friends, no." Steven caught the sparkle of Lisa's bracelet out of the corner of his eye. Too excited by the delight of finding this connection, he had to suppress the urge to keep talking to John in French. It was too rude, leaving Lisa out of the conversation. "Hopefully I can convince Lisa to learn, then we won't have to whisper secrets anymore. We could talk about people out loud at parties."

Lisa's bubbly laughter reminded Steven just how much he loved her. "If you'd said that's why I should learn, I'd have started when we were still in college together." She patted Steven's knee, forgiving him for kicking her earlier.

"So, Steven, are you at U-Dub now?" John asked. "Or elsewhere?"

"Yep. U-Dub."

"I also went there, but I wasn't nearly as enthusiastic about my studies as you seem to be. If you're always this eager to please, your professors must find you a joy to have in class."

Steven flushed in confusion, unsure whether John was complimenting him or teasing him for being so excited about school.

"I can't imagine you as a party boy in college," Lisa said to John, which saved Steven from humiliatingly blurting that he'd be glad to please John. It wasn't just the man's attractive face and graceful movements. Usually when Steven talked about school, people listened only to be polite, but John watched with an intensity that made Steven feel respected, truly heard. In the half hour they'd been acquainted, Steven longed to prove he was worth this man's time. Which was likely why John saw him as eager to please.

"Ah, I wouldn't say I was a party boy. I wasn't in a fraternity. I had more than enough of that kind of thing in boarding school." John sipped his espresso and looked thoughtfully at the Art Nouveau mural above Lisa's head for a second. The idea of a young John in an all-boys boarding school was too much for Steven at the moment. He filed the information away to consider later. Like maybe in the shower.

"Of course," John continued, "it was the late sixties, early seventies. There was partying, just not like today's keg parties."

Steven calculated quickly: late sixties meant his deduction about John being in his late thirties or early forties was accurate.

"I guess things were much more political then, too?" Steven asked, determined to push for the most information about John he could gain in the little time they might have.

"It's Seattle. Isn't everything always political?" Lisa asked.

John laughed. "Yes, I suppose it was. It was hard to avoid in the circles where I hung out. Still, I'd have been better off paying more attention to school work, given the opportunity I had."

"Doesn't seem to have affected your success," Lisa said. Steven nodded, although he was only guessing that John was successful. Unsuccessful people didn't have John's confidence and grace.

"I floated through school," John said, "studying things that wouldn't get me a job because I knew I'd have one with my father's company. I just imagined that I'd have a natural aptitude for business."

"And you didn't?" Steven asked. He leaned in to hear the answer, then aware he was hanging in John's space. He sat back, hoping to appear casual. Not letting Lisa catch his eye.

"I did, as it turns out. But my parents died a few years after I graduated. I wish I'd spent more time with my father to learn the business. I wish I'd learned something in school that he thought was useful." The pain of his loss flickered in John's eyes. He smiled sadly, as if apologizing to Steven for that answer.

Steven's stomach dropped. "I'm really sorry." He wanted to touch John to offer comfort, however inadequate.

"That's terrible, John. I am so sorry," Lisa said, her hand twitching on the tabletop, as if she too wanted to reach out.

John shook his head, as if releasing the sadness, sending it away. "It's been a long time. Though I do wish I'd listened to him more while he was alive. Not only to learn business, but just to learn about him. I suppose I still have daddy issues. But who doesn't?"

"Isn't that the truth," Lisa agreed.

"I don't think I do," Steven said at the same time.

John's inquisitive blue gaze caught Steven. "No?"

Lisa said, "Actually, that's true. He has weirdly normal parents."

Steven felt a bit awkward that, even after six years in the city, he still carried a suburban taint. Yet he answered, to allow John to see who he really was. "My dad is kind and loves me. He's interested in my life, but not so much that he's invasive."

"I didn't know there were families like that." John sat back, his brow wrinkling in contemplation.

"Ah well, not all American suburbs are pits of secret horrors. I do have issues with my mom. She loves me and means well, but my coming out was hard for her. She's not over it nine years later." Steven shrugged. "But overall, my family is pretty normal."

A smile lit John's face, his eyes glittering and crinkling at the corners. "Surely something must be wrong with you. You can't be well adjusted, smart, ambitious, and self-assured. That wouldn't be fair to everyone else."

"I'm red-haired, left-handed, and gay. If that doesn't make me the devil's own child, then I've been living my life all wrong," Steven replied, a cocky smile on his lips.

The pure mirth in John's laughter cracked open Steven's heart. Then John's focused smile shone on him again. "I'm sure you do very well at leading others into temptation when you put your mind to it, without having to claim devilish descent. Perhaps you need an angel on your shoulder to keep you in check."

Steven's body responded with a small shudder. John's voice had dropped slightly, and that growl went straight to Steven's groin.

"I'm pretty humble, usually." Steven fumbled, not sure whether he was being chastised or teased.

Lisa watched with rapt attention, as if this show was purely for her entertainment. Steven would never live down his attempts to flirt with John while she watched.

John's voice smoothed out, his tone turned amicable. "I'm convinced you have no reason to be humble. You certainly aren't what I expected, Steven." John lifted his hand as if he might reach to touch Steven's arm. Steven held his breath, unsure whether he could keep his composure if John touched him. But then John twisted his arm back to look at his watch. "I wish I could spend the evening talking with the two of you, but I do need to go. Can't keep people waiting." He put his hand out to Steven and spoke in French, "Steven, *it was a pleasure to meet you. Let the better angels of your nature prevail.*"

"*Merci*, John. *I'll try to be good.*" Steven blushed, feeling caught out. "It was nice talking with you." He switched to English, conscious of leaving Lisa out. The scratch of John's hand against his, together with their renewed language connection, left Steven lightheaded. He sipped at his coffee while butterflies tried to beat their way out of his stomach.

"Lisa," John said, putting his hand out to her. "I won't make you wait for an answer. If you're still interested, I'd love to have you. Call you in the morning to discuss the details?"

"Oh wonderful. Thank you, John," Lisa's incandescent smile, whatever it was about, made Steven even happier as he watched her shake John's hand.

Steven slumped in his chair, resenting that the steamy windows prevented seeing more of John after he walked out the door.

4.
Lint on Velcro

"What was that last bit about? And how do you know the most handsome man who ever lived?" Steven offered his most winning smile.

Lisa's gaze was soft and knowing. "That was an informal second job interview. I'm going to work for him. That last bit was him being kind and not making me wait to hear about the job."

"Oh rad! You've been needing a better job forever. I'm so excited for you!" The charge Steven got from his conversation with John sparked into gleeful happiness. Everyone got something good today. And Lisa working for John meant Steven would see him again. Soon.

"Thanks, sweetie. I hope it works out."

"So—" Steven steepled his fingers under his chin, trying to look grave and serious. "Do you believe in love at first sight?"

Caught off guard, Lisa laughed. "Why? Did you fall in love with John when you first saw him? Or did you wait until you heard him speak French?"

"What? No. Ridiculous," Steven said, disdaining the idea. "I'm wondering if he fell in love with me. At first sight." Laughter bubbled in his chest while he tried to look as innocent as possible.

"Sweetie," Lisa said, laughing, "everyone who knows you loves you at least a little. So if he doesn't now, I'm sure he will."

"Okay, but seriously, do you think he was flirting with me? Like, just a little? I couldn't tell for sure, but some of the things he said—well, I could read more into them if I wanted too." Steven leaned on the table, chin in hand, maintaining his solemn expression. Though he seriously wanted to see John again.

"I don't know, but you were certainly doing your level best to flirt with him. Not sure how effective it was," Lisa said. Steven made a face, wrinkling his nose at her. Thoughtful, she went on. "I don't think he dates younger guys anymore."

"Anymore?"

"Yes."

"So he has dated younger guys before?"

"I don't know him well enough to say what he does in his personal life. It's secondhand information. Sorry."

"You're not helpful. Anyway, he bought me cake." Steven looked at the nearly untouched piece of *fraisier* in front of him. He picked up his fork, glad to have this sweet bit of John left. "That has to mean something, right?"

"He can certainly afford the cake," she said, taking Steven's other hand. "Given the sparkle in your eye, I probably shouldn't tell you that he's fabulously rich, huh? If you were with him, you'd never have to work." Lisa arched an eyebrow suggestively, in the spirit of fantasizing about imaginary crushes.

"Handsome and a sweet sugar daddy?" Steven dropped his fork to the table and fluttered his hand to his chest. "Be still my heart! Ha. Really though, I just want to know how he kisses. God, did you see his mouth? And how strong his hands are? I'd like him use those hands to—"

"Please stop right there before we both regret where you're going with this." Laughing, Lisa waved a hand to cut him off.

"So what kind of lover do you think he is? He seems so nice. Like he's kind to animals and small children, right? But maybe a little kinky in bed?"

Her face pinched with distaste. "You really are the devil's child. I do not want to know how he is in bed. Do not want to think about it, especially if he's going to be my boss."

"Okay, we don't have to talk about his bedroom possibilities. But he's really great, isn't he? I could stand to have a really nice boyfriend." Steven took a bite of his cake, savoring its sweetness.

"I do hope you find someone nice, sweetie." Lisa squeezed Steven's hand, then picked up her coffee cup. "You deserve good things in your life."

Steven set his fork back on his plate. "What's not good in my life? I'm back in school, so you can't harass me about that anymore. What's left that's so terrible?"

"Adrian."

"What's wrong with Adrian?" He knew that Lisa hadn't liked Adrian since the beginning, but she usually just grimaced faintly at his name and let it go.

"I'm sure that his mother asks herself that every day."

"Don't be mean, Lisa. Adrian is my closest friend."

"And I'm sorry for that, Steven. You're so nice, and he's a bitchy drama-queen who hates everyone."

"No, he doesn't."

Steven's post-John euphoria crumbled as he chafed at the insult to Adrian, feeling both scolded and protective. Lisa couldn't see that her assessment of Adrian was wrong.

"Oh sure, he likes *you*—but only because you follow him around like his shadow. Adrian will never be there for you. I wish you could find someone who appreciates you. But Adrian will always come between you and anyone who's interested in you. He needs you to fluff his ego, so he can't let you get away. But the worst is that he barely ever drops you a scrap of affection."

"Wow, don't hold back." Steven sipped his coffee casually. He looked away, not wanting Lisa to see how much her judgment hurt.

"I'm sorry, sweetie. I don't like to see you treated badly. But it's as if you don't even see what Adrian does." She reached for Steven's hand again, and he let her pull it into her lap.

"You don't even know him, Leese."

"No, but I know you. And I want more for you." She leaned forward to brush her other hand along his jaw. "Your face *is* so pretty that people will judge you for it. You're so much more than some scene queen, swanning around with Adrian like Snow White and Rose Red." She shook her head when

Steven smiled at the description. "It isn't good. You look like beautiful, flashy club kids. All surface and no substance. It leaves a negative impression for a lot people who don't run in the circles you do. I want people to think more of you."

Steven delayed speaking. Lisa would never understand, because she'd never seen Adrian the way Steven had, curled up on Steven like a cat, crying that no one loved him, that no one ever wanted anything real from him, that he couldn't trust anyone but Steven. Sure, they were coming down off a weekend of opium and cocaine, and Steven *didn't* actually understand Adrian, but he did care. Steven didn't know how to make Lisa understand that if he wasn't there, then Adrian really would have no one.

Still, Lisa's comment about people seeing him as shallow was unbearable, especially if that was what John meant when he said Steven was different than he'd expected. He spoke up, bravely.

"I don't think John saw me that way."

"Sweetie, guys like John already have everything. They want something more than another pretty object in their collection. Even I can see how gorgeous John is. You think men aren't always throwing themselves at him? He could collect twenty twinks just walking from here to his house. They stick to him like lint on Velcro, but he always brushes them off. What makes you different? What makes you better? That's what you have to prove if you want him."

"Thanks," he said, coldly. "I'll take that into consideration the next time I'm swanning around."

The dig had hurt. Steven liked having a pretty face, liked that it drew other pretty boys to him, but Lisa knew he wanted to be more. He'd complained to her after every breakup that the last boyfriend didn't appreciate Steven's depth, didn't love the deeper side of him, didn't understand his intellect or his aspirations. She was digging into that wound while refusing to acknowledge that his friendship with Adrian had rewards—that someone besides Lisa saw all the pieces that made Steven who he was, the parts he shared only with the people he trusted most. It was an old fight that Steven was tired of. He was glad to let it go when Lisa reached out to him.

"Sorry. I don't want to upset you. I want good things for you. I just don't know how to help you get them, given the way your life is now." Lisa kissed Steven's hand in apology, and then released it.

"It's fine. No big deal," Steven said, his light tone masking how he felt. "But I came here to do homework, so I should get to it. Are you staying?"

"As fun as it sounds to watch you do homework, I have a date."

"Oooh, who's the lucky girl?" Steven asked, glad of the subject change.

"Actually, I don't know. Shane and Bash, the friends who introduced me to John, invited me for dinner to decompress after the interview. Shane is always trying to set me up with someone. At least I've figured it out now, so I show up looking nice."

Steven said, "You couldn't look any nicer than you do right now. If she doesn't fall in love with you immediately, then something is wrong with her. I can't wait to hear about it. And about your new job. John is so lucky to have hired you. He'd better treat you well."

Lisa rose to leave. She kissed the top of Steven's head and whispered, "Be good."

Steven pulled out his notebook and *Mathematical Foundations of Computer Science* textbook. He'd been looking forward to today's chapter, but now he couldn't focus. Bad feelings lingered from the conversation with Lisa. He shoved them aside, thinking instead of John's voice as it dropped into a near growl, of John's hands and how they might feel on him, of the warmth that had spread through Steven's belly every time John smiled at him.

Completely lost in thoughts of John, Steven ate the rest of the delicious cake John had bought him. Surely that was flirtation and not just taking pity on a poor college student?

5.
Exactly Like It Is

"THERE YOU ARE," ADRIAN SAID. He slipped into a nearby chair, startling Steven from his daydreams.

"Hey."

"Got tired of waiting, so I came to find you. Let's go out."

"I can't, Ade. I need to study." Steven waved his hands over his books. "I have both finals and work tomorrow." He felt defensive at Adrian's arrival after Lisa's harsh words, ashamed that he hadn't done more to defend his friend.

"Whatever. You're such a grandma since you went back to school." Adrian scrunched his nose up at the face Steven made. "Well, you are. And you're always gone. I miss you. Can't you at least do homework at home so I can see you?"

Adrian's need for Steven's attention was limitless, though uneven. They could go for days barely speaking more than a greeting, each comfortable in their separate worlds. But when Adrian's razor-sharp needs turned, they spent entire days together, never apart for more than an hour. Sometimes Steven was Adrian's audience, other times they just sat close, touching lightly as they both read. When Adrian wanted full contact, it was useless to argue that he distracted Steven from his work. But no one ever needed anything from Steven in the way Adrian needed his attention, so Steven gave it. Gladly.

"So then," Adrian continued narrating his day as they headed down Bellevue Avenue back to their apartment, "she pulled down another one. Pink satin. Satin! And I was like, 'Well, girl, you can't wear pink with your coloring and no one, no one, who is cool is wearing satin to prom,' and I thought for a second she'd cry. I wasn't even being mean or anything, I was trying to help—"

Steven cut in, since the story would go on long after they got home. "Wait, sorry, but do we have dinner at home? Before we head down the hill?"

"Oh! I checked and if we get meat, you can make spaghetti, okay?"

That Steven would cook was given. Adrian's cooking, whether accidental or on purpose, never once proved to be edible. Steven nodded his assent, so they turned toward the Broadway QFC grocery store before home.

As if the interruption never happened, Adrian continued. "So I'm trying to help and she finally gets it. It was so great. I finally sent her off with a short-sleeved deep turquoise velvet skater dress. You know: little flared skirt and all. And I convinced her to wear it to prom with thigh-highs and her 20-hole Docs. Like what is prom even for if you aren't going to look like yourself? And I'm sure her pictures will be totally dated in like five years, but who cares? She'll remember 1991 exactly like it is, exactly like she was."

"Sounds like a good day."

"It was. You know, I thought this job would suck. There's only like four things in that shop I'd wear. I'm fabulous, but I'm no drag queen, so prom dresses are pretty much right out, but I feel like maybe I'll actually do some good. It could be my calling, you know, hand holding the poor, frumpy masses and sending them back out into the world dressed a little better than I found them."

Steven laughed and squeezed Adrian's hand affection-ately. A staggering amount of thought and detail went into Adrian's outfits, and he often spent as much time fussing over Steven, so Steven knew exactly what the teen girls in the shop had been through that day. Yet when Adrian was on and flattering you, you definitely felt like royalty. So maybe that *was* Adrian's calling.

"I bet she felt great when she left," Steven replied as they toured the meat aisle at QFC. "What do you want?"

"Something better than hamburger. Something that tastes good."

Steven chose some hot Italian sausage. Different from what he usually cooked. Adrian would eat anything, but he'd be happier about it if he thought it was fancier. That was the secret to pleasing Adrian in any situation: tell him what he got was better than what most people had.

It was a pleasant, normal evening for their household. Their other roommate, Ryan Ikeda, wasn't home. They cooked, ate, and watched TV while Steven studied, until Adrian decided it was time to get dressed and go out. He didn't argue when Steven declined. An ordinary end to a day that had been fractured into pieces, normalcy crunched against the argument with Lisa and the elation of meeting John.

While chatting through Adrian's endless pre-club outfit changes, checking for cues as to whether he was supposed to reject or approve each one, Steven didn't say anything important. They discussed teal glitter versus silver, but Steven never mentioned the rasp of John's calluses against Steven's palm when they shook. He didn't say how John's voice echoed that same grit and strength.

After Adrian left, Steven went to bed. Sleepless, he pulled the pillow around his head to block out the world. Remembering John's voice and touch, Steven tried to shut out other thoughts. He'd kept John a secret from Adrian, knowing that neither would appeal to the other, Adrian surely too flighty for John. But more than that, Steven couldn't be sure of Adrian's reaction. He wanted his best friend to be happy for him, but he feared the possible truth in what Lisa said earlier. That Adrian might try to keep Steven from John was too awful to contemplate.

6.
Missed Connections

"THANKS, MAN, SORRY IF I KEPT you." The UW Bookstore was open late, but Steven was the last customer on a Friday night. "I appreciate it though."

"No problem." A tall, lanky, dark-haired guy rang up his book purchase. "We're only like a minute after hours. Plenty of time to close up. You got plans tonight?"

"Probably going dancing. I don't know yet." Steven answered thoughtlessly as he struggled to shove books into his backpack.

"Really? Where?" The clerk helped hold Steven's bag open. Steven glanced up to find he was being watched intently.

"Oh, I haven't decided." Steven licked his lips, conscious that this wannabe rock-star-looking surfer guy was probably hitting on him and not merely giving friendly service. "Usually Neighbours, but not always."

"Cool, I was gonna go catch a show at the OK Hotel but maybe I'll hit Neighbours instead." The guy's smile was an invitation. "I'm Chris." He put his hand out. Steven finished zipping his backpack and shook Chris's hand, acutely aware of how he lingered in the shake and reluctantly drew his hand back. It wasn't a surprise for Steven to get hit on, but usually it was in expected places, like bars. It didn't happen around school a lot.

"Hi, I'm Steven." He smiled, noticing the guy was actually pretty cute under the shaggy surfer hair and the scruffy goatee.

"I noticed your books. Are you taking Professor Kiehl's class?" Chris leaned on the counter as he spoke.

"Yeah, the condensed one, this summer."

"Good luck. I did it last fall. It was hard."

"Oh, are you doing Comp Sci? I don't think I've seen you around school," Steven said.

"Naw, Electrical Engineering, but I think it's all starting to kind of blend together, you know? Like there's a bunch of things I'm gonna wish I knew to study later, but computers seems obvious right now."

"Yeah, it feels like everything is changing, doesn't it? I heard Kiehl goes into a lot of speculation about future applications and stuff."

Steven's excitement about his upcoming courses bled into his voice. Chris gave a conspiratorial smile in response, like he got why it might be interesting to think about the future of computing.

"Kiehl's totally cool, man. Like he'll give you all these extra reading suggestions that are actually science fiction books, trying to get you to think about the future in different ways. I totally dug it."

Chris leaned closer, their hands almost touching. This wasn't merely a conversation about shared interests; this guy was using their nerdy connection to hit on Steven. He hadn't considered hooking up with cute guys at school before. The idea of having to see that person again in classes or around campus complicated everything. That veered toward dating. Did he want to date a schoolmate?

Steven glanced up at the clock. "That sounds cool. Fuck, I'm gonna miss the last Express 43, if I don't hurry. And I should let you close."

"No worries. It was nice to talk to someone who gets it. Hope I run into you later. We could talk more."

"Yeah, that'd be rad!" Steven answered, unsure if Chris's last bit had been a question or an invitation. Steven grabbed his backpack off the counter. "Sorry again that I kept you."

"It's no problem."

Steven headed out the door, feeling Chris's eyes on him.

He hadn't lied about the 43; he did have a bus to catch. His whole day had been stacked. Running between advisors and the registrar's office to get approval for an extra five credit hours for summer quarter had taken the whole day, leaving no time to get books, too. His last class on Friday was super late in the day. Who knows what he was thinking when he signed up for that? He'd made it to the bookstore with only twenty minutes to spare and five classes to find books for.

The bus was coming around the corner just as Steven made it to the stop. He sagged with relief into a seat near the front, his heavy pack on his lap. The University slid past the windows on the left as the bus headed toward Capitol Hill. He hadn't managed to catch an express, but it was fine. He sat back and wondered what he'd do if Chris showed up looking for him at Neighbours tonight. Sex would be hard to pass up today, just for the celebration and the relief of it.

The meandering ride through Montlake and over the back side of the Hill felt like a Zen exercise in patience. Time to let go of how rushed his day had been and think about the weekend. He had to work on Sunday, but he had no homework, which was worth celebrating.

◊

The apartment was quiet when he got home. Ryan's rent check was on the kitchen counter, which felt weird because he was sure it had been at least three weeks since he'd seen Ryan at all.

Steven was never sure if Ryan was always gone, or if they worked completely opposite schedules and so never crossed paths. It was too bad, because Steven liked Ryan, and Ryan seemed to like him and Adrian as well. Which was great because Adrian had chased off the last three roommates, causing Steven to worry that they'd have to find a cheaper, smaller place. So far, Ryan was a perfect roommate who seemed to use his room merely as a storage locker. It was hard to tell when Ryan was home, since the door to his room was always closed, and he never complained about the loud late nights that sprung up around Adrian.

Steven left his heavy backpack on the floor. He sat on the edge of his bed and unlaced his Docs before falling back and staring at the ceiling. He breathed slowly, thinking for a minute that he could fall asleep here. But no, he needed to get ready. He got up and stripped off the jeans he'd worn to school and headed to the bathroom.

The shower was warm when he checked it with his hand, but ran ice cold, then slightly too hot when Steven stepped in. Their apartment was convenient and cheap for the size and location, but, oh god, he hadn't had a decent shower at home in five years. He shampooed, trying to remember Chris's hands, wondering what they'd feel like on his skin. The door clicked open just as Steven ducked his head under the spray to rinse.

"Ooh, naked," Adrian declared by way of greeting, tugging open the corner of the curtain and peeking in.

"Almost done. Be out in a second. Unless you're coming in?" Steven teased.

"I showered earlier," Adrian said. He dropped the curtain back in place, declining to take the invitation seriously. "Isn't this the last weekend before summer classes start? We should celebrate."

"I can think of some ways we can celebrate," Steven said, opening the invitation again as he rinsed off the rest of the soap. Sex had been on his mind since his encounter at the bookstore. Steven had rarely been the instigator between them, but today having casual sex with Adrian offered better possible consequences than hooking up with a guy from school.

"I can too, and none of them involve me getting in there, so hurry up and finish," Adrian answered. Even if he was high or drunk, Adrian seldom accepted the passes Steven made.

"Towel?" Steven asked as he shut off the water.

A slim white hand popped through the curtain, holding a towel. Steven pushed back the curtain to see Adrian sitting on the closed toilet lid, examining his nails and ignoring Steven as he dried off.

"You look like shit," Adrian finally said.

"Fuck you." Steven wiped off the fogged mirror and then finger-combed his wet hair into order.

"No, I just mean you look tired." Adrian moved behind Steven, sliding his arms around Steven's waist. Steven leaned back into the heat of Adrian's body, his t-shirt sticking to

Steven's damp back. Adrian rested his chin on Steven's shoulder.

"Of course you're beautiful," Adrian said to their dual reflection, "but you look worn down, like you work too hard. Too much thinking." He tapped a finger against Steven's temple and kissed his cheek. "You need a good night out, so you remember what fun is."

Adrian bit Steven's neck hard as he released him and slipped out the bathroom door before Steven could respond.

"I'm going to find you something to wear," Adrian called from the hallway.

Steven spun through a thread of inadequate comebacks, all along the line of showing Adrian what fun was, but none were good enough in the face of Adrian's rejection of Steven's earlier advances.

In the mirror, Steven did look strained. If anyone had come on to him looking like that, Steven would have walked away, too. He forced a smile that looked so fake, he laughed out loud. There's no way he had looked like that at the bookstore. Chris wouldn't have given him a second glance. Or did Chris see something in him that Adrian didn't?

7.
Rainbow Brite

IN STEVEN'S BEDROOM, SEVERAL PAIRS of jeans and shirts were strewn over his bed. Adrian knelt on the floor to dig through the milk crate that held Steven's albums.

"Here we go," Adrian said. He settled a record on the turntable and lowered the needle.

At the first pulsing beat of the dub version of "Into the Groove," Steven twitched, body memory reacting to his favorite song. Madonna made everything better.

"Come on," Adrian said, raising his arms and shaking his hips. On the beat, he stepped toward Steven. "You're always happier when you dance. So dance with me."

Steven did, letting the towel fall to the floor since modesty was pointless with Adrian. He danced over to the dresser to fetch clean underwear. Adrian catcalled and whistled as Steven shimmied into grey Calvin Klein briefs. The possibility of sex removed, they stepped comfortably around each other, dancing in the small room. Steven closed his eyes as he moved, letting the song call him out. He could feel this free only when he was dancing, when the lyrics were exactly right.

Steven sorted through the clothes on the bed. When he bent over, Adrian ground against him. They both almost fell over as Steven stood up. Adrian caught Steven's arm and turned so he fell sitting on the side of the bed, singing along ardently, demanding that Steven prove his love. Steven was busy sliding into nicely fitted faded Levi's.

"What about this?" Steven held up a glittery pink-and-black bowling shirt, just as the record rotated to "Where's the Party?"

"Fugly. And kind of dykey, isn't it?" Adrian lay on his side, head propped on his hand.

"I don't know any lesbians who wear sparkly pink," Steven said, holding the shirt out to look at it again. He thought it was a cool shirt.

"That's the problem with lesbians, isn't it? Their lack of sparkle?"

"I don't think there are any problems with lesbians," Steven answered. He picked up a long-sleeved t-shirt, printed from shoulder to shoulder, neck to hem in the color bar pattern of an empty TV channel. It looked way too tight to wear. It must be Adrian's, because it definitely wasn't from his closet.

"You should wear that," Adrian said nodding at the shirt in his hand, "and spend less time with your dyke friends before their lack of fashion sense wears off on you."

The shirt was brighter and more colorful than Steven's usual choices, but not as tight as he feared. Definitely more body conscious than his usual style. But he felt good when he looked in the mirror. Eye catching. Also there was a subtle sense of rebellion in dressing outside his comfort zone, even if he was being told to do it.

"Come help me get dressed," Adrian demanded as Steven fussed with his hair in the mirror. "I've got shoes for you. And a present."

The present turned out to be an astonishing amount cocaine. "Not only for tonight," Adrian assured him. He cut lines for them on his glass-topped vanity before plunging into his closet to find outfits to model. Steven figured out long ago that Adrian planned his outfits in advance, but Steven needed to nix the ones that Adrian had already rejected. It was a ritual, part of the setup for the night.

Adrian had a CD player in his room, although they owned only six CDs between the two of them; the novelty of it was kind of exciting. Erasure was playing, a mix of "Oh L'Amour" that Steven hadn't heard before. Adrian must have been CD shopping recently.

"You're supposed to be dancing." Adrian chastised as Steven lay down on the bed. The cocaine rushing in him agreed, so Steven got up, shaking his shoulders to the steady click-track rhythm. Adrian stripped to his underwear and danced over to Steven. Looping a scarf around Steven's neck, Adrian pulled him in to dance close for a minute, grinding as if they were on display in a club.

"Don't you feel better already? Are you happy now? Have I made you happy?" Adrian was so near that his voice vibrated in Steven's ear.

"I'm happy. Aren't you going to get dressed?" Steven said, grabbing Adrian's hips and pulling him closer so they moved together.

"You're much more fun like this," Adrian taunted, wiggling away from Steven. "You have to help me choose." He held up a slithery, draping silver tank top to his chest. "Probably too cold for this, right?"

"Not if you had the right jacket," Steven answered, settling back on the bed but still keeping the beat with his body as the CD spun into "Who Needs Love Like That."

"It isn't worth wearing if I have to cover it up with a jacket," Adrian pouted. He tossed the shirt back into the closet and reached for a pair of yellow pants.

In the end Adrian's chosen outfit was white platform creepers, dark green jeans, a tight neon green t-shirt cut low enough in the back to display part of his tattoo, plus a thin white leather collar and black, white, and neon green rubber bracelets stacked on his arms. Steven watched from the bed as Adrian smoothed on foundation and faint green eye shadow, and then fine silver glitter across his cheekbones. He looked like a mythical creature that had come from the forest, pretending to be human.

"Want me to do your face?" Adrian asked.

"No, I'm good."

Adrian dug out shoes to complete the look he wanted for Steven: bright blue combat boots with rainbow laces, coordinating perfectly with the shirt Steven wore. The outfit worked, but was so Rainbow Brite that he'd probably be asked if he'd put it on just for Pride Week. But it looked good and would draw the right attention if Steven wanted it.

Almost ready to leave, Steven sprayed himself with the bottle of Chanel Égoïste from Adrian's vanity. He caught Adrian smiling when he put it back.

"See?" Adrian said, "We're going to have fun tonight. You remember fun, don't you? You like fun. Let's go prove how fabulous we are. Just you and me together against the whole world."

8.
In the Moment

I⸝ WAS A PERFECT JUNE Seattle night, the kind you wish would last forever: dry, clear, humming after the late sunset. Steven could exist endlessly in this run of perfect moments, everything as it should be.

They walked the long way to Neighbours, up Mercer Street and then all the way down the long corridor of Broadway, which was lined with shops, restaurants, and the city's brightest, most outlandish, and mostly gay denizens.

The walk was stellar. Adrian had cut rails of cocaine before they left, so Steven felt so *aware*. He loved being high like this, right at sunset, the air not chill but cool on his skin. Under the pervasive city smells of exhaust and human habitation, there was a soft perfume, like everything green in the city was just about to burst forth in bright bloom. The early-summer sense of primordial fecundity filled the air, even along this endless stretch of asphalt, concrete, and glass.

He felt such joy in attending to every interesting detail, but as soon as his interest shifted, whatever had last captured it ceased to exist. Like living perfectly in the moment, with no past or future, entirely in tune with the whole world around him. Steven saw smiling faces in the cars that passed, the sparkling colors everyone wore on the street, the glittering smiles of people in restaurant windows. His body was wired, on the edge, ready to move however he wanted, ready to carry him completely out of his head on the dance floor.

At times Broadway was a busy urban corridor, grey like the sky, filled with rushing pedestrians. Other times it was an ongoing party. Tonight, the streets were filled with brightly colored, dropped-low Japanese cars with racing spoilers alongside old Buicks bumping bass beats that shook everyone to the bone.

The Sisters of Perpetual Indulgence, spectacular drag queen nuns, graced the street with their presence, in several small groups, brightening everything they passed.

Gutter punks staked out the front of the 7-11, much to the manager's chagrin, a dark but sparkling counterpoint to the hippie kids begging for change in front of the bank down the block.

And men everywhere. All sizes, all kinds, dressed to the nines or barely noticeable in practical clothes.

Steven and Adrian knew everyone they passed, maybe not as a friend, or even an acquaintance, but all were people they saw regularly, nodded and smiled to acknowledge the daily passage through each other's space. This night belonged among those magical nights, where the street felt alive and pulsing, filled with possibility.

The liberty-spiked, leather-jacketed punk girls sitting on the steps by the Broadway Arcade waved as they passed.

Adrian called out, "Ooh, girls, look at you! You go! Take down the man!"

The girls laughed and pushed each other, then lit fresh cigarettes and went back to whatever girls like that talk about.

When a couple of big Bears cruised them, Adrian grabbed Steven's hand and said far too loudly, "Oh, save me, I might be eaten by a bear!" and threw his wrist up to his forehead like he might swoon.

Adrian blatantly cruised every halfway decent-looking man that passed, ending with a look of disdain when he deemed them unworthy. In between, he smiled for Steven, pointing out people they knew by sight or for real, and wondering aloud if either of them might finally meet a good man tonight.

When they passed the post office and crossed Denny Way, Steven saw two men in suits exit the steakhouse next to Kinko's. The men moved toward a waiting taxi. One held the door open, and the other man paused to touch his friend's shoulder in thanks. The gratitude and friendly intimacy of the gesture tugged at Steven as he heard, *"Merci."*

"De rien," the second man replied. He closed the door, circled to the other side, and climbed into the cab.

Too late to say anything in greeting, Steven recognized John in the taxi, his pale hair looking wrong under the sodium lights, his face too severe and angled, the dark suit and tie unexpected. He'd seen John only in jeans before. The cab pulled away just as Steven and Adrian came alongside.

A flash of recognition crossed John's face.

Then the taxi was gone, headed south on Broadway, the direction of Neighbours.

It was too much to hope that John would be at the bar tonight. Not dressed in that suit. Still, Steven shivered with a sense of premonition, certain the universe meant for him to see John again.

Had John really seen him? Was he thinking about Steven now? Or did Steven only imagine—

"Hello?" Adrian pushed his face close into Steven's, a block later, as they waited at the light to cross Pine Street. "Where'd you go?"

"Sorry. I, um, saw someone I know. I was just thinking about him." Steven still hadn't mentioned John to Adrian.

"Bitch, where? I did not see a man good enough to make you go all dreamy like that. Uh-uh, you point him out if you see him again."

At Neighbours, the broad-shouldered guy who minded the door nodded, recognized them, and did not ask for ID when they paid the cover. At the bar, Steven ordered water and a double vodka-cranberry. He leaned against the bar, drinking the vodka quickly. There was no show tonight. The stage was covered already with dancers who thought they were prettier than the rest, lit with the same purple lights that glowed from the rail along the half wall that went around the booths, filled with sorority girls thinking they were doing something risqué, and leather daddies, laughing together, just like the sorority girls. The black walls disappeared in the swirling lights, so the room felt like a limitless space, male bodies twisting to the music as far as the eye could see. Endless possibilities. The music thrummed through him, leaving him so glad he'd come. As tired as he'd been, this was definitely where he wanted to be.

The room held every kind of man—every kind except John. Steven looked carefully, just in case. Adrian shrieked with joy when Erasure's "Take a Chance on Me" flowed through the speakers, stopping Steven from thinking too much about John. He finished his water and let Adrian pull him onto the dance floor, both of them mouthing the words to the song.

The night passed in a blur of bright moments, nothing to worry about or remember, nothing in the past or the future, just music, bumps of cocaine in bathroom stalls, water and vodka from the bar, dance partners both beautiful and unworthy. Adrian was there, gone and back again, his own partners ever changing.

As the night wore on, Steven's bright, positive bubble cracked a bit. His muscles ached with exhaustion the cocaine couldn't mask, and the alcohol made him dizzy, diluting his earlier euphoria into an uneasy calm. Adrian appeared from nowhere when the last song ended. He grabbed Steven's hand, pulling him outside, where a tall, stern-looking guy in a leather trench coat waited.

"We're going to get breakfast," Adrian declared. Steven wasn't sure if the "we" included him or not.

"Where? IHOP or the Doghouse?"

"Arnold—"

"Arnaud," the man said in a thick accent.

"Yes, I said that." Adrian turned back to Steven, "Arnaud wants to go to Cafe Minnie's." He leaned in close to Steven's ear. "You're welcome to come but you have to find your own way home, because we're going to Arnaud's waterfront condo after. You could come too, but you never say yes to a threesome."

Adrian turned his mouth into a comical little pout showing that Steven's aversion to threesomes was a sad disappointment to him. Threesomes lacked intimacy, and Steven was sure he'd end up feeling left out if the threesome involved Adrian.

"I'll pass, thanks. I'm wiped. I'll see you later."

Adrian hugged him and turned his attention entirely to Arnaud, who nodded politely to Steven as they headed in the other direction.

9.
De Rien

TIME STRETCHED AND RIPPLED AS Steven headed down Pine Street and cut over to walk down Boylston, bypassing Broadway to avoid people as much as possible. The minutes lost meaning when they took so long to pass. Steven couldn't remember how long this walk was supposed to take, despite making it several times a week. It felt like a loop, the same buildings passing by.

The flat grey sky reflected Steven's darkening mood, his earlier exuberance sweated out while dancing, leaving him sketched out and anxious.

Glad to be alone—even Adrian would be too much company right now—he also felt unbearably lonely. He could have hooked up as easily as Adrian, though Chris had never appeared. Perhaps Steven misjudged his interest in the bookstore. It didn't matter. Complications in navigating school relationships aside, he knew Chris wouldn't compare to the man he imagined John to be.

Which was ridiculous. Steven didn't even know John. But surely a man couldn't have such fine eyes and not be an equally fine person?

His mind filled in the details: John was everything Steven could want. A magic union of qualities never before put together, but now made into the perfect man. More than John's chivalry or the gift of cake, Steven remembered most the way John had listened to him, the way John watched while he talked, as if Steven was going say something very important. Since then, every real man Steven met failed to live up to the ideal that John represented.

Inside the apartment, Steven put on Depeche Mode's "Music for the Masses," and then spun out the rest of his drug-fueled nervous energy by washing the week's worth of dishes and making scrambled eggs. Stars shot in the corners of his vision when he pulled off his shirt. His day had started twenty-three hours earlier. He'd been exhausted from the outset.

The brown glass vial of cocaine tumbled from his pocket when he took off his jeans. He picked it up. It was still half full. He contemplated it for a second. A gift from Adrian, promising fun. It had the same glitter and thrill as everything he did with Adrian. But had it been fun? He felt anxious, stretched thin. Any night out with Adrian was like a cocaine high: the brilliant glow, the rush of dancing in colored lights. And only emptiness at the end.

They never talked about the things that interested Steven. Chris would have done that at least, if he'd showed. But that wasn't enough either. There had to be more.

Steven set the vial on the dresser and fell into bed.

Even without more drugs, Steven lay sleepless, mentally replaying the small exchange he'd watched between John and his friend.

Merci.

De rien.

Small gestures of kindness. Everything that had been missing from Steven's own night. Adrian had never shown that kind of intimate respect.

Shoving away the emptiness that threatened to engulf him, Steven thought of John again. Who was that friend in the taxi? What was John doing now? What would he think of Steven, disheveled and strung out, the shallow and vain club kid that Lisa insisted men like John saw in Steven? Was Steven even worth John's regard? What could he do to earn respect and the intimate kindness John showed his friend?

Be better, Steven thought as he drifted off. *Show him who I really am, what I can give him.*

10.
Bubblegum Ice Cream

"Steven?"

The voice went straight through Steven, rising above the noise on the deck at the Cause Célèbre Café. Though it had been several weeks since he last heard that voice, Steven knew the gruffness and faint accent instantly.

John stood over him, impeccably dressed in a grey suit, a pale yellow shirt, and a lavender-and-yellow stripped tie, his blue eyes contrasting with the pale and neutral palette.

"John, hey."

Steven rose, his heart fluttering. He held out his hand, acutely aware of John's strong grip, the roughness of his calloused fingers.

"*Comment ça va?*"

"*Très bien, merci!*" Steven replied. His heart beat madly, overwhelmed that John remembered he spoke French. Steven continued in French, longing to maintain that small connection between them. "*Are you meeting someone? I have room if you want a seat.*"

"Yes, please, if I'm not intruding?" John answered, switching back to English, the warmth of his smile over-heating Steven.

"No, I'm just doing homework. I could use a break. Please sit."

"Thanks, Steven. Just for a minute or two." John set his briefcase on the deck by the empty chair.

"How's your day so far?"

Slipping off his jacket, John folded it over the back of the chair adjacent to Steven. Angling the chair as he sat down, John settled in so they were facing each other. "I might have given a different answer a few minutes ago, but my day is great now. It's gorgeous outside. And here I am on a breezy deck with good company, hopefully about to hear something exciting about computers or perhaps more secret truths about the hidden happiness in suburban families." As he spoke, John loosened his tie. Steven was transfixed by the slow drag of silk under nimble fingers, which then released John's top two shirt buttons with quick flicks. Steven swallowed, holding back the urge to slide the pad of his finger over the hollow of John's throat, to feel the pulse that fluttered there.

"I'm not sure how much new I have to say on either topic today. It's too much pressure to be clever on a hot summer day when I've had my head buried in books for hours."

"Homework in a coffee shop again? Where will I find you next, having chocolate while studying at Dilettante? Or perhaps further down the Hill at Café Paradiso? Hmm, you'd have to be there early in the morning for me to see you."

Steven filed away the new knowledge that John stopped at Paradiso on his way to work. He said, "Probably neither of those places very often. I like B&O best, but when I have a lot to do I come up here to get far enough from Broadway that I'm not distracted by friends."

"And here I am, keeping you from your work again."

"No, it's great, really. I've literally been here for hours. I won't retain anything I read if I keep at it. A conversational break would help me." Steven cringed at how eager he sounded, but he'd say just about anything to keep John near, talking to him. How would they ever fall in love if they didn't spend time together?

"In that case, I won't get my coffee to go. We can sit a minute. I'm on my way home, alas, with more work to do tonight. This feels like the day that never ends. But how could I choose poring through legal documents over good conversation and gorgeous weather?" John's smile was bright but Steven detected fatigue flickering behind it. "I'm going inside for coffee. Do you want anything? More coffee perhaps?" John looked into Steven's empty cup as he stood.

"Yes, actually that'd be great!"

"Café au lait?"

"Oui, s'il te plaît."

Steven smiled, flushed with pleasure that John remembered what he drank. He handed John his empty mug for a refill.

"I'll be right back."

Steven marked the place in his book and closed it, sitting back so he could observe John through the café's glass door. The noise of café patrons seemed celebratory, as if they laughed for his joy at running into John. The thin, early evening light together with the strings of lights crisscrossing the deck's trellis tempered the festive air, making it more romantic. Steven sighed wistfully.

John returned with a small tray loaded down with cups and small dishes. He set a steaming mug and a dish of ice cream in front of Steven.

"I hope you didn't get some earlier, but the special ice cream flavor today was handmade strawberries and cream. I remembered your cake. Alas, no *fraisier pour Monsieur Frazier* today, but I thought this might be a suitable substitute." John's eyes were alight with teasing mirth.

Steven sat up, excitement expanding in his chest. John remembered more than just his drink. "This is amazing, thank you. I didn't even look at the ice cream earlier. I just had a sandwich when I got here."

"Then it's definitely time for ice cream."

"Let me give you some money for it and the coffee," Steven said, reaching into his pocket.

"Don't be silly," John said, putting his hand on Steven's arm to stop the motion. His eyes met Steven's. "I'm sure you'll find some other way to repay me." He blinked, and then turned to his own coffee cup and dish on to the table. "Or simply let me treat you. A treat is good for everyone now and then."

"Well, thank you." Flustered, Steven covered by tasting the ice cream, the first bite melting on his tongue. "Oh my god, it's amazing."

"Good." John gave a satisfied smile and picked up his own cup of ice cream. Steven did a double take, seeing the bright blue contents.

"What do you have?" he asked before taking another bite of his own.

John laughed like he'd been caught out. "It's bubblegum."

"Bubblegum ice cream?"

"Yes."

"It looks—"

"Disgusting? Toxic?"

"I was looking for a more polite word," Steven said. "But yes, it's sort of an unnatural blue."

"It's my secret shame," John said, leaning in as if he was imparting a secret. "I love sweet, sweet things. Really terrible candy. Things any sane person over sixteen wouldn't put in his mouth."

"Like Bottle Caps and Smarties?"

"Exactly." John grinned, his teeth faintly blue.

Steven thought about candy he'd never eat. "Necco wafers? Gobstoppers? Blow Pops?"

"No one anywhere eats Necco wafers. And anyone who tells you they don't like Blow Pops is lying. Everyone enjoys a sucker sometimes. Though Tootsie Pops are better, because of the soft centers." John smirked. Steven's brows shot up at the obvious innuendo.

"What's your favorite, suckers or—?" Steven's face burned with his own attempt at innuendo. Best if he didn't try again.

John grinned, acknowledging Steven's attempt and then answered more seriously. "Hmm, Skittles, perhaps. Though anything made entirely of sugar, dye, and artificial flavor will do."

Of the many ways in which Steven had conjured John in his mind, the real John was entirely unexpected. Everything about John exuded class and wealth. Chemically flavored candy was neither of those things. "That's, huh, probably not what I'd have guessed if I was choosing for you."

"What would you choose for me, Steven?"

A curious eyebrow up, mouth pursed in a question, John spooned more of the toxically blue ice cream into his mouth. Steven watched, fascinated by the soft curve of John's lips, the glistening hint of his tongue, yet unsure of John's dubious taste in sweet things.

"Not candy. Probably tiramisu or marzipan, although I've never been convinced anyone actually likes marzipan. They just eat it because they think it's fancy."

"Marzipan is often very beautiful, and people do like pretty things. I have always assumed that was the reason for violet candies. Speaking of pretty things—" John wiped the last traces of blue from his lips and folded the paper napkin into his empty dish. "Was that your boyfriend I saw you with the other night?"

"The other night?" Steven blinked in confusion, startled at the sudden subject change.

"Hmm, two Saturdays ago? On Broadway and Olive Way. I'd just gotten into a cab. I thought you saw me."

"Oh right. Yes. I mean no, he's my roommate, my best friend, Adrian. But we're not—it's not like that." Steven flushed, wondering what John would think of those rare occasions when they were friends with benefits.

John sipped his espresso and studied Steven. "It's funny, you know. I never forget a face. I remember the first time I saw you."

"Yeah?" Steven croaked, his throat dry. Ice cream finished, he took a swallow of his café au lait to cover his nervousness.

"Yes, two years ago on Broadway. You were with Adrian. You were holding hands, and you both cruised my date."

Steven blinked and put down his cup. "I don't remember."

John laughed. "Well, I don't think either of you looked at me at all. It's okay, he was quite striking." John's expression softened. "Perhaps I only remember at all because I thought how beautiful you'd all be together, with your red hair, Adrian's white, and Tom's dark. Three very different, beautiful young men. Sorry." John looked apologetic. "That was probably more than you needed to know."

"No, it's fine. Like totally okay. Tom was your boyfriend?"

"He was." John's expression closed for second. Then the fondness returned. "It wasn't meant to be, but he was sweet."

"He was younger than you? You said 'three young men'?" This line of questioning bordered on the invasive, but Steven had to know.

"Yes, it didn't work out, as those things go. May–December might seem like a classic romance, but somehow it's always doomed."

"I don't believe you're old enough for May–December. More like May–August," Steven blurted.

John smiled at the compliment. "Anyway, sorry. We were talking about my love of dreadful candy, which is probably as uninteresting as this story."

"No, I'm always curious about other people. I'm truly interested in anything you have to say."

"What else should I tell you about then?"

Steven struggled to find something neutral and safe. *Tell me more about how you remember seeing me years ago,* his mind demanded. *What did you mean about beautiful boys? Are you into threesomes, or watching? Tell me if you'd consider dating someone my age.* Caution won out.

"You said you came to Seattle for college. But what made you stay?"

John settled back in his chair, his collar gaping slightly, teasing Steven again with the soft skin of his throat and a glimpse of the tangle of hair on his chest. John's long fingers stroked the edge of his little espresso saucer thoughtfully. Steven squirmed in his chair at the idea of John's hand stroking him.

"Ah, Seattle," John mused. "You know after a beautiful day like this one, it's impossible to imagine living anywhere else. Of course, we slog through so many grim days, but then the mountains finally come out, and the water reflects blue instead of grey. And from every view, it looks like you're standing on top of the world, able to scale every peak. It's hard to imagine living somewhere like New York, or even San Francisco."

John paused and sipped his espresso, politely ignoring Steven's intense scrutiny. In the pale evening sunlight Steven noticed that John's hair was sandy blond, streaked faintly with white, not the pale blond Steven had seen indoors. His nose was a bit off center, as if it had been broken a long time ago. Setting his cup down, but keeping his hand on it, spinning it in the little plate, John continued. "I don't think everyone gets it, but for some people, whether you're from here or moved here, Seattle gets inside you, and you can't help but love it."

Inappropriate responses rose unbidden in Steven's mind. *I'd like you to get inside me and love it. I can't help but love you.* Fortunately, his fear of public embarrassment overruled any such comeback. Steven licked his lips, looking away— he'd find a better response if he couldn't see John. He was supposed to be talking about Seattle, right? What did he like most?

"I've never lived anywhere else, but I've traveled a little. I've never seen anything as beautiful as a sunrise over Mount Rainier on a clear day. Even just catching a glimpse of the mountain driving over the 520 bridge is a reminder of how beautiful the world is. How we should all pay better attention."

"The view of Rainier at sunrise from Drumheller fountain on the UW campus is probably one of the most spectacular things I've ever seen," John said.

Steven nodded, wanting nothing more in the world than to watch the sunrise and the mountain with John.

"Speaking of UW," John said. "How come you're doing homework in July?"

"Trying to get through as quickly as possible. Summer means more credits in less time. And honestly, the classes are better. You only get the really serious students."

"Ambitious." John studied him.

"And what about you, John? What are you doing that you're headed home from work only to do more work? I confess I'm not exactly sure what you do. I know Lisa works for you, but I'm embarrassed to admit I don't have any idea what she does, except it involves finances. Or finance, which I know is different."

"Ha, finance, yes. Lisa probably doesn't want to bore you too much with the details. It's easiest to say that I'm primarily in investment banking. Lisa helps oversee a few other ventures I have."

"That sounds—"

"Boring?"

Steven laughed. "No, I'm sure it's interesting. So you research companies, right? Learn about different technologies? No, that doesn't sound boring at all. I want to know more."

John grinned. "Yes, indeed, I do those things. It isn't just moving money around."

While John spoke, Steven was again distracted by his hands: unbuttoning his cuffs and carefully turning them up to the middle of his forearms. The hair on John's arms was fine and pale like the hair on his head, though it might feel scratchy if Steven rubbed his cheek over it like a cat.

John continued to answer Steven's question, and Steven found that he was truly as interested in what John had to say as he was in discovering whether the skin on the inside of John's wrist was salty. Squeezing his thighs together again to push back the rising physical attraction, Steven focused on John's explanations.

"We make a lot of decisions about how much money to put where, and how to decide what kind of investments are best suited to each different investor. There's so much research to do, we often take advice wherever we can get it," John said. "If it's a small company doing something new, it's hard to gauge the market for what they are offering when no one has offered that before. Even with a restaurant, a new concept can make it hard to project what will happen."

"I can see that with restaurants. Like all the Asian fusion places right now? Who could guess that just Chinese or Thai food wouldn't be enough?" Steven sipped his coffee to keep more useless words from spilling out of his mouth.

"Exactly," John laughed. "I regret not investing in one of those when I had the chance. But I thought the same: why would you blend all Asian food together? Yet it does seem to appeal to a wider audience, though I'd be hard pressed to tell you why." He appeared at ease as he spoke, his hands turning in small gestures to punctuate his words. His crisp shirt and tie should be out of place on this porch full of people in scruffy jeans and flannel shirts, but his own innate calm made him appear he belonged here. When Steven first saw John, he'd pinned him as both out of place and fitting in perfectly, the same as now, though both the clothes and context were different.

"Do you invest in restaurants?" Steven asked, wanting just to listen. He enjoyed watching John talk so much.

"A couple, but just with friends I trust, and that I don't mind losing money with. Too risky. Small business investing is great, but there are surer bets than restaurants. I do investments in larger companies for other people as well. A good chunk of my regular income is from making money for other people."

"Wouldn't you be better off making all the money for yourself to begin with?" Steven leaned back, aware he mimicked John's posture. Except his own casualness felt forced. John inhabited a parallel universe where people had enough money to lose on investments.

"You'd think so, but where does the money come from? If I have only ten dollars to invest in a good opportunity, but suppose someone offers to invest a thousand dollars and give me five percent? If I can see there's a chance of a large return on their investment, then I have a chance to make even more money than I would on my own."

"Like gambling with someone else's money." Steven pushed back his discomfort at discussing money at all. His upbringing discouraged discussions like this, but John was obviously comfortable with it. This was like another kind of coming out, where you could speak openly about anything, including money or religion, not just sex.

"Not even *like* it. It *is* gambling with someone else's money. But it's also helping people succeed in ways they couldn't do on their own. It can be touchy if people don't understand what they are risking. But the rewards can be great for everyone." John sipped his espresso.

"Interesting. I'm reading a lot about software venture capitalism lately. It's a complicated situation when the nerd geniuses have to present a vision to people who can't understand the basics of what is happening with computers."

"Yes, there's likely a lot of missed opportunity right now. I know folks who've had IBM stock for decades are now finding themselves much wealthier. What will the future hold that we can't yet see? What tech opportunity will we wish we'd been in on from the ground floor?"

Steven struggled to hold on to the thread of the conversation, too focused on John's mouth.

"I feel like that about school right now," Steven said, shaking off fantasies about the thick pink curve of John's lips. *School*, he thought, willing down an ill-timed erection. "Computer science was the right choice, because I love it, not because it's a moneymaking opportunity. But everyone we read about seems to be on the verge of discovery. Like, all these new ideas are swirling around, nothing solid yet, but everyone waiting to see if they have the next big thing."

"What do you think the next big things will be, Steven?" John leaned forward, head tipped to listen to Steven's answer. Steven felt comfortably pinned under the intensity of John's gaze.

"I don't know. The Internet maybe. Access is becoming available to libraries all over the world. I can see information at a hundred other universities, just from my chair. And there's so much information stored, I wonder how fast technology will catch up with it and how it will be kept safe."

"Safe?"

"If we put all information on computers, then it's like everything else in the world, right? Some people will want to hide things away, others will want to steal it. And what about financial transactions?"

"What about that?"

"The software all has to work together so when everything goes digital, people trust it enough to use it."

John nodded. "I hadn't thought about it, but you're right. 'When everything goes digital.'" He looked thoughtful as he repeated Steven's words.

Steven went on. "Half my classes now are with students who'd be there anyway, who love math, or who get the way it works, like I do, and want to dig in and see what they can make. But there are others now, people more interested in thinking about what programs can do—and how they can make money off them. Not that that's bad, it's just a different outlook."

Steven drank the rest of his now-cold coffee. John settled his chin in his fist, body tipped toward Steven. It was gratifying to be listened to like that.

"It's made me think more about what I want to do," Steven said. "Not just whether I help design code for software, but what kind of software? What will it do? How will it help people? It's pretty exciting. It was like puzzle-solving when I took my first class. But six months later, I'm thinking a bit about how I can help change the world."

"I admire a man who sees when the road he's chosen isn't the right one and submits to finding the better road, the one that rewards him for hard work. You don't seem at all afraid of hard work." John's voice dipped on the last sentence. Steven blinked. It was a compliment for sure, but Steven's imagination and the gorgeous distractions of John's body blurred his thinking, leading him to find a sexual charge in benign statements.

Dirty thoughts aside, he was elated that John appreciated Steven's hard work. He rambled on, wanting the praise but not wanting to make too much of what he really did. Studying was merely time-consuming, not complicated.

"Yeah, it's still all school: reading, studying, solving problems I initially don't understand." Steven waved his hands over the books spread out in front of him. "But it does feel exciting, like I'm where something is happening. Does that make sense? I mean, nothing happens at school except people talking about ideas. But this isn't Philosophy. These ideas are going somewhere."

"What's wrong with Philosophy?" John said, smiling. "It's what I studied as an undergrad. But yes, I understand what you mean."

"Sorry, I wasn't trying to insult you. I just meant that Philosophy is more abstract. More like pure math than computer science."

John laughed. "I'm not insulted. I became neither a philosopher nor a professor. It was like what you said last time we talked, about Anthropology being appealing until you realize you'd have to work in academia forever. You figured that out much earlier than I did."

"How did you end up going from Philosophy to finance?"

"The easy answer is that I was given a choice between being a penniless academic or having a large financial stake in my family's business. Or, perhaps, what was exciting at eighteen seemed less practical at twenty-four, and I like to think I'm a practical person. Of course, many other things happened." John glanced at his watch.

"Do you have to go?" It was the proper question to ask, but Steven didn't want the answer to be yes.

"Not yet." John smiled. "Life has a funny way of pushing you in unexpected directions. Though sometimes it's good to be pushed to take direction. But I'm sure you know that."

John licked his lips. Steven was almost convinced that he was being teased. Honestly, the idea had never crossed his mind, but the thought of John *directing him*, telling Steven where to touch and what to do, burned through Steven's belly. He twisted slightly in his chair.

"So what do you do when you're not making other people rich? For fun?" In any other situation it would be laughable that Steven changed the subject away from school, because he was getting hot and bothered. Though if John was doing it on purpose, there likely was no safe subject.

"For fun? Depends on your definition of fun. I restore old furniture. It takes a little woodworking and a lot of sanding and chemicals, but once I learned how satisfying it is to repair old things, I couldn't stop."

"That makes sense."

When John looked quizzically at him, Steven explained. "Your hands. They aren't office guy hands." Steven cringed at what he'd revealed about how closely he'd observed John. "Why furniture?"

John glanced down at his hands and swiped his thumb over the calluses on his palm as he spoke. "I bought an older house and spent years working with a couple friends to restore it, to take the 1950s revisions out and get back closer to its original. I had to learn to do woodwork refinishing as I went along. When I was done with the house, I started furnishing it with secondhand furniture that needed as much love as the house did. It's become an addiction." John looked distant, dreamy. Steven became convinced that he'd just imagined the flirty, dirty undertone in John's comments.

"Where's your house?" As innocent as that question might sound, Steven was crossing a line.

"Sixteenth, off Prospect, near the Park." John tilted his head to indicate north, a few blocks from where they sat.

"Nice. Wow, nice up there. I live on Mercer and Bellevue. Totally different world."

"More apartments and fewer houses, for sure," John said.

"I'm sure your neighbors aren't all junkies and rock musicians. Well, mine might just be rock musicians and not junkies, since they can afford the rents. It's hard to tell the difference."

"Capitol Hill has changed so much in the last fifteen years, since I first moved here. I'm not entirely sure that my neighbors aren't all rock stars, or at least involved in some shady activity to afford the prices now." John again looked at his watch, and then up into the darkening sky. Steven's heart fell. "Look how late it is. I'm afraid I've kept you from your homework again."

"No, I asked you to stay, which kept you from your own work. Sorry I rambled on."

"If rambling is the charge, then I think we're both guilty." John winked. Steven smiled involuntarily. John's eyes stayed locked on Steven's. "As before, you've were very informative, Steven. You are full of useful information about technology. Do you mind if I make use of you and your knowledge?" John stroked his fingertips on the back of Steven's hand, a too-brief questioning touch. Then John's hand was back in his own lap.

Certain now that he hadn't imagined the suggestiveness in John's comments, Steven swallowed hard and tried his own game. He said, "Of course. Whatever you need. Use me any way you want."

John's eyebrows went up. His smile twisted into a promising smirk. "I'll definitely use you, Steven." Steven flushed, leaning toward John, wanting to feel John's fingers on his hand again, anywhere on him. John said, "Unfortunately, tonight I do have other people's money to gamble with. Or at least a lot of paperwork to that end. I should get going."

Steven smothered his disappointment. "Yes, and I should finish my homework. We aren't going to change the world sitting here drinking coffee."

"You never know. Maybe this conversation will set off a spark for you, set you on the right path. Though I'd say you're nearly there."

John stood. Steven did too, reaching for the touch he wanted from John's handshake. John gripped tightly, his fingers brushing over the pulse in Steven's wrist. He looked into Steven's eyes again.

"Steven, you've been a lovely diversion tonight. Perhaps next time we meet, I won't be pulled away by work. And we can take our time with each other."

"I'd like that." Steven felt his chest heave as the words came out. He tried to smile a normal, friendly goodbye.

John's smile curled in wry satisfaction. Steven had no doubt that John's word choices had been intentional.

Steven stayed standing, staring dumbly at the deck's empty steps where John had departed. He sank back into his chair, exhilarated and shaky.

The thrill of this fantasy was new, that an attractive, smart man understood him. This wasn't just about sexual desire. Trying to focus on the pages he needed to read, Steven strayed from wondering how John's mouth might feel pressed against his to imagining the house John had restored with his own calloused hands. He pictured them in the dining room, reading the paper together before work, discussing whether Apple would ever be a worthwhile investment. Or sitting in front of an old marble fireplace arguing the merits of Philosophy versus mathematical solutions. Would Steven do all the cooking? Or would John come in and help when they had dinner parties?

And now he was hungry, too. He might as well go home. At least there he wouldn't feel guilty about fantasizing about John instead of studying.

11.
Like Ronald Reagan Old?

"I'm home!" Steven called as he stepped into the apartment. His chest felt swollen with his crush, ready to burst if he didn't share.

"God, not so loud. What the fuck," Adrian grumbled from the living room.

He found Adrian stretched out on the couch, reading. The TV was on, the sound barely a hum in the background.

"I met someone, Ade." Steven crowded in on the couch. Adrian rolled over and curled around him.

"That's nice." Adrian's attention stayed on the book in his hands.

"No, like met-met. He's amazing."

Adrian set his book on the floor, rubbed his eyes, and propped his head in his hand. "Really? Boyfriend material? At school?"

"No, at Cause Célèbre while I was doing my homework. This guy, John, he's so good looking and smart. Oh my god, and his hands." Steven fell back across Adrian's hips and dropped his head against the edge of the couch. "And he told me he'd had a younger boyfriend. Well, I mean, not really—he was telling a story and—"

"Wait, what? He has a young boyfriend? Like how young? Oh, is this guy old?" Adrian kneed Steven in the back as he wiggled out from under him and sat up, interested. "Well, there's old and *old*. Like Tom Skerritt old? Or like Ronald Reagan old?"

"Definitely Tom Skerritt. I think he's in his thirties or early forties? He's so handsome, and he's so great to talk to. Like, we had the best conversation."

"Is he rich? Your new sugar daddy?"

"It's not like that. He's nice. And smart." Steven hid his scowl. He'd joked about having a sugar daddy before, but the idea of anyone thinking of John like that sickened Steven. He wasn't sure who got used in the worst way in those relationships, which were all about taking advantage.

"So you picked him up at the coffee shop?" Adrian prodded.

"No, he's Lisa's new boss. I met him a while ago. I talked to him at the club one night when I couldn't find you. Then I met him later with Lisa."

"You've been seeing him? Without telling me?" Adrian pushed Steven away, as if Steven had wounded him by not sharing sooner.

"Oh god, no. I just keep bumping into him places, and tonight we talked. Like, it isn't anything. Maybe it has possibilities, but I'm not sure what. Just—I know I like him."

Adrian studied him with raptor-sharp eyes. "So are you going to date him?"

"I don't know. We didn't talk about it. We talked about his work and what I'm doing in school, and stuff. We didn't exchange numbers or anything." Steven felt the swelling in his chest deflate as he explained. It had been such an incredible conversation with an amazing man. But what was he hoping for? To run into John over and over again until John asked him out? Steven sagged back into the couch. "I guess it isn't anything. I like him, is all. I liked talking to him."

"I'm happy for you," Adrian said, his voice flat. "I hope you see him again."

Steven closed his eyes, elation from those moments with John collapsing under the weight of Adrian's cold, hurt response. Steven didn't know how to make Adrian understand what John's attention meant to him. And he hadn't meant to hurt Adrian's feelings.

The couch shifted. Mouth close by Steven's ear, Adrian said, "Don't be sad. I bet he likes you, too." He'd misread Steven's expression. "I bet he's too nervous to ask you out."

Steven didn't answer. John was confident; he'd never have a problem like that. But Steven felt a gap open inside him, where loneliness flowed in. He'd had only a few moments' connection with John; and then trying to explain it disrupted his connection with Adrian. Steven rested his head on Adrian's shoulder, seeking comfort.

"Plus, it's great if he's got money," Adrian said. "You'll soon age out of being able to cash in on your twinky good looks, so you should make the most of this while you can. Let's face it. You aren't going to be anyone's Boy Friday, but you could still find a decent sugar daddy."

Steven sat up, pushing Adrian away. "What the fuck, Ade? You're older than I am. And I'm not some twink. Fuck, why do people keep saying that? If I was looking for a rich daddy to take care of me, why would I bother with school?"

Adrian laughed. "I bet he thinks you're sexy when you're angry, too. Or has he made you angry yet? You're all flashing green eyes and indignation. It's totally cute." Adrian scooted back over and twisted his arm around Steven's waist. "Don't be mad, dollbaby. I love you. I'm sure this guy will, too. I'm just saying you have lots of options in life, but they won't always be open to you, so maybe you should take advantage this time."

Exasperated, Steven now wanted to forget the whole conversation. He leaned into Adrian again, letting him stroke his hair, but irritation buzzed inside as they sat watching court shows flicker across the TV. Adrian's indifference dismayed Steven. It was as if Adrian didn't care at all about Steven's true happiness.

"Are you going out tonight?" Steven asked, changing the subject. The bubble of his beautiful evening shattered, real life now filled the bright space that had moments before contained dreams of John.

Adrian slipped his arms around Steven's waist and rubbed against him suggestively. "Don't you want to go out with me and have fun tonight?"

"Ade, you know I can't." Steven waved his hand over the text books on the table in front of him.

Adrian cupped Steven's chin and turned his face. He hovered close, his mouth an inch from Steven's, their eyes locked.

"Are you saving yourself, trying to be pure for your sugar daddy?" Adrian said huskily. "Because he doesn't know what we have, what we share that no one else does."

"Adrian, no—"

Adrian's mouth closed softly over Steven's, tongue pushing for entry. Without thinking, Steven opened to him, feeling his body heat up in response.

Breaking the kiss, Adrian pressed his mouth against Steven's neck.

"It's fine," he said softly, though a bitter edge came through. "I guess you just won't need me anymore once you get your man. Wasn't it always us against them? Are you going to abandon me now?"

Guilt poured through Steven. He would never abandon a true friend for a boyfriend. It went against his nature. But he had no solid way to prove to Adrian that he'd always be there—except to simply be there when Adrian needed him.

"Where are we going?" Steven said, resigned to another late night.

"Oh!" Adrian exclaimed, sitting up and clapping, his face bright with joy. "You'll go? I was thinking maybe something different. Brass Connection? Unless you have a better idea? Hmm, you can't wear that. C'mon, let's find you something," Adrian headed for his closet before Steven could answer.

◊

Later, head spinning from too much vodka and alone in bed—Adrian off with the trick of the night—Steven remembered what Adrian had said: *Us against them*. More specific than his usual *you and me against the world*.

Who was "them?" Boyfriends who might come between them? Older men, in specific? Had Adrian been hurt in a way Steven didn't know? Even after all these years, there was so much Steven didn't know about the mystery of Adrian.

Desperate to sleep before dawn came, Steven pushed away those thoughts. He closed his eyes and slipped into a different vision of the future, of reading the paper over breakfast with John. So simple, but so much more than he had in everyday life right now.

For the first time, he could picture a relationship with the man of his dreams. It wasn't about money or being madly in love at first sight. It was just about being listened to, and another person trying to understand the things you cared about. But how to get that?

12.
Button Up, Boys

STEVEN WAS HIRED AT BUTTON Up Boys the same day he'd started at the UW. Back then, he imagined the store would be less stressful than working at Fred Meyer. Instead, he'd traded helping harried mothers and screaming children for waiting on entitled rich jerks. At that particular moment, Steven had his best Button Up Boys smile in place, while secretly coping with exhaustion from last night's clubbing.

"I can't believe you don't have this in blue, in my size," the man huffed, hand on his hip, his face warped with the ill temper of a thwarted toddler. The door chimed behind him. Steven's boss Marcus entered.

"It's so typical," the man sneered. "The one thing everyone wants, and you don't even have it."

"Sir, I'm sorry," Steven started to explain that their small store couldn't possibly carry enough stock to appease every need. John surely dealt with rich guys like this all the time. Steven couldn't imagine John apologizing, not to a guy with insipid complaints.

Steven smiled and started again. "I'm sorry you don't understand how our store chooses merchandise. We don't expect our customers to be looking for what everyone else already has. We expect that our customers come here to find something no one else has."

The man looked suspicious, unsure whether he was being insulted. Steven laid it on thicker, "The blue is more last season, although it's a great color. I can see why everyone was attracted to it. But the gold is so much nicer."

Steven lifted the sweater off the stack and unfolded it, shaking the wrinkles out of the lightweight silk. He held it up to the man. "It'll carry you into fall if you put a layer or two under it. Plus this tone is so flattering with your hair color."

When the man turned to the mirror, holding the sweater against his chest, Steven knew he'd won. He busily straightened the disarrayed sweaters while the man responsible for the mess paid Marcus for his gold sweater and left.

Marcus came around the counter. "You are a miracle worker," he said, patting Steven's shoulder before leaning in to help tidy the stacks of sweaters on the wall shelves. "That guy actually seemed happy, although I thought he was going to punch you when you said he didn't understand how the store worked."

"I thought I'd completely fucked up for a second," Steven said. The loose, open texture of the sweaters he folded had the kind of slouchy glamour Steven wished he could wear. Adrian always pulled off that look, but when Steven had tried, he just looked disheveled.

"I hope it wasn't like that here all day," Marcus said as he rehung brightly colored dress shirts.

Steven, in a spring-green poplin shirt and grey cotton pants, felt underdressed next to Marcus in his seersucker shorts, short-sleeve broadcloth shirt, and sockless loafers. It was the kind of look that Marcus could pull off because he was from Atlanta—and fond of saying how much better men dress down there. The pale summer palette looked striking against his polished-walnut complexion. Marcus and his life partner Mitchell had been the first black business owners on Broadway when it started to become a gay destination. Mitchell died of AIDS six years ago. Marcus now seemed to keep the store open from that memory, rather than for business ambitions.

Steven put up the last sweater and straightened. "Yeah. There were some good people. Sales were good. But definitely more assholes than usual. Plus, I'm tired." He sank on to the stool behind the cash register. His hangover felt distant now, just a lingering melancholy and weak muscles.

"Out late with Adrian?" Marcus asked, sipping from the carry-out coffee he'd left on the counter.

Steven shrugged and nodded. He rearranged the endless stacks of flyers that Marcus's friends always brought in, advertising AIDS hospice fundraisers and retro dance parties.

"I don't know how you do it," Marcus said. "I don't think I ran as hard as you do when I was your age. But maybe it's worth it when you know what you're running for." He raised his eyebrows, asking a question his tone didn't.

That look meant this was their regular check in, Marcus making sure Steven was sticking to school and not fucking up. After a year of working together, it was familiar, comfortable support and not the abrasive questioning of his intelligence Steven had mistaken it for the first time Marcus talked to him about school.

"Maybe?" Steven let doubt show on his face. Steven couldn't tell whether the regular pressures were getting him down—the day's tests and then work, the week, school—or if his lingering discomfort from telling Adrian about John was coloring everything. Still, he needed to talk. Relief washed over Steven with the realization that Marcus would at least try to understand all the emotional clutter buzzing in Steven's brain.

"Maybe?" Marcus repeated. "You don't know where you're running to anymore? Or you don't know if it's worth it?" He pretended to sound incredulous, as if he couldn't believe Steven didn't have it totally together.

"I know what I'm doing." Steven was always reassured by the faith Marcus had in him. It made him feel unstoppable, as if someone was cheering from his corner even when he stumbled. "I go out dancing. I go to school. I come to work. I'm just not sure why anymore."

"You come to work so you can pay for school. You go to school so you don't have to work jobs like this anymore, because you're too smart to have to put up with shit from guys like the one who just left." Marcus indicated toward the door with his coffee cup, and then stared at Steven expectantly.

"Yes," Steven agreed, knowing better than to argue. "But what about everything else?"

"What else?" Marcus scoffed. "Bars, school, work. You got sex, money, and mental stimulation covered. What else do you want?"

Steven turned to fiddle with a rack of sunglasses behind the counter, not able to meet Marcus's eyes.

"Oh," Marcus said, drawing out the word. "You want love. Did you meet someone?"

"I just think there should be more to strive for in life than financial success," Steven said stiffly, uncomfortable to have been discovered so easily.

"Uh huh. That's right," Marcus said. "What's his name?"

"John."

"And going out with him is making you rethink what you want out of life?"

"I haven't gone out with him yet." Steven straightened the pens by the register and tugged at the receipt tape, still not looking at Marcus.

"Why not?"

"I don't think he's—well, maybe I'm not his type."

"I have met very few gay men who don't like hot guys. You're hot. What's the problem?"

Feeling the weight of Marcus's attention, Steven looked up to find Marcus leaning on the counter, watching him intently.

"Maybe we're too different," Steven hedged. He was embarrassed to say what he worried about: that John might think of him as just an immature club kid. And if Steven said it out loud, Marcus might confirm it as truth.

"What's different about this one?"

"He's older than me. Successful."

"Age usually isn't an obstacle, unless he's a lot older than you. Like fifty-five or sixty?"

Steven shook his head.

Marcus crossed his arms. "And you're also successful."

"I'm a twenty-five-year-old college junior who works in a clothing store." Steven rushed through a summary of how he'd been thinking John must see him. "No offense," he added, not wanting to insult Marcus's business.

"I'm only offended that you've got some self-pitying bull-shit I've never seen from you before. You work harder than anyone I know. You never let anyone's opinion keep you from getting what you want. So I suspect you don't really know what this guy thinks of you?" Marcus raised his eyebrows, asking. Steven shrugged again, as if admitting to just that. "So you need to go find out what he thinks. Then decide if you're 'too different.'"

"When you say it like that, I sound kind of annoying."

"'Kind of'? Self-pity don't look good on a man, but it's especially bad on you, when there's no reason for it."

Marcus's scolding left Steven wanting to crawl under a rock. Instead, he faced the criticism, shaking it off.

"I am usually pretty smart."

"Usually." Marcus nodded in agreement.

"And I'm pretty hot." Steven put a hand behind his head and the other on his canted hip, clowning to divert them both from his moment of self-indulgent defeatism.

"Blind people can see you're hot," Marcus laughed.

"And I've only got a year left of school. What's a year?" Saying it out loud was making Steven feel better.

"Nothing. So you go out there and get this guy, if that's the last piece you need to make you happy." Marcus encouraged Steven, sounding like a coach. "What does Adrian think of this new man?"

"He didn't—he said he hoped it worked out, but he didn't take it seriously." Steven shifted uncomfortably on the stool, glancing out the window. "He also said some not-nice things."

"Teasing?" Marcus asked, again with his brows raised.

Steven nodded, though it had been worse than that. "But that's Adrian, right? It's hard to say what he'll think tomorrow. And he hasn't even met John yet."

"Does it matter, Adrian meeting John?" Marcus studied Steven while he spoke, though his response was casual.

"If he doesn't like John, it's a sign I could never make it work." Speaking the words solidified Steven's vague fears. "I think I've worried myself sick about all the possibilities. But Adrian's my best friend. His opinion matters a lot, don't you think?"

Marcus put a finger to his lips, thoughtful. "You know, when Adrian quit this job, he said he liked working for me just fine, but you needed more shifts than I could give if you both worked here. He said he wanted you to have a boss who looked out for you, who treated you better than you were treated at your last job."

"I didn't know that." Steven's heart beat in a way that only Adrian ever evoked, where love and anxiety mashed together in never-ending confusion: how Adrian could be so kind, and then so hard, almost cruel, when Steven didn't respond the way Adrian wanted.

"I think he usually looks out for you," Marcus said, an echo of Steven's thoughts. "But maybe—just maybe—he doesn't know what's going to be best for you, even if he thinks he does?"

"Adrian's done a lot for me." He didn't want Marcus to see what had been worrying him for the past night and day. Perhaps it wasn't John he wanted most. Maybe, after all these years, what Steven still wanted most was for Adrian to be there for him.

"Maybe he has. But would giving this guy up make Adrian give you what you want from him? And if you did, are you sure that would make you happy?"

The words hit too close, shots fired right into the heart of Steven's fears, as if Marcus could see right through him. Discomfited, Steven steered the conversation away from Adrian. It didn't seem like happily ever after existed in the real world, but Steven wanted Marcus to tell him he was wrong.

"That's way too heavy, since I don't even have this guy to give up." Turning away from Marcus, Steven laughed, as if it wasn't such a big deal. "If John's not interested, then there's nothing to talk about."

Marcus shook his head. "I thought we covered this already? You're smart. You're hot. Do I need to make you say it again?"

"It's more than that." Steven flashed back to that conversation with Lisa. "I'm pretty sure John can get 'hot and smart' for a dime a dozen. And I didn't make a great first impression. Most likely he thinks I'm a drug-happy, club-hopping twink."

"If you're ready for it, I can give you the answer to one of your life's great mysteries." Marcus put both hands on the counter and leaned in, as if prepared to reveal a deep truth.

"What?"

"Stop fucking getting high and spending every night in clubs. See? Look at me, solving all your problems today." He stepped back, waving his dismissal at Steven's problems.

"I'm not ready for that." Steven shifted to look out the window again. Outside, the usual afternoon pedestrian traffic streamed past on Broadway. Steven hoped none of them decided they needed designer jeans or silk shirts while he was spilling his guts to Marcus.

"Really? What's holding you back?"

"It's my only psychological relief," Steven said, knowing it was bullshit, but he wasn't ready to say what he knew to be true. Giving up that part of his life meant giving up Adrian, which Steven certainly wasn't ready for.

"Relief?" Marcus said, shaking his head, having sensed the bullshit. "People get high just to feel good."

"Relief from everyday ordinary life. Relief from being me," Steven said, masking the real part: keeping his place in Adrian's life.

"Didn't we just agree that being you was pretty great? But maybe not. Maybe there's more you're not telling me?"

Steven shook his head.

"Then you need to decide if you like being you better or not being you. Pick which one will make you happy. And find another way to get psy–cho–logical relief."

"It isn't that easy." He could never say the only times he'd come close to finding relief was with Adrian, both of them naked and pushing the limits of friendship.

"It is definitely that easy." Marcus squeezed Steven's shoulder. "That easy for sure. Be true to yourself. Sounds like cheesy bullshit, but it works. Now c'mon, this *is* getting too heavy, and you're supposed to be off the clock."

"I'll figure it out," Steven assured him, reaching under the counter for his backpack.

Marcus came behind the counter and straightened the watches in the glass display while Steven gathered the books he'd had out, stealing time to study.

"Hey, Marcus," Steven said. He zipped his backpack and then hitched it up on to his shoulder. "Thank you. I'm sure you're right."

Marcus nodded. "Let me get your check before you go."

"Payday isn't until tomorrow."

"Do you work tomorrow?"

"No, but it's no big deal for me to come by."

"Well, maybe you can use it to take out your man and impress him with your wealth." Marcus laughed like he'd made a great joke. He headed to the office in the back of the store.

Steven decided to take this year while he finished school to get to know John. That'd be enough time for John to see that he and Steven could be right together. Enough time for Adrian to acknowledge the importance of their relationship.

"Thanks for tidying up the office, Steven," Marcus said. He handed Steven the check. "Don't know what I'll do when you finish school."

"No problem." Steven hitched his backpack up higher, headed for the door.

"Be safe out there, kid," Marcus called after him.

Steven smiled back over his shoulder. If Steven could be as kind as Marcus was to people around him, he'd be nearer to accomplishing his new goal: becoming a man worthy of John's affection, while also keeping his most treasured friendship.

13.
All's Well That Ends Well

Ryan was standing in the kitchen eating a peanut butter sandwich when Steven came in. He wore a suit, which meant he was coming from or going to his job, which involved charming old ladies into spending money in the women's shoe department at Nordstrom. His usually tousled black hair was combed neatly. His only outward signs of nonconformity were the two thick steel hoops in each ear.

"You look good. Just getting home?"

"Just going out," Ryan said.

"Ugh, late shift. Glad it's not me." Steven dropped his backpack on the kitchen table and sifted through the pile of mail to see if there was anything for him. He tore open an envelope from his mom.

"It's not so bad. I had the day free," Ryan said around a mouthful of peanut butter. He swallowed. "Sorry." He held up the last bit of the sandwich apologetically. "I'm in a hurry."

"No big deal." Steven split his attention while he talked, glancing through the letter to figure out what the tickets clipped to it were. A French language production of *All's Well That Ends Well* that his mother couldn't attend, since she'd be out of town.

Steven stared at the tickets.

There was only one person he could invite to something like that.

He swallowed, feeling like he might choke on the idea of what he'd have to do: call Lisa to get John's number, and then call to invite John to go out with him. Too weird? Too much to deal with.

Steven turned his full attention to Ryan.

"I haven't seen you in forever." Steven smiled, repressing the excitement and anxiety about having some place to invite John to go with him.

"Yeah, I haven't been around." Ryan smiled like he had a secret.

"New guy?" Steven opened his backpack to take out his books.

"Not exactly. It's complicated." When Steven raised his eyebrows, Ryan shrugged evasively. He said, "Speaking of new guys, someone called for you. John?"

The book Steven was holding slipped out of his hand and thumped onto the floor.

"Did he say—well, what did he want?"

Ryan's face split into a mocking grin. "Christ, Steven, you look like you're going to puke. Or jump up and down shrieking like a little girl who just got a pony. He didn't say anything, just to have you call him. The number is on the pad by the phone."

Steven grabbed the cordless phone and the note from the living room. Ryan had stuffed the last of the sandwich in his mouth and was washing his hands while he chewed when Steven came back.

Steven sat at the kitchen table staring at the phone. The French play tickets lay next to it. If he called John, he was going to ask him to the play. And he had to call John now, didn't he? At least to learn why John had called him?

"Hey, are you okay? I gotta go."

Steven looked to see Ryan hitching his own backpack onto his shoulder.

"I'm fine, just wasn't expecting this."

"School? Work? New boyfriend? Ah, I can see it on your face. Hope he's as cute as he sounded." And then Ryan was gone.

Steven still stared at the phone. He'd psyched himself up about John on the walk home from work. The part of his plan he couldn't nail down was how to get onto John's radar, how to see him beyond accidentally running into him at a coffee shop or forcing Lisa to invite Steven to their office.

The note, in Ryan's loopy handwriting, read:

Steven call John, not urgent, before 7pm or anytime tomorrow is fine.

And then his number. Steven dialed slowly and then listened to it ring while he tried to remember how normal people breathed.

"John Pieters."

The rough timbre of John's voice went through Steven like a spark. Giddy, he tried to keep from catching on fire.

"John, hi, Steven Frazier. You called?" He forced his words to be as businesslike as possible, though he was out of his chair and pacing as he spoke.

"Steven, hello! You said I could use you whenever I needed. And I need you."

John's tone was light, but the implications of his words made Steven's breath hitch, his dick stirring as if it had been called into the conversation. Steven's pulse thudded in his temples. He dropped into one of the kitchen chairs.

"You need—" he stuttered, "You need to use me how?"

Steven put his hand on his knee to stop it from jiggling under the table. Hope flared in his chest. Steven didn't know John well enough to distinguish genuine interest from teasing, although he felt fairly sure John was teasing him with an opening line like that. But Steven didn't know what to do now. Every one of his relationships had started as a one-night stand; without that kind of forced closeness, he wasn't sure if he should take John's flirting seriously.

"I'm looking into an investment opportunity for some clients. All the financials look good, and it comes highly recommended. But it's a computer thing. I was wondering if you might have any insight?"

Steven's leg stopped jittering. This was not what he expected, though he had no real expectations. Only hopes. Still, being useful to John could help win him over. Steven said, "Maybe. There's a lot I don't know, though. But ask away."

"Microsoft has a new operating system in the works—" John started.

"The next generation of OS/2." Disappointed that John had called just to ask simple computer questions, Steven answered shortly, cutting John off.

"Yes. I trust your opinion about the future of software and computers. I'm curious if you think Microsoft will have the winning hand over the next decade. I need to talk it out with someone, and I knew right away you're the one I need." He paused.

Steven's heart kept beating.

Then John said, "The software part seems like a given, but what about networking for desktops? Should I encourage my clients to invest in Microsoft or Novell?"

Steven's disappointment crumbled to ash in spite of John's warm statement of trust. But this is what he'd hoped for, a way to be useful to John, a wedge to open the door to John's world. He said, "I think it's obvious to everyone by now that Microsoft is worth investing in. Novell is maybe just as big? Well, no, not yet, but it seems like they will be. I think they've got a lock on the Ethernet part, and that's where connectivity is going to come from. Remember how I told you about libraries everywhere sharing information? Companies are trying to, too, as I'm sure you know. But they won't be doing it without Novell's software and Ethernet cards."

Steven took a breath and pushed on, wanting to give John as much accurate information as possible.

"I don't know enough about investing to guide you. But 32-bit computing and networking will be *the* thing. At least until the next big discovery. So, yeah, I wouldn't choose between Microsoft and Novell, I'd split and go with both. The Microsoft and 3COM networking stuff are still kind of lame."

"Great, yes, good answer, Steven. I confess that's what I was hoping to hear." Steven sat up straighter, as John went on to his next question. "Do you know anything about this Paul Allen guy? He's got an outfit in Bellevue that's doing hyper words or, wait, I'm not sure that's what it is."

Steven knew that answer, too. "Hypertext. Yeah, that might be exciting. Apple did it first as an application. But hypertext only matters if the CSNET and TCP/IP networks are allowed commercial traffic." Steven couldn't shut his mouth; knowing didn't help. He rambled on about communities growing on the Computer Science Network, playing with hypertext, how his prof said it was going to revolutionize academics and libraries.

"Sorry," he said, winding down, "I got carried away again. You didn't need to know all of that. But that's how we'll research everything in the future."

"Never apologize for enthusiasm, Steven." The rasp of John's voice reassured him. "Now that I know how important you think this is, it gives me the best ideas for where to start with my own research. I'm impressed with your whole-hearted dedication to giving the most honest answer you can." John's tone moved to a lower, gruffer scrape.

Steven shifted in his chair. He felt so out of his depth with John. This was just business, right? Every one of those words was a simple, kind reply to Steven's answers, so why did he feel like each sentence was a coded message? Was this a weird artifact of his extreme crush?

"I'm happy to help. I don't think I said anything that impressive though." Steven knocked his head against the wall. Could he sound more desperate for praise?

"If you're game, I think we can help each other in the future." There it was again. A friendly, neutral offer for future collaborations? Or a hint at a more intimate relationship? Remembering Marcus's scolding, Steven tried to err on the side of the second possibility but stumbled through, too unpracticed.

"I'm game. To help you out. You can do what you want with me. I mean, I'll help. Whatever you need." Steven flushed, certain he heard a muffled chuckle on the other end of the line.

"I'm sure we'll find many ways to help each other out."

Steven shivered in anticipation. John was playing at something, and Steven wanted to learn the rules. This was also his chance to ask, before John got off the phone. Steven began. "You could help me out this week, if you're free on Thursday night?"

"I could probably do Thursday. What kind of help do you need?" John's voice was low, with a deeper grind to it. Steven shivered again, thinking of all the kinds of "help" he could ask for.

"I have an extra ticket to a play Thursday." Steven tried to remember what his mom's letter said. "It's *All's Well That Ends Well*, in French. I don't know anyone to invite who would understand it besides you."

"Shakespeare in French?"

"Yes, it's by a group out of Quebec, with some sort of performance art Separatist movement aspect to it. Though I'm not sure how that'll work."

"When and where?"

"Thursday. It starts at—" Steven picked up the tickets to see. "At 6:00 at the Fremont Palace."

"I think I can do that. Should we meet there?"

"Sure. I'll be coming right from work, so that's probably easiest. Outside at 5:45. You know where it is?"

"I do."

"Great."

"If this is the kind of help you're going to need, I'm certainly glad to offer my services. It's not exactly a burden. There are so many harder things you could have asked for." John's voice dropped to a low growl again.

Steven's mind raced for the right answer and then, startled when the front door slammed, he almost dropped the phone. Adrian came into the kitchen.

"Thanks. So Thursday then." Steven heard his breath across the mouthpiece of the phone, masking what he wanted to say: *There is something you could make harder for me.*

Clearly recognizing that Steven was trying to end the call, John said, "Yes, Thursday sounds great. I'm very much looking forward to giving you a helping hand."

"Of course, in return, I'll help you, anyway I can, in the future." Steven bit his tongue. Anything he said, Adrian would hear. That was more than he could deal with right now.

"There's nothing to eat," Adrian declared loudly, slapping the fridge shut.

"Sounds like I should let you go," John said. "Take care, Steven. See you soon."

"You too. Bye." Steven clicked off the phone.

"Who was that?" Adrian slumped into a kitchen chair.

"It was John, Lisa's boss." Steven clutched the phone as if holding it proved that really just happened.

"Your crush? Did he ask you out?"

"No." Steven straightened up and smiled benignly at Adrian. "He had questions about some computer stuff." It wasn't a lie, but Steven's heart pounded like he was sneaking around. There were things that Adrian didn't need to know.

"Too bad. What are we doing for dinner?"

"I don't know. We could go to the store." *We could do anything that would distract you from asking about John.*

"Ugh, I hate the store. Unless you're going to cook for me?" Adrian batted his eyelashes.

"Maybe. But—" The phone rang. Steven lunged for it. "Hello," he gasped. Adrian rolled his eyes.

"Hi, sweetie, it's Lisa. What are you doing Thursday?"

"Hey. Are you at work?" Steven shuffled his notes on the table so he wouldn't see the faces Adrian was making.

"No, I just got home. Why?" Lisa's voice was muffled, as if she was cradling the phone on her shoulder while she worked on some task.

"John called me to ask about some computer stuff and investing. I wondered if you suggested it." Steven could feel Adrian watching him, but he had to tell Lisa that John called, even if it meant once more trying to explain to Adrian why John mattered.

"He called you for advice?" Lisa's voice became clear and loud, as if she moved the phone. Steven had her attention. And she hadn't made John call him.

"Yes." Steven smiled, unable to suppress his glee at the idea that John had been sitting somewhere alone, thinking about Steven enough to look him up in the phone book and call him.

Lisa said, "He doesn't need investment advice from college students, not at his level. Maybe it was an excuse to call you?"

"No, it was just business." Steven bristled. "More stuff he and I talked about when I saw him the other day. You and I don't talk about it, but I do know things." After the way John had listened to him go on about networking, Lisa's attention, though kind, felt lacking.

"I know. You're smart. It just seems weird." Her voice shifted again, becoming distant. Steven heard papers shuffling in the background. "Anyway, I have an extra ticket for the Sonics' game on Thursday. My date bailed. Do you want to go?"

"I can't. I have a thing."

A game would have been fun, but an almost-date with John was better. Yet he was dying to talk to Lisa about John. However, Adrian was right there at the kitchen table, his eyes on Steven.

"Oh boo. Now I have to find someone I don't like as much as you. Call me soon and we'll get a drink?"

"I will. Bye, Leese." Steven set the phone back in its cradle by the answering machine.

"What did your lesbian lover want?" Adrian asked, disdain dripping from his words. Adrian was no more a fan of Lisa than she was of him.

"Jesus, Ade, don't be such a dick about her all the time."

"Well?"

"She had an extra ticket to—" Steven trailed off. "A thing, but I have to work. Though she doesn't think John was just calling me about work." The words slipped out. Instantly Steven wanted to grab them back, but it was too late. What had just happened with John was too big, too good, and Steven couldn't contain it.

"Why do you even care? Obviously he's not good enough for you if he can't just ask you out." Adrian flipped through a magazine, demonstrating his indifference.

"I'm glad he called. Don't make this shitty, okay? Let me have my moment."

"Whatever." Interest blinked out of Adrian's eyes like a light going off. "So, about dinner."

"Let's just go get food. I don't want to cook."

"You never cook for me anymore. Always too busy or too tired. I bet you'd cook for your John." Adrian spat the last word.

"Pagliacci's sound good?" Steven asked, ignoring Adrian's pique. He could manage pizza, but no more than that. He was already preoccupied, wondering what to wear on Thursday. He'd have to go straight from work, in case Adrian was home and asked where he was going.

"Can we stop at the library on the way back?" Adrian said. "Aw, don't look so sad. What did the library ever do but bring you joy and love?"

Once again Adrian confused Steven's thoughtful expression with sadness. An ache tugged at Steven's heart. Had Adrian always been this oblivious to what Steven was feeling?

"It isn't that," Steven said as Adrian slipped his arms around Steven's waist.

"I know, dollbaby. I'm sure this guy likes you, but you don't need him anyway, do you? You have me, and I'll always love you the most. Us against the world." Adrian kissed Steven on both cheeks. "Come on, I'll buy you dinner. Maybe that'll make you smile." Adrian released him.

"Ooh, sugar daddy, I can't believe my luck. A $2.50 date? I wish I'd worn a nicer outfit."

Adrian slapped Steven's ass as he went out the door. "I wish you had, too, but your butt looks good enough in those jeans that I'm only slightly embarrassed to be seen with you."

"Bitch, please." Steven answered the teasing tone in Adrian's voice. "You wish you could have this ass."

"Dollbaby, we need to find you a man worthy of that sweet ass of yours."

John was worthy of his ass, Steven was sure, though he didn't answer Adrian, who simply didn't fit inside the bubble of Steven's elation.

John had called him.

14.
Separate Vanities

AT THE LIBRARY, WHILE ADRIAN found his books, Steven browsed the *Puget Sound Business Journal*, looking for news about the companies and topics John had mentioned. When Steven carried the papers back to the rack, he saw all the local phone books stacked on the end of the counter. He couldn't resist.

Steven shoved over the Thurston County and Tacoma books to get the Seattle White Pages. It took him a moment, trying possible Belgique spellings, and there it was:

J. R. Pieters, 946 16 Ave E

With the number Steven had dialed earlier. John had called him from home. The address was right off Prospect, like John had said, but it didn't matter. He was the only J. Pieters listed, it was definitely his house. Steven wrote the address down carefully on a piece of scrap paper with one of the little golf pencils at the checkout counter. He put it in his shirt pocket next to his heart, and went to see if Adrian was ready.

When they left the library, the evening sky was still bright, the August evening warm around them, a familiar calm, like a childhood memory. As they walked, Steven took half the books from Adrian, noticing a title as they headed down the hill to their apartment.

"Rudolph Nureyev?" he asked, seeing that every book was about the dancer.

Adrian shrugged. Adrian read celebrity biographies, a different celebrity every week.

"I can see the attraction." Steven held up a book. "He's beautiful."

"He was gay, too." Adrian's celebrity obsession was with those rumored to be gay, known to be gay, or involved in a vast conspiracy to hide their gayness. "There will never be anyone like him for me in this town."

Steven stifled a giggle. Competition for the mirror would be incredible if Adrian dated a superstar; they'd have to have their own separate vanities. How could Adrian date a man who got actual applause? "You'll find someone worthy of you."

"What about you? Where will we find someone for you?"

"I don't need to find anyone." It wasn't a lie. Steven had a plan. He thought of the phone call and the paper in his shirt pocket. He was one step closer to making it happen.

"I hope that guy from the phone isn't your someone." Adrian made a face. "He should have asked you out already. Forget about him and move on."

"I didn't say anything about him, did I?"

It stung that Steven couldn't share his not-quite-a-date elation. A space opened in the sidewalk between them, lined with Adrian's obvious disdain for a man he hadn't yet met, and filled with Steven's few small secrets about John.

"Defensive much? You spent all of dinner inside your head, obsessing over that phone call. What you could have said differently. Reading more into everything that guy said." Adrian crowed in triumph about reading Steven's thoughts. Steven had been thinking about John but wouldn't admit that now.

"Nope. I was too busy listening to you go on about Arnaud's condo to even think my own thoughts."

"You don't have to lie to me, Steven. No one else has what we have. I know you better than anyone." It sounded like a threat the way Adrian said it. "I don't want to see you get hurt. Especially since this clearly isn't even a thing. Take me and Arnaud, for instance."

Steven sighed. Too loudly.

Adrian shot him a warning look. "Obviously, this isn't forever. Arnaud is handsome and has money, but he isn't good enough for me, you know? Still, it's fun for now. That's how we've always done it, isn't it? And your John," Adrian said the name like an insult, spelled with a lowercase j, "isn't even fun for you, is he?"

"It was a business call, Adrian. He asked for information. I offered help like I'd do for anyone." Redirection typically worked with Adrian.

"Good. I was afraid I'd have to cancel on Arnaud tonight and babysit your sad ass. Now," Adrian unlocked the apartment door, "come help me decide what to wear."

Steven believed it each time Adrian said they shared something no one else did. It meant Adrian knew him, really knew him. For the first time, Steven started to doubt the truth of those words, to doubt that Adrian would understand that Steven had found one of the good ones in John. The rift between Adrian and Steven seemed small, mendable. Yet at that moment, their connection felt so delicate that Steven knew going out with John would send him into unknown territory with Adrian.

15.
I Want Candy

"CAPE COD. WHISKEY SOUR. ANYTHING else right now?" the server asked as she set down their drinks in front of them.

"I think we're good, thanks." Steven stirred his, so the cranberry juice wasn't floating on the vodka.

Across the table Lisa looked like she'd smack him if he didn't start talking.

"Okay," she said, "now we have drinks. What's so important that you needed emergency happy hour on a Wednesday? Because I know you didn't just have a sudden need for Burgerama Happy Hour at the DeLuxe." She leaned back in the small booth, the last empty one at the DeLuxe Bar & Grill that night, the whole of the Hill having decided they needed burger-and-drink specials.

Steven's maniacal grin strained his face. He felt like the comic-book Joker or that Hatter from Alice in Wonderland.

Lisa eyed him, suspicious. "So what's going on, sweetie?"

"I'm going out with John tomorrow. That's why I can't go to the Sonics game with you."

"Out out? He asked you?"

"I asked him."

Steven tried to relax his face, though he couldn't totally stop that goofy grin. He sucked at his drink through the small straw, trying to look boastful and innocent, like he was as together and ready for this as *I asked him* sounded.

Lisa's mouth rounded into an "o" of surprise. "Well done. Wow, I'm impressed." She raised her glass in a little cheer.

The room around them bustled with unintelligible conversations, clanking cutlery, and music, making a wall of sound that isolated Steven with Lisa in a little padded corner of the world. He felt his smile break though again as they clinked glasses. "Yup. I'm going out with John."

"You go, baby. This is exciting, but your face is kind of freaking me out. Is this your 'about to explode from happiness' look, or 'rigor mortis has set in' because you're dead from the shock?"

"Both?"

"Okay, so tell me about it."

"My mom sent me these tickets, and all I could think of was to ask John. But I'd already talked myself out of getting his number from you—"

"You mean, tussling his number *from* me," she said.

Steven shook his head. "It wasn't about wrestling you for it, I was chickening out when he called me. To talk about that networking stuff."

Lisa raised an eyebrow. "Yeah? You told me on the phone that you were talking about work."

"We *did* talk about work. I did help him," Steven insisted. "But then I didn't want to lose a chance, so I asked him to come to a play with me. And he said yes. And it's tomorrow."

"So fucking exciting." Lisa beat on the table happily, like she also couldn't contain herself. "I'm amazed that you have the restraint to sit still. You look like you're about to start whirring around like a top. So what are you going to see?"

"Shakespeare in French, basically. Some political Quebecois Separatist thing. I know, right?" Steven said in answer to Lisa's expression. "It might be just awful, but then, of course, years from now when we're telling the story of how we got together, we'd be able to laugh about terrible it was."

"'Years from now'?"

"Obviously this how it all starts. Although I'm sure we'll include you in the meet-cute story at the coffee shop."

"You sound very sure of all this."

"Do I? Excellent! Because I am so not sure." Steven slumped back into the booth and took a long pull on his drink. "I'm in so far over my head, I don't even know what I'm in."

"Oh sweetie, tell me all your worries."

"Really?"

"Yes. I'm sure we can write them all off as utterly ridiculous. Because you're being kind of a drama queen right now."

Steven scowled at Lisa, but then smiled and sat back up. "It's not ridiculous to worry about someone's intentions."

"Whose intentions are we worrying about? John's?"

"Yes. What if this is just a pity thing? Like he thinks he's doing me a favor?"

"Oh god! Body-snatched?"

"What?"

"Who are you and where is my Steven?" Lisa didn't look like she was joking.

"Okay, funny."

"No, seriously, what the fuck? You have never been like this over a guy. Adrian must be ready to smother you in your sleep if you're mooning around the house like this."

Steven blew out his breath, deflating. "I didn't exactly tell Adrian."

Lisa shook her head again, closing her eyes for a second. She knocked back the rest of her drink, looked at Steven's, and signaled the server for two more. Her teeth looked sharp when she smiled, as if she'd just as soon eat him as help him. "Sweetie?"

"Yeah?" Steven didn't meet her eyes.

"You know I love you?"

Steven looked up, dreading it. "Yes."

"Then just tell me what's really going on. I'm hoping this isn't some new thing with fucking Adrian that you want to drag me into. But even if it is, I will listen and try to be fair."

Steven toyed with his drink for a second, drinking the last quarter of it, and then setting the glass aside.

"I don't know why I'm so nervous," he said. "It's not like I've never asked a guy out. And he said yes. I just feel like something is happening that I don't understand."

"Okay, this is just about John?"

"Yeah," Steven answered. It wasn't lying if you only told the important parts.

"Go on."

"This sounds stupid, but what do you think he wants from me?"

Lisa smiled kindly, as if he was slow-witted and needed her to explain a simple thing. "Okay, did you ask him out?"

"Yes."

"And he agreed?"

"Yes." Steven nodded, feeling his weird smile crack again. The glee from John having said yes was hard to contain.

"And he knows where you're going?" Lisa asked.

"Yes."

"So, I think he wants to go out with you. Based on that evidence. I know you are very smart, sweetie. I'm sure you can come up with one hundred and six reasons why this isn't a date, but at its core, this is the actual definition of a date. Maybe it's more of a casual date than you wanted, but that can be good. It gives you guys time to get to know each other, find out if you really want him, or if you've just imagined him as some ideal."

"My imagination is currently the problem." Steven drew his finger through the wet circle his glass left on the table.

"How so?"

"When I saw him the other day and in the phone call, he keeps saying all these things. Like, I think he's flirting with me, but I can't tell."

"What do you want me to tell you, baby? He's definitely a flirt. He flirts with me, with his clients, and with Shirlene, our secretary who's sixty-five. So I'm sure he's flirting with you, too. But maybe he's trying to tell you something."

"You think so?" Steven asked hopefully.

"I don't know, sweetie. Maybe you're just reading too much into it, because you really like him. Explain the flirting to me. Thank you," she nodded to the server as fresh drinks were set in front of them.

"I know he's flirting, but that kind of flirting doesn't really mean anything. This something else. He says things that sound normal in context, but it feels like there are hidden meanings in what he's saying. So I try to play along. Really badly, I might add. It turns out I am not good at some things." He gave a "who knew" look. Lisa laughed. "So he says things that could be benign, or might be flirting, as if he's trying to elicit a response from me. His voice drops and his tone is—well, it makes me hard. Sorry," he added, seeing Lisa's expression. "But it does. And what he says are these kind of sexy daddy things. So I get really confused."

"At the risk of sounding crass, isn't that why guys like you go for guys like him? The sexy daddy thing?"

"Well I don't. I never have. And, honestly, the sex I have is pretty vanilla."

"Sure. Right." Lisa looked incredibly doubtful.

"What? It is." Steven didn't know whether to be offended or proud that she thought him so much wilder than he was. "A hook up isn't kinky just because it's gay and in a bar bathroom or in an alley." Lisa made a face, but Steven ignored her. "What if John's comments are like S&M code, and my responses mean something I don't intend?"

"Oh my god, you are ridiculous. I can assure you that John wouldn't tie you up and spank you because you gave a secret-coded answer to a mystery question. He'd talk to you first. Which is a method you might want employ: talk to him. Because sitting around thinking and even talking to me is clearly making you crazy."

"I do feel kind of crazy," Steven said. "And I know it's ridiculous. I have rational moments, short ones, in which I realize that this is just pre-date jitters. Which I'm not used to. I don't know how to act with a guy like John. Find a pretty boy in a bar, find out he wants me too, make out in an alley, fuck in a stranger's apartment—I can do that. Two months later, the fun is gone and one of us stops calling. Whatever is going on with John is so different from that. Like I'm in the championship game of a sport I've never seen played, trying to guess the rules." Steven leaned back against the booth and stared at the ceiling for a second, listening to music above the ambient restaurant noise, trying to give his brain a break from all the bullshit he'd been thinking all week.

Lisa's voice was clear over all the other sounds. "Go out with him. Relax. Be yourself, and whatever other crap advice I can give you. I can say for certain that you will have to work for this one. More than you have ever worked in your life."

Steven sat upright. He grimaced, remembering their last conversation. "Yes, I know. Men like him have tons of guys throwing themselves at him."

"And you're not used to having to work for guys either. They just come to you. This kind of pursuit is different. You have to understand, John is you. You in fifteen years. So put yourself in his place: you've lived, you've had your heart broken, probably more than once. You have a whole life of friends and work, and then some kid shows up and starts panting after you. What do you do?"

"Some kid?"

"You know what I mean."

Steven sank back against the padded vinyl of the booth. He looked back at the ceiling, as if searching for the right answer. What would he do? Be himself, for starters—which wasn't the insecure mess sitting at this table with Lisa.

Spine straight, Steven smiled at Lisa again, losing all the strange, strained mania. "Since we know the pursuer is totally hot and smart, I'd probably go out with the kid." Steven wrinkled his nose, showing his distaste for being called a kid. "At least to see what he's really like. Age shouldn't matter, if we really connect."

Lisa nodded.

"So I guess all I can do is go out tomorrow and hope for the fucking best?" Steven picked his drink up and stirred the melted ice into it before taking a sip.

"If it helps, I don't see how he could help falling in love with you."

"If he doesn't, will you tell him to fuck off, quit your job, storm out of the office, and run away with me?" Steven managed excellent deadpan.

"No." Lisa's deadpan was even better.

"Well, then I better make him love me." Steven laughed, relaxing, caught by how absurd he was to worry about things he'd never be able to control.

Lisa grinned. "I have faith in you. Now—" She raised a dangerous brow. "Do you want to talk about why you haven't told Adrian about this date?"

"No, I definitely do not want to do that," Steven answered, feeling his body tense again.

Lisa studied him for second, then apparently decided not to press the Adrian issue. Bow Wow Wow's "I Want Candy" played over the other diners' conversations and Lisa drummed the riff on the table.

"I love this song," she said. "I so wanted to be the girl in this video when it came out, but I don't think I could have pulled off that mohawk."

There was much to be said about friends good enough to know when to change the subject. Steven listened to the song, remembering time spent watching the video during his high school years, wishing he had "candy" like the guy in the video. Candy.

"Leese!" Inspired, elbows on the table, Steven pushed as close to Lisa as he could. "This song is a sign."

"How dumb is this going to be?"

"Hear me out. I'll bring him some candy for the play. Like Skittles or Tootsie Pops. You know, instead of first-date flowers. Right? Is it good, or is it dumb?"

"Dumb on what scale? Like against average humans, or against other things you've said tonight?"

"Fuck you. I'm serious." Steven imagined pulling a roll of Lifesavers out of his pocket, the tropical fruit ones that taste weird, and giving it to John while they waited for the curtain to open. *You remembered*, John would say, and he'd look at Steven like he was truly considering him as a partner.

Okay, yeah, it was dumb. But Steven didn't want to back down now that he'd asked.

"Why would you bring him candy? I mean if you want to do that, at least go to Dilettante. Get something good."

"Oh god, he does keep it secret." Steven paused. If Lisa, his employee, didn't know that about John, it was gossip. And he only wanted to gossip about John if it was to tell about their first kiss.

"What?" Lisa was genuinely confused, not humoring him. Steven didn't have a choice but to answer.

"He loves crappy candy. John does. He ate blue bubble-gum ice cream when I saw him at Cause Célèbre. We had a whole conversation about it. He joked that it was his dark secret. Since I know, I can bring him some. To show him I remembered our conversations."

"Hmm, maybe. Huh."

"What?"

"Nothing really, just remembering the he has a really nice vintage milk-glass covered dish on his desk. I peeked once, and it had Skittles in it. I assumed they were for a specific client, but oh my god he's just sitting in there eating candy with the door closed." Lisa's delight made Steven happy he'd shared. "Sure, candy, why not? I don't think it'll change the outcome, but it's cute."

"Buy candy. Be myself." Steven ticked off the advice. "Don't worry about what I can't control. Talk to him as if I really want to know what he's thinking. Which I do."

"Yep, that sums it up. Are we getting another round? Or are you going home to freak out until tomorrow night?"

"Do you need to be anywhere?"

"Nope."

"More drinks then." Steven flagging the server.

"Then do you want to tell me how good I look while we have our drinks?"

"Didn't I say something when I came in?" Steven did his best to look horrified at his own bad behavior.

"Nope."

"Fuck, I'm the worst." Steven felt lighter immediately, back in the right balance between them, his free-form anxiety about John temporarily drowned by vodka and smothered by good friendship.

"You are," Lisa agreed, but her expression was kind. She reached across the table and stroked the back of his hand.

"You do look incredible. Did you wear that to work?" Steven asked, giving the short red sheath dress the attention it deserved. On closer inspection, the fabric was elaborately embroidered, red on red.

"I did, but under the blazer that goes with it, so it wasn't this sexy."

"Matching shoes?" Steven leaned over the side of the table to look.

"Nope." Lisa stuck out her foot, revealing purple pumps that went with her purple feather earrings.

"God, you're amazing. Will you come to my house and dress me?"

Lisa squeezed Steven's hand, then let it go. "Now this is the conversation I was expecting. Have you started picking out outfits yet? Is this play thing casual?"

"It's Seattle, so..."

Freed by falling back into normal conversational territory, Steven rattled on about his outfit possibilities (most involved jeans and shirt choices), school, recent work days. By the time they eased into discussing what was going on in Lisa's dating life (nothing), Steven felt a lifting of the burden of gloom he'd been carrying.

Excitement and anticipation thrummed just under his skin. John was a grand unknown, an unexpected ride. Steven couldn't do anything but hang on and see where it went.

16.
Blow Pop

"*I* ADMIT, *I* WASN'T EXPECTING *much. But it was quite good, wasn't it?*" John asked in French. He rested his elbow on the back of his seat, angling around to face Steven.

His spoken French was comforting. After hearing only French for two hours, Steven thought English would have sounded strange. He was glad John felt the same.

The theatre was emptying very slowly, and their seats were right in the center of the row. They were stuck until everyone else cleared out.

"*I wasn't sure, exactly how* All's Well That Ends Well *would fit the separatist theme. But it worked out better than I imagined. The costumes were great,*" Steven said. He'd been sitting next to John in the dark for two hours, breathing that green, woodsy scent. And not touching him.

"*And the sets...minimal, but very effective.*" John smiled, indicating past Steven. The row to Steven's right had emptied finally. John stood, waiting while Steven grabbed his jacket, and then they headed toward the exit.

"*S*hakespeare *in French was better than I imagined as well,*" Steven said over his shoulder. John followed close behind him.

"*Y*es, *I'm glad they didn't try for archaic French. I'm not sure that would have worked.* Watch the steps," John cautioned in English as they reached the end of the row.

Looking forward, Steven felt John's hand ghost across his lower back, as if to catch him, should Steven lose his balance. Steven went carefully down the steps, wanting to lean back and press into the light touch that disappeared as soon as Steven hit the last step.

In the lobby Steven shrugged on his jacket to fend off the early fall chill, wondering how best to suggest they draw out the night. He'd vibrated with excitement all day, barely able

105

to sit through his one class, and then driving Marcus crazy by speculating whether John thought this was a date or just a casual social meeting.

Steven had arrived with minutes to spare. Flustered by trying to pick the perfect candy for John, Steven left the store with nothing. He caught the last possible bus, which was delayed by traffic Steven hadn't anticipated, because he so rarely came to this side of town. Bus, then the drawbridge, another too-long wait for rich people's boats to pass. Steven walked the two blocks to the theatre quickly. John was waiting outside, looking like he'd stepped out of photo shoot from GQ magazine. Chinos neatly pressed, a moss-green dress shirt, and a cotton sweater, dark green and cream stripes, warding off the cool September air. In black jeans, black-and-white checkered button-up shirt, and a blue denim jacket, Steven felt under-dressed next to John's perfectly understated casual look.

"Not a minute to spare," John had said, smiling, his hand out for Steven to shake.

"I'm so sorry. I had no idea what traffic would be like at this time on a Thursday."

"I haven't waited long. But we should take our seats."

And now here they were, on the sidewalk in front of the theatre, having had barely enough time to say hello since they sat down two hours ago.

"Did you eat before?" John asked, relaxed, hands in his pockets. "There's a great little place around the corner. We can probably get a table." He looked at his watch and nodded in agreement with his own statement, raising his eyebrows in question.

"I didn't eat. I came straight from work. The Longshore-man's Daughter? Or Yak's Deli?" Steven didn't care where they went, relieved that John suggested dinner, saving Steven from asking.

"Longshoreman's Daughter. I'm sure they're open for dinner during the week. Though Yak's does have its charm."

"Sounds great. I've only been there for brunch."

The cafe was crowded and bright, with colorful art on the high white walls and the rowdy clatter of silverware on dishes and friendly conversation.

"Two?" asked a brusque waitress, passing by with a tray of food.

"Yes."

"There's one left, and it's all yours. I'll be with you in a sec," she said, pointing to a table in front of the big window that looked onto the sidewalk.

They sat in red vinyl chairs, new but looking like they came from a diner forty years ago. Glittering strings of white lights twinkled around the square white columns spaced around the room. The table had a vintage-looking tablecloth printed with oranges and flowers, and a little vase filled with blossoms, leaves, thorns, and tiny orange salmonberries.

"Oh how funny. I was listening to this album while getting ready to come meet you," John said.

Steven's brain caught the song slowly, not able to match it all with what he might have guessed John would listen to. He frowned as threads of the song resolved into the whole and Johnny Marr's jangly guitar on "This Charming Man" rose over the chatter of the restaurant.

"This is The Smiths."

John laughed. "You look confused."

"No, not all, sorry. Just couldn't hear the song at first." Steven covered for what had indeed been confusion.

"It's okay. In your place, I wouldn't have expected that answer from me, either." John grinned. Steven felt warm, pleased at how relaxed and easy-going John always seemed.

"I hadn't thought about what you might listen to." Steven lied. He'd never admit that he'd once imagined John schooling him in classical musical, explaining all the great composers. "Now I'm curious about what you do like."

"Most of my musical education when I was younger was from boarding school music appreciation classes. And, of course, the Beatles. They were hard to avoid back then, even at a remote all-boys school in Switzerland. But I always liked the Kinks better."

Boarding school in Switzerland was something Steven expected to hear from John. Recognition of alternative rock bands, not so much.

John said, "I like all kinds of music, though I admit that my knowledge of popular music is more scattershot than wide ranging."

"Menus," the waitress said, materializing at Steven's elbow and dropping them on the table. "There's no specials tonight. Anything to drink?"

John turned his attention to her. "I'm fine with water. Oh, unless you have something sparkling?"

"Pellegrino coming up. You?" She looked at Steven, as impatient as before.

"Water's fine for me, thank you."

She nodded and was gone.

Steven picked up his menu. "So The Smiths just fell into your scattershot knowledge of music? Heard it one day on the college radio station and loved it?" he asked, watching the graceful movements of John's hands as he laid his napkin in his lap and flipped over his own menu.

"How old do you think I am?" John laughed.

"No, no, I didn't mean anything like that. I don't ever think of the Smiths and businessmen together. I let that shade my thinking." Steven covered his guilt again. But John's smile was warm and amused. Steven relaxed as John explained.

"My friend Shane is a great lover of music, and he often brings me what he thinks I'll like. He's rarely wrong. I do like everything he offers. He's opened me to a lot of music that I never would have given a chance otherwise. Although, while I think Shane wants to be altruistic, he doesn't exactly share music just for the joy of it. He has an odd need to match people up with what he thinks they need, including new music, clothes, or boyfriends. He just keeps bringing things over and over until something sticks. Once he knows which things you like, he'll tailor what he brings to your liking as he understands it."

"That sounds kind of fun."

"It is, as long as he isn't trying to make a project of you." John shook his head, obviously affectionate toward his friend, but also annoyed at being or having been one of Shane's projects.

Not wanting to poke too deeply into what kind of project Shane might have made of John's life, Steven asked, "So what's some music that you really loved?"

"Things I got from Shane? Hmm. Joan Jett and the Blackhearts. Lush. The Smiths." John nodded in acknow-ledgement, his eyes sparkling, "Squeeze. The Psychedelic Furs. Dolly Parton. But I've found plenty on my own or have carried it with me for years."

"Like what?" Steven leaned in, anxious to absorb new information about John.

"Chaka Khan, Blondie, David Bowie, The Commodores, The Righteous Brothers, Melba Moore. Throwing Muses." John dipped his head to acknowledge the song now finishing in the restaurant. "I don't want to bore you listing them all."

Steven was sure he couldn't be bored. And John's list was so unexpected. "That's a very—"

"Eclectic?"

"Yes. A very eclectic bunch of bands."

"What were you going to say? Sorry, I didn't mean to speak for you."

"Eclectic is probably better. I would have just gone with 'weird.'" Steven gave an awkward shrug. It *was* a weird collection of bands.

"You think I'm weird already, and here we've hardly gotten to know each other." Amusement teased at the corners of John's mouth.

"Is that good or bad?" Steven asked, also starting to smile. John's casual friendliness infected him, leaching away all that pre-date anxiety.

"You tell me."

Steven forced a thoughtful look, worrying his lip like he was making a big decision. "Good, definitely. I like weird."

"Then I'm glad you think I'm weird." John's smile lit his face again, an eyebrow up, like he was letting Steven in on a joke. "Now what will we eat?" John turned his menu again, his hands barely holding it, resting it gently on his fingertips.

Steven imagined that light touch on his back, what those fingers would feel like on his skin. He sucked in a breath, trying to focus on what was happening in front of him. Everything on the menu looked good, or at least what Steven could read of it. He was having a hard time focusing. The chicken, he decided, so he wouldn't have to choose.

"You should get the ravioli," John said, unprompted. Steven looked up to find John watching him.

"Yeah? Everything looks good. It's hard to decide."

"The owner makes them by hand every night. You don't find butternut squash ravioli like this many places."

Steven read the description. He wouldn't have chosen it, but now the chicken seemed so unsophisticated and boring.

The waitress returned with water glasses and a tall green bottle. "We only had the big ones," she said as she set the bottle down, "I figured you could share. Now, do we know what we're eating?"

Steven ordered the ravioli, feeling John's smile, as Steven tried to keep his eyes on the waitress. John ordered ceviche, and Steven wished he hadn't handed away his menu, so he could peek for a reminder of what that was.

John poured water for both of them and offered his glass out to clink in a small toast when they both reached for their glasses at the same time.

"To unexpectedly good things, like political activism in French theatre," John said.

"John?" asked a deep voice just behind Steven's shoulder. Steven only caught a glimpse of the man's face before John was standing up to embrace him. A good-looking man about John's age, with burnished cocoa skin, a shaved head, and thick silver rings in each ear. Red scarf looped around his neck, white t-shirt, black jeans, jewelry glittering at his wrists. Everything about him was stark, bright, and buzzing with exuberance.

The man said, "I thought that was you. But then I thought, 'What would John be doing in this neighborhood?' And then I thought, 'What am I doing in this neighborhood?'"

John laughed in reply, relaxed and open in a way that Steven hadn't experienced. As jealousy shot through him, Steven scooted back to get a better view of the interloper.

"Whatever reason you're in Fremont," the man said, "it's good to see you. Slumming it on this fine September night?"

"We were at the theatre around the corner. And this place is always worth coming to when I'm in the neighborhood. What about you? Kicked out of every place on the Hill?"

Nose wrinkled at John's tease, the man answered, "No, we're coming back from a dinner party. I just had to run in when I saw it was you. Ricardo is waiting outside, because he says I won't lollygag if he doesn't come in." Outside, an older man with long, black hair, strikingly shot through with silver and braided down his back, stood with his arms folded across his chest. He smiled and nodded when everyone looked his way out the window.

John finally stepped back, running his hands affectionately down this man's arms. Steven had been acutely aware of the intimacy of John's grip on this guy's biceps as they spoke.

John waved outside to Ricardo and then turned, smiling at Steven. "Gabriel, this is my friend Steven. Steven, Gabriel."

Gabriel stepped back to look at Steven and then stuck out his hand, which Steven dutifully shook.

"Sorry I can't get up," Steven waved his hand, indicating how he was hemmed in by Gabriel's position.

"Oh no worries, honey. I can see you just fine." He leered, then turned back to John. "I can see we have some catching up to do. I'll call you soon, okay? I really should run. Ricardo is waiting. Nice to meet you, Steven, really lovely, hmmm."

And Gabriel was out the door. Steven watched through the window as Ricardo slipped his arm around Gabriel's waist, and Gabriel said something. They both looked back, smiled at Steven, and hurried down the street.

"That was—" Steven started then stalled, trying to choose the right word. Annoying? Bizarre? Unexpected was the most polite word.

"—my ex. It's been many years, but we're still close."

"That was unexpected," Steven finished what he'd meant to say. He'd tried not to guess at John's past, his other relationships, besides Tom who haunted Steven with imagined youthful beauty. Gabriel was not what Steven would have anticipated as an ex.

John met Steven's eyes, his expression soft but speculative, a kind turn to his mouth. "Yes, unexpected at the very least. Also, awkward."

"No, not at all. Seattle is, like, such a small town. And it's always the places where you think you won't see anyone, right?" Steven tried to smile convincingly.

It wasn't jealousy, but a new feeling settled in his chest. A reminder of how far removed he was from John's world. It was a void that he yearned to fill with all possible knowledge of John. It now held only a few tiny stars of information that shone in the void's vast emptiness.

"So, Gabriel, how—how did you meet him?" The awkward phrasing wasn't nearly as bad as what was churning in Steven's brain, worrying that it was ill-mannered to ask. He had no idea, besides ignoring the whole thing, what the social niceties were in this situation.

"You know, I'm not exactly sure how we met. It was a very experimental time in Gabriel's life, and mine too. I could say we were in love, except we were young and both damaged, so we clung to each until we realized we should have been just friends from the beginning. But then, everyone has that ex, don't they?" As he spoke, John's fingers traced his lower lip, drawing Steven's attention.

"I don't think I do," Steven said, distracted. No one had stayed around that long, and none came back to be friends.

"You aren't friends with any of your exes?"

"Maybe. How long do you have to have been with someone to consider them an ex?"

"I don't know if there's a rule about that. But I'd say three months is enough time to get really settled with someone."

"Then I only have three exes. One moved to New York and we hardly find time to catch up, but we might have stayed friends if he hadn't moved. Most guys I've been with, I didn't even know well enough when we ended it to know if I wanted to stay friends with them." Steven's face burned as stupid, immature words fell out of his mouth. "Not that I'm running around picking up strangers and dropping them. I just—you know how it is. Sometimes you don't click enough with a person that you don't share anything with them, and then you don't realize it right away because you're blinded by some other connection." At that moment, Steven would willingly lose a hand if it would to make him stop babbling.

John looked sympathetic, though whether from hearing Steven's half-assed explanation or pitying Steven's obvious discomfort, Steven couldn't tell.

"It sounds like you haven't yet met a person willing to meet your needs."

John's hand was on the table next to his water glass. Steven could simply reach out and touch it, curl his fingers around John's. Just the idea of John's pulse against his, their palms together, was calming. Steven clenched his hands together in his lap to keep from reaching out and making this more awkward.

"Or maybe I have and I didn't know it. Or he didn't know it."

"Anything is possible." John's smile was benign though Steven felt the full weight of his attention. John tipped his head, brows drawn together. His tongue slipped over his lower lip, just a flash. He looked like he was about to say something when the waitress bustled up again, dropping plates in front of them.

"Anything else?" she asked, already stepping away.

"No, this looks great. Thank you," John said.

"Yes, thank you," Steven said to her back.

Grateful for the well-timed interruption, Steven carefully cut one of the huge, round raviolis into quarters and swiped a bite through the sauce in the bottom of the wide bowl before putting it in his mouth. He chewed slowly, with an apologetic tip of his head: *Sorry, can't answer with my mouth full.*

"This is really good," he said when he could speak, fork pointed at his plate. "How's yours?"

John picked up a tortilla and spooned some of the colorful shrimp mixture into it, then wrapped it closed and took a bite. "Surprisingly good. You know, I haven't been here in years, but I don't remember if it was this good before."

He began to tell a story about getting second-degree burns on his hand while making ceviche in the Caribbean. The lime juice that causes the reaction that cooks the shrimp did the same to John's hands in the sunlight when he failed to wash them well enough.

The restaurant clattered and hummed around them as they ate. Steven's fantasies shifted. The image of sitting in front of a fire with John, being lectured about classical music, crumbled to dust. In its place, Steven imagined them cooking together on a Saturday night, talking and laughing while listening to the Cocteau Twins in John's kitchen, which surely must be nicer than any Steven had seen. Steven's fantasy ended with no accidental burns, although he couldn't deny he liked the idea of John tending to him and worrying over him.

"That was excellent," John said. The waitress whisked away their plates and left dessert menus in their stead.

Steven studied the short list of desserts. Nothing appealed and he was too full to eat more, though he considered ordering, just keep them at the table.

"Anything look good?" John asked, waving the small menu card.

"Not really."

"I saw not one strawberry on this list. No *gateaux fraisier* for you tonight."

"I do like other things besides strawberry," Steven said, setting aside his own card. "And you? I suppose you'll just get a Blow Pop on your way home? Something to suck on later?" He teased, boldly pushing the flirting he was certain they were doing.

The openness and intimacy that John had shown Gabriel was present in his laugh. Like a secret they shared, as if he was surprised and pleased with Steven's jab.

"You remembered," he chuckled. "Yes, I'll go home with something sticky and sweet, wishing I had something even sweeter to devour. My only satisfaction will be knowing that you'll be eating strawberry jam right out of the jar, muttering about how you do too like other things, just strawberries are best." John's eyes sparkled with amusement.

"My aunt does make really excellent jam," Steven said, managing to keep a straight face.

When he finished laughing, John asked, "Besides all the jam you've eaten, Steven, tell me: what was the best part of your week?"

"Tonight's been pretty great so far." Steven wished he knew the right smile to suggest he'd like to have many more nights like this, out with John.

"Besides tonight." John set aside the small card he'd been turning over in his hand.

"Let's see—" *When you called me earlier this week*, probably wasn't the best answer. Nor was *lying awake thinking about you*. Fortunately the waitress returned to take their refusal of dessert and John's request for the check, giving Steven time to think of something safe to talk about. "I didn't do a lot besides go to work and go to school. I had a great Applied Mathematics class this week. A big piece of it just fell into place for me. It's really satisfying to find an answer that's been eluding you. Especially with math: it's, like, *clean* in this weird way. There aren't any decisions to make. You just find the right steps and then the answer is there for you."

"You like having decisions made for you?" John's tone didn't quite have the inflection of a question, but Steven thought that must be some effect of his accent.

"I'm not— I decide things for myself. But with math, it's not like Philosophy where you can endlessly argue grey areas and then simply decide that you won't agree and nothing has changed. With math, you do it the correct way, you get the answer, and you're done. You have a solid solution."

"You're happier when you have set goals and know the boundaries for reaching them." John sat with his elbow on the table, his ring and pinky fingers bent to follow the line of his cheek bone, the other fingers resting on his brow, framing his bright eyes.

The inflection missing yet again.

"Is that a question?" Steven asked.

John nodded though it came across as more of an indication for Steven to keep talking, rather than an affirmative.

"I like knowing where I stand, and I always know that with math. There are no hard choices, just finding the solutions." Steven was uncomfortably aware of John's regard, as if each of his responses was being cataloged. He felt a strong need to give the right answers, but he had no idea what those were.

"Would you rather not have to make any choices?" John asked, this time the questioning inflection fully there. Had he merely made statements before, revealing his observations about what he thought of Steven? Or maybe this was simply a conversational gambit.

"Is this a philosophical discussion?" Steven had never felt this out of his depth. John was a math problem for which Steven didn't have the full equation. There's not enough information to solve for x.

Again John's shrug was more encouragement than answer. So Steven answered.

"Okay, it's philosophical. I like having free will. Isn't that our gift, the best part of being human, that we can choose any path? Then we go and prove ourselves the winner by making the best decisions? Everyone is trying to show what a strong leader they are by making the correct choices?"

"Sometimes it's easier not to have choices. Strength doesn't necessarily come from decision making." John sat back, his hand dropping to the table, once again close enough for Steven to touch. But he refrained. "True strength can come from how you face the unknown. How you deal with what you can't control."

"Some days it feels like the only thing I can control is the computer code I'm writing, or the math I'm working through."

Steven moved his hands to his lap again, twisting them together.

"Is that why you like it so much? The sense of control it gives you?" John asked, his eyes alert and curious.

"No, I think it's just so clear cut in the end. There are rules, there are formulas. There's structure to it. This sounds ridiculous, but it just feels safe. Like, as long as I follow those rules, I'll always get the answer, I'll always make the code work. Knowing I can trust that feels more secure than the rest of life."

"That doesn't sound ridiculous at all. I completely understand what you mean."

Steven's breath came out in a whoosh, like the release when he finished a test, the pressure gone. He had felt in their earlier conversations as if John was really listening, trying to understand. Hearing it said out loud was such a relief. It didn't mean anything, of course, just two new friends talking. But the possibility that John might laugh at him was gone. The idea that he was saying things that made sense to someone was more comforting than any math solution.

"It's good to have someone understand. Sometimes I'm not sure I understand myself," Steven joked, meeting John's eyes as he spoke.

John held his gaze, until Steven began to feel awkward again. Then John's smile came, soft and light, and only for Steven, as if Steven had performed admirably.

"We should let the poor folks still waiting have our table," John said, breaking the moment. He pulled a fold of cash and cards from his pocket, peeled off some bills, and laid them over the check.

Steven reached for the check. "How much was mine?"

"Don't worry," John said, "You provided the tickets for the great show tonight, so the least I can do is pay for dinner. Especially when you've been such good company."

Good enough company, Steven hoped, that John would want to kiss him good night, at the very least.

17.
Elephant Car Wash

ON THE SIDEWALK OUTSIDE THE Longshoreman's Daughter, they stood close to the building, out of the flow of pedestrian traffic. Though the neighborhood didn't have the vibrancy of Broadway, Fremont had a surprising number of people out this late. They all seemed to be moving between restaurants and bars, loud and joyous but without the whimsicality Broadway offered late at night. The people looked more like Steven's classmates than his fellow club-goers. He judged the lack of vibrancy as the difference between straight and gay neighborhoods.

"Are you parked near here?"

John pulled jingling keys from the pocket of his jeans, drawing attention to how well John's jeans fit him. It couldn't possibly have been comfortable to squeeze those keys into that pocket.

"I didn't drive. I'll catch the Number 36 bus downtown and walk up the Hill. It's only a couple blocks up Denny to my place."

"Don't be silly. I'll take you. I have to get up the Hill anyway."

"Okay, thanks."

"I'm just over here."

They headed west on Northeast Thirty-fifth, past dingy secondhand stores and loud bars, and then cut over to a pay parking lot. John's car was a new-looking shiny black Lexus. He unlocked and opened the passenger door for Steven.

As he buckled his seatbelt, John asked, "Have you seen the Troll yet?"

"No, I haven't."

"Neither have I. Let's drive up that way and see if we can get a view in the dark. I think it's on Thirty-sixth."

They looped around, out the parking lot and headed up Northeast Thirty-sixth. After a block, the shops ended. Houses with perfect picket fences lined the road on either side, like fairy cottages in lush gardens. Two more blocks and John slowed the car, stopping under the far northern end of the Aurora Bridge.

"You can see it. Just not well."

Steven leaned forward, peering past John out the driver's side window. A massive concrete troll sat under the bridge, one of his eyes reflecting the streetlights. The troll seemed to be crawling out of the ground, only his head and upper torso visible, his giant hand closing over a VW Bug.

"Is that a real car?" Steven asked, moving closer into John's space to see better, breathing his green, woody scent.

"It looks like it is. Amazing."

They peered at the figure in the bridge's shadow for few more seconds, Steven close to John. If John turned too quickly, they'd knock heads; slow enough and it wouldn't be much for their lips to meet. Steven let out a shuddering breath and sat back.

"Seen enough?" John asked, turning his attention back to Steven.

Steven nodded, unsure what he might say while still under the spell of having been so close to John. Whatever was happening between them, Steven knew for sure he wanted it. The vague, nebulous "it." In this moment, he'd do anything to keep John's attention.

"Where are we going?" John said.

To your place, Steven thought, *somewhere private, somewhere I can be sure you'll kiss me.* Yet he said, "I live on Bellevue, just off Mercer on the west side of the Hill."

"Denny Way is the easiest then."

John turned right, down the hill on the road under the bridge. He followed the arterial along the water and back to the heart of Fremont, and then over the drawbridge that had almost made Steven late for the play.

"So, Steven," John said, breaking the companionable silence as they wound around the bottom of Queen Anne Hill, circumnavigating Lake Union to get to Capitol Hill. "What does the rest of the weekend hold for you? What do you do when you're not studying, clubbing, or discovering unusual theatrical productions?"

Steven wanted to beg John to confirm that he was really asking how much free time Steven had, how John could fit into his life, and that he wanted to know as much as he could about Steven. But he feared that John was simply making polite conversation, filling the silence in the car. He answered factually, wishing he knew how to casually suggest that they should spend more time together.

"I'm not that interesting, really. Clubbing is sort of a break from boring old me. I mostly just go to school, do homework, go to work. At home we—" Steven paused acutely aware that he was as hesitant to talk to John about Adrian as the other way around. "I just read a lot."

"What are you reading right now?"

"Texts for class, plus some theory books for computational mathematics."

"Nothing to relax."

"I just finished *Fried Green Tomatoes at the Whistle Stop Cafe,* which was much better than the movie. And I started *Significant Others*, the most recent Tales of the City book. Though I guess it's been out for few years, and I'm just catching up."

"How is it? I always find Armistead Maupin to be a little precious."

"I like it so far. Less bat-shit crazy than the earlier ones, with the Jonestown stuff and whatever. I read all the other books back to back my senior year in high school. I'll definitely finish the series, however much he writes, because it meant so much to me when I was seventeen to find stories about gay people just being in the world. I learned more about cruising and gay life from those books than anywhere else."

John laughed. "Must have been a shock to get out and find the world had become very different since 1979."

"Yeah, this book touches on that a little, I guess. I mean Michael Mouse has HIV, and everything is more like now than when the first book started. And this book is kind of nuts too, with the weird lesbian plotline. The militant lesbians I know aren't really like that."

"Maybe you have to be in San Francisco to find them."

"Maybe."

Steven glanced out the window. The Elephant Car Wash sign flashed pink where they waited at a stoplight on Denny Way. A few more precious minutes, and they'd be at Steven's apartment.

Even after a full evening together, everything between them felt casual and tentative. It would be awkward if he invited John in. And impossible to chance it. If Adrian was home, it might be more than just romantically awkward. But this evening left Steven desperate to know more about John, to see him more. To end the night without a kiss or a promise for more would be crushing. He braced for it.

"Thanks for going out with me tonight. It was great. The play wouldn't have been nearly as enjoyable alone." Steven said, wanting more time together, tonight or another night.

"My pleasure, really. I'm impressed at your discovery of the play. I need to do better at finding events like that."

"Well, I'll let you know what I hear about French language stuff going on. My mother forwards me the newsletters for Alliance Française de Seattle. That's how I hear about some of it."

"Great, I'd like that. Let's see," John said as he turned on to Bellevue Avenue, "it's how far? Four, five blocks down?"

"Yep. Almost there." Steven chirped, as if he wasn't expecting any more out of tonight. "It's on the left, just on the other side of Mercer."

The street was deserted this late. Brick apartment blocks and trees slid past the windows, bringing them too quickly to the end of the night.

"Right there." Steven pointed. "The Amherst."

"What a nice old building," John said. He slowed to a stop in front of the door.

"*Oui, il est magnifique.*"

"Merci, Steven, for the invitation tonight and the conver-sation. Both are very much appreciated."

A kiss and promise of a date? But Steven couldn't ask for either. He nearly laughed out loud, remembering their earlier conversation: all he wanted now was for John to take control. Wanted John to lean in and slip his hand around the back of Steven's neck, pulling him close. He wanted John to declare that he had to see him again right away.

None of which was going happen. That tension he felt hanging between them—it was only his imagination.

"Merci, John," he said, his false cheerfulness back, "I had fun. I'm glad you came. And thanks for the ride."

Steven's hand was on the door handle, pushing it slowly open, as if there might still be a chance that John would close the space between them and capture Steven's kiss. "Well, *au revoir."*

Steven reluctantly rose from the soft leather seat, step-ping out of the car, away from John's imaginary embrace.

"Bonne nuit, Steven. Sorry I kept you out so late." John tilted his head, looking out the open door at Steven.

"No, no, it was fun." Steven said, bent like he might just get back into the car if invited. John only smiled.

John waited as Steven unlocked the front door, the car idling behind Steven while he fussed with the stiff old locks. He turned and waved as he pushed the door open. The street-lights illuminated John's brilliant smile, his small nod, before he drove back toward his own life.

The apartment was quiet. Ryan's door was closed as always, Adrian's open but his room dark. Relieved not to have to converse, Steven left his jacket and boots in his room and headed to the bathroom.

The shower was hot and the water pressure strong this late at night in the old building. Steven's skin was pink with the heat when he soaped up. Lathering the curls at the base of his dick, Steven let his hand slide up, squeezing gently until he was half hard, then stroking through the soap bubbles.

He closed his eyes and thought about the kiss he never got: John's mouth would be hot on his, tongue pushing for entry. Steven would open to him, moaning. John's hands would be even better, slipping under Steven's shirt as they walked from the car to the house. Steven imagined those needy touches, John wanting Steven as much as Steven wanted him. In Steven's imagination, John's bed was a huge soft white square in the middle of an undefined room where Steven lay naked, as John held him down and made him come over and over.

John's name echoed off the bright tile in the bathroom as Steven came hard. The blue lightning of orgasm and the false memory of John's fingers on him left him shuddering. Sticky come washed off his hands and down the drain.

Emptied of thought, Steven crawled into bed, not bothering to find the boxers he usually slept in. Everything faded out, fantasy mixing with memory as dreams took apart Steven's reality.

Steven's eyes snapped open when he heard the heavy front door clap shut, and then the jingle of Adrian's keys and the sound of Adrian undressing in the bathroom. It had to be Adrian; Ryan always came home quietly. Steven lay in bed listening to the water run, the barely audible hum of Adrian singing whatever song he'd last heard, not loud like he did in the mornings, a modest concession to the late hour.

When he heard the water shut off in the shower, Steven knew with certainty, hearing Adrian humming now, that he'd have to choose. If John was interested in Steven, Adrian wouldn't let it play out the way he had with Steven's earlier relationships. He'd insert himself, make it about Adrian and what they shared that no one else had. Steven's world would split, with Adrian on one side and John on the other, along the fracture that opened when he first told Adrian about John.

Adrian's humming in the shower turned to song, the lyrics of Chaka Khan's "We Can Work It Out" coming clearly through the wall. Steven took it as a sign and relaxed. He drifted off believing that when Adrian finally met John, it would all work out.

18.
This Charming Man

ADRIAN, DRAMATIC IN MONOCHROME DEEP purple, wore heavy black boots that balanced his tight, violet jeans. His long-sleeved purple top was cut wide and low across the neck to expose his sharp collarbones. The shirt's back was slashed into a ladder of fabric ribbons, showing off his spine, the arch of his shoulder blades, and the shadows of that angel-wing tattoo. His skin and platinum hair were pale against the dark fabric. His milk-blue eyes shone brightly.

Going out with Adrian meant forcing yourself to blend into the background. Nothing Steven wore could ever be flamboyant or bright enough to outshine Adrian.

Steven checked the full-length mirror again, wondering whether he should change his shirt. Grey silk shirt, un-buttoned low enough to display his collarbones and to show that he had nothing underneath it. Black leather pants, borrowed from Adrian—being the same size had its advan-tages. And his trusty black Doc Martens.

"I don't have any color. Is this too dull?"

Adrian assessed Steven.

"I don't know, darling. Maybe a nice navy blue bandanna to fly in your right pocket? Or, hmm, maybe mauve or gold?" Adrian smirked, like he'd made an excellent joke at Steven's expense.

Steven scowled as he dug through his drawer. "I don't even know what those last two mean. And I can find partners with-out advertising my preferences for everyone to see."

"Hanky code isn't just about advertising. It's shorthand. Code to get what you want without wasting time." Adrian, looking triumphant, held out two handkerchiefs. The top one was red.

Steven shook his head, disgusted. "Gross, Ade. Red? Really? Do you think that of me? Fist fucking with strangers?"

Adrian laughed. "Not every bandanna is about hanky code. Sometimes you just need to match an outfit. Or wipe your nose." He tossed away the red one and handed Steven a light blue one. "This is for you."

"Fuck you," Steven said. "I'm not advertising that I suck cock. I'm going dancing in a gay bar in tight leather pants. Everyone knows what I'm interested in."

Adrian shook his head as if tragedy had struck. "Fine, but you should at least sparkle if you're going to wear only grey and black." He reached in his bag and retrieved a rhinestone collar, which he fastened around Steven's neck.

"You don't think it's too much?" Steven asked, running his fingers along it. The mirror showed that the necklace made his eyes bright and his grey shirt looked silver. It drew attention to his neck and his bare collarbones.

"Do *I* think anything is too much? You look lovely." Adrian studied Steven for a second and then moved in and wound his arms around Steven's neck. "You look great, really. Are you being insecure because that guy never called you?"

When John hadn't called four days after their date, Steven broke down and told Adrian everything. Now, a full week since the play, Adrian was still solicitous, periodically remembering that Steven needed to be treated to with care. The extra concern wasn't necessary, but Steven let his head tip and rest on Adrian's arms, taking comfort in the embrace.

"He was never worthy of you, dollbaby. He didn't call because he knew he'd never be good enough, and he didn't want to embarrass himself further."

"Thanks." Steven answered automatically. Adrian was way off base, but Steven had no idea why John hadn't called, so he couldn't defend John against Adrian's assessment of the situation.

"Now c'mon, we're off to find you a boy worthy of your time. If we get there too late, all the best boys will be gone. And don't I always make sure you have a good time? Open up." Adrian stepped back and pressed his fingers against Steven's lips.

"What is it?" Steven asked, unintentionally giving Adrian the opportunity to shove it into his mouth.

"Just X. We're going dancing, darling. Don't you want to enjoy it? It's pharmaceutical, from Texas. Really clean."

Steven worried for a second what it meant for the night. But as much as he hoped for it, John wasn't likely to reappear at Neighbours or show up anywhere else they went: Rebar, Tugs, R Place. Steven swallowed the pill dry, tasting its acrid bitterness.

"Let's go," Adrian said. "This ugly room is cramping my style. I need lights and disco balls and hot men vying for my attention."

"Are we meeting Arnaud?" Steven asked.

"No, most definitely not. We are not meeting Arnaud ever again."

Steven ran his hand through his hair, wondering if he should ask or let it go. He looked to see if Adrian also needed commiseration, with both of them abandoned the same week. Adrian adjusted his bracelets, unconcerned, Arnaud already forgotten.

Best to let it go.

Steven slipped his ID and some cash into his pocket and then looked in the mirror once more.

"Ready?"

◊

When Steven and Adrian approached the club, a lanky figure peeled off the wall and moved toward them. His jet-black hair spiked up a couple of inches, he was clad in tight black except for his blood-red cowboy boots and leather trench coat.

"There you are, darling," he said in a deep voice, speaking with equal parts affection and disdain.

Steven's stomach turned. He'd never taken an instant dislike to anyone before. Maybe a weird side effect of the ecstasy coming on. Adrian launched himself into the stranger's arms. They kissed roughly, aggressively, but with no visible affection, simply a show for everyone passing on the street.

"When did you get here?" Adrian asked when they pulled apart.

"This afternoon."

The guy pulled cigarette from behind his ear and lit it with a Zippo, closing the lighter with a practiced flip, then disappearing it back into his red coat.

When Steven coughed, Adrian turned around, his lips and cheeks flushed. He grinned.

"Steven! This is Philip, my best friend—well, at least until he abandoned me for San Francisco."

"Hi, Philip." Steven put out his hand.

"Everyone calls me Flip. So you're the Steven that got my Adrian?" he said, shaking Steven's hand.

He snaked a proprietary arm around Adrian's waist and pulled him close as his eyes raked Steven. Steven didn't often feel like anyone towered over him, and Flip couldn't have been much more than an inch taller. But between Flip's hair, the cowboy boots, and his attitude, he left Steven feeling reduced.

"You're visiting from San Francisco?" Steven said, cringing at his awkwardness. "Rad. I've always wanted to go there."

"I live in L.A. now. There just isn't a club scene in Frisco at the level I work," Flip said. Steven recoiled at the pretentiousness. Even he knew better than to call that town Frisco.

"Flip's a promoter," Adrian said. "He puts on the best raves on the West Coast."

Steven nodded, not sure what to add to this bullshit. When he'd heard Adrian talk about Flip, he'd imagined a high school boyfriend who Adrian came into the city with, who'd left for bigger things. But he'd assumed someone less imposing, mousier; a boy that a young, arrogant Adrian could boss around. Of any two people least likely to be friends, he'd definitely pick Adrian and Flip. They didn't make sense together.

"Should we, ah, go in?" Steven asked, wanting a drink, music, noise. He needed the prospect of dancing and attention from a man who actually wanted him. With Flip present, Adrian had joined John in the ranks of those who had better things to do than hang out with Steven. Inside the club were

endless handsome, willing possibilities for forgetting his romantic misfires.

Flip said, "Actually, I got a line on a warehouse party over
off Leary Way that's supposed to be the best thing in Seattle
on a Thursday night. Whatever that means."

He dropped his cigarette and crushed it under his boot
heel as a commentary on the Seattle scene.

"Yeah?" Adrian said, interested.

"Let's check it out first. It's bound to be better than this."
Flip nodded toward Neighbours. "I'm parked around the
corner, so let's go," he said to Adrian. They started off
together. "You coming?" Flip acknowledged Steven again.

Steven felt the first creeping tug of the ecstasy that Adrian
had forced on him, leaving him calm and warm despite the
cool September air.

"I don't know." He stalled.

"You have nothing better to do." Adrian reached for
Steven's arm. "We're celebrating tonight. It's a reunion and I
want to go to a party. We always come here. Don't you want
some real excitement?"

There was no one specific to meet at Neighbours that night,
Steven reasoned. He could pick up someone wherever they
went. Plus, he'd already taken Adrian's ecstasy. The prospect of
staying at the club, alone and high, wasn't inviting.

"Yeah, let's go."

Not entirely convinced he'd made the right choice, Steven
followed them to Flip's huge black car, a shiny relic from the
sixties that likely got five miles to the gallon. Perfectly suited
to Flip's overly dramatic appearance.

◊

The warehouse party was invitation only. A guy with a
clipboard took covers and cards from people in line. Flip
bypassed the line, with Adrian and Steven in his wake. Steven
smiled at the bouncer as he passed, finally floating high on
the ecstasy, which was indeed clean and jitter-free. He
entered the club feeling full of love for everyone, ready for

magic to happen, the past week's miseries slipping away under the golden waves of his high.

Inside, the thumping bass and the crush of bodies twisting under the strobe lights pulled Steven further out of his dark thoughts. Potential hookups and past mistakes forgotten, Steven danced his ass off, the beats and loud music taking over his body. He moved like silk, every song a new level of bliss. The universe was composed only of the bright glow in his chest, his love for every beautiful thing, the people around him, the rhythms that rattled his bones, the sensuous twist of his body as every muscle responded like it loved him right back. And it went on forever. There was nothing but gorgeous now, as long Steven moved to the music.

Steven's endless dance ceased only for more water or the bathroom. Throughout the night, Adrian and Flip disappeared and reappeared over and over again. When they danced, Flip touched Steven as if he had a right to him, gripped his hips and ground down on him, the same familiarity he exhibited with Adrian. When Flip and Adrian danced together, they put on a show for the crowd, so breathtakingly beautiful that (even when the drugs whispered to Steven that he'd lost Adrian, too) he couldn't be hurt. Everything was love as long as the music played on.

◊

When the lights came up, the blissful bubble in which Steven had been dancing finally burst. He found Adrian and Flip outside, and they all piled into Flip's gas guzzler and headed across town to the Hill. Back to real life. Within the warm cushion of the ecstasy high, disappointment hovered, waiting to move in when Steven came down.

On the Hill, at the twenty-four-hour IHOP on Madison, Adrian and Flip ordered only coffee, still buzzing from whatever they'd taken in addition to the ecstasy. Steven ordered eggs and hash browns, knowing he'd be sorry later if he skipped food. The music was bleeding out of him as his high wore down, leaving him brittle, stretched too thin. He could barely follow the chatter Flip and Adrian exchanged about people Steven had never heard of, places he'd never been. Adrian was uncharacteristically relaxed. The Adrian that Steven knew had sprung fully formed in the middle of a club, set on being fabulous at all times. Steven couldn't imagine Adrian and Flip in high school. Once again he questioned how well he really knew Adrian.

"Are your eggs that bad?"

"What?" Steven put down his fork.

Adrian addressed him. "You look fucking pathetic. If your eggs are that bad, don't eat them. Or did you miss me tonight?"

"I was just thinking."

Flip smiled, but it didn't look friendly. Like he was tolerating his toy being played with, waiting patiently for it to be handed back.

Adrian frowned. "Are you still sulking about that old guy? Oh my god, seriously. You look this miserable just because he didn't call? What's his name? John?"

"It's about more than just a phone call," Steven shot back, wishing he had more control over his emotions, over his words. Fighting with Adrian about John would not end well.

"Unrequited love? Or just some fantasy crush?" Flip asked.

Steven hated how his words came spilling out. "Neither. I met him. I liked him. We went out. He didn't call." Steven was relieved that more personal truths stayed in his head. How he knew John was something special, meant for him. He just couldn't understand what had happened.

"Stop being such a drama queen." Adrian poured more coffee. "You act like you're in love with him but you barely know him."

"Just lust, then. Find him, fuck him, and be done with it," Flip said with authority, like he'd solved the problem.

"That never seems to work for Steven," Adrian said. "He's a romantic." He turned to Steven. "This guy, he's a fag, right?"

"Yes, Adrian, he's gay." Steven hated the way Adrian made *fag* sound so ugly, the way the guys in his high school used the word, rather than the endearment it should be.

"Then this isn't even unrequited lust. I mean, look at you. You're the perfect picture of young male virility, pretty enough to turn anyone's head. This guy was too stupid to even see you. Why obsess?"

"Are you jealous, Adrian?" Steven picked up his coffee cup. A sense of foreboding had overtaken the last wisps of his good ecstasy high. Spilling the wrong words, spoiling for a different fight. Steven was not in control. He shouldn't have let Adrian bait him.

"Of you? Never. Just look at me."

"No, of John."

"Don't be ridiculous, dollbaby. Don't think so highly of yourself." The cruelty was so bright in Adrian's eyes that Steven bit his tongue to keep from saying something that would only make the situation worse.

The waitress swooped in, asking if they needed a fresh pot of coffee, giving Steven a second to shake off the sting of Adrian's words. He felt caged by Adrian's nastiness, unsure where to turn in the face of a force he'd only watched before, never been subjected to.

"Oh honey, good, you can help. We need another opinion." Adrian batted his eyelashes at the waitress. She was about twenty, with frizzed-out blond hair and too much green eyeliner. "My friend here," Adrian pointed to Steven, "seems to think he's all that, and everyone one wants him. So tell, me, do you want to fuck him?"

"Adrian," Steven warned, anger bubbling up under the painful prick of cruelty.

"Sweetheart, do I look like a fool? He is pretty." She smiled at Steven, who returned his most apologetic smile, negativity swirling behind it. "But boys like him don't think about girls like me. Or girls at all." She patted Steven's hand and left with the empty coffee pot.

Adrian's face pinched into a moue of distaste. He glared at Steven and then turned to Flip. "What Steven needs is someone like you." He ran his finger over Flip's jawline. "What we have, no one else does. He just doesn't understand what it's like to really share a connection with someone." Adrian's finger trailed over Flip's chest and then lower when Adrian leaned in to kiss him.

Steven sat frozen, trying not to recoil as if he'd just been slapped.

They began to make out in earnest, putting on a show for Steven, who tried to believe it was only Adrian's problem...it was the drugs...an apology would come tomorrow.

Steven caught the waitress's eye and signaled for the check, smiling apologetically again. She rolled her eyes.

"I've seen worse," she said softly when she dropped the check on the table. Steven paid the whole check, trying to get out as quickly as possible without further discussion.

As they gathered their things, Flip had his hand down the back of Adrian's pants. Adrian leaned in and kissed Flip's neck and fussed over him. Steven had long since stopped being embarrassed by Adrian, but he did feel sorry for the normal people trying to eat breakfast. It was rude.

"It's always been you and me against the world, hasn't it, baby? Even when you're far away?" Adrian spoke only for Flip, but loud enough for Steven to hear.

Steven's stomach turned at Adrian's complete disregard for the last six years. Who the fuck was Flip that Adrian fawned all over him, as if Steven wasn't even there? That Adrian suddenly had only poison for Steven?

They'd parked way up Twelfth Avenue, a couple blocks past the Lamborghini dealership, by the cop shop in the no-man's land of industrial store fronts. Each block felt like forever. Steven slowed as they walked, letting Adrian and Flip get ahead of him, Adrian coming as close to giving Flip a hand job in public as he could. Steven had no desire to watch. Only his exhaustion propelled him toward the car, the promise that he wouldn't have to walk the mile and half back to their apartment.

"Steven?"

At the sound of his name, Steven immediately recognized John as the figure coming down the hill toward where they were stopped, waiting to cross Pine Street. This was how deer got caught in headlights.

Steven gasped. "John!"

Adrian turned to look.

"I thought that was you," John smiled warmly, putting his hand out. Steven stared at it for a second before shaking it. John wore a navy suit and a charcoal grey overcoat, as always perfectly put together, like a man outside of time, able to fit in anywhere. "How are you?"

Steven didn't answer quickly enough. Adrian wedged in between them.

"John?" Adrian asked. Steven reached to grab Adrian's wrist to pull him away, but Adrian slipped his grasp. It was too late. "We were just talking about you, John. Weren't we, Steven?" Adrian gave Steven a cruel, slit-eyed glance, then turned back to John, smiling like a shark.

"Oh?" John gave Steven a questioning look. The blue of his eyes was so clear in the morning light that Steven's breath caught, a sharp mix of both longing and mourning bleeding into the dread that overwhelmed Steven as soon as Adrian spoke John's name.

"Yes," Adrian said, his voice a silvery bell, carrying in the empty morning air. "I was saying that of course if you were a fag, which clearly you are—" Adrian ran his eyes up and down John, measuring, weighing his worth. "—then you must want to fuck Steven." Adrian turned and put his hand on Steven's shoulder, shoving him forward. "I mean, who wouldn't—look how pretty he is with that red hair and those green eyes, all hopeful longing and innocence. I can tell you, with authority, that his ass is as sweet and tight as you could hope, and the innocent part is totally an act. He's very dirty. You could say he's been well used, but maybe you already figured that out, and that's why you never called him after your date." Adrian smiled like a satisfied cat that'd just dropped a tortured bird.

"Adrian!" Steven's jaw muscles tightened, his hands balling into fists. This might be the day he killed Adrian.

Adrian flashed that shark smile and stepped into the street. Half way across, he spun around and called out, "I'll leave you boys to get caught up, since I have more important places to be. So nice to meet you!" His words to John sticky with saccharine, he then smirked at Steven. "You can tell me *everything* later."

"You bitch." Steven gritted his teeth. Adrian swanned off to meet Flip on the other side of the wide intersection.

Cheeks blooming, red-hot with humiliation, Steven turned to John.

"I'm sorry," he said.

"Yes, he's quite the bitchy queen, isn't he? Nice friends you have." John, the pink curve of his mouth turned down, examined Steven.

"We just had a fight and it's been a fucked-up night, what with fucking Flip showing up, and I didn't—" Desperate, angry, and embarrassed by how smudged, limp, and rumpled he looked in the thin morning light, Steven let the words pour out before he put them in order to make John understand. "And I talked about you just now when I shouldn't have."

John studied him, dissatisfied in a way Steven hadn't seen before and wished never to see again. The silence grew thick between them. Steven tried to not fidget while bearing the horrible awkwardness, his punishment for Adrian's action.

"I should go," John said finally, sadness replacing the other possible expressions Steven hoped for. "I'm expected at work. And you need to go home and get some sleep."

Steven nodded like a kid caught doing what he shouldn't. The situation couldn't be salvaged. Yet Steven tried.

"This isn't what it looks like," he said, ready to do whatever it might take so that John never again looked at him with so much disappointment.

The sad expression on John's face became a blank mask. "It looks like you've been out all night and were headed home with your friends, one of whom wanted to do his level best to embarrass you."

"Yes," Steven agreed, "but I'm not—"

He trailed off, not sure how to explain to John that this wasn't him, that he was the guy whose company John enjoyed that night at dinner, that he was the smart guy John had asked for technology advice. That this Steven, this fucked-up kid, was a thing of the past, only out killing time until something good enough, someone like John, came along to fill the hole that drugs and dancing temporarily covered.

"You're not what?" John prompted.

"Not like my friends," Steven finished, miserable.

John's expression softened. "Get some sleep," he said. "I'll see you around." His hand on Steven's shoulder, he squeezed gently and then was gone.

"It was nice to see you," Steven said, his hopes crumbling while still feeling the heat of John's touch on his shoulder.

John nodded goodbye, setting off down the hill toward his work. Steven watched him go, a wrenching sense of loss filling the void that opened as John walked away.

Part Two

Fall/Winter 1991

19.
How to Use a Knife

A GLASS OF RED WINE in hand, Steven supervised Lisa while she stirred thinly sliced peppers into the pan with the onions and garlic.

"Like this?" she asked.

"Just like that," Steven agreed, watching as she shifted everything around with a spatula.

"And then what?"

"And then we watch it for a couple minutes with the heat up high enough for the edges to blacken, but not so much that all of it burns."

"That calls for more wine. This is rough work," she joked.

"I did all the heavy lifting," Steven teased, as he refilled her wine glass and topped off his own. "Next time, we're going to teach you how to use a knife."

Lisa leaned back against the counter. "I can use a knife just fine. I just don't need to use the huge one like you do."

"Yes, you do. It's called a chef's knife for a reason. If you're going to learn how to cook, you're going to learn the right way to cut things."

"We'll see." Lisa had the stubborn look she always got before she gave into Steven's needling. The look that said she knew he was right but didn't want him to know.

"We'll see—we'll see if you burn those peppers when you don't stir them and pull them off the heat in time."

"Fuck." She slid the pan to an empty burner and jammed the spatula in, tossing the peppers and onions.

"No, they're perfect, Lisa. You did great. If you'd paid close attention instead of talking to me, then you'd have over-stirred them, and they'd be soggy and not crispy black on the tips."

"That's it?"

"Yep. Plate up so we can eat."

Lisa's dining room table was covered in dishes for making fajitas: sour cream, guacamole, steamed tortillas covered with a napkin, chicken she'd cooked, shredded, and simmered all afternoon in green chile sauce, shredded cheese, cilantro, rings of olives and jalapeno peppers.

Steven made room for the dish of peppers and onions that Lisa carried, and they both sat down.

Raising her glass, Lisa said, "To friends you can trust to help with anything!"

"Even teach you how to use a real knife," Steven said, clinking her glass. Lisa gave him a fake frown. "Come on, I've been dying to eat since I came in and smelled the chicken."

"I hope it's edible. I've never done anything like that with chicken before. I appreciate you walking me through it on the phone. But that doesn't mean it's good."

"I'm sure it's great."

They loaded tortillas with a little of everything on the table. Steven made a point of spearing a little of the chicken on his fork and tasting it solo. "It's fucking amazing. Seriously. You're a cooking prodigy. A couple more run-throughs like this and you're going to be so much better than me. I mean, once you learn to use a knife."

"Okay, enough with the knife!"

Outside, the sky was already darkening. This far north, the just-past Equinox meant winter-dark skies in autumn. The waning of the light was the worst thing about living in Seattle. The few trees that dressed in brightly colored leaves couldn't make up for the impending darkness. Even this early in the season, Steven dreaded what was coming instead of enjoying what light was left.

Yet here in Lisa's comfortable dining room, surrounded by bright paintings and amazing food, windows steamed over from their cooking, Steven was at ease. That was the best part of the coming winter: cozying in and eating and drinking.

"I can't believe I made this." Lisa reached for a second tortilla.

"It's so good. Seriously better than when I make it."

"Don't you always tell me that food tastes better when someone else makes it for you? What do you call it?"

"The peanut butter effect. Anything someone else makes for you automatically tastes better. Even a peanut butter sandwich. Especially a peanut butter sandwich. You just said yourself how good this food is." Steven also reached for another tortilla. "So imagine how good I think it is. Awesome. Best I've ever had."

"You're such a flatterer."

"Someone has to remind you how great you are." Steven blew Lisa a kiss.

She set down her fajita and reached for her wine, watching Steven wrap up his second tortilla and take a bite.

"What?" he asked around a mouthful as she kept staring.

"This is the first time I've seen you smile in a week." Lisa picked up her fork and started to eat from the mess of meat and vegetables that had fallen out of her unfolded tortilla. "It's nice. I was missing it. Although I've loved seeing you this much even though you haven't been smiling."

In the week since he stood on that empty street corner watching John walk away, Steven had slept in his own bed, but he'd spent every waking minute out of the apartment. There was so much time to fill when it isn't possible to sit and relax at home.

Unsure what was coming, Steven reached for his wine. He said, "You're going to make me talk about this, aren't you?"

"Sweetie, I don't want to make you do anything but you showed up at 7:00 AM, upset with this awful story about fucking Adrian undermining everything with John. And you've barely left since, except to sleep and get clean clothes. So am I going to make you talk about it? No, but by now you must have things you need to say."

"There is something I need. A favor."

"Anything."

"I will never ask you to talk to John for me, of course. But if he mentions anything, could you just tell him I'm sorry?"

Lisa finished the last bites on her plate, her expression unreadable. She picked up her wine glass, emptied it in a long swallow, and then refilled it. Steven nodded when she tipped the bottle toward his glass. She poured the rest of the bottle into it.

"No," she said.

Steven sagged back against his chair. Lisa was his last connection to John. If she couldn't relay an apology, then it was really over.

"And I'll tell you why." Lisa set down her glass and focused sternly on Steven.

"Please," he said, certain he did not want to hear this at all.

"I won't because you're not apologizing for your behavior, but for Adrian's. And I won't be part of defending him."

"I don't want to fight about Adrian. Not now, please. If you don't want to talk to John, it's fine. It's fair. I know it's over anyway. I just wish it ended differently." *Or not ended at all.*

"You can call John yourself, like an adult, if you need to apologize." Lisa picked up her fork and went back to her food.

"The whole thing is already too fucked up. I give up. I'm over it. I'm already moving on." Steven felt cracks in the tight shell he'd been living in all week, hiding his own feelings.

"You are so full of shit, I don't think you even believe your own lies. You want that man, and it's not impossible. But maybe you need to take a step back."

"A step back to where? There's nowhere left to go." Despair leaked in, the dread Steven had avoided, the crash that would surely come now that he was looking at his situation.

"You can apologize to John, but I don't know if it would even matter. It's all happened already. You've got to regroup and get yourself in order before you try again. Let's clear all this shit out of your life and get you self-sufficient and happy, because that's what's going to get you where you need to be."

"I'm not so fucked up over this that I need therapy," Steven said, feeling defensive, yet not convinced that he didn't need some kind of help.

Lisa reached over to hold his hand. "Maybe you do, I don't know. But this isn't about that incident with John. It isn't about Adrian. It's about how you've been living your life. You skate by because you're good looking and smart, so minimal effort gets you more than the average person. It's a shitty way to live. So start over. A new you. Work harder. Drive yourself to be better. Then do better. Find people who will cheer for you and raise you up instead of holding you back—"

"I thought you said this wasn't about Adrian."

Lisa raised an eyebrow. "Then you admit that he's holding you back? You should be done with the little shit. If it wasn't for Adrian, you could be out somewhere nice with John right now instead of listening to my shit. Adrian is never going to let you really be with someone else. Not as long as he can keep you worshipping him."

"He's been my friend for six years. He showed up when I didn't know my ass from my elbow and gave me the keys to living in the city. It wasn't just an apartment, you know. We shared everything. He bought me clothes, introduced me to people, took me in, helped me find my way when I was just a dumb suburban kid."

"How long has it been since he did any of that? What has he done lately to look out for you and not just for his own benefit?"

Steven closed his eyes, feeling raw and exposed.

All the nights blurred together: Adrian telling Steven where to be and how to dress, disappearing each night when he found someone better than Steven, sweaty frantic hook-ups that happened only at Adrian's whim and were refused if it was who Steven offered.

Every time he and Adrian fucked, Steven hoped it would be the time that Adrian finally wanted him, finally saw Steven for who he was. No hope for that now. There never had been.

Steven pulled his shaking hand back from Lisa. What he'd been avoiding seeing all week wasn't the result of what Adrian said to John. This had been coming for at least a year, ever since Adrian first pulled Steven close, slid his hand into Steven's jeans, and whispered, *"Don't I always look out for you? Take care of you? Don't you want to fuck me?"*

Steven stared at the colorful painting behind Lisa, its bright, modern splashes of paint not representing much more than emotions. Steven wasn't much more than emotions right then. The painting was a safer focus than the conversation, but Lisa wasn't going to let it go.

"Don't you see how toxic Adrian is? He needs you to be his acolyte, his shadow, for his own ego. But then he humiliated you. Who the fuck does that to their friends?"

"I fucked everything up, Lisa, I really fucked it up."

"No, baby, this isn't on you. It's him, you just need to get away. He'll never let you be happy."

Steven closed his eyes again, not wanting to see her face when he spoke. "I've been sleeping with him."

"With Adrian? Since when?" Her disbelief was clear in her tone, Steven opened his eyes, facing up to all of it.

"About a year now. Since school started last year. No, don't say anything else," he said when Lisa opened her mouth. For second it looked like she wouldn't be able to restrain herself, but she did. "I can see it all clearly now. I guess I've known for a while, but chose to ignore it. I thought—I don't know—that even if we didn't end up together, that he'd be there for me when I finally found someone else. He's my best friend, that's what he's supposed to do, right? But it was never going to be that way, was it?"

His sense of loss widened into a gulf Steven couldn't cross, misery on this side, happiness so far away on the other side that it was only an idea. But tears didn't come, instead a cold humiliation burned in Steven's chest. He'd been disappointed before, hurt when boyfriends didn't call again, lonely at home on a Sunday night, heartbroken for his friends' break-ups. But he didn't know what suffering was, he didn't know what pain was. The whole structure of his life was a lie. A lie that he perpetuated, that he helped build.

Adrian was poison. Steven had been drinking it for years.

"Sweetie, are you okay? I know this is a lot. Talk to me. We're gonna fix everything." She scooted her chair closer and wrapped her arms around Steven's waist. He let his head down on hers, his cheek resting on her hair.

"I'm fine, it's fine." His voice sounded weird. "It's just that I always told myself that I'd never leave him, even the few times he was awful to me, because he'd have no one and he needed me, it was always supposed to be us, together against the world. But that wasn't it at all, was it?"

"What do you need? You can stay here. Anything I can do, money, moral support. Help finding a place? Packing? Anything, just ask. But let's start by getting you out of there."

"Yeah. I'll figure it out. I'm good, really. It'll be fine."

20.
Terrible Choices

"Is FLIP HERE?" STEVEN ASKED. Adrian sat alone in the living room watching TV. The apartment hadn't been Flip-free since the day he arrived.

"No. Went to see his parents."

"I need to talk to you." Steven hovered in the doorway between the living room and the kitchen. After most of a second bottle of wine and full night's sleep, Steven decided the best course of action was to get out as cleanly as possible, with as little drama as possible.

Adrian flicked off the TV and dropped the remote on the coffee table. He pulled his legs up under him on the couch, patting the space next him. "Tell me all your problems."

Steven sat down. "It's not a problem, Ade. I'm moving out." He rushed on, getting it out before he got cut off. "I need a quiet space to study, to be more focused on school. I can't get those things when I'm living here."

Adrian returned only his flat, predator's stare. Steven held his gaze.

"I need to make realistic choices about finishing school. This isn't about our friendship."

"I hope not," Adrian said. "Because if you're doing this because of what I said to that guy, it'd be pretty pathetic. Or maybe it's because your fucking friends hate me. Did Lisa tell you to move out? You've been spending a lot of time at her place lately. Or did your sugar daddy finally come through for you?"

"Don't do this," Steven said, bracing for the fight that was going to end all of this.

"Don't do what?" Adrian's eyes narrowed.

"Say mean things you'll regret later. Try to make me hate you. I don't want it to be like this. I'm not trying to hurt you."

Adrian looked out the window, his back to Steven. Steven moved instinctively to reach out to Adrian, but stopped. Nothing would make this better.

"Why are you doing this to me?" Adrian spoke in a small voice that he used only when he was most hurt. "Is this about Flip? Because I met him long before I met you."

It was about Flip, it was about John, but most of all it was about Adrian and Steven. Once the truth hit Steven—how badly Adrian treated him, while Steven always wanted more from Adrian in a way that was never possible—there was no going back. Steven rested his hands on Adrian's shoulders. The silence stretched until Steven felt light headed, as if pushing back all he wanted to say had cut off his air. So he let the truth rush out.

"Adrian, I've waited all this time for you to fall in love with me. But that isn't what I want anymore, and this isn't who I'm supposed to be. I don't know what to do except change everything."

He caught Steven's wrists, holding them. "I do love you," he said, blinking. Tears ran down his cheeks.

"Whatever we're doing together, it isn't good for either of us. It's comfortable, but it's codependent. It's keeping both of us from being happy."

"Lisa definitely told you that. Only lesbians talk like that."

The stereotype annoyed Steven but he let it pass. Now wasn't the time for that battle. "Look, I need to finish school. I need to find something that's mine."

Adrian let go of Steven's wrists. "If you go, you'll miss everything good."

"I'll miss you," Steven said, hugging Adrian. His recent cruelty notwithstanding, for years Adrian had supported Steven, listened to his problems, and, recently, kissed them away and let Steven get lost in the heat of Adrian's body. But now he felt manipulated by Adrian's tears. Had all of the kindnesses been a manipulation of Steven's affection? He had to leave now or else risk ending their friendship forever, which Steven didn't want to do.

He kissed Adrian behind his ear and lied so hard it hurt. "You'll always have me. You can always call, and I'll always come when you need me. But it can't be like this anymore. I want something else."

"Like John?"

"I told you, this isn't about that."

"But it is, isn't it?" Adrian wriggled out of Steven's embrace. His face was dry, all evidence of tears gone. "I saw how you looked at him, Steven. You never looked at anyone like that, even me. You're doing this because of him."

"No," Steven insisted, uncomfortable with how close Adrian came to the truth. *I'm doing it because I was always going to have to choose, and because you would never choose me.*

"You think I never pay attention to you," Adrian said. "But I see you. I know how you are when you've made up your mind. So go. Move out. Try and get him to notice you. When you get hurt, I'll be here. Like I always am."

Steven stiffened at the change in Adrian's attitude, the insult under it, the lashing out. But it hurt, as it always did. That was why Steven needed to change his life. Not because of John.

◊

Everything was okay on the surface for a few days. Adrian insisted that he understood and wanted what was best for Steven. He laughed through the evening they spent separating their wardrobes. He insisted Steven take the CD player and all the CDs.

But the last couple of weeks in the apartment were awful. Adrian pushed, trying to force Steven to go away mad. Steven did his best to ignore it. He stayed on Lisa's couch a few times. He spent long hours at school and fled to the coffee shops whenever possible. Yet more than anyone, Adrian knew how to drive Steven crazy.

Jolted awake when the front door banged open, Steven looked at the clock: 3:30 AM. He had a test in five hours.

Although in each interaction Adrian had been solicitous, even helpful, while Steven packed and made plans, every fucking night for a week he and Flip had had loud sex with no regard for Steven's schedule. Steven rolled over and pulled the pillow over his head. There was a loud thump on his bedroom door, as if one of them fell onto it.

"Jesus, you're fucking hot for it, aren't you?" Flip's voice snarled. "You look so good, everyone was watching only you at the club."

"Can't wait for you to fuck me. No one else there was good enough to fuck me. You're the only one who really gets me," Adrian said. Another bump and thump, like a knock on Steven's door.

Fully awake now, Steven let anger bubbled up in his chest. Adrian might be acting out, hurt that Steven was moving out, so Steven had been forgiving all week. But there were limits. Steven pulled on jeans as the rustling and thumping continued outside his door. This was on purpose, not Adrian being drunk and inconsiderate. It had been calculated all week.

Steven yanked the door open. Adrian and Flip almost fell into his bedroom.

"Oh shit, sorry," Flip said. He pulled himself upright, disentangling his hands from under Adrian's shirt. "Didn't mean to wake you." An insincere smile.

"Are you guys fucking kidding me with this?"

Adrian smirked. "I'm sorry. Were we too loud?"

"Yeah, Ade, you're too loud. Tonight, and every night this week. I need to fucking sleep."

"Sorry. I didn't realize you'd be home." Adrian smiled his sweetest smile. For once, Steven felt the urge to punch him.

"This is bullshit, and you know it."

"Can you give us minute, Flip?" Adrian asked.

Flip cast a disdainful glance at Steven, then headed down the hall. Steven crossed his arms, waiting for Adrian to speak.

"If you're upset because your old-man crush rejected you, you don't have to take it out on me like this, Steven." Adrian leaned in the doorway, the hall light making his platinum hair glow like a halo. "I warned you. I tried to protect you, you know. That's all I've ever done, is try to take care of you."

"Don't, please. Just go. Be quiet and let me sleep tonight. We'll talk tomorrow."

"Steven, I didn't want to tell you, but your *John*," Adrian spat the name like an epithet, like it implied that Steven was a whore, "isn't right for you. So I tried to cut it off before you got in too deep."

"Please stop."

"No, you need to hear this. We saw him tonight with his big bear of a friend. They propositioned us, me and Flip, you know, for a foursome. And that wasn't even the first time. I was surprised though, because I'd heard that John likes them much younger. That's why he never called you, right? I mean, you're gorgeous, but you're already too old for him."

Steven squeezed his shaking hands into fists. "I have never done anything to you, Ade, nothing bad enough to deserve to be lied to and treated like this. Why are you spewing utter bullshit?"

"I never lie to you. You know I don't. I'm the only one you can trust to tell you the truth. All your other friends, your fucking dyke friends, Lisa and Ryan and Marcus—they only tell you what you want to hear. They think you're too delicate, too stupid to deal with the truth. But I'm looking out for you. That's what I do."

"Shut up, Adrian."

"Aren't we best friends? It's my job to tell you what an old creep that John guy is. I mean, he had his hands all over me at the bar tonight. It was all I could do to get away from him."

"Stop lying."

"You've never done anything except follow me around like a little bitch, have you? Now you think you're better than I am? You think you're in love with some fucking guy who won't give you the time of day. I didn't think you were stupid, but maybe you are if you can't see how wrong for you he is."

"Why are you doing this?"

"I wanted to spare you, but you need to know. He broke up with his last boyfriend when the kid turned nineteen. Because that was too old. John likes them young, dollbaby. And dirty. You're not either of those things, are you?"

"Whoever told you this is full of shit. John isn't like that."
His heart about to burst, Steven clenched his fists tighter.

Adrian was clearly high, but his gaze was sharp, focused on Steven, a smirk tugging at the corners of his mouth.

"Why are you lying to me like this?" Steven demanded again. "I've never done anything to you to deserve this."

Adrian's mouth turned down, his body tensing. "You've never done anything to me at all, bitch," he spat out. "I've never felt anything for you but pity. I'm trying to help you, but it's clear you think you're too good for my help."

"Fucking don't do this. I know you. I know all the games you play. Don't fucking try them on me."

"You don't know me. You told yourself a story about me when we first met. But you were never my friend. You only care about yourself. You're the most self-centered little bitch queen I've ever met."

Adrian stormed down the hallway, slamming his bedroom door. Steven could hear the faint murmur of voices. After a few minutes, Steven went into the kitchen to make coffee, since he wasn't going to get any more sleep.

◊

His books open on the kitchen table, Steven was staring blankly when Ryan came in at six o'clock.

"Hey, man, I didn't think anyone would be up," Ryan said.

"Yeah, bad night. Adrian and Flip are in Adrian's room. I don't know if they're up or not."

"Man, those guys were practically fucking in the living room when I came home the other day. Who is that Flip guy, anyway?"

Steven shrugged. Ryan went on.

"Ade said that you're moving out? Did you guys have a fight? Is it about this Flip guy? Because he's not nearly as cool as you. I always wondered what would happen when you guys broke up."

Steven put down the pencil that he wasn't taking notes with. "We were never together. Me and Adrian have always been just friends."

Ryan poured coffee and sat across from Steven. "Sure, okay. I'm gone a lot, but I live here too, and you guys are not just friends. I have friends, and I'm not like you guys are with any of them."

"It's complicated." The only answer Steven could come up with.

"It always is." Ryan sipped his coffee. "I figured you guys had an open relationship. But honestly, I always thought you could do better. He never treats you well." He shrugged apologetically. "If you weren't together like that, then maybe you need better friends. It's probably good for you to move out."

Steven folded his arms on the table, glaring at Ryan.

"Sorry. I shouldn't talk shit when I don't know what's going on."

"No, it's cool," Steven said. "It's like everyone else can see my life better than I can."

Ryan studied him for a second. "If you're trying to do better, then you're already ahead of the game, you know?"

"Thanks, Ryan."

"Yeah. I need to get to work. Do you need the shower?"

"Nah, go ahead."

Ryan headed into the hallway.

"Hey, Ryan?" Steven stood up, his hand on the back of his chair. "How come you're never here? It's not my business, but I feel like a shitty friend, never even asking what you do."

"It's cool, man. I've been, you know, out making my own terrible choices." Ryan ran his hand over his face. "Sticking by someone I probably should have given up on. Let me know if you need help moving. And maybe we can get coffee soon. Cool?"

"Yeah, that'd be great."

Steven listened to the city waking up outside. The traffic on the interstate usually faded into the background, like ocean waves, but right now it roared while Steven tried not to think about how much of his life he'd lost that night.

21.
Filling Space

THE SCHOOL'S LAB HAD A DEDICATED Ethernet connection, so Steven was spending a lot more time there. He'd found a bunch of bulletin boards with people from other schools talking about the same computer science texts and theories he was studying. Although he intended to stick to that resource and a few others he'd stumbled across, he ended up looking at new boards that popped up every day, people talking about TV shows, books, and music.

Yesterday he found a whole group devoted to cataloging club mixes in New York and Chicago, arguing about who the better DJs were. Today he'd found a French-language computer science board, mostly students in Paris as far as he could tell, but his technical French knowledge was just a little less than he needed to follow along or join in.

Steven was closing out of that board to check his school electronic mail account when he felt someone hovering behind him.

"Hey, Steven? Your name is Steven, right?"

Steven turned around. One of his classmates stood there grinning manically.

"Yeah, hey, what's up?" Steven looked up into surprisingly kind brown eyes, boring down on him with questions, expecting Steven to have answers.

"I was wondering if you could help me with yesterday's class? If you had a few minutes." Bleached-blond skater bangs fell over the guy's eye, and he constantly flipped them back as he spoke.

"I'm sorry, but I missed Tuesday's lecture." Steven turned his hands out, apologetically.

"Did you do the reading? Because you always seem to really get stuff when we're in lecture. I don't get this algorithm thing, and I think you do." He turned the open book he held toward Steven, finger marking equations on the page.

Steven recognized pages he'd read them that morning to catch up for class. It was information he'd covered before and understood.

"Sure, yeah, I have time now."

The kid seemed relieved. He sat next to Steven. "Awesome. I knew, man, I fucking knew. I was, like, this guy knows the shit and he'll help me."

"I'm sorry, what's your name again?"

"Davy."

"Nice to meet you for real, Davy." Steven put out his hand and fumbled as Davy pushed through a complicated hippie handshake that ended in a fist bump. Davy was not what Steven expected his classmates to be like, though he hadn't put a lot of consideration into that until now.

As they poured over the equations, Steven did his best to explain it in the way he understood the material, not just repeating what the book said. The math was pretty clear to him. Simply another language. He sketched until he saw understanding dawn in Davy's eyes.

"Do you get it?" Steven asked.

"Yeah. Fuck yeah! It makes way more sense the way you explain it. Like, dude, how come the book doesn't just say that?" Davy's skater bangs were perpetually in motion as he spoke, falling down and being flicked back again.

Steven laughed. "I don't know. Actually, part of it was in one of the recommended readings. Wait, I'll tell you which one, because it helped me a lot." Steven dug in his backpack until he found the suggested reading list to show Davy.

"This is so cool, man. You could, like, totally teach this."

Steven wasn't interested in teaching, but the idea that someone thought he was good enough for that was heady. Surprised at how much pleasure the compliment gave him, Steven said, "I'm not sure I'm ready for that. I'd rather just do the work."

Davy nodded. "Yeah, it must be easy for you."

"Really, sometimes it kind of clicks for me, and I can see my way through it."

"I wish I was like that. Oh fuck, are you going to lecture today? We should probably go."

Steven glanced at the clock and hurried to log out of the workstation. He followed Davy out the door and across the Quad to their afternoon lecture.

"Mr. Frazier," Professor Green boomed as they entered in the room. None of Steven's classes had enough students to hide in, but this one was even smaller. There was no blending into the background when only twenty-six other students were present. "Pleased you've joined us today. It isn't the same without you here."

"I'm sorry, sir. I had to move to a new place before the end of the month and it fell in the middle of the week," Steven said, chagrined that he'd missed class yesterday. Professor Green was a great guy. Always making sure everyone got what he was explaining. The guy knew by the second week of class who needed extra help and who didn't, but he never shamed anyone in his class about needing extra assistance. Green seemed genuinely concerned that everyone learn and did whatever he could to help.

Several times he'd asked Steven to explain things back to him when he was lecturing. Steven loved that. It made him feel the way that explaining to Davy had, like he really got it and could help other people get to where he was if he explained it right.

Steven found a seat. Davy sat next to him.

"Life always gets in the way; you just have to find time once you've committed to learning. I hope you've all done the reading?" Professor Green asked, his eyes on Steven before he turned his attention to writing equations on the overhead projector.

Steven copied what Professor Green was writing, even though he knew it was straight from the book. His detailed lecture notes were what kept him from falling apart at test time. He took down verbatim whatever his instructors said, including all questions and answers. Often it was the second explanation, given to a question Steven would never have thought to ask that made the understanding click and stick with him. He liked to have a record of that to refer to later.

At the end of the hour, Steven was going through his notebook, drawing stars next to the parts he'd need to look up before the next class when Professor Green approached. Steven put down his pen and looked up as his teacher settled on the desk next to him.

"Missing three classes in the first month of the quarter isn't going to hurt your grade, especially since your test scores are so high."

Steven nodded, waiting for the expected scolding.

"But you aren't doing yourself any favors borrowing notes from other students when you're out. You're missing discussions that are beneficial to your learning. And you're depriving the other students of your brilliance. We can't have that, can we?" Professor Green smiled like he'd cracked a great joke. He clapped a hand on Steven's shoulder when he stood.

"Yes, sir, sorry. I have a much better living situation now, with nothing to distract me from school. I appreciate how much attention you're paying to my work. I'll do better."

"Don't do it because I asked. Do it because you want to be the best at this. I can see you do, so whatever's been holding you back, find a way past it." His teacher's expression was serious now. Steven nodded again, to show he understood. He packed his books away slowly.

Lisa was right when she'd accused Steven of skating through. All last year he accepted Bs instead of working for As, asserting that time out clubbing with Adrian was as important to his self-development as school. That lie echoed hollowly in his head today. Breezing through was fine, self sabotage wasn't. As he walked out of the classroom, Steven resolved again that he was truly committed to working harder this year, because now he had nothing stopping him.

"Hey man."

Davy, waiting in the hall outside, startled Steven from his self-reflection.

"There's this big Halloween party on Friday, like massive, if you're interested. A bunch of Comp Sci guys will be there, other cool guys I know, a DJ, a keg, the works. And, like, girls and stuff, too. You don't have to wear a costume, but it would be way more awesome if you do." Blond skater bangs flicked rapidly as he spoke. Steven resisted the urge to reach out and tuck them behind Davy's ear, wondering if that would make him hold still.

"Oh, well, thanks. But I have to work Friday, so I can't. But ask me next time, okay?" Steven said as they exited into the Quad.

"Totally, dude."

Davy put up his hand and Steven struggled with his backpack and books for half a second before slapping it the way he hoped Davy intended.

◊

"Steven!"

He turned at his name, expecting someone else was being called. Students were thick around the fountain, and his name wasn't uncommon. Steven had taken the long way, by the medical school, to catch his bus, enjoying the sunny October day.

The man approaching him was familiar, but Steven couldn't quite place him at first.

"It's—" he started, his hands in his pockets.

"Chris," Steven said, finally placing the face. "From the bookstore last summer."

Chris had shaved his goatee, and his shaggy surfer hair was pulled back with a head band. "You remembered."

"Sure. How are you?" Steven asked. Chris was more handsome than he remembered.

"Good. Hey, sorry I never showed up that night." Chris shuffled uneasily, taking his hands from his pockets and putting them back in.

"No big deal. It wasn't a plan, right? Just a loose possibility. And a long time ago," Steven said, checking Chris out as subtly as he could manage, finding that he hoped Chris's nervousness was because he was still interested. Maybe he was wrong, thinking he shouldn't hook up with anyone from school. What could it hurt, as long as they didn't have classes together?

"Yeah, I wanted to be there, but something came up. Anyway, I am for sure going out tonight, and I just saw you walking and," Chris paused and flushed, "I don't know, it seemed like a sign or something that you're right here. Any chance you're going out tonight, too? Maybe we can hang?"

"Yeah, wow, man, I wish I could. But I just moved and I've missed some classes. I have a test to get ready for."

The way Chris's chest stretched his t-shirt added to Steven's regrets, but he'd just recommitted to being responsible. However, having someone to talk to besides Lisa and Marcus would be great after the last couple weeks. "I'd love to another time, really."

"Cool, yeah, no big. Just thought I'd ask since I saw you. Next time." Chris stuck out his hand and gave Steven one of those complicated hippy handshakes that everyone but Steven knew how to do.

"Definitely," Steven confirmed.

◊

He unpacked and set up the turntable before he did anything else. For the first two days, all Steven had was a bed, records to listen to, and boxes to dig through whenever he needed anything.

Patti Smith's "Dancing Barefoot" played while Steven emptied the boxes of dishes and kitchen necessities that his mom had brought from his parents' garage. The plates were from his paternal grandmother's house, packed away since she died: 1950s stoneware with a twisty Atomic pattern on each, like something Steven drew with a Spirograph when he was little. Definitely way cooler than anything Steven expected to come from his family.

When Steven sat down to study at his little yellow kitchen table, he looked around, satisfied. The kitchen, dining, and living areas weren't separate by more than the lines on the floor where the linoleum ended and the pine floors began. Today he'd added an old overstuffed chair and a coffee table. Two boxes of books served as his side table, though records already lined the bottom of the wide book shelf his parents had brought over. There hadn't been time to shop for more living room furniture, so he'd taken what Marcus was giving away. The small bedroom held Steven's bed, his dresser and, and an alarm clock on a flipped-over milk crate. But it was home now.

The record ended, and Steven listened to local sounds for a minute, making out the faint hum of human and car traffic on Broadway two blocks over. A dog barked nearby. A car honked, and nearby a voice in the courtyard of his apartment building shouted, "I'm coming!"

Steven felt empty, clean, as he cracked open his text book. The school year had started awkwardly while the drama rose with Adrian, but that was all over now. He had a quiet place. For the first time, he had a place that was entirely his own. After the last month, the quiet loneliness of not having anyone there to talk to was a relief. Still, he wondered how he'd fill all the space he suddenly had in his life. Would Chris pop up again, still interested? Could he find someone to compare to his memories of John? Though they hadn't spoken in a month, on this quiet night the emptiness seemed to be shaped like John.

22.
Strawberry Cupcake

"SO WHAT IS IT YOU DO, Steve?"

"It's Steven." He smiled cautiously. "I'm studying computer science at U-Dub."

"Really? I thought Marcus said you worked in his store." The man lifted an eyebrow in a way that made his round face unpleasant, the question an accusation. Steven regretted giving this guy the benefit of the doubt, that he'd genuinely misheard Steven's name. No, he had an agenda of some kind.

"I do, but school is the biggest thing in my life right now." Steven swallowed the rest of his beer and picked at the bottle's label.

"See, that's so interesting, because of course I've seen you and your little blond friend at the clubs. I assumed you were biding your time, working for Marcus until you found another sugar daddy. I mean, that's what pretty boys like you do, right? Hook lonely old men into spending all their money on you?" The man's voice dripped with disdain, making Steven responsible for the sins of someone else. Steven didn't have time for it. He'd come here to meet people, not be taunted by bitter, lonely trolls.

"The thing most people don't realize about pretty boys like me is," Steven smiled and leaned forward, as if ready to reveal a secret, but actually armed and wary after an earlier run-in with rude strangers that night, "even though it looks like we survive on poppers and cocaine, we're actually vampires and have to be careful not to literally suck our victims dry. But don't worry, you're in no danger. We only bother with older men who have manners and class. Excuse me."

Steven gave his most insincere smile, waved his empty beer bottle to demonstrate the need for a refill, and escaped to the kitchen, trembling with exhilaration at having told off a nasty jerk.

Marcus's party hadn't been terrible so far. Though twice now, Steven walked away from vicious old queens out to insult him for no crime other than being young and good looking, as if his very existence affronted them.

In the kitchen, the fridge was held open by an exceptionally pretty girl with dyed black hair and heavy eyeliner. She glanced over her shoulder at Steven.

"You need another?"

She handed him one from the fridge without waiting for his answer. In her early twenties, she wore a Ministry t-shirt, what might have been a black skirt or part of another shirt, black leggings and combat boots. She wasn't what Steven expected to find at Marcus's birthday party.

"Thanks!"

"Sure." She closed the door and twisted the top off her own beer. "It isn't free though. There's a price for that beer."

"Oh?" Steven held the bottle away in mock horror before taking a sip.

"Yes. I need you to answer for your entire gender."

"I don't know how qualified I am for that. But what's the question?"

"Finney here," she pointed to a stern-looking older butch in a black polo shirt, khaki chinos, and black three-hole Doc Martens. Leaning on the counter, Finney raised her beer in greeting, a heavy silver cuff flashed at her wrist.

"And Rae." She indicated a woman dressed in flowing midnight blue with curly grey hair. "We've been discussing the merits of single-sex reproduction. Science is working on it. Rae said that asexual reproduction would produce only female children that way, and the males would die out. But I think there's value left to your gender." She poked him in the chest. "So what say you?"

"Hmm." Steven pondered the question. "Based on my recent experiences with the male population, I'd say we don't have much to offer. I wish I could make a case that I'm one of the good ones, but not everyone has that opinion of me."

"You're one of the good ones." Finney's voice was scratchy, like she'd been smoking filterless cigarettes for a hundred years.

"How can you tell?" Steven asked.

"You're Lisa's friend, right?"

"Yes, how—oh, we met once at Ernie Steele's right?"

Finney nodded.

"That's good enough for me," Rae said. "What's your name, last good boy on Earth?"

"Steven."

"Hi, I'm Jess," the pretty black-haired girl said. Steven awkwardly shook hands around the room. "I haven't seen you at Marcus's parties before."

"No, this is my first."

"What brings you out tonight?" Rae asked, clearing a space on the counter behind her and hopping up to sit on it with surprising grace.

"Short answer or truth?" Comfortable in this bright little corner of the party, with this unlikely group of women, Steven was ready to answer either way.

"Truth," Finney bellowed and slapped the counter like she'd made a joke.

"Well, I recently lost my best friend—"

"AIDS?" Jess asked softly, putting her hand on his arm.

"No, he's not dead. He's just an asshole."

Finney's laugh boomed through the room, warm, inclusive, and friendly. Jess and Rae smiled and nodded sympathetically, so Steven went on. "And now I'm reassessing my whole life. All my past choices. I have to worry about the repercussions of where I go when I go out, who I might run into. So a party where I'm not likely to know people seemed like a good idea."

Finney stepped close, dropping a friendly arm over his shoulder, and pulling him against her. "Aw, cupcake, friend breakups are the worst. Then you don't even have anyone to talk over the breakup. I wish we put emphasis on friendships and support at times like this in our society."

"Yeah, shitty. I'm sorry, man," Jess said.

"But you have us now." Rae raised her beer.

"Yes. And you are pretty enough to be an honorary girl." Jess grinned.

"With this mouth? For sure, he's a strawberry cupcake if I ever saw one." Finney cupped his jaw, examining him like a farm animal.

"Do you need rescuing from these mad women?" Marcus asked as he came in. He pulled a beer from the fridge.

"We're making friends," Finney said, tipping her head to the side. She rubbed her grey crew cut against Steven's cheek like a cat, causing everyone to laugh.

Marcus put a hand on Steven's shoulder when Finney released him. "Good, because he's the best worker I've ever had. I wouldn't want your lot scaring him off."

"How do you all know Marcus?" Steven asked.

"At a bright time when we were young, the bars weren't separated by gender. Everyone was full of free love and bad hairstyles. I think it was the 70s, but I hardly remember it because of all the drugs." Finney laughed, as if she'd made a great joke.

"We've been friends a long time," Marcus agreed.

"After ten years together, I know most everyone Finney knows," Rae said.

Steven turned to Jess and tipped his head, questioning.

"We volunteer together at ACT UP. You should come sometime. We're about to start a safe sex campaign in the high schools. I'll get your number before you go, okay?"

"Jess is one of our best recruiters," Marcus said. "You'll find she's hard to say no to once she's got her claws in you."

"What about you?" Jess asked.

"I work for Marcus at the shop. The friend I recently broke up with introduced us." Steven turned to Marcus. "I was telling them my sad, personal drama, because apparently I've become That Guy."

"It's okay," Rae said. "We already like you more for it. Tell me about this safe sex thing," she said to Jess.

The kitchen was bright and cluttered. Cheery yellow paint covered the walls and all the cabinets. The chatter of his new friends was comforting, like the friendly rushing clack of a mountain brook in summer. Jess's dyed black hair proved to be disheveled from running her hands through it, which she did as she described the safe sex campaign she was working on. She detailed making flyers and organizing folks to hand them out at schools. Finney watched them, clearly amused by Jess's zeal.

The warmth and friendliness kept Steven in the kitchen for the rest of the party. People came in and out, shaking hands, smiling as they grabbed fresh drinks. Steven wondered whether any of them knew John, if John came to parties like this with his own friends on Saturday nights, or was drinking at the Elite or dancing at a white party at Tugs.

"Wait, where was this?" Jess asked. Her concerned tone pulled Steven back from a daydream into the story he was missing.

"In the Rockies, not the little mountains around here," Finney said, drawing her shoulders back and squaring her stance, as if she was settling into the story for the long haul.

"And there was a bear at your campsite?" Jess's brows knit together in confusion. "Did he come with you?"

Finney howled with laughter. Even Rae was wiping away mirthful tears when they all calmed down. "Oh baby," Finney said, a bright grin splitting her face, "a grizzly bear. *Ursus arctos horribilis*. Big, hairy, and wild, not big, hairy, and usually a leather daddy."

"Oh. Oh! I couldn't figure out why you were so scared about chasing him out of a campsite. I mean, what with all you do, I figured you'd have some technique for controlling even non-submissive Bears. But I guess not grizzly bears."

Steven laughed, throwing a companionable arm around Jess's shoulders, so she'd know he wasn't laughing at her. Coming into the story late made it so much better.

"I assure you," Rae said, "even the leather daddy Bears know when to be afraid of Finney. She's mostly fun, but that grizzly should have been worried about the kind of punishment she can dole out."

"Let's not scare my new cupcake, talking like that," Finney said, pinching Steven's cheek. "We want to keep him around, so he'll tell his stories, too."

"I don't know any good stories," Steven said.

Jess slipped her arm around Steven's waist. "Of course you do. Tell us something embarrassing. Tell a good story about your asshole friend, so you can shake off the bad memories."

Adrian was still a raw wound in Steven's heart, but any funny story he had would certainly involve Adrian. Steven thought for a second while fetching another beer out of the fridge. "This is more embarrassing than funny—"

"That's all I wanted," Jess interrupted, her face lit with mischief.

Steven smiled and tried to set up the story, though he'd never been good at telling it right without Adrian's help. But since he was doing without from now on, Steven did his best. "One time he chased a bear for me. A muscle Bear, not an escaped zoo animal."

Finney's delight was evident as she put her elbow on the counter, chin to fist, and said, "Ooh, tell us."

"I wasn't twenty-one yet, not even twenty, I think. It was about six months after I moved here, and I definitely still had a suburban taint on me."

"I bet you were a twinky little treat, not the perfect cupcake you are now." Finney bared her teeth and snapped like she was going to take a bite. Marcus came and leaned in the doorway, listening.

"I wouldn't say I was innocent, but I wasn't well versed in gay life yet, though I'd had a crash course. I just didn't really understand everything yet."

"Naïve," Rae supplied.

Steven nodded. "Yes, exactly. I think we went to the Brass Connection first and then Tugs in Belltown, the old one, and we had taken MDA. I was dizzy from the never-ending smell of poppers—remember how it was?" Steven was looking at Marcus, but he saw Finney nod her head as well. "I was dancing and felt hands on me. I thought it must be Adrian, so I sort of ground against him and then turned around into this huge wall of muscle, hair, and leather. He sort of backed me up against the wall—I remember it was brick in there—and put a hand on either side of me, and just started saying the dirtiest things you can imagine."

"Well, not that Finney can imagine, but probably the rest of us, yes," Rae said, making Finney laugh.

"It's funny," Steven said, "I can't remember what he said, but I'm sure if I heard it now it would probably sound like nothing but—" he shrugged, "nineteen, high, and naïve, it was dirty. I was just sort of stunned. I'd somehow imagined that like always stuck with like. The pretty young boys danced together, the Castro-clone leather men stuck close, the flaming queens all cackled together at the bar, right? So I couldn't understand that he actually wanted the things he was saying from me."

"Bears and twinks. Like chocolate getting with peanut butter." Finney grinned.

"So Adrian comes up—he's my height, my size really, with white blond hair and makeup out to here—" Steven drew his finger under his eye like Adrian's dramatic eyeliner. "He shoves the guy, whose nipples were at my eye level. Well, maybe not. The guy probably wasn't seven feet tall, but it felt like it when he had me pinned against the wall. So the guy steps back and looks at Adrian, who just slaps him across the face and says, 'Daddy, this honey isn't yours to eat. You better find another tree to bark up!' And the guy was so surprised that he turned and walked away." Steven swallowed the rest of his beer, remembering how worried Adrian had looked, like Steven was in danger. "Adrian said, 'You almost got eaten by a bear!'" Steven did his best to mimic Adrian's overly dramatic delivery.

Finney's laugh filled the room. "You might have liked being eaten by a bear."

"Maybe." Steven made a face to show he was considering it. "I still haven't tried it."

"I'm sure there's plenty out there that would glad to oblige you if you got curious," Marcus said from the doorway. Steven smiled, raising an eyebrow.

"Are you suggesting I should try?"

"You should try everything once, kid." Marcus raised his beer to toast the idea.

"How else will you know what you like?" Finney asked.

"So how come you and Adrian aren't friends?" Jess asked, leaning back against Steven, her head on his shoulder.

"He turned on me, like the proverbial wild bear, and destroyed all my chances with a guy I really liked." Jess rubbed her hand in circles across Steven's back. He said, "It's clear to me now how toxic our relationship was. It was never going to end well."

"Sorry I asked," Jess said, clearly worried she'd upset him.

"It's fine. I'm in a better place. "

"You're the one Lisa told me is studying computers, right? I want to hear about that," Finney said, getting herself another beer.

The night flowed on, still comfortable and warm, and the darkness around Adrian and John couldn't dampen how good Steven felt in this company. He explained his classes to Finney. Rae talked about students at the private high school where she taught. Jess teased Steven about being a secret nerd. He basked in the cheery glow of their attention until they drifted off at the end of the night, back to their lives.

◊

When everyone was gone, Steven wasn't yet ready to return to his empty apartment, preferring to help Marcus clean up.

"Are you doing okay?" Marcus asked, as Steven swept empties and abandoned paper plates into a trash bag. "With the whole Adrian thing?"

"Sure." Steven dropped things into the bag one at a time. "It sucks, but we were so codependent. It's best this way for both of us."

"Did you learn that word from the dykes tonight?"

"What? Codependent? No, I—" Steven started to say *No, of course I already knew that word*, but stopped. "No, I know other lesbians."

Marcus laughed. "Okay, joke and change the subject. But you did lose someone important and you should process that. If you need anything, ever, call me, okay?"

"I'm fine. It's not like when you—" Steven stopped, leaving *when you lost your lover* hanging unsaid between them.

"It's all loss," Marcus said, putting down his own trash bag and setting Steven's aside. He pulled Steven into a tight hug, which Steven returned uncomfortably, not sure if he was supposed to be giving or receiving comfort. Marcus finally stepped away and returned to cleaning up.

Eager to fill the silence between them, Steven said, "I had fun tonight. And I wouldn't have if Adrian had been here. So my life is already better."

"Good, I'm glad. Just watch out for those girls."

"Who? Finney and Rae? They seem great."

"They are great. But Finney likes pretty boys like you, so be careful." Marcus seemed more amused at the prospect of Finney liking boys, teasing Steven with the news rather than actually warning him.

"That might be more information than I need." Steven laughed. "I thought she and Rae were together?"

"They are, but Finney's a Dominatrix. Like a professional. She takes both pretty sub boys like you, and women." Marcus watched Steven, to see if Steven was shocked.

Not much shocked Steven any more, but he raised his eyebrows and widened his eyes in a parody of shock, playing along. "That was definitely more information than I needed. I don't think I'm in danger, there. Not exactly a sub boy."

"Sorry, I thought you—I'm overstepping. Sorry."

"No, it's okay," Steven offered, glad when the conversation turned more casual while they finished cleaning.

◊

The whole walk home, Steven couldn't shake the idea of Finney as a Dominatrix, finding it both terrifying and comical to imagine, but for a while it diverted him from thinking about why Marcus assumed he'd be a sub in a situation like that. The majority of his sexual experiences had been pretty much plain vanilla. Likely most people hadn't had as much sex in relatively public places as he had, but, like he'd told Lisa before, occasional bathroom and back-alley sex was convenience, not kink. He never thought he'd missed anything by not being kinkier, however much Adrian used to tease him about it. He wondered if, because he'd been abstinent for months, he now needed to push his previous boundaries.

That awkwardness with Marcus and worries about Dominatrixes aside, the party proved he could make new friends. For the first time in weeks, he hadn't felt isolated, hadn't missed the idea of John, or even missed Adrian. Personal misfortune had been replaced with laughter and kindness.

The late November air was cold, but Steven didn't regret rejecting Marcus's offer of a ride. Walking from Marcus's house on the far north edge of Capitol Hill, Steven stayed on Fifteenth Avenue East, walking the long way around Volunteer Park instead of cutting through to Federal Avenue and his new apartment. Though small, the apartment was all his, which was the first time Steven had ever been able to say that. And it now felt like home, everything unpacked.

He stopped at corner of Prospect and Fifteenth Avenue, looking up into the dark park. He could cut through, but he risked running into creeps and freaks among those cruising for anonymous sex in the bushes. Better to head down a couple blocks to Roy Street and then walk straight down the Hill. But Steven didn't. He turned east on Prospect Street, walking another block out of his way.

It's no big deal. I happened to be in the neighborhood. It doesn't hurt to look.

He continued rationalizing his actions until he turned onto Sixteenth Avenue. John's house was two in from the corner, all the lights out at 1:00 AM. The sleek black Lexus plus an old orange Datsun and green Subaru station wagon were parked close to the house, on the street instead of in garages, like most of this part of Capitol Hill.

The front yard was small and tidy, shaded with trees and filled with rhododendrons and japonica bushes in the spaces around flower beds that sagged with the last hardy fuchsias and chrysanthemums. It was a yard someone cared about, spent time in. A bench swing was anchored into the crossbeam of the porch, and the front door was set with an intricate panel of leaded glass. Steven resisted the urge to creep up the steps and peek through the windows on either side of the door. Spellbound, he watched the quiet house, mentally playing back the fantasies of the kind of life he once imagined having with John: Saturdays trimming the bushes and sweeping the porch before walking to the park to read together on a bench. A window over the sink, for Steven to look out at John's workshop as he made dinner for them. Tiny domestic moments that would fill their days together.

Eight weeks and he hadn't run into John. He wanted to bring it up with Lisa, but she'd been so good helping Steven move, listening to him talk about Adrian, that he didn't want to put any more on her.

Standing here wishing would not change one thing. Still, Steven was reluctant to abandon his fantasies of life inside John's house. Steven walked slowly up the street, not looking back, finally cutting over on the next block and hurrying down the hill.

Inside his apartment, out of the cold, the light flashed on his answering machine. Steven pressed Play, optimistic that other magic could happen that night. But the two messages were only from his mom and Ryan.

No surprise messages from John, asking after Steven.

This late at night, there was nothing to be done but go on with life. Shaking off the dejection that had crept in, Steven dug out Toni Basil's "Mickey" and danced while he undressed, reveling in having space to do whatever he wanted, free of judgment, free of drama. Tomorrow would be better, setting out on the path to the life he dreamed of.

23.
Business Casual

Nᴇʀᴠᴏᴜꜱ, Sᴛᴇᴠᴇɴ ᴜɴᴅɪᴅ ʜɪꜱ ᴛɪᴇ and started over, trying for a tidier knot this time. When he'd last seen John, the knot in John's tie looked like it came from a fashion magazine. Steven wanted to at least get his to be even.

When Steven called to ask, Lisa said to dress "business casual" for her office holiday party, whatever that meant. Steven hoped he had it covered by wearing his best wedding/church/job interview outfit: shirt and tie, black pants, and a V-neck sweater. It was businessy enough, or casual enough, or, he hoped, both. The last occasion when he was this nervous dressing for an event might have been his high school prom.

He had to face John for the first time in almost three months, and he didn't know what to expect. But the invitation to their office Christmas party came from John, not Lisa. Lisa said it was an open house for clients and friends, so not to read too much into it. Yet hope bloomed in Steven's chest when he opened the envelope. If nothing else, it meant John wasn't averse to seeing Steven again. Perhaps he'd thought of Steven in the intervening months.

The invitation included "Steven Frazier and guest," which seemed generous, given John's last run-in with one of Steven's friends. Steven was going only to see John. Of course Lisa knew that, but he didn't want to seem too obvious about it, so he'd enlisted Ryan to come as his date. Steven needed all the support he could get.

Ryan's arrival was a welcome distraction. Steven kissed his cheek. Ryan started laughing immediately.

"What?" Steven asked.

"I can't believe that's what you're wearing," Ryan said, still grinning.

"What's wrong with it?" Steven looked down, seeking a defect he hadn't seen in the mirror. When he looked up, Ryan was unbuttoning his peacoat to reveal that he was wearing exactly the same thing. Where Steven's sweater was green and tie was grey, Ryan had a grey sweater and a green tie.

"Oh. My. God."

"We look like we planned it," Ryan said as he buttoned his coat back up. "I didn't know what 'business casual' meant, so I dressed for church."

"Me too," Steven confessed. "Should I change?"

"Into what?"

"I don't know! It took me forever to figure this out." Steven studied Ryan. They weren't really on a date, so was this any different than if they both wore jeans and t-shirts, or similar suits? Steven said, "I don't care, if you don't care?"

"I don't think anyone is going to mistake us for twins."

Steven nodded. Ryan's Japanese heritage was only the beginning of the differences between them, though the most obvious. "People might think we're a super cutesy couple," Steven warned.

"I can live with that." Ryan grinned again. "I could do better, but you don't look so bad. You clean up all right."

Steven scowled, then smiled. "You look handsome too, jerk. Should we go? What's it like out there?"

"Dry enough that we can walk. Or wait, where is this thing?"

"Pioneer Square. On Occidental."

"Hmm, we could still walk if we aren't in a hurry to get there by a certain time."

Steven looked at the clock. The invitation said 7:00 PM to 10:00 PM, and it was 7:35 right now. "Maybe the bus?" he asked.

"Whatever you think is best. This is your gig, man. Actually, what is this gig anyway?" Ryan asked.

"You know my friend Lisa from before, right?" When Ryan nodded, Steven went on. "This is her office Christmas party. She works in finance and investments, but her boss—" Steven tried to be casual about mentioning John "—is gay and knows a lot of people. So it's kind of fun, kind of business?"

"Sounds good," Ryan said. "I like your place. What I saw of it."

"Oh yeah, sorry," Steven said as he locked the door. "I'll give you the tour another time. It's like two whole rooms though, so the tour is pretty boring. Imagine our old apartment without your room, Adrian's room, or the kitchen."

"It didn't have a kitchen? Where were we standing then?"

"It does. It's just small and built into one corner of the living room," Steven explained as they headed through the courtyard and up the alley to Broadway. A bus was pulling up when they crossed the street. Steven followed as Ryan ran for it. The Number 7 bus seemed surprisingly empty for this time on a Saturday night. They found seats near the front.

"So," Ryan said, leaning back, not looking at Steven. "It's okay to tell me to shut the fuck up, but have you talked to Adrian recently?"

Steven tensed at the mention of Adrian. "Ah, no, not really. We've exchanged relatively polite hellos when we run into each other, but we haven't talked. Did something happen?" Steven realized how cut off he was, and, worse yet, he wasn't sure how he felt not knowing anything about Adrian's life. It was kind of a relief.

"Oh no, nothing bad. You know Flip's still there, and I'm moving out at the end of the month?"

"I didn't know any of that. Ugh, Flip must have burned all his bridges in L.A., huh?"

"If he ever had any. That guy is a whirlpool of chaos."

Steven nodded. "Is Adrian doing okay?"

"Yeah, man, I guess. That cat always seems to land on his feet, doesn't he? He lost his job again, although he doesn't seem concerned about it. Who knows, maybe Flip has rent covered? But Adrian's jobs never seem to pay enough. Like where does he get his money from? Do his parents give it to him or something?"

"I don't know. He's from Wenatchee, which doesn't mean his family isn't rich, but he's never talked about them. I'm not sure he speaks to them at all," Steven said, aware of how little he'd known about Adrian, even after six years living in each other's pockets.

"Maybe he has some benefactor? Like a sugar daddy?"

"He always said I needed to find one, so maybe? Still, I think in six years that might have become apparent to me. But then I wasn't paying the right kind of attention."

Ryan nodded, then he broke into a crazy grin. "Oh! Oh god, do you think he's actually a hustler?"

"Adrian bends over for a lot of guys. I don't think he's charging any of them, but maybe he should." Steven could imagine Adrian accepting cash, but he couldn't imagine Adrian ever asking for it, making solicitation unlikely.

"Okay, then," Ryan continued speculating, "do you think he steals from them? Or maybe he steals from his job, and that's why he's always leaving them?"

Steven shook his head. "This conversation is exactly why I always ignored how he could afford whatever he wanted. Because nothing good can come of guessing where the cash comes from."

"It's kind of fun though. Hmm, I bet it's something lame, like his mommy gives it to him, and he tries to make it look like he hustles it because it fits his image better."

"I feel like I never knew anything about him at all," Steven said, ending the joking. "For all I know, his parents are dead." He didn't want to stomp on Ryan's fun, but talking about Adrian wasn't easing his anxiety about seeing John again.

Ryan, not quite getting it, said, "Well, for what it's worth, I'm glad you got away from him. You deserve better. I don't know that you guys had such a healthy relationship."

"Yeah, I hope he's okay." In spite of everything, he'd spent too much time with Adrian not to wonder regularly how Adrian was doing.

Ryan nodded. "Yeah," he said as if considering his words carefully, "even with Flip there, Adrian is actually partying a little less than you guys were together at the height of your, ah, whatever. And once he's over this Flip thing, which, given how much they seem to argue, is probably soon, I'm sure he'll be fine."

"Good. Now let's talk about something else." Steven felt disappointed that his departure didn't seem to have affected Adrian. Or maybe it did. Adrian was always a mystery. But once he'd seen Adrian's true face, he could never return to the halcyon days of their friendship, however hard it was to end the years of habit, caring about Adrian's well-being.

"Sorry, I shouldn't have brought it up."

"No, Ry, it's cool. I didn't realize I was worried about him."

"Yeah, I can tell. Sometimes, like now, your face is a full picture window to your inner thoughts."

Steven shivered, uneasy that he could be read so easily. He said, "Right now my inner thoughts hope there's an open bar at this party."

"Wait, there might not be? Because I didn't sign on to talk to a bunch of suits while sober." Ryan looked horrified. Steven laughed, instantly feeling better, like he was entering the lion's den with a brother in arms.

"Oh god, what if there isn't a bar, for real?" Steven fretted.

"I promise I'll take you somewhere else. I have no idea who all is going to be at this party."

"Why are we going again? For your friend Lisa? Does she need moral support?"

"Uh, no, I know a couple of people there," Steven dodged, unwilling to explain the whole backstory to Ryan, the unintentional role John played in Steven's break up with Adrian, especially.

"What is your face right now? Oh fuck me, this is about going to see a guy you like, isn't it? You just started dating? Nope, I can see it's something else. Who? Oooh, tell me!"

Steven shook his head, embarrassed, worried that everyone could read him this easily.

"It's cool," Ryan said, leaning back again. Then he smiled slyly. "I'll figure it out when we're there. It'll keep me entertained."

Steven punched him lightly on the shoulder.

"Should be easy, too." Ryan grinned. "But since you and he aren't a thing yet, I'll be cool. No worries. Damn, I can't wait to see this mystery man. Oh my god, it is a man, right?"

Steven punched him again, harder this time.

◊

After the bus ride, walking eight blocks from Second and Cherry down to Occidental Avenue in the cold, through the scruffy edges of downtown into the older part of Pioneer Square, Steven felt his anxiety rising again. He was in a better place than he'd been the last time he saw John, but how could he prove that?

Maybe John had been a fever dream that Steven used as a distraction, to stay blind to how out of control his life had been. What if John wasn't what Steven remembered? He didn't even know John, only the idea of him that Steven had fantasized about so often.

"Hey man, relax," Ryan said as they got to the door, his eyes serious. "It's just a party. He's just a guy. Whoever he is." He smiled kindly.

"Am I this obvious about what I'm thinking to everyone? Or is this a special power you have?"

Ryan smiled crookedly and straightened Steven's tie. "You look like you need extra attention tonight." He pushed at Steven's hair. For a second Steven thought they might kiss, until Ryan broke the spell. "You look perfect. Let's go find your man." He pulled Steven through to the door and up the stairs in search of Lisa.

Steven tried to take in the room as he reintroduced Ryan to Lisa. He looked for John but didn't want to seem too obvious, and he didn't want Ryan to zero in right away and guess who his target was.

"The bar is back there," Lisa said, pointing. "Get a drink. You look like you need it." She kissed his cheek and turned to greet the men entering behind them. Ryan and Steven moved out of the way, taking off their coats and heading to the bar.

"You can put your coats in there." The bartender nodded, indicating a door next to the bar. Having shed their winter burdens, Steven and Ryan came back to the smiling bartender and braced themselves with liquor, preparing to make small talk with strangers.

Ryan surveyed the room. "Hmm," he said, "you didn't give yourself away by spotting him right off. So either he isn't in the room or you're cleverer than I thought."

"I am an evil mastermind," Steven said. "You'll never figure me out in this lifetime."

The room seemed huge for an office. It took up the entire second floor of the building. Some walls had been removed to open the space, though several doors still led to other rooms. The far corner held a huge table covered in food. Chairs were lined up against the wall like castoffs from a big board meeting. The rest of the room was filled with couches and chairs in small clusters, designed for entertaining and casual conversation. The furniture was nicer than what Steven was used to, and he assumed most of it was antique—heavy cocktail tables and dark, looming armoires along the walls. Steven wondered if any of the pieces were ones John had refinished. The floors were old, stained concrete, polished to a high shine, with huge, colorful Persian rugs. It looked more like an antique gallery than an investment office, everything expensive, old, and too nice to touch. But then, he supposed, if you were going to let someone invest your money, you wanted it to be a person who appeared to have money themselves, someone successful. This room felt successful.

"This is nice," Ryan said softly. "I don't usually come to parties like this."

"Me neither." Steven swallowed the rest of his drink and turned back toward the bar. When he rejoined Ryan, he focused on the people in the room, not the room itself. There were maybe thirty or forty people milling about, women in slacks or short dresses, men in jackets or sweaters. Steven relaxed, feeling more like he fit in. At least he didn't stand out in the wrong way.

He spotted John on the far side of the room, near a glassed-in office. He was as handsome as Steven remembered, maybe more so, and had several other men with him who seemed to be chatting amiably. He didn't appear to notice Steven.

"So, where is your mystery man?" Ryan asked.

"You think I'm going to give myself away if you simply ask?" Steven countered.

"It was worth a shot, to see if you'd let down your guard after one drink."

"Ha, I'm not that easy."

"Good to know." Ryan arched one brow and gave a crooked smile like he was keeping track. "Should we see what the food is like in a place like this?"

Tense again, Steven followed Ryan. To get to the food, they had to pass where John stood. Steven couldn't interrupt John's conversation with his actual guests, but it would be awkward to walk by without acknowledgment. It didn't matter in the end. John turned, pointing out the window, his back to Steven as they passed.

"Damn it," Ryan said when they arrived at the food table. "Something happened but I wasn't watching close enough to see who you were worrying that I might notice."

Steven smiled, feeling like this hadn't been such a good idea. What if he didn't get to talk to John? Oh god, what if he did get to talk to him? Steven was unready for either scenario.

They picked over the food, examining every morsel as if they were in a foreign country. Ryan made it seem fun, rather than weird. They talked, awkwardly balancing drinks and plates. Steven kept his back to the room.

Glad of the company, Steven narrowed his focus to their tiny little corner, trying to stave off the feeling of impending doom at seeing John again. Ryan's face was animated as he told about working in retail during the holiday season.

It was no wonder Ryan was never home; he must have guys crawling over him all the time. Without Adrian in the way, clouding Steven's judgment, he realized that Ryan was really hot.

24.
An Artist and a Mad Scientist

"So, is it Tom of Finland over there that you're all worked up about?"

Steven glanced in the direction Ryan indicated, his eyes widening. "Nope, but holy shit, is that guy real? He literally looks like he stepped out of the comics. I've never seen anyone like that, even at a gay bar." Steven turned back, trying not to notice what John was doing on the other side of the room.

"Okay," Ryan said, dropping voice and leaning in. "If your man is tall, handsome, and slightly older, then I think he's headed right for us, right now."

Steven, keeping his face neutral, fought the urge to turn around. He dropped his empty plate in a nearby trash can and shifted hands with his drink.

"You must be Steven," a tall, dark, severe-looking man said, holding out his hand. Steven felt Ryan's curious look while he shook the man's hand.

"Yes. Hello, and you are?"

As the man looked him over, Steven remembered the rake of those eyes from the first night he'd seen John at the bar. "Shane," the man said, releasing Steven's hand and turning to Ryan.

"This is Ryan," Steven said.

"Ryan Ikeda." He shook Shane's hand.

"So you're John's computer genius friend, right? And are you the roommate?" Shane smiled like a prowling tiger. Steven felt consumed, judged and spit out.

Ryan looked confused for a second, and then said, "Actually yes, I was a roommate, though Steven moved out several weeks ago. But maybe you're thinking of Adrian?"

"Are you the boyfriend then?" Shane asked.

"Nope, just came for the food." Ryan lifted his plate to prove it.

"So you're both single?" Shane's tiger smile became pleasantly solicitous.

"Yes," Ryan said, "though very recently for me."

"Excellent. So, Ryan, what do you do?"

"I'm an art student, and I work at Nordstrom."

"Perfect. An artist and a mad scientist."

"Mad scientist?" Steven wasn't sure what was happening.

"Computer genius, whatever." Shane waved his hand. "Smart, anyway. And arty and both so very nice-looking."

"I'm sorry," Ryan said, picking another stuffed mushroom from the buffet. "Who are you exactly?"

"Shane." The scold in John voice's resonated through Steven, the roughness making him shiver. John approached from the left and joined their group with another man, the bearded giant from that first night at Neighbours. "You aren't trying to recruit our friends into your matchmaking schemes, are you?"

"You excuse my partner," the other man said, with a distinct Russian accent. "He collects pretty young friends, but he means no harm." He reached a hand to Steven. "Sebastian Kamenev. You can call me Bash."

Steven shook his hand. "Steven Frazier. This is my friend, Ryan Ikeda." Ryan put out his hand politely.

"Ah, I don't know why I assumed you'd met before. I'm sorry. Yes, this is Shane and Bash," John said to Steven. He turned to Ryan. "I'm John Pieters. Hello, Ryan. Welcome to our party."

"Nice to meet you, John. Thank you for having us. This place is beautiful." Ryan glanced to Steven as he released John's hand, his eyes searching, reading Steven. Finding what he wanted, he grinned at Steven and turned back to John. "Did Steven tell me this is your office? It looks like an antique dealer's show room."

"He makes the office look opulent for clients. And sometimes then he does actually sell the antiques to them. So tacky," Shane said, filling a plate with everything on the table.

"It's all business," John laughed. "Antiques are just another investment for many people."

Steven wished desperately that he had another drink. He hadn't expected this. Some small talk with strangers, lots of standing in a corner with Ryan and Lisa. Maybe a little conversation with John, another apology for their last meeting, but not surrounded and hemmed in by John's jocular friends.

"So what do you do, Ryan and Steven?" Bash asked, taking a sip of his own drink. "Not in investments or antiques?"

"What gave us away?" Ryan asked.

"Not the matching outfits. The young brokers I see are always dressed alike. Did you guys plan that?" Shane managed to smile, eat and talk all at once, and still look intimidating.

"It was an accident," Ryan said.

"It's cute," Shane said around a mouthful of crab. "You should do it all the time. I bet you'd both end up with dates. Everyone loves coordinated sets, even when they are only choosing one piece."

"*I wouldn't suggest taking fashion advice from Shane,*" John said in French, grinning at Steven. Shane frowned, clearly understanding what was said. John went on in English. "You do look nice. Green suits you, although you probably hear that a lot."

"Yes. Something about the red hair. *You look great as well,*" Steven added in French, pushing close to the line of flirting. Ryan's eyebrow went up, his mouth twisted into a tiny, knowing smirk at Steven's response in French. Steven couldn't help it. The drinks, the party. And John looked so good. After the horror show with Adrian, Steven wanted to get back to how he'd talked with John when they first met.

John wore a French blue shirt, open at the neck, with grey wool pants and loafers, but his cufflinks, his watch, and how he moved made him seem more dressed up than he was.

"It's been a while, Steven," John said, pinning Steven once more under that gaze. "How's school? Still as eager as ever? Learning anything in particular to make yourself useful?"

Out of the corner of his eye, Steven watched Ryan study John, curious whether Ryan heard the shift in John's tone that made the simplest questions sound like innuendo. Or perhaps Steven imagined it, out of his desire to get back to where they were three months ago.

After all that time replaying his conversations with John, Steven wished he'd tried harder, flirted better. No time like the present. "I'm taking a much larger course load this year. So everything is tighter," Steven tried a casual smile. "Hopefully, what I'm learning means everyone will want to use me when I'm done."

"I'm sure that's true," John said, his eyes sparkling, corners crinkled as if he was trying not to laugh. Ryan caught Steven's eye. Steven flushed, aware of how he sounded, how bad he was at flirting.

"So what do you have for me, Steven? Still working on networking and software? Or is there something new in hardware I don't know about yet?" John asked, his eyes bright. Steven's chest felt tight, his dick stirring slightly at the idea that John was teasing him. It had to be on purpose. Everything that came out of John's mouth couldn't accidentally sound like an invitation to something dirty.

"I've been spending a lot of time on different networks, not just for school. Lately, it's like everyone has gotten online, so you can find anything you need if you know what to ask."

"And do you know what to ask for?"

Steven's pulse raced. He inhaled slowly, trying to keep his breath under control. With nothing to lose, Steven tried to score in whatever game John was playing.

"I know what I want," he said, keeping his eyes locked on John's for a second until he felt his cheeks burning and had to look away from John's wolfish grin.

"I bet you do," John said. "So how are you finding what you want? Do you have a modem at home?"

Ryan, Shane, and Bash watched the exchange intently, leaving Steven feeling even more exposed. Yet lightning hadn't struck him down for bold flirting. Maybe they were now back in safe territory.

"No, I use the connection at school to dial into CSNET or elsewhere. You can't believe the amount of information that is popping up everywhere. More than academic stuff. It's a new kind of information sharing."

"Yes." Bash stepped in, rescuing Steven, perhaps unknowingly, from straying off course again. "I'm finding all kind of forums. People talking about everything from restoring old cars to long rants about the government."

"That seems interesting, but what can you do with it for me?" John asked Steven, as if Bash hadn't spoken.

"For you?" He licked his lips unintentionally, pinking again as John's eyes tracked Steven's mouth.

"As a businessman," John amended, "will your networking, and your software, and your hardware help me out?"

"You could get stock information on your computer from all over the world in minutes. No more waiting on tickers. You'd see it right away, all at once."

"This just got boring," Shane interjected. "You're all too smart for me. We need more drinks to get you all back down to my level."

"Yes, do you need another drink?" Ryan asked, close to his ear, taking pity on Steven while Bash agreed with Steven about the need for all offices to get connected with modems if they were going to succeed in the future economy.

"Yes, let's go to the bar," Steven said, grateful to have a friend ready to rescue him from his babbling.

"No, stay and talk to your friend," Ryan countered with a sly smile. "I'll get it. Vodka and cranberry, right?" Steven nodded. The conversation couldn't take a worse turn than the way Steven had already steered it.

"I'll go with you," Shane said, taking Ryan's elbow. "You can tell me about your art and what you like in guys."

"Do you work in computers, Bash?" Steven tried to watch John discreetly while Bash spoke. "You seem to know a lot about it."

"Yes. I am an engineer for Boeing, so with computers and airplanes, not so much software and modems like you are studying. But I'm always curious."

"I feel like I run into engineering with everything. Like I can't do anything computer-related without it touching some kind of engineering. I wish I knew more about it; I'm always curious too."

"Does your enthusiasm meet your curiosity in all aspects of your life?" John raised an eyebrow. Steven's heart fluttered.

Before Steven could answer, a short, round man stepped into their circle. "I'm sorry to interrupt, John, but Sheila and I wanted to say goodnight. We don't mean to run, but we have other reservations."

"Mick, I'm so glad you and Sheila came. Did you get the information you needed from Lisa?" When the man shook his head, John said, "We should find her. Excuse me," John said to Steven and Bash, with an apologetic look.

When they were alone, Bash said, "John speaks highly of your knowledge. He's in high spirits tonight. I can't remember the last time I saw him drink this much. Or smile this much. Good to see him like this. Maybe we need to do this more often." Bash winked at Steven just as Lisa arrived with Ryan.

"Hello, sweetie." She kissed Steven again, her cheeks flushed, "I see you finally met Bash and Shane."

"Yes, your friend is very smart and cute." Though Bash was addressing Lisa, he smiled at Steven when he spoke. "Shane tried to recruit him right away. He knows quality when he sees it."

Lisa laughed. "Speaking of Shane, he wants you by the bar. He needs you to settle an argument."

"Always arguing," Bash muttered, nothing but fondness in his words. He took his leave. Steven, who regretted losing a chance to talk to Lisa, told her that John had just gone looking for her.

"Do you want to stay?" Ryan whispered. "I might end up too drunk for a nice party like this if I have to keep standing around making small talk. But I'm willing to make that sacrifice since the drinks are free."

Steven looked around. John was surrounded by a ring of people again. The room was full, all people John knew and Steven didn't. Another opportunity for Steven to attempt flirting didn't seem likely. Lisa came back to them.

"We're going," Steven said. "This was great. Thank you so much. Where is John? We should thank him too."

"Yes, we should find him." Ryan elbowed Steven in the ribs and smiled conspiratorially at Lisa.

"You sure you want to leave? John will be here for a while." Lisa grinned.

Steven made a face. "He has important people to talk to. I'll slip away before I embarrass myself. Or before one of you embarrasses me."

"Adrian isn't here, so I think you're pretty safe in that regard. I don't think Ryan or I could match that."

"The line to fuck off forms to the left. You can move to the front of the line if you have anything else like that to say to me." Steven smiled sweetly as he spoke, not revealing how the jab hurt.

"I'm just saying," Lisa said, pinching Steven's cheek. "I don't have to tell you, that you could do worse than friends like us, since you already have."

"Oh, were you off to talk to your work people? So sad," Steven kissed Lisa on both cheeks and patted her butt. "So sorry you have to go. See you soon."

"Oh you're so clever," she laughed. "I do have more important people to talk to. Ryan, it was nice to see you again."

"You too," Ryan answered as she walked away. "What was that about Adrian?" he asked Steven.

"I'll tell you later. Come on, we should go while we can. Before I get drunker and say something I really shouldn't."

25.
Sneaking Off

THEIR GOODBYES WERE QUICK, SINCE John was occupied with his guests. Steven felt a twinge of disappointment at not being able to keep John's attention, but as they moved through the crowd to the door, a hard pinch on his ass jolted him. He whipped around, ready to confront the offender.

"Hello, cupcake."

"Finney! What are you doing here?"

"John does some work for me. And of course, Lisa." She grinned. She wore an argyle sweater vest over a crisp dress shirt, the sleeves rolled up to mid forearm, her wide silver cuff flashing at her wrist.

"You look very dapper," Steven said, reaching to adjust her collar.

"Thank you." She took his hand away from her collar and squeezed it before letting go.

"Is Rae here?" Steven looked around, wondering if maybe they should stick around for a while and visit with his new friends.

Finney shook her head. "She's in California with her family. I'm going down tomorrow." Her face flushed, she looked positively gleeful as she turned to Ryan. "Who is your handsome friend you seem so eager to leave with?"

Ryan put his hand out. "Ryan Ikeda," he said as he shook Finney's hand.

"Not just handsome but nice manners on this one. You could do worse," Finney said in a sideways stage whisper to Steven. "I'm Phineas Valentine, but you can call me Finney, since you're obviously close with my cupcake, here."

"Cupcake?" Ryan asked, amused.

Steven ignored him. "Ryan and I aren't—"

"Aren't sneaking off to have sex, because that's what it looks like you're doing."

Slow from all the alcohol, Steven searched for the right denial, but Ryan answered. "No, we've been here a while, already seen everyone we came to see."

"Or you just don't want to be in those cute matching outfits anymore?" She waggled her eyebrows with comical Marxian perfection, so it was impossible not to laugh.

Ryan put his arm around Steven. "We're twins. Our mother has a hard time telling us apart, even now. We switch up the colors, but after a minute or two, can you remember which wore the green tie and which was in the grey? There'll be a quiz later."

"I like him!" Finney said, slapping Ryan on the back. "Go give him the blow job of his life, cupcake. I'll see ya soon." With that she rejoined her companions.

Steven shot Ryan an apologetic glance, but Ryan was about to choke from trying not to laugh.

"C'mon, man," Ryan said, pulling it back together. "She was great."

"Yeah, she's pretty great," Steven answered, disconcerted that she'd assumed he was with Ryan. He'd only seen her a couple times since the party at Marcus's, but Finney always seemed to see right through him. She must have been drunk to make such a mistake about Ryan.

After that, their exit was easy. John was still occupied, Shane and Bash nowhere to be seen, and they hadn't met anyone else at the party. A cab waited outside the door and they piled in, Ryan telling the driver to go to Broadway just as Steven realized that the cab must have been waiting for the person who'd actually called it.

"So what now?" Ryan asked.

Steven leaned back in the cab. He was tipsy for sure, but not yet done with the night. "Do you want to go out? It's still pretty early for Saturday." He wasn't ready yet to be alone with his thoughts of John.

"Sure, whatever you want. I didn't make other plans."

"We could get a drink somewhere," Steven suggested.

"The Double Header is near here, right? I've never actually been. Does that make me a bad homo? Am I missing some key history?"

Steven considered. "I've only been once. I don't think you're missing anything. But I want to change before we go out. I can't take looking like the Bobbsey Twins wherever we go, Tugs or whatever. I have something you can wear if you want to change, too."

"Your house first, then," Ryan said, obviously understanding that Steven didn't want to risk running into Adrian at their old apartment.

As the cab headed up Capitol Hill, Steven enjoyed the trees wrapped in white lights, the streets shiny, regular wet Seattle Christmas cheer.

"John's got a little bit of Dom-Daddy thing going on, doesn't he?" Ryan asked, as the taxi moved up Pike Street slowly in late night traffic.

"What do you mean?"

"He just sort of steers you when you're talking, doesn't he? Totally gives off that vibe that he'd really take you in hand in bed, you know?"

"Sure," Steven lied, suddenly imagining what Ryan might mean: John holding him down, making him come, making him beg. His cock twitched. Pulse racing, he couldn't shake the feeling, even though Ryan was watching him closely.

"I didn't realize you were into older guys," Ryan said.

"I'm not, it's, he's..." He trailed off, unable to say what it was about John, not without revealing his current dirty thoughts.

"He's incredibly handsome and rich?" Ryan filled in.

"Yes, but that's not it. There's something about him. It doesn't matter anyway."

"Why not?"

The thump of Steven's heart tipped from arousal to anxiety, his body tensed. "We went out, kind of, once. And then right after that, actually the day Flip showed up, we were coming home from an all-night warehouse party and ran into John on his way to work. Adrian taunted him about having not fucked me, and then said some really awful things about me to John. Tonight's actually the first time I've seen him since all that happened." Steven felt sick, describing it.

"Oh shit, man. I guess that's what Lisa was talking about?"

"Yeah."

"Did Lisa invite you tonight to see him again?"

"No, he invited me." Steven's chest warmed, recapturing the feeling he'd had when he'd first seen John's name in the invitation, his swirling signature.

"See? Yeah, that past shit doesn't matter. Not with the way he was looking at you, like you were naked and he was trying to decide what to do to you. It was really hot actually."

◊

"So this is it," Steven said, laying his coat on the couch. "The one room." He took three steps and opened the bedroom door. "And the other room."

"Where do you pee?"

"Ah, there's another secret room, hidden inside this one." Steven stepped into the bedroom, flipped on the light, pointed.

"Thanks." Ryan headed into the bathroom. Steven went to the closet, looking for clothing that was less "business casual" and more "gay bar," which was most of his wardrobe.

He had pulled his sweater over his head when Ryan came back into the room.

"Let me help you with that," Ryan said, loosening Steven's tie. They both stopped, their faces inches apart, Ryan's hand on Steven's collar, Steven's hands trapped between them, still bound in his sweater, his head flushed with vodka and this sudden intimacy.

"It's funny, isn't?" Ryan said, so close Steven could feel the heat of his breath. "How your friend Finney thought we were running off to fuck. It's like she could see that John's obvious interest in you made me look at you differently. Seeing you there, cheeks flushed, as he teased answers out of you, like he wanted to jump your bones. But he didn't. So I get a chance now." Ryan moved in closer, his mouth right by Steven's ear. "Have I mentioned how good you look in a tie?"

Steven shuddered as Ryan's hot breath tickled over his ear. Ryan let his hand slide down Steven's tie, but kept ahold of it as he drew back, looking into Steven's eyes.

"You're confusing your own interest for everyone else's." The idea of kissing Ryan wasn't new, but he'd never assumed he'd have a chance to act on it.

"I am very interested tonight." Ryan's intense gaze radiated desire. Steven licked his lips, aware how Ryan's eyes followed his tongue, just as John's had earlier.

"Yeah? What are you going to do about it?" Steven challenged, more boldly than he felt.

Ryan leaned even closer. "Is this okay?"

Steven nodded, unsure what he agreed to. Then Ryan's mouth was on his while Steven was tugging the sweater sleeves off his hands, drawing Ryan against him. Steven fell back against the wall as he yanked at Ryan's sweater. After he pulled it off, Ryan cupped Steven's face and kissed him slowly, deeply.

"Fuck, I've wanted to do that all night," Ryan said when he broke the kiss.

"Now you have. Does that mean we're done?"

"You're funny. There're other things I want to do, too." Ryan started to unbutton Steven's shirt.

"Like what?"

"Let me show you. That'll be better than telling you."

Steven loosened his tie, pulled it over his head, and flung it down. Ryan dragged Steven's shirt down his shoulders, but stopped at his wrists, trapping them against Steven's hips. Steven stepped toward the bed and Ryan followed, tumbling them both on to it.

The silk of Ryan's tie felt cool against Steven's bare chest. Ryan still seized Steven's bunched sleeves around his wrists, holding him down to the bed as he kissed Steven again and slipped his thigh between Steven's legs. Steven ground against him. He tried to lift his arms, to pull them out of the sleeves.

"No," Ryan growled, twisting to capture Steven's wrist in his grip. "Just let me show you, please?"

Ryan's pupils were blown wide with arousal but Steven saw no ill intention there. He nodded. "I'm yours." Heat rose from his chest up to his face, his own arousal awakening at the loss of control. Ryan pulled the sleeves the rest of the way off Steven's wrists and pinned Steven's hands above head before capturing his mouth again, then biting his ear and nibbling his neck.

It had been so long since anyone had touched him tenderly, since he'd felt so desired. Steven twisted and shivered when Ryan moved down his chest, finally going so low that his hold on Steven's wrists was compromised.

"Keep them there. Don't move until I say," Ryan whispered.

"Yes." Steven stretched out, overwhelmed.

Straddling Steven's hips, Ryan carefully stripped off his tie and shirt while Steven watched, obediently keeping his wrists crossed above his head. He shivered, though the room was warm enough.

Ryan's gentle dominance was a surprise, stirring an intense response in Steven. He felt lighter, as if he'd discovered what he'd always wanted but never knew how to ask for it. Adrian always bottomed, though Steven had had a few boyfriends and partners who'd taken some command in the bedroom. Those times seemed like luck when they happened. Now with Ryan, Steven slowly opened to the idea of his partner taking control.

In the dim incandescent light of the bedroom, Ryan's skin was the color of sun-warmed honey. Steven put his tongue out to taste. Finding it both salty and sweet, he went for more, licking down the column of Ryan's neck and across his collarbones.

Ryan undid Steven's belt and pants and tugged them slowly over his hips, stopping to untie Steven's shoes and pull off his socks.

"Okay?" He asked again, coming back to kiss Steven's breath away.

"Yes. So okay."

"Tested recently?" Ryan asked, his voice still soft.

"Yeah, a couple weeks ago. You?"

"About a month, but I haven't been with anyone since," Ryan said. He took off the rest of his clothes, except for his incredibly sexy black briefs. Steven felt awkward in his boxers, wanting to explain that they were more comfortable under dress pants.

"You look amazing like this," Ryan said, as if Steven's thoughts were visible on his face. He stretched over Steven and kissed him again, pressing his erection into Steven's hip. Steven started to reach for him, to pull him closer and grind against him. But he remembered and raised his hands back above his head.

"Good, so good," Ryan whispered as he slid down Steven's body. "Hands up there until I tell you otherwise."

"Okay, yes." Steven took a shuddering breath. Ryan's lips felt hot against his chest. He lifted his hips to grind against Ryan's thigh again, but he couldn't get enough contact. He groaned in frustration.

"Shhh, I'll take care of you."

With delicious torture, Ryan skipped kisses and licks over Steven's abdomen while slowly sliding his boxers down. He kissed his way over Steven's hips and thighs, never quite touching with enough pressure to satisfy, teasing constantly, moving closer to Steven's dick and then away again while Steven whimpered and considered begging, or grabbing Ryan's head and directing his mouth onto his cock. But he'd said he wouldn't move his hands, so he didn't. By the time Ryan closed his mouth over the head of Steven's cock, Steven was unbearably hard from anticipation.

Ryan was a more attentive lover than Steven had known in a long time; he kept teasing, pulling Steven close to the edge and then pulling back. His blow job, like his teasing licks, made Steven want even more. When Ryan slid back up his body to kiss him as he wriggled out of his briefs, Steven thought, *finally, finally he's going to really touch me.*

Roughly grabbing Steven's hips, Ryan pulled them together. He threaded his fingers through Steven's hair in a tight grip as they kissed, rubbing the silky length of his cock against Steven's. When Steven thought there would never be enough contact, when he was right on the edge of begging for more, Ryan said, "You can touch me now, while I make you come."

Steven whimpered. He let his hands crawl over Ryan's chest and hips, feeling the hard plane of his stomach muscles, the steel of his thighs. Ryan spit into his hand and wrapped it around both their cocks, jerking hard and tight for the first time all night. Steven kissed him hard then, trying to take control as his orgasm coiled at the base of his spine. He reached between them and squeezed his hand over Ryan's when Steven started to spurt, the rush of his orgasm flashing blue behind his eyes.

"Fuck fuck fuck," Ryan said. He felt Ryan pulse under their combined grip. Ryan's warm come splatted Steven's chest and stomach. Steven kissed him again, deliriously happy that he'd made Ryan come.

They lay there, kissing gently until Ryan cleaned them off with the corner of the sheet and pulled Steven's head against his chest. Before long Steven was asleep, dreaming of ocean waves that thrummed in the rhythm of Ryan's heartbeat.

◊

Steven's head hurt. Someone pulled at his shoulder.

"Hey, you."

Steven opened his eyes. He rolled over to find Ryan blinking sleepily at him.

"What time is it?" Steven asked softly.

"Like five o'clock, too early to get up."

"Okay."

"Okay?" Ryan asked.

"Okay, let's not get up." Steven closed his eyes and nuzzled against the warmth of Ryan's neck. After a minute Ryan stroked his hair. Steven twined his arms around Ryan's waist. He could feel tension in Ryan's body.

"You alright?"

"Yeah, you're the first person I've been with since Hector and I broke up. It feels weird. Sorry."

"No, it's cool. That stuff can be weird. What can I do? Do you want to go?"

"No. Go back to sleep. I'm fine."

Steven nuzzled against him, holding him tighter. As he started to doze off again, Ryan said, "It wasn't because I was drunk, you know."

"Yeah?" Steven struggled back to wakefulness, ready to listen to what Ryan needed to say.

"You know how it was at the party. I couldn't stop thinking about sex after that, the way John looked at you, the things he said to you. And I've always thought you were hot."

"What else at the party?"

"Your Finney assuming we were running off to fuck. And I assumed Shane and Bash went to fuck in the bathroom when we left."

"Why do you think that?"

"Did you see how Bash looked at Shane?"

Steven shook his head. He hadn't noticed. He hadn't noticed anything but John and his own anxiety.

"Shane said they'd been together for like nine years. God, I hope I find someone who looks at me with that much passion after nine years. Nine years. Can you even imagine?" Ryan said.

"They didn't look that old."

"I think they were younger than us when they got together. Man, I want what they have."

"Ryan, I'm sorry," Steven said, uncomfortable that Ryan wanted more from him than he could give.

"Not with you, asshole," Ryan laughed. "Not that I don't want you. It could be anyone, someday. Later. I don't know. Not right now. I'm still too fucked up over Hector. This was just a hook-up. That's okay, isn't it? I got the impression you're into that John guy."

"This was definitely just friendly," Steven said. The silence stretched after his words, but it was calm, the tension gone. Steven started to nod off again when Ryan spoke.

"Hey."

"Yeah?"

"I have something friendly to show you." Ryan's fingers circled Steven's wrist. Steven's dick twitched as Ryan pulled

Steven's hand to his own erection. "I'd like to show you some more friendly appreciation for last night."

Steven laughed and kissed Ryan as he started to stroke him. "I can definitely do friendly," he said and ducked down to demonstrate with his mouth, hoping Ryan wouldn't regret this in the full morning light. He was hard again already, and Ryan was so hot and already in his bed. He licked and sucked wetly over Ryan's dick, trying to repeat whatever made Ryan moan and swear above him.

Ryan's hips rocked up and he gripped Steven's hair, pushing him down. Steven let Ryan set the speed as he rutted his own erection into the bed.

"Christ, fuck, your mouth is amazing."

Steven grabbed Ryan's hips and rolled them carefully onto their sides, Ryan's dick still in his mouth. He pulled back enough to spit in his hand and then he worked his dick hard while he sucked Ryan. Ryan thrust and bucked into Steven's mouth.

"Not gonna last," Ryan grunted. "God, your mouth is so fucking sweet."

"Come," Steven said, then sucked Ryan back into his mouth. He wrapped one hand around Ryan's cock, letting his mouth wet it as he went down. He kept the head in his mouth and jerked Ryan as hard as he stroked himself.

Their rhythm kept breaking, stuttering, and then coming back together again. Steven did his best to open his throat and let Ryan thrust forward, though lying on their sides made it awkward.

Unexpectedly Ryan shoved Steven back and grabbed his own cock. Steven moved, trying to help. Ryan cried out, "Coming, fuck, I'm coming already," and Steven felt the first hot spurt hit his collarbone. Some of Ryan's come shot up and landed on the corner of Steven's mouth, the rest landed on his chest. They both lay panting for a moment, then Ryan scooted down in time to see Steven lick the come off the corner of his mouth.

"Oh god, you're fucking dirty," Ryan said, his voice filled with awe. He reached between them and wrapped his hand around Steven's straining erection, wiggling until they faced each other. Ryan kissed him and then pulled back.

"You are a dirty boy, aren't you?" he whispered. He scooped up come from Steven's collarbone with his fingertips and pushed his fingers into Steven's mouth. Steven licked and sucked them like he had Ryan's cock moments before. Ryan gripped him and stroked Steven's cock harder before closing his mouth over Steven's. The kiss was fierce, intense. Steven bucked in Ryan's grip, pushing right to the edge as Ryan slipped his fingers into the crack of Steven's ass, pressing lightly at Steven's entrance. "You going to come for me, dirty boy? Yeah, come for me, make a mess."

Steven's pulse felt tidal, rolling through him, carrying him to the edge. He closed his eyes and imagined John slipping a slick finger inside him, gripping his dick, and commanding him to come like a good boy. In his imagination he could hear John's gruff accent asking if he liked it rough like this, and Steven tumbled over the edge, coming hard in Ryan's hand. He shuddered through the aftershocks, slowly aware of Ryan caressing his hip and pulling him closer.

"Good morning," Ryan whispered into his hair as Steven's breathing slowed and he curled in closer to Ryan.

Steven laughed. "Good morning. Holy fuck, waking up should always be that good."

"Yeah, totally. Shower?"

"Yes, please, I'm all sticky. Together?"

"Yeah. I don't think I have another round in me, but I am curious to see where else you have freckles."

"Everywhere," Steven laughed again. "Come on. I think I even have clean towels."

"Oooh, fancy. Are you this good to all your tricks?"

Steven swatted at Ryan as they got up, but Ryan pulled away, stumbling and laughing toward the bathroom. Steven caught him in the doorway.

"Hey." He pulled Ryan against him. "Thanks."

"Yeah, man, I didn't expect that exactly."

"Sex?"

"That, but also I've heard you fuck Adrian—I'm sorry, but you guys were loud—and I didn't expect you to be so receptive, taking orders like that. Until I kissed you, I thought you always topped, but there's more to you, isn't there?"

Steven blushed. "I, um, thanks for making me feel safe."

"I hope you find someone who does that right for you someday. Now let's shower. You're covered in come, you little slut."

"Hey!" Steven shoved Ryan into the bathroom, following him in.

Ryan stroked gentle touches over Steven's back as Steven leaned down to adjust the water temperature.

"Freckles everywhere for real," he whispered.

26.
Season's Greetings

STEVEN WOKE UP HARD AND disturbed from dreams of Ryan telling John how to suck Steven off while Adrian watched and laughed and claimed none of them really knew what Steven wanted like he did.

He spent all morning trying to shake the haze of the dream, the sense of foreboding that came with it. Going to work was a relief, for the distraction, if nothing else.

"Merry Christmas, kid," Marcus called when Steven entered the shop.

"You too, Marcus." Steven felt awkward, like Marcus would know he'd had sex, though he felt absolutely no guilt. "Busy today?"

"Steady. I always wish it was more than that this time of year. Then I feel swamped if it happens. So steady is good."

"Anything I need to know?" Steven said, perching on the stool behind the cash register.

"Did you hear that Jess got arrested?"

"Shit, I meant anything at the store. But wow, that's unexpected. What happened?"

"Her safe sex campaign was deemed offensive. She got busted for handing out inappropriate material to minors."

"Oh god, is she okay? That sounds like it could be bad."

"They didn't charge her with a felony. I think she'll just have to pay a fine."

"That's a relief."

"You should call her though. We need to keep her spirits up until she goes to court."

"I will, for sure. So, now I'm afraid to ask, but anything I should know about the shop today?"

Marcus looked tired. "Some sweaters in the back need to be put out. Sorry I didn't get to it. I'll be back in a bit to help, if you get swamped. I need to go to the bank and run a couple errands."

"Okay, cool. I'll be here."

The bell on the door jingled and two very athletic men came in. Marcus raised an appreciative eyebrow and whispered, "Good luck, I'll be back." He headed out the door.

Steven helped the men, who wanted to see everything in the store up close, but had no real idea what they were looking for. It set the tone for the day.

Lots of people in and out, ready to buy but not sure what to choose. Christmas shopping was much different from their usual clientele of gay men shopping for themselves. This week had been filled with women shopping for their partners and family. Steven met lots of neighborhood people that he'd never seen in the store before.

It was chaotic, but even at Christmas time Marcus's store was better than Fred Meyer or waiting tables. By the time Marcus came back, Steven was glad of the help. The sweaters still weren't out, and Steven was starving.

Marcus offered him a twenty from the till. "Run next door and get us some take out? My treat for making you work through lunch."

To say Steven got teriyaki at Hana all the time was an understatement. It was inexpensive, right next door to work, and delicious.

Steven ordered and sat near the front window waiting, glad of the short break from the store. At three o'clock, the restaurant wasn't so busy that he felt guilty taking a seat while he people-watched through the window.

All of Capitol Hill seemed to be shopping on Broadway. Families, couples gay and straight, teenagers, and old people streamed past the window, all looking hurried. When Adrian and Flip passed, Flip in his ugly red leather trench coat and Adrian in a silver puffy down jacket, Steven fought the urge to duck, but neither of them looked his way. Still, the tension stuck with him. He jumped when Adrian said his name behind him a minute later.

"Hey," Steven replied, unsure whether to be ready for some kind of confrontation.

"I thought that was you."

Steven nodded. "Just getting some food and heading back to work."

Adrian watched him for a second, then finally spoke when the waitress came with bagged boxes of food for Steven. "I just wanted to say Merry Christmas."

"Merry Christmas, Ade."

"I should—"

"I wa—"

They both spoke at the same time and stopped. Steven indicated Adrian should talk.

"I should go. Flip's waiting outside and it's cold." Adrian looked toward the door, then back to Steven. "What were you going to say?"

"Nothing."

Adrian looked like he didn't believe that, but nodded. "I'll see you around."

"Yeah." Tears pricked at Steven's eyes as he watched Adrian walk away. He sank back into his seat, not ready to face either Marcus or customers.

For months Steven and Adrian hadn't spoken, maintaining a silent détente. No exchange meant no friendship, but it meant no anger either. Right now Steven felt all of it, missing his friend, angry at being so mistreated, pain for the whole world not being what he expected.

What had he been about to say to Adrian? *I've been so lonely for you.* Or: *I don't miss you at all, you asshole?* Both were equally true.

Steven gathered his take-out and his emotions and carried both back to the shop. As ever, it seemed his face showed his feelings, clear as glass.

"You okay?" Marcus asked, Steven set the food on the counter, away from the cash register.

Steven shrugged. "I saw Adrian."

"Oh, honey." Marcus came around the counter and hugged Steven tight. Steven wanted to sag into him and cry at the unfairness of the world. But he could see customers stealing sidelong glances, wondering about the drama. Steven pulled back.

"I'm fine," he said, straightening his sweater.

"What did he say?" Marcus asked, as a woman came to the counter with three pairs of pants.

"Sorry," she said, acknowledging the interruption.

"No problem," Steven said.

"Can I exchange these later if they don't fit my husband?"

"Of course!" Marcus said, chatting amiably with the woman as he rang her up. Steven stayed busy opening containers of teriyaki and rice on the back counter, glad to be saved from an awkward conversation. He didn't want to talk about his feelings. He'd felt too raw since he woke from tangled dreams, and didn't need anyone poking around in that wound.

◊

Steven stayed in the alcove that protected them from the wind while Marcus locked the shop door.

"You okay?" Marcus, asked, putting the keys in his pocket.

They didn't step out into the sidewalk. The wind was fierce, bringing real winter to Seattle just in time for Christmas. The doorway offered some small shelter.

"Yeah. I didn't mean to be such a drama queen earlier."

"I know you're with your family tomorrow, but you call me if you need to talk, or if you need anything at all. Promise?"

"Of course," Steven said. Marcus enveloped him in a hug.

The tension of the day, of the last few months, seemed to drain out of Steven's body. He buried his face in Marcus's shoulder. Affection from someone who didn't expect anything from him made Steven feel like the dam of tears might burst. Too soon, Marcus pulled back, his hands on Steven's shoulders.

"You deserve so much more than a boy like that. You deserve someone who's going to treat you right."

Steven nodded, fighting tears. A voice behind him said, "Steven?"

It was John, his grey wool coat buttoned up and his hair covered by a black knit cap. "I thought that was you. Everything okay?" John looked from Steven's face to Marcus.

"John, hi!" Steven put out his hand. John's was covered in warm leather, his gloves smoother than the calluses of his hands. "Yeah, fine. We were just closing up."

John smiled at Marcus, who put out his hand. "Marcus Tucker."

"John Pieters." John shook Marcus's hand before turning back to Steven. "Sorry, if I interrupted something. I wanted to say Merry Christmas."

"Merry Christmas," Steven echoed the greeting. "Are you out shopping?"

"No, just heading home from work."

Steven nodded.

The noise of Broadway traffic behind them couldn't fill the silence between them, though it couldn't have lasted more than two seconds. Steven, drowning in the emotional waterfall of his day, wasn't sure what to say.

"I shouldn't keep you out in the cold. You don't even have a hat." John ruffled Steven's hair, then quickly pulled his hand back to his pocket, as if he'd made a mistake. Steven shivered as John spoke, hoping he'd attribute it to the cold and not the unexpected touch. John's voice was scratchy, thick. "I'll see you around. Take care." He nodded to Marcus. "Nice to meet you."

"You too." Marcus said.

Wanting to find some way to hold John there, if just for another second, Steven said, "Merry Christmas again. I hope you have a Happy New Year if I don't see you."

John turned back, as if he could see right inside Steven, to his fears, his longing. Then John's smile was so bright, Steven was glad of the too brief encounter. "You too, Steven. I hope it brings good things for you." He set off up Broadway. Even given John's heavy coat, Steven could see the strength of his frame, the grace of how he moved. Marcus's arm settled around Steven's shoulders.

"Who the fuck was that?"

"Ah, that was the reason Adrian and I fought." Marcus's eyebrows shot up, so Steven went on. "I've talked about him enough, and now you see what I was so excited about?"

"Oh, *that* John. Why aren't you running after him and making *that* happen for you? Shit, I haven't looked at another man since Mitchell died, and I'd give up my best friend for *that*."

"It's been kind of weird. Not just the mess with Adrian, but I went to John's party a couple days ago and uh—"

"'And uh' what? What happened?"

Steven's face flushed hot, despite the bitter wind. "I slept with someone else after the party."

"So?"

"So I don't know."

"Do you like him? John, not whoever you fucked."

"Yes."

"Well, in my limited forty-five seconds acquaintance with him I think he likes you too. Just based on how he looked at you. How he lingered when there was nothing to say." Marcus shook his head. "I've never understood men. Always out boldly asking for sex, fucking whoever. But as soon as we like a guy, we clam up. Let me guess, you've been wistfully hoping that he'll ask you out and he hasn't?" When Steven nodded, Marcus said, "You need to make that happen. You won't be satisfied until you do."

"I think I'm not his type."

"I think you're an idiot. But it's too cold to stand here arguing. Do you need a ride home?"

"No. It's about as far to walk to your car as to my house."

"Okay. Be good, kid. Merry Christmas." Marcus pulled him into another quick hug. "I hope Santa brings you enough sense to go after what you want instead of waiting for it to come to you."

◊

Steven waited for his father to pick him up and take him back across Lake Washington, to the suburbs to help cook Christmas Eve dinner for their extended family. Meanwhile, he searched for festive clothes, but nothing so over-the-top as to make his mom worry about what his aunts might think. Not that it mattered. Everyone knew he was gay. Unless he showed up in assless chaps, which he didn't own, he couldn't actually offend anyone in his family at this point.

Most every morning since he'd gotten a radio in his bedroom at age twelve, Steven danced while he got dressed. Some mornings it was slight hip twitches as he rushed not to be late. Music always carried him through the best days and buoyed him up on the worst. This was his time to dream, to get ready to face the world with a smile. Today it was The Waitresses' "Christmas Wrapping," which felt strangely prescient: *that guy I been chasing all year.*

But as Marcus had pointed out last night, Steven hadn't been chasing John at all; he'd merely been waiting. It wouldn't pay to dwell on that today though. He prepared for the questions his mom would ask, now that Adrian wasn't coming with him on anymore visits.

Steven danced around his room, shaking off thoughts of Adrian and John, letting the music clear his head. By the time he was dressed in his green sweater, with a t-shirt this time, and some dark burgundy jeans, he felt festive and ready to deal with whatever the day brought.

The drive with his dad to the suburban domesticity of the Issaquah Plateau was relaxed and easy. Home was where they always had to take you in. Steven's earlier self-pity wriggled in, making him glad of his family, of people who had to love him no matter what, even if they didn't always agree with him.

Once he and his mom had prepped most of the main courses, the only thing left was the cheesecake, which Steven made every year from his grandmother's recipe. While Steven crushed up graham crackers in a bowl with some melted butter, his mother did her worst casual questioning.

"So, are you seeing anyone new?" She smiled like a sitcom mom. Steven stifled the urge to laugh. She hadn't yet come to terms with his sexuality, but she tried, and the cheerfulness in her tone as she asked was an indication of how hard she was trying.

"No, Mom, I'm not seeing anyone."

She looked at the pastry knife in his hand. "You could have used the food processor."

Steven shrugged. He didn't like to dirty more things than necessary. The food processor seemed like more work to clean than the effort it saved by using it. He wondered if he was off the hook that easily on the dating questions.

"What about your friend I met when you moved? Lisa? She seems nice." Nope, not off the hook. His mom leaned on the counter next to where he worked.

Steven set down the pastry knife. He poured more melted butter into the bowl full of crumbs and stirred it around as much as he could with a fork. He took a deep breath to tamp down his exasperation. "Ma, do you remember the gay thing?"

"You two seem to get along so well."

"Hand me the pan, please? She's a lesbian. There are too many hurdles to overcome with that one." Steven dumped the crust mixture into the bottom of the pan, focusing on it and not his mom. Sometimes it was like she came from another planet, or like she didn't want to deal with reality. He was happy that she had no problem with interracial relationships, even if she couldn't quite love the same-sex ones yet.

"Anyway," she said, moving to the sink to wash her hands, "I'm glad you left Adrian. He was never nice enough to you."

"He wasn't my boyfriend." Steven reached for the cream cheese. His mom had remembered to take it out early this morning so it was soft. She was amazing in the kitchen. Amazing in general. He wished his being gay didn't upset her still. She must have known all his life, unless she deliberately chose not to see it.

"I don't know what you kids call it, Steven, but you were with him a long time, so 'partners' or whatever the cool lingo is. This is hard enough without you trying to make it harder."

"I'm not trying to make it hard for anyone, Ma."

"Leave him alone, Maggie. He's fine the way he is." Steven's dad patted him on the shoulder as he came in. He headed for the fridge.

"Thanks, Dad."

"Of course, I won't complain if you choose to stay single forever." He could hear his dad's grin in his tone, but Steven looked annoyed anyway. It was his role here, and he played it as best he could, even though he was supposed to be an adult now.

"Dad!"

"I'm kidding, I want you to meet a nice boy, or do whatever you want to. No one cares anymore. Didn't we finish fighting this battle in the seventies or something? Just as long as you're being safe."

"Oh god, Dad, no. I mean, yes, I'm always safe, but no we aren't ever going to discuss sex."

"Language, Steven." His mom sounded strained.

"See? Mom won't even let me say 'sex.'"

"No, I was objecting to your use of the Lord's name."

Since his father seemed to become less and less religious while Mom ramped up her devotion, Steven had one more thing to tiptoe around. Best to change the subject. "Is anyone else coming? I'm not stuck with the two of you all night, am I?"

His dad said, "You can move back in, if you miss us that much. I'm sure your mom won't mind giving up her quilting room. Then she wouldn't have to worry about you dating men either. Who wants to date an adult who still lives at home? She could keep you a little boy forever."

Steven laughed. His mom tried to swat his dad with a potholder.

"Your aunt Lillian should be here soon with your cousins. Kelly got engaged and I think her young man is coming. And the Iversons and the Forssblads. Let's see, I don't think your uncle Frank is bringing his family for dinner, but they might come later. His girls are all married now, you know?"

"I do know. I hope you aren't telling me that like you think it's going to make me get married, because I think we need to change some laws before that will happen," Steven said.

"The problem with you kids is you don't protest like we did in the sixties. You're never going to get anything changed."

His dad mixed himself a drink. Steven wanted one too, but he wasn't sure if he should ask. Odd how being at home made you feel young. Perhaps feeling Steven's eyes on him, his dad grabbed a second glass and gestured to Steven who nodded, relieved, as his dad poured a second whiskey and ginger ale.

"Yeah, Dad, that's definitely what our problem is. Not the economy or our representational government that doesn't represent any of the people."

Steven loved good-natured arguments with his parents. It felt especially comforting this year, solidity in an unchanging role. His mother might never accept that she'd never get a daughter-in-law out of him, but she'd come a long way in eight years. His dad never seemed to take anything too seriously, which was comforting in its own way.

Steven got the cheesecake together and into the oven while arguing politics with his father, who blamed everything on Steven's generation's lack of hippie ethics, which was pretty funny, since his father had never been a hippie in the sixties anyway. It was fun, easy to be with them today. It was like the dessert he was making: follow the same steps every year and hope for the best.

His mother stopped him as he headed to the garage to help his dad get the extra tables.

"I just want you to be happy, you know?" she said, her hand resting on his arm, her eyes sad. As an adult, he'd never connected with his mother in the way he had with his father. They didn't see the world the same way. Still, he loved her and wanted her to be happy, which roused vague guilt that he'd never give her grandchildren. She'd have made an amazing grandmother, even if her motherly questions made him uncomfortable.

Steven kissed her forehead. "I know, Mama. I am. I will be. Please don't worry about me."

It was a kindness to his mother, but it stuck with Steven through the New Year. Would he be happy? He didn't know if he was ready to take Marcus's advice, but he was going to have to try in the coming year—to start looking for happiness, instead of waiting for it to come to him.

27.
Free Throw

"THANKS FOR BRINGING ME TONIGHT, Leese. This is rad." Steven balanced his beer between his knees, wishing the narrow stadium seats at Key Arena allowed a place to put his elbows or his cup.

"I've been asking. But you keep saying you have work or something. I thought maybe you didn't like basketball anymore and didn't want to tell me." Lisa sucked the top centimeter off her beer and then banged elbows with Steven trying to get settled.

"Who doesn't like hot guys running around in little shorts and bumping into each other? Although these new longer shorts are kind of a disappointment."

"I'm definitely not here for the guys." She rolled her eyes.

"Well, I'm not just here for the guys. It is the only sport worth watching."

"How un-American of you. What about baseball?" Lisa asked, looking faux-scandalized.

"Too slow, although it does seem to have a decent amount of ass slapping, so I can respect why people watch it." Steven sipped his beer.

"People do not watch baseball for the ass slapping."

Steven raised one eyebrow. "Don't they?"

Lisa laughed. "Maybe they do. I'm more of a softball girl anyway."

"Yes, you are. All cutely butch with your short hair."

Lisa rolled her eyes.

"C'mon," Steven went on. "Isn't it at least getting you all the ladies?"

"I do all right."

The horn sounded, ending half time and saving him from following up. They watched as the Sonics ran hard against the Lakers. They were up by nine points, but they'd lost a large lead in the second quarter.

"What about you?" Lisa asked.

Steven wasn't going to get away with avoiding the subject this time, but he stalled anyway, "What about me?" He wasn't bothered by Lisa asking, but there was nothing to tell. His life had become nothing but work and school. Late at night when he was desperate and took himself in hand for relief, he always pictured John's mouth, imagined John's hands on him. But he might as well be thinking about Gary Payton or one of the other players on the floor in front of him for all imagining John did.

"What about you? I literally haven't seen you in nearly a month. So? Anyone special? How's Ryan?" Lisa pushed.

"Ryan is fine. He's not special though. Well he is but he's not my special...thing." Ryan would be even more amused than Steven at the idea that they'd get together. It had been fun after the party. Not just relief, but closeness that both of them needed, but he couldn't see it happening again. Ryan wasn't ready for another serious relationship yet, and casual wouldn't work for Steven. They got along great, but Steven didn't think they'd be compatible.

"You seemed to be getting along at Christmas." Her voice was sing-songing, like she was about break into a nursery rhyme.

"I'm not going to date Ryan, Lisa."

"Why not?"

"I don't think that's in the cards for us." Steven drank his beer and turned back to court in time to see Gary Payton make a good two-handed dunk, looking like he hovered on air as he jumped. Steven leapt up and cheered with the crowd.

"What is in the cards for you, sweetie?" Lisa asked as they settled back into their seats. "It doesn't seem like you're even trying anymore. You and Ryan seemed like you were enjoying hanging out."

"Trust me. Ryan and I aren't going to become a thing, okay? We hooked up. At Christmas. After the party. We've talked about it, we're not getting together." If the conversation was going to keep going this way, Steven would definitely need more beer.

"Because you're waiting for John." Lisa wasn't asking. That wasn't fair, because he couldn't say for certain that she was wrong.

"I'm not waiting for John," Steven asserted anyway. He saw movement at the corner of his eye. The guy on the other side of Lisa settled back, like he'd been leaning forward and listening. Just what Steven wanted, every Sonics fan in Seattle knowing his business. Not that it mattered, since he didn't have any real business.

Lisa sat forward, elbows on knees, her eyes on the court. But her attention wasn't there. "Okay, well, as long as I've known you, you've been telling me about your crushes, your boyfriends, and your hook-ups and I haven't heard anything from you lately, so what's going on?" she asked.

Steven waited until she met his eyes. "Right now? You want to talk about this right now?" He waved his beer toward the court where Nate McMillan was making a free throw.

Lisa held his gaze, her mouth set in that serious line that made Steven fear for her children, if she ever had any. She would never have to punish them, just look at them like this, and they'd always spill their bad deeds.

Steven resigned to giving her what she wanted. He said, "Okay," and Lisa nodded, waiting. "Well, what? I'm not dating right now. It's too hard. There are only six weeks of classes left. I'll finish in March. Then I have to find a job, even if I have to wait until June to graduate, I need the head start to find work when everyone else isn't looking. I should probably make a serious decision about graduate school sooner rather than waiting. I need to put in a lot of hours at Button Up Boys to pay for school and my apartment. So when am I supposed to be dating? It's no big deal."

Lisa finished her beer and raised her arm to flag the vendor carrying his wide tray of beers up the steep steps. While they waited for him to get to them, Lisa said, "You are so full of shit, I can't believe your eyes aren't brown." Then she turned back to the approaching vendor, digging in her jeans pocket. She held up two fingers and handed a ten to the guy, waving off her two dollars change. She handed one of the beers to Steven.

"Why am I full of shit? Because I'm getting my life together? You're the one that told me I needed to work harder."

"Because if you're not outright lying to me, then you're lying to yourself. Is this because of what happened with Adrian?" Lisa wasn't trying to be casual about it anymore.

"No, nothing to do with him." Steven finished his first beer and settled the second one into the empty cup, sipping off the top to keep it from sloshing out.

"Liar."

"This is a basketball game, Leese, not a therapy session."

Lisa said, "It can be both."

"There isn't anything to tell right now," Steven repeated.

"Why not?"

Steven leaned back in his seat and drank some of his beer, watching the figures below toss the ball back and forth on the court. Lisa settled back in next to him, but Steven knew, even while they cheered and yelled and watched the game, she wasn't going to let it go. He only had two options, he could keep arguing with her, which meant keeping his own counsel as he had been for the last month. Or he could tell her what he'd been thinking through all the lonely nights since Christmas, when his small apartment felt more like a monk's cell.

When the quarter ended, he picked the second choice and said, "Because I'm holding out for John."

"Ha! I knew it." Lisa reached up and ruffled his hair, letting her hand rest protectively on the back of his neck.

"I'm not waiting for him. That isn't what I said." Steven sipped his beer, unsure if he'd made the right choice. Continuing to protect his feelings might have better than exposing them.

"So, what? You're going to ask him out?" Lisa stroked his neck and pulled her hand back.

"No. Well, maybe. I don't know. Look, I have a plan. I need to get through school, and then we'll see," Steven said.

"That's your plan, get through school, and then maybe ask him out? That's a shitty plan." Lisa rolled her eyes.

"It's a pretty shitty plan," said the guy on the other side of Lisa.

Lisa nodded and waved her beer toward the guy.

Steven shot them both an incredulous look. "Thanks, I don't need strangers weighing in on my life. I think you can see I have enough shit from my friends." The guy shrugged and turned his attention back to the court. Steven lowered his voice, "It's not a shitty plan. I made a resolution that I wouldn't wait for things to happen to me. And I'm not waiting for John. I'm trying to get my life to a place where I'm ready for him. Or someone like him."

"What does that mean?"

"It means it doesn't have to be John and it doesn't have to be now. It just has to be someone as good and kind as I think John is, who will treat me well. Someone I can build a life with. And I can't ask anyone to commit to me unless I can give a hundred percent back." Steven sat back, tired of the subject. "So I'm finishing school. And then I'm getting on with my life," he concluded, looking at Lisa again.

"Still kind of a shitty plan," she said. Steven thought he saw the guy next to her nod slightly in agreement.

"Well, it's my shitty plan, so I'll carry on with it," Steven said, just as the buzzer honked the start of the last quarter. "Besides, you're the one who told me to take a step back and get my shit together last September, so I'm doing that."

The Sonics were up by twenty-one points now. The audience vibrated happily around them, cheering and talking.

"I think you have a chance with John, you know. He asks about you." Lisa spoke softly her eyes still on the game.

Steven's heartbeat sped up. "He asks what about me?"

"Just how you are, if I've seen you recently." Lisa looked at Steven. "He's casual about it, but he never asks me about our other friends and acquaintances."

"Maybe he sees your other friends more than you do?"

"Maybe. But I think he'd say yes if you asked him out."

Steven thought about it. He sipped his beer turning back to the game. "I have a plan."

"Okay, but don't be too slow with your plan. I want good things for you. Someone good. And John is one of the good ones. Don't miss your chance."

28.
Don't Duck

"THAT WAS AMAZING," DAVY SAID, patting his belly. "Thanks for coming with me, dude. I couldn't face lunch in the student union after that test. Had to get off campus because nothing but falafel would do."

"Glad to do it. I needed it too—the break, not necessarily the falafel. Although it was awesome."

"Cool if we stop by the bookstore on the way back?" Davy asked. Their friendship had grown fast in the past month. Explaining the previous class's lessons to Davy gave Steven a better understanding of them, and after a while Davy's weird exclamations and hyper-effusiveness became kind of endearing. Lately they'd started spending class breaks together, and when they weren't studying, they were talking about books, movies, and the best places to skateboard in Seattle. Steven didn't have much use for that knowledge, but it was like being let in on a secret underground culture.

"Yeah, I don't have anything else but lab time this afternoon," Steven answered, gathering his book-heavy backpack from the chair next to him.

"Me too, but, man, I need my lab time this week. Bookstore will only take a second. I need to look for this book my uncle told me about."

"Cool."

As they walked up from Forty-third Northeast to Forty-fourth on University Ave, Davy regaled Steven with stories of his most recent party. Steven was assured that it was the bomb and the next one would be better, though Davy had stopped inviting Steven after his third polite pass.

Steven followed Davy as he deftly wove through the shelves, skateboard in one hand, backpack on one shoulder, but somehow he managed to not hit any other patrons. He found his book quickly and they headed to the cash register by the main door, hoping for no line at this time of day. Instead they found Chris.

"Oh hey, Chris," Steven greeted him, feeling awkward. They hadn't run into each other since his rejection of Chris's last invitation. He smiled apologetically. "Nice to see you. It's been a long time."

Chris smiled, open and friendly. "It's cool, man. I'm sure you've been busy elsewhere." He raised his eyebrows at Davy and looked back to Steven.

Steven laughed, getting it right away. "Yeah, some shit went down in my life. I got distracted, but no—" he nodded toward his friend, "not by Davy, I don't even think he knows I'm gay."

Davy looked comically offended. "Hey, I pay attention. I know what's going on. How do you know *I'm* not gay?"

"You're not gay," Chris and Steven said in unison, both laughing.

"How do you know?" Davy challenged.

"Sometimes you can tell when someone's straight," Chris smirked and Steven agreed.

"Sorry, Davy, he's right."

Davy pushed his lip out in an exaggerated pout. Steven couldn't help but smile again. Davy was always surprising and ridiculous. Steven imagined if he'd had a little brother, he'd be as charmingly obnoxious as Davy.

"But you're cute," Steven said, knowing Davy could take teasing as well as he dished it out. "We both think so." Steven looked to Chris for support.

Chris nodded. "Way cute."

"Okay," Davy grinned wide, showing all his teeth. "That's good enough for me. I'll leave you to your gay flirting. I'll be outside, Steven," he said over his shoulder, waggling his eyebrows suggestively like he was one of the Marx Brothers.

"That kid is weird," Chris said as Davy walked away.

"So weird," Steven agreed. "I like him. He's funny."

"So," Chris started, leaning forward on the counter like he had that first day last year. "I haven't seen you around. Anywhere."

"Yeah, sorry. Life got really crazy, and then the holidays and, well, you know." Steven set his backpack on the counter between them.

"I do know." Chris cocked his head and studied Steven for a second. It was intense enough that Steven wanted to step back or look away. Finally Chris said, "So, is the third time a charm or should I stop asking?"

Steven shuffled. The Chrises of the world weren't part of his plan. "Um, it's just—"

"It's cool I can take a hint." Chris didn't drop his gaze but his expression was slightly sorrowful, like he expected rejection.

The expression made Steven want to explain, to tell about the last four months of his life, how everything was different and he wasn't completely sure how he wanted to navigate relationships and hook-ups any more. But it was too much to say, so instead he went with, "No, no hints. It really has been crazy and I haven't been out there. Like that."

"I get it," Chris said. "Whatever happened, bad break up or new relationship, makes you not want to commit." That wasn't exactly it, but Steven nodded. Chris went on, "Okay, how about this: Steven, do you want to get a drink some time? I won't hit on you unless you tell me you're interested. Purely friendly."

"That sounds great, Chris."

"Well then—" Chris pulled a small card advertising a children's book from behind the register, flipped it over and wrote on it, "—here's my number. When you're less busy or ready to get 'out there,' call me."

"I will. I promise." Steven slid the card into his pocket.

Chris leaned in again and said in conspiratorial whisper, "Your weird friend is peeking in the door at us."

Steven laughed, grateful of the escape opportunity. "I should go." Steven smiled his goodbye and walked through to the door, feeling Chris's eyes on his back.

"You got his number? Good work!" Davy slapped Steven on the back as he stepped outside.

"Maybe. It's complicated."

Davy shook his head. "Dude, only as complicated as you make it. Maybe we could make a deal," he said as they headed across the parking lot back toward the main campus and the waiting computer lab.

"What kind of deal?" Steven side-eyed Davy. He'd already learned that most of Davy's ideas were convoluted and dramatic in a way that probably wouldn't benefit anyone.

Davy looked confident and paused for dramatic effect, then declared, "You keep helping me with math, and I'll help you with the dudes. I know about dudes."

"What do you know about dudes?"

"I have two dads," he said matter-of-factly. "I've been around their friends all my life. I have seen depths of gay drama that no man should have to face." He stared into the distance, eyes and mouth wide in mock terror. "The things I've seen," he whispered softly.

Steven didn't laugh. "How come you never said anything?"

Davy snapped back to his usual goofy expression. "Do you go around telling everyone, right off the bat, that your parents are straight?"

"That's fair," Steven said. "I appreciate the offer of secret dude knowledge, but I don't need help in that department."

"Then how come you're still single? I've never heard you talk about anyone. I thought maybe you were trying to keep it secret that you're gay, but it's not that. And guys are giving you their numbers, so that isn't your problem. He was hot, too. I can say it, I'm not ashamed to say when a guy is hot."

"You don't seem ashamed of much, Davy."

"That's true. Maybe I could teach you to be as chill as me."

"Maybe," Steven said, trying not to laugh at the idea that Davy was chill.

"Might be tough, though, if your parents are super uptight. Hard to shake that off." Davy's face got serious. "For real though," he said, "if you ever want to talk, I'm good with advice and shit."

As they crossed campus, under the grim late winter trees, Steven weighed confiding in Davy. There was a safety in talking to someone who didn't know any of your friends. And apparently Davy knew more gay men than Steven did.

"I could use some advice," Steven said, deciding.

"Yes!" Davy put his arm around Steven's shoulders and pulled him into an awkward side hug as they walked. "Tell me your troubles, man."

"I met this guy last year. He's handsome, older than me—"

"Oh, a twist, I like it. Tell me more."

◊

As they crossed campus, Steven detailed for Davy how he'd met John, and the times they'd run into each other over the year. Steven tried to explain his attraction.

"And it isn't just because he's good looking and smart. There's something when I talk to John, like he's really listening. I feel like I could talk about the most esoteric math or the most complicated coding, and even if he didn't get it, he'd try to understand, because he'd see what it meant to me. I've never had any one listen like that before. When he listens, I feel special, like he really sees me. And when he asks me questions, it's like being rewarded for knowing things. Or just, well, more than that. I don't know."

Davy's forehead furrowed. "Dude, didn't you have nerd friends in high school?"

"Not really. I think they were afraid the gay would rub off on them. I mostly hung out with the girls from drama club and my boyfriend."

"You had a boyfriend in high school? That is so cool."

"Yeah, it isn't helping me now." Steven shrugged.

"No, I guess not. But I don't see the problem. You like this guy. He wouldn't be paying you the kind of attention you're talking about if he didn't like you." Davy looked up thoughtfully, troubling out the problem. "He's gay, right?"

"Yeah."

"So he probably likes you, so what's stopping you?"

"I'm not sure I've left the best impression." Steven still felt a twinge of embarrassment when he remembered standing on the corner with Adrian and John. John's friendly conversation at Christmas hadn't erased that.

"What happened?" Davy asked.

Steven paused and considered how much to tell. There wasn't anyone in the computer lab but them. Still, he spoke softly as he did his best to explain Adrian, the clubbing, and that terrible morning.

"So," he concluded, "here's this successful, totally together guy John, versus me looking sketchy with horrible friends."

"Okay. One, did this happen before or after he invited you to his Christmas party?"

"Before."

"And two, holy shit, dude, I didn't think you were that kind of guy, all dancing high on poppers in tight little shorts." Davy grinned and Steven started to point out that he wasn't ever into either of those things, but Davy kept talking. "I can see it though, you'd look good all sparkled up for the clubs." Davy shook his elbows like he was dancing. "But wow, yeah, I thought you were all studious and nerdy like most of the guys in Comp Sci."

"Um, thanks." Steven wasn't sure from Davy's tone if that was an insult or a compliment.

"So, I think you're underestimating how nerdy you are. If this guy has listened to you explain something like I have been forced to repeatedly—" Davy rubbed where Steven popped him lightly in the shoulder "—then he knows how smart you are, crazy gay drama aside. I think you're putting too much weight on that."

"Even if I am, I'm still in school. John's a successful guy, I don't know how to step into his world. I don't know if I'd fit into it at all. I think I need to get to where he is before I'm ready for him."

"I tell you what. In ten years we're all going to be at the reunion, and everyone in this class will be working some slacker job for Boeing or something, and you're going to be the next Bill Gates. Better, even, because you won't have dropped out."

"I don't think that's—"

"Nope, believe it. Fuck, most of us have been nerding around with this shit all the way through high school and you've been doing it what, two years?" Steven agreed and Davy went on, "And your encryption project is way beyond any of us. I mean, we understand it, but we couldn't make anything like that. Not on our own, not yet. So, you're successful. Maybe you haven't seen the rewards of it yet, but you are."

"That doesn't help me much with John."

Davy rolled his eyes. "Sure it does, I bet he can see it in you. If I can, he can, trust me. So what if you don't fit into his world, you will. You go and figure it out. If it's not too late. When the universe throws him at you again, don't duck."

"What?"

"You'll figure it out," Davy asserted, satisfied with himself.

Steven knew he looked as skeptical as he felt. He said, "I'm not sure this was helpful."

"Do you feel better for having said that all out loud? Sure you do. You just need to think about what I said."

"You didn't say anything helpful."

"It's like a Zen koan. You'll get it eventually." Davy patted Steven on the back as if he were a slow child that needed encouragement.

"You're crazy."

"Yep," Davy agreed happily. "Now talk to me about yesterday's assignment, dude. I can't figure any of this shit out anymore unless you explain it to me. And after that, you can explain to me why you don't just go hook up with that hot bookstore guy. Or are you some kind of magic homo who abstains from the easy score?"

29.
A Piece of Meat

CHRIS CLINKED HIS BEER BOTTLE to Steven's vodka glass in a toast.

"I'm glad you called," Chris said for the second or third time, leaning in close so he could be heard over the music.

Steven smiled and nodded, watching the dance floor. The unmistakable beats of Madonna's "Vogue" filtered through the dwindling of Pet Shop Boys' "It's a Sin."

"Oh, I love this song," Steven said, setting down his empty drink and putting his hand out.

Chris took his hand and followed him on to the floor. The crowd at Tugs was different than Neighbours, though Steven couldn't put his finger exactly on how. Even though it wasn't one of their infamous underwear party nights, everyone seemed more naked, more ready to fuck. A little sleazier. But it was about what he expected from place that sold shirt shirts emblazoned with: *I am not just a person. I am a piece of meat.* Steven felt like a piece of meat as Chris ground against him from behind, clutching at Steven's hips and holding him close.

"You really like this song?" Chris asked, his lips touching Steven's ear.

"I do," Steven said nodding in case his words were lost in the music.

"So cliché though, right? Club-going gay boy loves pop divas. It's cool, whatever you or anyone likes. I try not to do cliché myself."

Steven turned so he was facing Chris, who grabbed his hips again and pulled him in, pressing their dicks together as they danced.

"Just dance," Steven said in Chris's ear, hoping to avoid any more conversation.

The night hadn't been terrible. Chris had suggested dinner and Steven agreed. Why not? He hadn't been on a real date with anyone but John in more than a year. But dinner turned out to be burgers at the Madison Bar & Grill, and then Chris decided Tugs Belmont would be better when the crowd in Madison's back bar was all lumberjack Bears.

Steven and Chris hadn't connected in conversation, although Chris didn't even seem to notice that, which was more disturbing to Steven than the obvious incompatibility of their world views.

As rocky as the night started, they rolled together smoothly on the dance floor. It wasn't dancing for a release from the cares of the world, like Steven usually sought, but it felt good to bump and grind against a hot, hard body.

The music spun around them and Chris's hands were always on Steven, tugging him back in possessively when Steven strayed too far, or holding him close as Chris aggressively rubbed his dick against Steven's ass.

Chris stripped down to a tight tank top that left little to the imagination. His t-shirt hung from his back pocket, his ubiquitous flannel shirt left outside in the car. Chris's torso was chiseled, tight, anatomically perfect curves, slick and glossy, inviting lips and tongues to explore him.

"You're so fucking hot," Chris said into Steven's ear before burying his face in Steven's neck and scraping his teeth over the thin skin there. His thigh slipped between Steven's and wedged them together perfectly, Chris's fingers digging into Steven's hipbones through his jeans. They moved together like that, still finding the beats as their hips rocked together, each seeking more friction.

Steven started to get hard, his body thrumming with the music, his head spinning with the vodka. He wanted Chris's mouth on him, some payoff for this connection they'd stumbled into. His hands on Steven's waist now, Chris rested his forehead against Steven's.

"Do you fuck like you dance?"

Steven felt his own laughter rumble in his chest. "I don't know, but we should go somewhere. Somewhere much more private."

"Just what I was thinking," Chris growled, reaching for Steven's hand and leading him off the dance floor.

There wasn't anything to stop him from hooking up with Chris. Steven knew he'd feel awkward when they saw each after this. Sex wouldn't make that worse. But he wasn't inviting Chris to his place, for fear he'd want to stay over.

"Any good ideas where to go?" Steven asked smiling suggestively, aware that Chris probably wouldn't realize that Steven was in this only for the easy hand job and hoping for no invitation for further dates.

Chris looked thoughtful and said, "I have an idea. Let's go."

Chris drove a rattly old orange Datsun. He took them up Pine Street and north on Fifteenth Avenue.

"Where are we going?"

"You'll see. It'll be great." Chris's hand massaged Steven's thigh, high up, never quite touching Steven's prick, but ramping up Steven's arousal.

Steven watched out the window as they passed the darkened businesses. The Teapot Café. Group Health Hospital. Rainbow Grocery. Matzoh Momma's. They could be going anywhere. Maybe Volunteer Park for a seedy hook up in the bushes. Or perhaps someplace more creepy and secluded. He'd told Lisa, Davy, and Jess where he was going tonight, so if Chris turned out to be a serial killer, at least they'd know where to start looking when they didn't hear from Steven. He wondered how many days would pass before anyone would worry. Still, he was getting harder under Chris's hand, which now just lightly brushed over Steven's erection. Steven surrendered to the physical feelings; it was the whole point of the night.

Steven was surprised back to full awareness when they turned right on to Aloha Street and immediately left on to Sixteenth Avenue. Steven's fabricated speculation on bad outcomes became real panic.

"What is this? Where are we going?" he asked as Chris pulled the car in between a familiar black Lexus and a green Subaru wagon. He tried to figure out what he'd ever said to Chris that would bring them here. When he got out of the car,

John's house loomed in front of him, a window on the upper floor still lit, blazing the possibility of John's presence into the dark, quiet street.

"It's my parent's house, but they're out of town," Chris answered, leading Steven up the steps of the house next door to John's.

Disoriented, Steven followed Chris inside.

The house was nice. Leaded glass front door, wide entry hall between what looked like a living room on one side and some sort of office or den on the other, stairs heading up next to the kitchen door. Steven didn't see much of it though, as Chris grabbed him and kissed him, backing them toward the stairs.

"This is a bad idea," Steven said, trying to disengage. He pushed Chris's hands away. "I should go." The proximity of John made Chris much less shiny. Steven's erection had diminished when they pulled up here. Steven's attention was pulled to the house next door and he moved a little ways away from Chris.

Misunderstanding, Chris said, "Don't worry, man, I'm clean and tested. There's nothing to stop us. My folks are gone. I've been feeding the cat and bringing in the mail. They're in Arizona looking for a house to retire to. Won't be back for like a week."

Steven stepped back and Chris reached for him again, crushing his mouth over Steven's and backing him against the wall at the foot of the stairs. Steven's body responded quickly, already amped up from Chris's teasing touches and their bodies grinding together all night. Steven pushed back off the wall so Chris could get his jacket off him, letting it fall to the floor behind him. Steven was half thinking of John. It felt wrong, to do this so close to him, but he wasn't a possibility right now and Chris was right here, hard and ready to make Steven come. Steven took advantage and spun them, pinning Chris to the wall as he they kissed.

"Fuck yeah," Chris said into Steven's mouth, reaching between them and undoing his own jeans and pushing them down his hips.

Steven caught Chris's hand, stroking his own dick, and curled his fingers through Chris's both of them jacking his erection. Chris pulled back, letting Steven take over.

After a minute Chris said, "You should put your pretty pink mouth on it," and pushed Steven's shoulders down.

Steven dropped to his knees, catching his weight with his hand just before he hit the hardwood. He nuzzled his face in as Chris bucked forward a little, rubbing his dick against Steven's cheek. Steven turned his head and mouthed around the side of the shaft, slowly wetting it, teasing. He licked and kissed over Chris's dick, dipping down to suck his balls, repeating each tease over and over until Chris's fingers twisted into Steven's hair.

"Fuck, just suck it." He reached down and rubbed his cock head over Steven's lips. Steven opened up and took it.

Chris did most the work, jerking his hips and holding Steven's head. Steven drifted, his hand tracing the taut muscles of Chris's abdomen, tracing up to pinch his nipples.

"Fuck yeah, yeah, you've done this before." His thumb traced over Steven's lips, pushing a little at the corner of Steven's mouth before Chris's hand dropped lower and gripped Steven's face, thumb and forefinger pressing at the pressure points in the hinges of his jaw. "You look good sucking my cock. Yeah, fuck yeah, take it."

Of all the things Steven had heard from hook ups, this was nowhere near the dumbest, but it broke him out of his drifting haze. He wanted to make Chris come, not because he gave a shit about Chris's orgasm, but just to get up off the floor, and do something about his own hard dick. He quickly switched from passive to active, grabbing Chris's cock around the base, squeezing and jacking while he sucked hard and used his tongue all down Chris's hot length. It wasn't more than a couple minutes before he had Chris babbling above him, both hands on Steven's head, holding him like he needed him there desperately.

"Fuck, I'm close, so close. You want it? You want my load, cocksucker? Yeah, take it, take it, fuck yeah."

Chris shoved Steven back. Steven watched as Chris took himself in hand, pumped come onto Steven's face, neck, and collarbone.

Steven sat back on his heels, and Chris crumpled down until he was kneeling on the floor, head dropping forward onto Steven's shoulder.

"Fuck that was awesome," Chris said as he breathing slowed. He sat back and stripped off his tank top, using it to wipe the come off Steven's face, before kissing him hard.

"Now it's your turn." Chris looped an arm around Steven's waist and tumbled them both back onto the stairs, pulling Steven up until he was sitting on the fourth step, his legs stretched in front of him bracketing Chris, squatting in front of him, mouthing over Steven's cock through his jeans.

The tease was delicious. Steven relaxed into it, letting his head rest on the step behind, as his cock got harder and Chris made a wet spot on the front of Steven's jeans. Finally, Chris sat back, flipped open Steven's buttons, and pulled his dick out.

"Yeah, nice," he said, tugging Steven's jeans down his hips a little. "Yeah, you're a real fucking redhead. Shit, have I told you how hot you are?" He rose up and kissed Steven awkwardly, before settling on his knees and taking Steven's hard prick all the way into his mouth in one long swallow.

Steven bucked up into the wet heat, moaning at the hot suction as Chris drew back and then plunged down again.

Chris's hands roamed, combing through curls at the base of Steven's dick, grazing his hip bones, flat palms running up Steven's chest until Chris found his nipples to pinch. Steven arched into the touch and let his mind wander.

It had been too long since someone sucked him off, too many nights with just his hand and his thoughts of John. Steven's eyes snapped open. John was practically here, only a few dozen feet away, through two walls and a narrow strip of yard. Was he in bed, light just snapped off? Steven shuddered at the thought of John so close, possibly naked, maybe jerking off right now so he could sleep more soundly, like Steven sometimes did.

Steven closed his eyes, letting the fantasy roll out, picturing John naked, stroking himself, Steven's name on his lips as he came. Chris's incredible suction and the fantasy drove Steven forward, tumbling into orgasm faster than he expected. The first wave of it shimmered at the base of his cock. Steven grabbed Chris's hair.

"Gonna come, fuck gonna come."

Chris didn't pull back, just sucked harder, his fist at the base of Steven's dick, squeezing tightly as Steven's orgasm crested and broke, rushing through him like dark water. He keened as his hips lifted off the stairs, his come pulsing into Chris's mouth.

Steven sagged back onto the steps, taking slow deep breaths to push back the slight dizziness. Chris kept sucking, gently now, almost affectionately, careful not to put too much on Steven's most sensitive spots, until Steven finally pushed him back.

Chris crawled up the step and sat next to Steven, leaning in to kiss him again.

"Should we go find a bed or do you want something to drink?" He asked when the kiss ended.

Steven took another breath, regret filling him. He didn't want to fuck Chris. The idea of spending the night with him seemed unbearable; the morning after, a torture, trying to make conversation. And shit, what if he ran into John outside in the morning as he left?

"I can't. I'm sorry. I need to go."

"What the fuck?" Chris's face creased with confusion as Steven got up and grabbed his jacket from the floor, struggling to get his jeans up and closed. Steven was halfway down the steps when Chris came out the door. "Hey, where are you going? Do you need a ride?"

"I'd rather walk," Steven said over his shoulder without pausing.

He saw the light in John's window flick off from the corner of his eye. He hurried up Sixteenth Avenue, hoping Chris wouldn't yell or cause a scene that might bring John outside.

"Was it something I said?" he heard Chris grumble behind him. Then it was quiet as Steven fought the urge to run. He wanted to be as far away as possible.

He walked down Aloha Street, feeling safer in the privacy offered by the canopy of huge, old chestnut trees that lined the road. The giant old haunted-looking houses were all dark and still. Steven slowed his pace as he became aware of how fast his heart was beating.

The front of his jeans were still wet where Chris had sucked him, now cold in the night air. He was right, it was going to be awkward when he saw Chris again. He didn't know how he could explain what had happened. But then, he didn't owe Chris an explanation.

It was coincidence, of course. A random accident that Chris would take him right to John's house. If it had been anywhere else, Steven would probably be in Chris's parents' bed right now, sucking his dick back to hardness.

Steven didn't believe in predestination. It was a fluke. Still, it was tough not to feel like the universe was trying to give him a message, trying to remind him that there were better possibilities than settling for the Chrises of the world, even if just for casual sex.

As he turned on to Thirteenth Avenue, almost home, a cat darted out and rubbed against his leg, nearly tripping him. Steven bent down to pet it.

"What do you think, buddy?" Steven whispered at the purring cat. "There's something better out there, isn't there? Don't I deserve more than hamburgers, sleazy bars, and guys who insult my taste in music before they get off with me?"

The cat didn't answer, just slipped back into the bushes.

Part Three

Spring 1992

30.
But Not Tonight

IT WAS THE LAST DAY of classes before spring break, but it was the last day of undergraduate classes forever for Steven. He'd accumulated more than enough credits to graduate. There was no point in spending the extra tuition to stay in school. He'd still walk in the graduation ceremony in June. Now he just needed to get on with the rest of his life.

Like some magic gift, this beautiful Friday had been part of that strange week every early spring in Seattle, when blue skies and temperatures in the fifties cause cherry blossoms to shudder out, blanketing streets in the fairy confetti of their petals. It was as if the universe knew that no one could sustain happiness through a dark Pacific Northwest winter and an uneven, gloomy spring. So it slipped in this one week to remind people there was beauty and joy in the world.

Steven spent the afternoon on campus, walking through quads filled with riotously blooming trees. The shirtless jocks tossing or kicking balls around didn't hurt the eyes either, but the blossoms were a sign that spring was coming, change was coming, every single thing was new.

That evening, lacking anything better to do, Steven let Jess drag him out to the Underground to go dancing with her, the only place she could get in, since she wasn't twenty-one.

The front wall of the DJ booth was mirrored, and Steven danced by it, blending in to the crowd of gothic black-clad bat-caver kids in tight black jeans cuffed up over black creepers, black t-shirt with the neck band cut out, not too wide, but enough to accent the lines of his neck and collarbones.

He'd found Adrian's rhinestone collar in his dresser and put it on, feeling nothing about it other than it was pretty. The bad mojo was gone from that fateful morning when Adrian turned on him and pushed John away. Steven smiled in the mirror wall when the collar sparkled with the lights. When he glanced up the DJ was smiling at him. Dapper, with heavy dreads streaked with red that stood out against his umber skin and cute white-framed glasses, the DJ had taken Steven's one request graciously and played it right away. Steven danced in view of the DJ booth all night, feeling eyes on him. He wasn't interested; just feeling wanted made dancing better. Unlike his usual bars, few people here approached him and that was fine; he kept dancing, stopping only to get water and to make sure Jess hadn't abandoned him. She bounced between a group of people at a corner table and Steven on the dance floor.

The lyrics of the Pet Shop Boys' "It's a Sin" rolled through Steven. He fell into the beats, his heartbeat matching the thrum of the underlying house beat when the intro to Nine Inch Nails' "Terrible Lie" wound its way out the end of KMFDM's "Virus." It wasn't music he usually listened to, but it carried his body just like he needed. Rage pushed through him, making him shaky as he moved. The terrible lie was Adrian and everything he'd ever told Steven about really being there for him. But as the song ended, Steven was empty again, freed the way only dancing to exhaustion in a room too loud to talk to anyone could really do.

He had plenty of partners. The goth girls were more respectful of personal boundaries than the sorority girls that came to gay bars to slum it. Steven loved the swirly circles they danced around him. Men came too, though far fewer than if he'd been at a gay club, and they were more respectful, too, like they were unsure. No one grabbed him and pulled him in, but every partner was fun, a new way to move, to share, to forget everything else.

◊

Steven was on his way to get more water from the bar when Jess found him. He'd been sweating on the dance floor for probably an hour since she disappeared off to a corner with her friends. She wore her usual combat boots with black-and-white striped tights and a very small black dress. Both arms were weighed down with silver bracelets and leather straps.

Her hair stuck up in all directions, framing her heavy black eye make-up. She had a battered leather jacket, scrawled over in white paint, listing phrases, or maybe band names that Steven didn't recognize.

"Sorry about my friends," she said. "I went to high school with most of them. They don't understand there aren't cool kids once high school is over."

"There are still cool kids everywhere. I'm not sure it ever goes away."

Jess frowned at that and put up two fingers to the bartender, who bypassed the line waiting for service and handed her two waters. She gave one to Steven. He cracked the bottle open and drank half of it.

"Remember when we met and I told you how I'd broken up with my best friend Adrian?" Steven asked, playing with the cap on his water. Jess nodded. "He's one of the cool kids, as much as that ever matters in the gay bar scene, and maybe it matters there more than anywhere else once high school is over."

"Does that mean you were one of the cool kids too?"

Steven shrugged. "Maybe, by extension, but it's a catch-22. The less you care about being cool the cooler you look; the harder you try, the worse it comes across. But I guess I wanted to be cool. I wanted Adrian, and I thought if I was cool enough he'd notice me."

"How could anyone not notice you?"

"Adrian's beautiful. And despite how cold and cruel he can be, he's charismatic as fuck. I was always a little in love with him, even when I couldn't admit it."

"He didn't feel the same way?"

"I doubt I'll ever know what he felt," Steven said. "I was just his audience, there to tell him how great he was when he wasn't too busy with someone else."

Jess's forehead crinkled. "I can't picture you putting up with that."

"He was a jerk sometimes but I forgave him everything, and never acknowledged who he really was. Maybe Adrian made himself a hard person to love on purpose, for protection. Maybe

233

I wanted to be him. Free, flamboyant, able to say anything to anyone. But all that is a façade for him."

"So is that why you guys broke up?" She asked, setting her water down and leaning against the bar.

"Kind of. It would have fallen apart anyway eventually. I can see now how toxic it was for me. Though it did have its good parts." Steven looked over the dance floor at black-clad kids writhing under rainbow lights. It wasn't quite the gorgeous gloss and gleam of a pack of shirtless guys at Neighbours, all vying for Adrian's attention, and Steven's by association.

Jess looked expectant, so Steven went on, "Everything fell apart at once. Adrian's old boyfriend, a real creep, showed up in town. We had a fight. Adrian was an utter asshole and humiliated me in front of a guy I like."

"What happened to the guy you liked?"

"I don't know. Nothing yet, maybe nothing ever."

Jess nodded. "That sucks."

"Dance with me?" Steven asked, ready to not think about Adrian or John.

Hours later, when the DJ intoned, *This is the last song of the night*, over the mic, Steven was aware of how not-high he was. He ached from the unaccustomed long dancing and the long day. Depeche Mode's "A Question of Lust" ramped up, so Steven danced on. The DJ deftly threaded the song into the extended remix of "But Not Tonight," leaving Steven feeling weirdly superstitious, like the universe was calling out to him, giving him signals. When the song wound down and the lights came up, he found Jess waiting at the foot of the stairs, ready to ascend to the real world.

◊

University Avenue was busy for 2:00 AM. As they started to round the corner on Forty-fifth, a false, deep, drawn-out, bellowing voice called out, "Jess!"

Before Steven identified the source, Jess hollered, "D-dog! What is up?" in the same falsely deep bellow to a group of skater kids crossing University Ave toward them. As they got closer, Steven recognized the one in the red cap as Davy.

"Steven, my man, what is up, yo? With my girl, Jess—did the bookstore boy freak you out so much that you're on to girls now? I think Jess might disappoint you." As he spoke, Davy put up his hand, palm out and Steven slapped it. Jess punched Davy in the shoulder at the end of his sentence.

"Davy, hey man, I didn't know you knew Jess."

"Yeah," Davy said, putting an arm around her shoulder. "She's my girl since way back. It's a small town, brother. Pretty soon we'll all know each other."

"We've gone to school together since like third grade," Jess supplied. "Otherwise I wouldn't have time for a useless shit like this one." She hugged Davy affectionately. Davy's friends milled behind then, hopping skateboards off the curb and talking to each other.

Davy asked, "What are you kids up to this fine evening? Meeting for the secret gay cabal? Plotting world domination?"

"We went dancing," Jess said.

"Oh nice. Did you find someone for Steven to date? Or at least to hook up with?"

"No, was I supposed to?" Jess looked at Steven as she asked. He shook his head.

"Yeah, man," Davy said. "He's got trouble in that department lately. He needs all the help we can give him." He released Jess and wrapped his arm around Steven's shoulders. "You can't let the bookstore boy keep freaking you, man. It was a sign from the universe. I told you to look out for those. You gotta go get what you want."

Jess raised her eyebrows at Steven.

"We're going to hit the parking garage," one of Davy's friends called. "You can catch up."

"Naw, man, wait, I'm right there." Davy said. He turned to Jess. "Tell him he won't fuck anything up if he gets a handy from a nice-looking guy, but he needs to go for the real deal, okay?" Davy raised his chin, acknowledging Steven again, "Get it, man, get it." And then he dropped his skateboard and slipped off with his crew.

"What was that about?" Jess asked as they continued around the block to where the car was parked. "And how do you know a little shit like Davy?"

"He's in my program at the U. We're—" Steven paused, making sure what he said was true. "We're friends. Actually he's been great."

Jess grinned. "Yeah, he's pretty great. I've known him so long he's like an annoying brother or something. He was always at my house because my mom was always feeding him. She thought his dads—you know about that?" She unlocked Steven's door for him and went around to the driver's side.

"Yeah, he told me."

"My mom thought he wasn't taken care of, not because of the gay thing, I think she believed two men couldn't properly feed a child. She's old-fashioned in weird ways." Steven tried to imagine his own mother dealing with a kid with gay parents. He decided it was probably for the best that he didn't want children of his own.

◊

"This bookstore guy that Davy talked about, is that a thing? You never talk about anyone you're dating." Jess said, turning the car onto Campus Parkway, toward the University Bridge.

Steven considered how much he wanted to tell her. He wasn't embarrassed, but he didn't know how much he wanted to relive the old shit he'd been trying to forget on the dance floor.

"That's because I haven't been dating anyone. The bookstore guy, we went on a date. It didn't end well."

The car rounded the curve up on to the bridge. The lights of Queen Anne Hill glittered on the other side of the lake. It was like an imaginary land, a place Steven never went, far away with nothing he needed there. The memory of the night with Chris felt like that now, a place that didn't need to be visited. But he was already there, so Steven pressed on.

"Remember earlier how I said that my break up with Adrian involved a guy I like?"

"That was the bookstore guy?"

"No, it's John. He's—I don't know—nothing ever happened with him. It almost did, or felt like it was going to, and then Adrian insulted him and me in a massively humiliating moment."

"Shitty." In the dark Steven could only see Jess' face in the flash of streetlights they passed under.

"Yeah, and stupid and complicated and six months later I can't even sleep with some asshole who took me on a date—"

"Bookstore guy?"

"Yep. I'm still so fucked up over John that no one else seems good enough. I keep telling myself that maybe I just need to find someone like him, someone who knows himself well enough that I can see his happiness, see that he loves me for who I am, not for what he can get from me. But then I think that's a bunch of bullshit, and I really only want John and I'm just making excuses for being too chicken shit to go after him."

Jess was quiet. Steven watched the houses and apartments rush by as they drove up Tenth Avenue.

"I'm glad I found you, Steven." Jess said, finally. "Actually I'm glad you found Davy too. The world is kind of weird, isn't it? Like you never know where you'll end up?"

"It's definitely weird. I miss Adrian, even though he was so awful to me. We were together for so long that there's a hole where he was, you know?"

"Totally."

"But it's getting better. Like it was hard to admit at first, but everything is better without him. I love having my own space after living with him for so long. And I think I chose not to notice what a tight little bubble we lived in. If he and I were still friends, I never would have met you, or Finney and Rae. I might never have talked to Davy beyond class stuff."

"Okay, tell me to shut up, but I feel like you're so close to having your ducks in row—sorry, my mom used to say that—you just need to find the last pieces. You definitely need to pay attention to what the universe throws your way. Like how it gave you me and Davy. What else is there that you might not see just because you weren't looking at it the right way?"

"Thank you, sensei," Steven said, smiling so Jess would know he was teasing. "I see you have learned well from Master Davy. I will do my very best."

"Fuck you," Jess laughed. "Don't make me force my problems on you now," she threatened.

Steven got serious. "I'm always here to listen, if you need."

"I know. Don't worry, I'll take you up on that. Just not tonight. Is this the right turn?"

"Yep," Steven answered as they turned left off Broadway on to Republican, then back on to Tenth Avenue.

When they pulled up in front of his apartment, Steven felt pleasantly empty, relieved of his burdens, cut off from his worries. Exactly what he wanted from a night of dancing. He was glad to find the feeling was still there, without Adrian, without hooking up, without getting high.

He awkwardly hugged Jess over the console. "Thanks for an awesome night. I didn't know how much I needed this."

Jess's smile reflected his growing happiness. He was glad to be home.

31.
Backwards and in Heels

SATURDAY NIGHT WAS WIDE OPEN. No homework in his future, Steven decided to find something that he wouldn't usually do, something he hadn't had time for when he was in school. He read through the *Seattle Weekly*, finding a Fred Astaire movie playing at the Harvard Exit at 6:30. He could barely remember the last time he'd gone to a movie theater.

As he walked the four blocks to the old theater, Broadway was shuffling from day shift to night shift. Employees closing up shops, families heading to dinner, too early yet for the punks and drag queens. He didn't have enough time to stop at Rocket Pizza on the way, so popcorn would be dinner.

The line at the Exit was short, but long enough that Steven felt the late March chill while he waited in his light jacket.

"What a pleasant surprise." That voice.

Steven spun around. "John! Hello."

John put out his hand, and Steven shook it, relishing its warmth, the familiar calluses. It had been months since he'd seen John, though he'd invoked him in conversation with Jess the previous night. Now here he was. Coincidence of course. Or the insane possibility that Davy was right and the universe was throwing John at him.

"Are you here alone?" John looked around, as if someone might appear to join them.

"Yeah. Last minute. I just saw *Daddy Long Legs* was playing and I didn't have anything better to do."

"Lucky you." John smiled. "Lucky me."

John's pleased smile at having discovered Steven here sent heat surging through Steven, shutting out the cold breeze.

The short line moved forward quickly, bringing them to the ticket window before Steven was ready.

"Here, let me," John said, pulling out his wallet and stepping up to the window before Steven could get his own wallet out.

"You don't need to do that," Steven said, flustered.

"No, please," John said. He slid bills through the hole in the ticket window. "Let me take care of yours." Steven relented, pleased this meant they'd surely sit together. "And of course," John went on, reading Steven's mind and flashing a warm smile, "now you're obligated to sit with me, and talk afterward."

"I'd like that." Steven couldn't muster anything more coherent. He wanted to laugh. To dance. To call Jess and Lisa tell them that his stupid plan of waiting and hoping had worked. Tell Davy that he could finally see the signs from the universe when they were this awesome. To tell Marcus the good thing Steven always wished for was finally happening to him.

Steven deserved an award for making it through the popcorn line and into the theatre without falling or saying anything inappropriate. John had paid for the popcorn too. Now they were sitting close—relatively—while John Waters instructed them from the screen not to smoke in the theater. Steven wasn't sure he could focus on the movie with his own John right next to him.

"I wouldn't have pegged you as a Fred Astaire fan."

"How would you peg me?" The implications of his words only formed in Steven's head as he said them, but he was as pleased as if he intended them. Perhaps he was actually figuring out how to flirt with John, if the wide smile that broke across John's face, like a bright reward for having the right answer, was any indication.

Looking thoughtful, John said, "Hmm, I'd have said you'd pick bad boys. Brando maybe, or James Dean."

"I'll take a gentleman any day. Fred Astaire was a gentleman, and gentlemen always make sure you come first—" he was John's eyebrows shot up in amused surprise "—you know, pulling out your chair, holding open doors. It's much preferable to waiting around for bad boys to decide if they can look away from the mirror long enough to notice you." Intending to tease, Steven knew the words were true. It was the difference between John and Adrian, the real difference about what he knew now that he wanted in a partner.

"Smart boy," John whispered as the theater darkened for the feature.

As Steven watched the movie, he couldn't help drawing parallels from the plot to his own life. The wealthy older man takes an interest in the smart young thing, Steven as Julie Andre, John as Jervis Pendleton. Had their night of dinner and theatre in Fremont last fall been Jervis and Julie's night of dancing in New York? Was Adrian like Alex the angry ambassador, driving a wedge between them so that John/Jervis severed ties suddenly, leaving Steven/Julie wondering had happened? It seemed too kind a role for Adrian, but Steven wouldn't complain if there was a fairy godmother like Alicia Pritchard to bring them together at the end once John/Jervis realized nothing should stand in their way.

It was a flight of fancy, the same daydreams Steven had been having for months, magical intervention finally bringing them together, John realizing his true feeling went deeper than flirting and teasing Steven.

When the curtain came up, John followed Steven out, his hand again on the small of Steven's back, balancing him as they went down the steps. The audience streamed out the wide doors in the concessions room, but John directed Steven back to the counter.

"Are you still serving coffee and maybe something sweet to have in the lobby?" John asked.

"Sure," the kid at the register said, "we'll be open in there until the second show ends at about nine-thirty."

The huge lobby, all marble and giant windows, with grand piano in one corner and elaborate Persian rugs across the expanse of it, felt more like a palace ballroom than a comfortable cafe. They settled down with cafe au lait. The counter kid came out a minute later with two plates of strawberry cheesecake.

"So your love of the gentleman Fred Astaire brought you out tonight?" John sat back in the old overstuffed armchair, across the small table from Steven, his full attention on Steven as he sipped his coffee.

"It sounds so cliché, but I loved musicals when I was a kid. My mom always let me stay up if they were on TV. We had season tickets to the Issaquah Community Theatre, so I saw four or five shows a year when I was in elementary school, and then when I was about fourteen, we came into the city to see *A Chorus Line* at the Fifth Avenue Theatre."

"You have quite the history of musical theatre for a small-town boy."

"My mom didn't get gay panic from my love of musicals, though. She just thought it was dancing I loved. Especially after she caught me at ten dancing with her scarves to the Bee Gees."

John smirked at that image. "What did she say?"

"Not much, although she signed me up for ballroom dancing. I'm not sure if she thought that was going to straighten me up or if it was some acknowledgment."

"Ballroom dancing? Did you stick with it?"

"I can still dance, if that's what you're asking. Though it's served me mostly only to be able to really impress my aunties and other old ladies at weddings."

"I'm certain it's more than just old ladies who want to take a turn with you when they see you on the dance floor."

Would you like to take a turn with me? Steven knew was the right answer in the game they were playing of teases and casually suggestive phrasing, but he knew too, that they weren't quite there, so he diverted. "What about you? You don't strike me a musical theatre aficionado, but then you've surprised me before with your musical tastes."

"I do like a good musical, but I just love the movies. I always have. When I was a child, before boarding school, before we moved to the States, we went to the movies every Saturday. It was always late-run American movies with subtitles or, later, more French films. I was sixteen when we moved here, old enough to know better, but I think I was still a little surprised to find America in the mid-sixties wasn't anything at all like the movies of the thirties, forties and fifties, but I never lost my affection for those movies, and movies in general."

"Is this your usual Saturday night, the movies?"

"Not as often as I'd like. But now everything is coming back on video, so every week feels like discovering a movie I hadn't seen in years. Decades even. Less reason to go out to the theater. Of course there's something to be said for things you can do in the privacy of your home, that couldn't be done in a place like this." John smirked. Steven shivered thinking of the things they could do in private.

"Some things could distract from a movie." Steven licked the corner of his mouth as if chasing a stray bit of cheese-cake, gratified to see how John watched the movement.

"Depends on the movie." John's eyes tracked Steven as he took another bite of his dessert, the silence growing when Steven didn't respond. Though he knew the rules now, Steven didn't trust the truth of John's responses. His interest felt genuine, as Ryan claimed it was at Christmas when John was a little drunk, but it was, after all, a game. Steven had no way of knowing if it was just a bit of fun for John.

Breaking the silence John asked, "So what's the best movie you've seen recently?"

"I feel like I've barely seen anything since I started school, but I know that isn't true. I loved *Cry Baby* and *Edward Scissorhands* as much as I loved *Dead Poets Society* and *Steel Magnolias*. Sometimes though, and this sounds stupid, I want to reject things that I'm supposed to like, like *Steel Magnolias*. I resent being told I'm supposed to like some-thing." Steven laughed. "I prefer to decide for myself. So I don't want anyone to think I like *Steel Magnolias* just because I'm gay."

"Nothing wrong with knowing your own mind, as long as you're open to new possibilities. And you seem very open."

"I am always open," Steven answered, forcing a smile as his cheeks reddened. With John, he needed to think more carefully before he spoke if he could be caught out this easily, even when he was trying to play along.

"From our previous conversations about your passions, I imagine you're very receptive to new ideas. Always ready for the next thing."

Afraid this made him sound flighty, Steven fumbled out with, "I don't quit for something new and shiny. I always finish what I start." His cheeks burned.

"J'ai dit ça comme un compliment," John said, noting that it was a compliment, with an amused expression on his face. "But diligence in working toward completion is an excellent trait as well."

"Thank you. I appreciate it." Steven replied, struggling both with the right French verb conjugation for "appreciate" and his intense pleasure at a compliment from John.

Steven looked down at his last bite of cheesecake. He lifted it carefully with his fork, wishing he could force attention away from his face as his blush faded. If this conversation went on like this much longer, he was going to declare his love for John, based entirely on his fantasies of their imaginary relationship. Which was beyond inappropriate at this point. He changed the subject. "So, this is your Saturday night out? Or do you have other plans?"

John laughed. "Are you telling me that you have somewhere else to be?"

"No. No! I thought you might have something better to do than listen to me ramble on."

"No. Nothing better." John said, his smile was so warm that Steven felt enveloped by it, like it would protect him through the worst of times. "What's better than the movies? Even when I shouldn't, sometimes I stay up watching the late movie on KSTW." Steven recalled the light on in John's upper window at two in the morning. John said, "At the risk of sounding trite, I just like the way movies are a window into something that isn't our everyday lives. Not that I need escape. I just love the drama, the new stories."

"Yes, without that my life might have been very different since movies did help me figure out that I'm gay," Steven admitted.

"Really? What kind of movies?" John's smirk returned.

Steven shook his head, denying John's implication. "I remember seeing *Superman* in the theater when I was about twelve. I was obsessed with it, but it felt like a secret I had to keep. Somehow I knew that how I felt about Christopher Reeve was how I was supposed to feel about Margot Kidder. I was right at puberty, so I knew enough not say anything that might make people think I was different. But I was suddenly aware of how different I felt. Then, later that year, I saw *La Cage aux Folles*—"

"Your parents let you see that at twelve?"

"Actually, they took me, because it was in French. My dad went and on about how hilarious it was. I can't remember if my mom ever said anything about it. Certainly no one talked to me about the homosexual relationships in it, but seeing an actual gay couple on screen cemented how I felt about Christopher Reeve."

"You aren't alone in making that discovery at the movies. I had my share of young crushes on movie stars. Although I learned more about being gay from books, though it was more subtle than what kids get today."

Steven nodded. "Books definitely helped too. Not long after that that I discovered Walt Whitman and Christopher Isherwood from other kids whispering about how gay those books were. I devoured every book I could find that looked a little gay after that."

"Did your parents know? Do they know?" John asked.

"Yeah, I came out to them in ninth grade. My dad's always been pretty matter-of-fact about it. My mom's still kind of having trouble with it. She just wants me to be happy. In her mind that means getting married and having kids. I think she's worried being gay will cause me to get hurt or have a harder time in the world."

"She's not completely wrong."

"No, but I think I'm lucky to be born when I was. Any earlier and things would have been very different. There certainly wouldn't have been things like La Cage aux Folles to go see, to show me early on that it wasn't only me, that a whole world existed of people like me. Still, I can't believe my mom didn't already know between the scarf dancing and my expressed love of watching Gene Kelly." Steven finished his coffee, feeling that he was talking way too much. "What about you?" Steven asked, emboldened by the moment they were sharing.

"Did my parents know I'm gay?"

"Yes, or when did you know?"

"Perhaps I always knew. Or at least by puberty, like you. I knew I wasn't interested in girls. It's hard to explain what it was like in Belgium after the war, even twenty years after. No one wanted to be associated with the Nazis, so if Nazis persecuted gay people, well then the Belgians could surely casually look the other way if some men never married and kept only the company of other men. As long as you never talked about it or made a big deal about it, it didn't matter too much. I came out when I was twenty-one to my parents. It was 1969 and we'd already been in America for four years so it was both easier and harder than it is now. Then it was both a political statement and an expression of the 'free love' everyone was talking about. I'd just finished college and was hanging out with radical hippies. That wasn't my thing, the politics or the hippies, but the drugs were great and it was a space to be yourself for a lot of gay people back then."

"I can't imagine you like that. Did you have long hair and bell bottoms?" Steven hadn't considered young John until now. He must have once been a rambunctious pink-cheeked child. A gawky teenager. Both seemed impossible; surely John's calm and grace were innate? College hippy John sounded like a mythical creature to Steven.

John laughed. "I did. Fortunately there are very few pictures."

Bravely, Steven took the opening. "I'm sure you look good in anything." *And nothing*, but his bravery only went so far and he couldn't get the last part out.

John grinned, about to respond, when his attention was caught by a café employee who'd come up behind Steven.

"Sorry, you guys, we're going to be closing here in few minutes. Do you need anything else?"

"No, thank you so much. Sorry to keep you." John smiled at the man and then turned to Steven. "That's our cue to leave. Which way are you headed from here?" John asked, pushing his chair back and folding his jacket over his arm.

"I live off Tenth and Republican now." Steven gathered his jacket slowly, wishing he could invite John home, or otherwise cement that this connection between them, make it happen again.

"Not too far out of my way. I'll walk with you. That is, if you don't mind."

"Great." Steven smiled.

On the corner of Broadway and Mercer, John stopped Steven with a hand on his shoulder.

"Let's see how your ballroom dancing skills are," he said pointing down to the pavement, and the instructional steps set in brass, arrows directing which way to move between the foot prints. "Do you want to lead?" John's hand was still on Steven's shoulder.

"I thought you didn't dance?"

"When did I say that?"

"That first night, at Neighbours. I asked you."

"Ah. I wasn't much for dancing that night. I was out under duress. Shane thought I needed to socialize more."

"Dancing isn't socializing?"

"Not when you aren't in the mood. But now, having just seen your gentleman, Fred Astaire, I'm in the mood. So do you want to lead?"

"No, you can. I'm sure I can still do it better than you, even backwards."

"And in heels," John finished the famous quote.

"Hey now, I'm no Ginger Rogers, but I'm pretty good."

"Show me."

They stepped through each move once slowly and then again at speed, John humming a waltz into Steven's ear. "Again?" He asked when they completed it smoothly.

"Faster," Steven said.

They went through two more times, John rushing it until Steven stumbled on the last step. They were both laughing.

"I assure you," John said, holding Steven's hand up as if formally thanking him for the dance, "that a gentleman never trips his partner. Forgive my clumsiness."

"Of course," Steven replied, bowing slightly. "We were going too fast." *But we can go faster if this is how you fall in love with me.* Steven caught his breath at the gift of John's smile and turned away, ready to cross Mercer Street when the light turned green.

"So what's next for Steven Frazier? A long Sunday of homework in one Capitol Hill's many coffee shops?" John asked as they cut across Broadway, already to Republican Street.

"No, I'm done with homework for now. Friday was my last class until, well, forever, maybe. It still feels weird."

"I thought you were graduating this June?" John asked, as they reached Steven's apartment building and stopped in front of the gated entry to the courtyard.

"I'm finished with classes a term early, Taking summer courses and extra credits during the year helped a lot. But I'll walk in the graduation ceremony in June, yes."

"What will you do now?"

"Get a job. Maybe consider graduate school, but I need to work before that."

"This might be another chance for us to help each other out." John smiled, though there was no hint of smirk in it, no impression of other intention.

"How?"

"I don't know if you'd be interested, but I'm purchasing computers for all the office staff. I could use help researching what to buy and then getting everything set up and running in the office."

"Wow. I'm not sure what to say."

"Of course, I'd pay you fair consultant fees. We'll need to get together to discuss time and expenses, but I'd certainly make it worth your while."

"That sounds great." Steven's head was spinning, too much to take in. The notion of working with John, even for a short time. He wanted that so badly. Yet. "You know I don't have any professional experience doing this. But I could totally do it. We'd have to be clear about what you expect and what I can provide."

"Of course. We'll talk through the details beforehand and make a contract. Call me at the office on Monday, and we'll talk. I'd hate to keep you talking business tonight."

Steven would gladly be kept talking about anything with John, but he recognized his dismissal. "Thank you, John. For the movie and everything. I had fun."

"It was my pleasure, Steven. Thank you for being such a good company. You'll call on Monday?"

"I will."

John put out his hand and Steven shook it. It was warm from John's pocket, and Steven worried that he clutched it too long.

An hour later, Steven was still tracing his own fingers over his wrist where John's had lingered.

32.
Changing Room

MARCUS'S SLY HALF-SMILE WHEN STEVEN and Ryan came into Button Up Boys was welcome. It hadn't been much more than a week, but Steven was used to seeing Marcus more often.

Marcus leaned forward on his elbows on the counter and looked Steven over. "I know you don't work today, so you must just miss me."

"Can't stand a week without you." Steven stopped and kissed Marcus on the forehead.

"Ryan! Hey, man." Marcus straightened as he put out his hand in greeting.

"Marcus, we need some clothes for my friend here," Ryan said, shaking Marcus's hand. "He's got himself a job and he needs to look good fast."

"Another job? Does this mean I'll be seeing even less of you?" Marcus asked, his face crumpling into a comical frown.

Steven tried a subtle smile of his own and failed, feeling like he might burst with the excitement of telling Marcus where he was going to work. He tried to draw it out. "Hopefully you'll see more of me if you have the hours for me to work. This new thing isn't full time. I just show up when I need to do something, so it's pretty flexible."

"You need to figure out how to make this your career now. We should all only have to show up when we need to do something. That would be awesome." Ryan slapped Steven on the back like he'd succeed at life.

"If you want that, don't open a store," Marcus said. "It'll take all your hours away. So, kid, what kind of trouble have you gotten yourself into that you have a job where you just show up when something needs doing?"

Steven tried to force down his goofy smile. "I'm doing a computer installation for an office, so I need to go figure out what they need, price it, order it, and install it. Not exactly nine-to-five, but great money and good experience."

"What our boy here neglects to mention is that this effort is for John's office—you know, *John.*" Ryan looked meaningfully at Marcus, who glanced between the two of them, his smile growing. Steven's grin broke through all his attempts to maintain.

"I see," Marcus said, one eyebrow cocked, the sly half-smile back. "So he needs some clothes with which to impress his future ex-boyfriend. I don't think his one sweater-and-tie combo is going to carry him through the next few weeks." Ryan smirked.

Steven ignored Ryan's jab. "And they'll have to serve as interview clothes, too. Something I can wear to my next job, assuming anyone ever really hires me after graduation."

"Okay," Marcus rubbed his hands together, coming out from behind the counter. "Where should we start?"

"Ties," Steven said.

"Shirts," Ryan said.

Marcus laughed. "Shirts, and then ties to go with them. Do you maybe need to bring Ryan with you everywhere? If you're always doing things backwards like this, it's no wonder you haven't caught your man yet." Marcus reached to ruffle Steven's hair, but Steven ducked away wrinkling his nose.

Ryan started flipping through shirts on the rack nearest to them. "I can't believe you're going to work for John. It will either be totally awesome or end in tears, although I'm not even sure whose tears yet." Pink shirt in hand, Ryan turned to Marcus, "Have you heard the way John talks to him? If this job thing isn't a ploy to get closer to Steven, then I'll turn in my gay card and start kissing girls."

"I haven't heard," Marcus twirled the rack in front of him. "But I saw the looks between them once, which was enough to know they should be knockin' boots by now. Maybe Steven can finally suck it up and ask John out, and we won't have to hear the whining anymore."

"Hey," Steven said, indignant.

"I dunno, Marcus." Ryan picked a couple of shirts out and laid them on the counter. His mouth was pinched tight with glee, like he couldn't stand how funny he was. "I think he wants John to ask him out. To just show up all masterful and tell Steven that they are going out. I'm not sure being the one to instigate is in Steven's fantasy. He's kind of a romantic and there's a hard submissive streak in him."

Steven pushed aside the stack of pants he was looking through and glared at Ryan. "Okay, one, let's not talk about me like I'm not here." Steven made a warning face at Ryan. "I'm not just some mannequin for you to dress up. I can hear you. And two, I'm not submissive. I top all the time. Everyone I meet wants me to top." Steven sighed, exasperated with his friend trying to be clever.

Misinterpreting the sigh, Marcus said, "Oh, honey, listen to yourself. No real top complains about everyone wanting to be topped. How did you get to be twenty-five, as free and open as you are, and not know about this stuff? It's okay to want your man to be a little dominant. You can't help how you are. Nothing wrong with being a bit submissive."

"Of course I know about it, but I'm not really interested in becoming someone's little leather slave, even John's." Steven turned back to the shelf of pants, feeling the color rise in his face. If he admitted to them now how much the idea of John giving him orders turned him on, he'd never hear the end of it. It was just John's voice, Steven thought, the way it dropped into gritty sexiness. That was what Steven wanted, not necessarily commands.

"You're still not getting it. This isn't about leather or being someone's slave," Marcus said casually as he pulled a couple pairs of pants off a rack and put them on the counter. "This is about finding balance with someone in a partnership that completes both of you and gives you something that you were otherwise lacking in life. Mostly it plays out in the bedroom, but it can go deeper and safely bleed over into everyday life. Submitting isn't slavery."

Ryan came up behind Steven and grabbed him around the waist. "Plus I know for a fact you like to be held down and told what to do," he said over Steven's shoulder.

"Oh? Oh, *you're* the Christmas boy." Marcus laughed and moved to a rack of shirts, flipping through them and pulling out a couple to add to the pile for Steven. He turned and winked at Steven. "Now I see why you were being cagey about it. Hooking up with your friends, dirty boy."

"You're both supposed to be helping me find clothes, not making inaccurate speculations about my sexual preferences and gossiping." Steven knew he sounded stiff and annoyed, which itself was annoying because that's what they wanted, but this was all little embarrassingly open for shop talk in the middle of the day.

"Alright," Marcus agreed, "let's get you some clothes your new Daddy will like."

"Sugar daddy," Ryan said. "I've seen where he works—the guy is loaded."

"Not to ruin your fun, but cut it the fuck out. The sugar daddy thing is gross and saying that's what I want from John insults both of us." The flush returned to Steven's face, real irritation now, not just trying to hide mortification.

"Aw, princess," Ryan said, kissing his cheek and then slipping away before Steven could punch his shoulder. "I'm sorry. It's funny though, how different you are from Adrian. He'd be all over the sugar daddy thing. I'm still positive that's where he gets his money. Unless he's turning tricks. God, I hope he's hustling!"

"You're awful," Steven said, trying not to laugh at how gleeful Ryan looked.

"And wrong." Both Steven and Ryan looked at Marcus, who shook his head, palms up apologetically. "The way he's going, Adrian will end up as someone else's sugar daddy. Didn't you know? He's got so much money from his parents' estate, he probably never has to work again."

"What?" Steven said, staring open mouthed, unsure if Marcus was fucking with him.

"Which explains why he never cares about keeping a job," Ryan said.

"Actually it's to his credit that he keeps getting new jobs when he loses them. And that he hasn't just blown through the money. He's got it set up so he has a limited monthly allowance for bills and clothes. The money was in a trust until he was eighteen. Mitchell helped him set up the accounts and budget it out for about twenty-five years of expenses. It was actually one of the last things Mitchell was well enough to do before he died."

Steven shivered, imagining he could hear Marcus's loss in his voice whenever Mitchell came up. The idea of young Adrian, before Steven ever met him, sitting down and carefully planning his finances for the rest of his life seemed insane, impossible. And how did Steven not know Adrian's parents were dead? Too many gay friends cut off from their families to make it seem unusual that a young gay man never talked about his family? "I don't know what to say. Are you fucking with me?"

Marcus looked sad, whether from the memory of Mitchell or Steven's disbelief, he couldn't tell. "I don't know how you lived with him for six years and didn't know this. I mean I know he was careful about it and didn't tell people, but I guess I assumed he'd have shared it with you."

"I didn't know a lot of things about Adrian." Steven knew his bitterness was clear as day in his tone. Each time he thought he was over it, past it, something else came up.

"This is fucking nuts," Ryan said. "You're telling me he's rich and ultra-responsible with all this inherited money? Like he's just living like a normal person, but he has accounts full of cash?"

"I don't know about normal. I've never met anyone so concerned with presenting a very specific appearance as Adrian is, but, yeah, he could probably survive another twenty-five years without working. If he was very careful and stayed in that old apartment. Although I think he works so he doesn't get caught out someday when the money runs out. Eventually, if he wants to live better than he is now, he's going to need to commit to a real career. It's not like he can live fancy forever, but he's taken care of for now." Marcus looked apologetic again, liked he hadn't meant to make this into something.

"This is not what I was expecting out of today," Steven said. Ryan laughed and Steven looked at him, questioning.

"I'm disappointed. So disappointed. Hustling would have been awesome. Or endless secret sugar daddies." Ryan shrugged, not caring about the face Steven made. "But being responsible with his own money is like the most anti-Adrian thing I've ever heard."

"Maybe that's why he doesn't want anyone to know. Who can say? He's a weird cat." Marcus shrugged.

"I can't deal with this. Are we here to talk about the past or get me dressed for tomorrow?" There was so much in his head already with John, with work, with school ending and his whole life changing. Steven could deal with new clothes. And maybe choosing where to have dinner. Trying to understand again how Adrian was different from how he'd always thought was beyond his emotional capabilities right now.

Marcus looked sympathetic, "Yeah, kid, let's see. Ryan, will you pick out three or four more shirts from over there?" Marcus pointed to the rack along the back wall of the store while he went through the rack directly across from the register.

"What do I do?" Steven asked.

"Stand still," Marcus said, picking through the clothes he'd amassed on the counter and holding a shirt up to Steven, rejecting it and reaching for another one.

Ryan came back, shirts hanging over his arm. Marcus took the shirts, adding them to the pile. He said, "Let's get to this. Jacket off, shirt off."

"Changing room?" Steven asked, slipping out of his Levi's jacket.

"No one coming in here will complain about eye candy," Ryan said, reaching for the hem on Steven's t-shirt and tugging it up.

Resigned, Steven let them undress him from the waist up. He looked at the stack of shirts in Marcus's arms.

"Am I going to have a say in any of this?" Steven asked.

"See how pliable he is," Ryan teased, "He just wants to be told what to do."

Steven rolled his eyes. "Not if it means keeping all of those shirts. I get it, I look good in green, but that doesn't mean I need to have a wardrobe like a fucking leprechaun."

"He's not wrong," Marcus said, sifting through the shirts. He handed three green ones back to Ryan. "Can you see if we have those in blue, or any other color in his size? Thanks."

Ryan headed to the rack at the back of the store. Marcus continued holding shirts up to Steven, going through three before he handed him a dress shirt, cream and forest green vertical stripes. "Try this." Marcus held the shirt out for Steven to slip his arms into and then carefully buttoned it while Steven stood still, arms out, feeling faintly ridiculous.

"Nice," Ryan said, "and not too leprechaun-y." He held a new stack of shirts.

When they'd made it to the third shirt, lavender with woven flecks of grey, Marcus led them to the shelves along the wall beyond the cash register where a hundred ties lay, in a rainbow fan of color.

"Both of you pick out some you like. Not too many patterns, I think. Go more for solids or two-color stripes."

Steven stood patiently as Marcus took the ties Steven had picked and looped them around Steven's neck, to see them against the shirt. He set a few aside and instructed Steven to change shirts.

It was slow, every shirt change requiring three or four ties to be judged against it. Customers came and went, Ryan taking over in comparing combinations when Marcus was busy, keeping up the banter as if this was a party and not a shopping expedition.

"John won't be able resist you now," Ryan said quietly, while Marcus rang up a customer. He pushed up the knot of the tie he'd just put on Steven. "You look good in all of this. Sharper, not just more professional. I'd believe anything you told me, you dressed like this."

Steven looked down at his pale blue Oxford shirt and deep purple tie, so dark you almost couldn't distinguish the black diagonal stripes on it. "Thanks," he smiled, catching Ryan's eye. "I mean it. Thanks for helping me choose clothes and just being my friend."

Ryan reached and adjusted Steven's collar, not looking at him. "I'd have snatched you up myself if things had been different." Ryan looked in Steven's eyes, his expression wary. "But I'm still too fucked up over Hector for that to be fair to either of us. And I need you to be my friend more than I need to ruin it by trying to date you."

"If things were different," Steven said, reaching to run the back of his fingers along Ryan's jaw, "I'd be begging you to hold me down and take me," he grinned at the surprised shock on Ryan's face, "but I'm glad we're friends. I need it, too. Not just because Adrian's out of my life, but because you're great."

"Are we having a moment? Do you want to go into the changing room and I'll look the other way and turn up the music?" Marcus asked as he joined them again.

Ryan laughed. "No, I think it's passed. Just admiring how good we made our boy look and telling him how lucky I am to know him."

"Very lucky indeed. Hold on—" Marcus hurried into the back office. Steven undid his purple-and-black tie and took off the blue shirt. Ryan grabbed Steven's t-shirt off the counter and handed to Steven. Marcus came out of the office balancing three small paper cups in his hand. He gave them each one.

The acrid vapor of whiskey bit at Steven's nose when he lifted the cup to it. Marcus raised his in a little toast. "To Adrian!"

"Adrian, really?" Steven asked.

"Without him I might never have found you," Marcus said, smiling kindly.

"Me too," Ryan agreed, slipping an arm around Steven's shoulders. "To Adrian!"

They pressed their small cups together and drank.

"The world sometimes gives you what you need, just not in the ways you'd expect," Marcus said. "Here's to finding the good in the worst things that happen to us."

Love surged through Steven, full of gratitude for the friends he had now, the life he had now. Without Adrian, he wouldn't have any of that. Silver lining. Even devils were fallen angels. Afraid to say too much lest he get sappy and silly, all he could manage was, "To finding the best."

"And to the next thing," Ryan said. "To starting over. New jobs, new lives—"

"Someday a good man for each of you," Marcus offered.

"And for you," Ryan said.

"Maybe." Marcus nodded smiling. "But for now, let's get this kid outfitted and ready for John to sweep him off his feet."

33.
Sweet and Pink

IT TOOK AN AWKWARD THREE days, observing the office and talking with John, Lisa, and their assistant Shirlene, to figure out what was needed. They all shared a desktop PC in the office for bookkeeping and other records. After listening to everyone and learning that they were getting ready to hire a second assistant, Steven decided they needed three more computers, two printers, and a fast, new 14.4 kbps inline modem to get the office up to speed.

Steven had been alone with Shirlene all morning while he made phone calls trying to find the best prices and availability, so he could show John just how good he was at taking care of things, that he was earning the ridiculous amount of money John was paying him. If the tentative budget John suggested when they'd negotiated Steven's contract was any indication, John was doing very well indeed. But Steven never liked wasteful spending, and he wanted options that would show John that he cared about John's resources, about his business. He was headed for the fax machine to fetch the price list from the third vendor when John walked in.

"Hi," Steven said, tamping down the giddiness he felt the first time he saw John each day. John looked striking, if slightly damp, in a navy suit and a brightly-patterned tie. Not as well-dressed as John, Steven still felt well put together when John looked him over. In that grey-flecked lavender shirt and deep blue tie, with grey pants and darker grey vest, Steven was glad of his new clothes.

Only three days of working together and Steven was conflicted. He wished this job would last forever so he could keep seeing John. However, dating his boss seemed unprofessional, and he needed to be professional to prove to John that he was capable of responsibility. As long as the job lasted, Steven would be second-guessing whether he should simply ask John out. But waiting was the right thing to do, if only until the job was over.

"Hello, Steven. Join me for lunch today? Take a break from the office monotony?"

"That sounds great!"

"We should go now then, to beat the rush."

"Whatever you say. You're the boss."

John paused, looking amused. "Yes, I am your boss."

"You are definitely the boss of me." This could hardly be called flirting with his boss. This was just awkwardness.

"And how am I doing at it?"

"Great, you can boss me around any time."

"Good to know. Get your jacket, it's drizzling. I was thinking Elliott Bay. Is there anything there you like?"

"Yeah. That'll be great."

They walked down a block to the Elliott Bay Book Company, to the cafe underneath. It had always been one of his favorite bookstores, but he rarely came to Pioneer Square. Now that he was here every day for a while, he needed to take advantage of it and check their computer books. At the counter, John had Steven pick what he wanted to eat and then waited for the food after shooing Steven off to secure a table.

This isn't a date. Strictly business. Steven avoided gawking at how well John's navy suit and bright tie complimented his eyes and his golden coloring.

"You look nice," John said, sitting down with the trays of food. "Did you get all polished up just for me?" He smiled, obviously teasing.

"Thanks," Steven said, desire surging through him. "I thought I'd better look good enough for your fancy office. I never did get the hang of tying a nice knot, though." He touched his tie. "My dad showed me, but he's quite proud of not having worn a tie since 1968, so he didn't have anything impressive to teach me."

"I could show you something about knots sometime." John's expression was unreadable, but his voice was low; it wasn't quite the grind that Steven already associated with sex in his fantasies, but close enough to make butterflies flutter in his belly, imagining John standing close behind him, his arms over Steven's shoulders as he demonstrated a knot.

The high of the fantasy robbing him of his better judgment, Steven said, "I'd like that. When?"

"Whenever you like. Some time when I'm in my office, stop by and I'll show you in the mirror there."

"Okay, yeah, definitely," Steven answered what he was hoped was casually. He pushed away the vision of John standing close behind him. "How's your day so far?" Steven asked. He took a big bite of his sandwich, hoping John wouldn't notice his flushing cheeks.

"Good, so far, and getting better already." John set down his fork as he spoke. "I had breakfast with a potential new client and then a good meeting with a long-standing client who's going to invest in some pretty interesting new ventures. A good start to a day. The rest is all paperwork and paying bills. What have you been up to?"

Steven held up a finger as he finished his bite. His sandwich was delicious but the sourdough bread was difficult to chew. He finished, feeling awkward. "My day is good," he said, wiping crumbs from his hands on his napkin. "I'm putting together price options for you. I think I've figured out the equipment lists. Now I'm shopping for the best place to get everything."

"Do you move this quickly with everything you do? You're on top of things, Steven."

Steven's attempt to repress inappropriate responses to John's compliment failed. "Once I know what I'm doing, I like to just go all in." He licked his lips and turned his attention back to his sandwich, unready to see John's response.

◊

Consulting was strange. After years of hourly-wage service jobs, it felt wrong to get paid to spend afternoons reading. It felt like playing hooky. Steven always headed down to John's Pioneer Square office around midday, leaving less time to be disappointed if John was out with clients in the morning. The day before the computers were to be delivered, Steven got what he most hoped for: another invitation to have lunch with John.

"Are you ready for graduation?" John asked. They stood at the wide concrete railing around Pier 54, eating Ivar's fish and chips out of baskets and watching the ferries come and go. The weather was finally nice enough to make the half-mile walk to the waterfront enjoyable.

"Yes. Though it feels like walking through a door where you don't know what's on the other side. I feel confident about what I know and what I want to do. But I still don't know exactly what's going to happen next."

"I'll happily help make sure you know what to do," John said. "I have people I can introduce you to. Clients. They'll be happy to interview someone I recommend. You've been a real asset to me. I'll vouch for your competence, skill, and eagerness to please."

Steven nodded, not wanting to take too much advantage of John's kind offer, but grateful for it. "Thanks, I appreciate it. And this job, too, it's generous and much-needed right now. So thanks, for that, too."

"My pleasure, Steven." John reached and dusted crumbs from Steven's lapel. "You've been incredibly good. I'd like to hire you for a longer time to keep you close to me, but arranging another job for you is the best I can do right now. And I'm glad to have you doing the work, knowing I can trust you."

"I just want to make sure I do everything I can for you." Steven heard the other possible implication to his words, and rushed to say the right thing. "Once I get everything set up, I'll make a manual and notes for you guys. Then you'll know as much as I do."

"I look forward to knowing what you know, Steven, although I doubt I can get it all from a manual." John crumpled his napkin into his empty chip basket and leaned on his elbow, regarding Steven closely.

Flustered, Steven focused on the manual, not the other possibilities of John's words. "It's good practice in computer programming to document what you do. When I start arranging your computer files, I need to get the process down, so you aren't lost without me."

"Lost without you," John repeated. "Yes, I'd like to find some way to keep you." He looked out over the water, at the ferries slowly rolling back into the harbor.

Steven was lightheaded. He knew since the movie that even when he was reading too much into what John said he wasn't entirely wrong, that John was at least flirting with him. But this was different, John sounded almost wistful. Was now the time to ask, to finally know if John felt the way he did? But when Steven opened his mouth he couldn't do it.

"John?"

Smiling, curious, John turned.

"Yes?"

"Um, just thanks, really, for this opportunity. I hope I've been useful."

John's hand came down firmly on his shoulder. "You've done excellent work. I'm really pleased with you."

"Thanks." Steven stuffed the last of his fish in his mouth to hide how pleased he was at John's compliment.

Watching the ferries come in, Steven wondered what he'd do when he didn't have this time with John anymore. Already he'd need to stay occupied this weekend to avoid worrying about what he'd do after the computers were installed and life was no longer occurring inside this amazing bubble of lunches with John and working specifically to please John. Soon he'd need to be brave enough to take Marcus's advice and ask John out, even if there was no guarantee John would say yes. Steven understood why they were called crushes, because he would definitely feel crushed if John rejected him.

"Okay?" John asked peering into Steven's face, his accent scraping through the word as they stepped back from the harbor-side railing, back toward work, life. "You don't look happy anymore."

Steven forced a smile, hoping it being solely for John was enough to make it real. "Oh, no, just thinking about things I need to do. Like I said earlier, the future is uncertain. I'm trying to get my ducks in a row, mentally."

"Ducks?"

"Yeah, it's something my mom says. Or a lot of moms say," he added thinking of when Jess had used the expression. "It doesn't—sorry, it's dumb." Steven felt shy all of sudden as John moved closer and touched Steven's tie, straightening it.

"We'll make sure you're ready," he said, his face inches from Steven's. If he leaned ever so slightly forward, their lips would meet and then—

His heart sped up. Steven shoved away the thought; if he didn't get it together, he'd be panting with desire at the thought of John's full lips against his. Oh god.

"I have a meeting I should get to." John's voice was deeper, gruffer, as he released Steven's tie and stepped back, breaking the spell. Steven wondered what John had seen on his face, if John read him as easily as his friends did.

"Yes, I should go, too," Steven said, feeling like something too big to grasp had happened.

"Are you going back to the office? Or are you done for today?"

"I'm just heading back up to the Hill."

"We'll walk together, let's cut up through the Market. I need to be on that side of downtown anyway."

They made their way across Alaskan Way and up the wide park steps from the Waterfront to the Pike Place Market, coming into the quieter lower Market, a long maze of tiny shops built into the hillside below the famous open Public Market.

"This way."

John led Steven through the snaking corridors to a tiny candy shop wedged between two overstuffed tourist-trap souvenir shops.

Midday, on a weekday, there was no one in the shop but them, which was good because it wasn't much more than a glorified closet full to the top with candy. Another person wouldn't comfortably fit.

"Hello, Miss Marion," John greeted a cheerful looking grandmotherly woman behind the cash register. She looked so warm and friendly Steven wished she'd just give him a hug and tell him everything was going to work out just fine.

"Hello yourself. Stocking up or just stopping in?"

"Just stopping in, needed something sweet after lunch."

She reached behind the counter and held up small, white paper bags. "One or two?" she asked, looking at Steven, kindly, curious.

"Two, thanks," John said taking the bags from her and moving to wall of binned, loose candy.

Steven watched while John seemed to consider each clear plastic container, filled with colorful treats. John's face was relaxed and happy. *Like a kid in a candy store,* Steven thought, smiling. The sun broke through the clouds and streamed in the wide windows lining the back wall of the shop, overlooking the waterfront.

"Sweetie?"

Steven looked over. Miss Marion was holding out a tiny wrapped candy. Steven took it and put it in his mouth. Lemon. "Thank you." He smiled, the candy gift and warm sunshine from the windows felt like the hug he'd just wished for.

Marion nodded to John. "He's been coming here since before I bought it a decade ago. Glad I'm not responsible for his dentist bills." She winked at Steven. John turned to them, his even white teeth displayed by the smile he gave the shop owner.

"I bet you see more of my money than my dentist does. Good genes, I suppose."

Marion laughed and took the bags from John to weigh them. He pulled a fold of bills in silver clip from his pants pocket and paid her. John and Steven left the store, heading north through the underground market, going up each set of stairs they came to until the third one spit them out at a small park.

"Over here," John said.

Steinbrueck Park was covered in late lunchers and tourists stopping to rest. They found a seat on the low concrete wall that encircled the grassy mound in the center of the park, looking out over the water toward the Alki peninsula.

John opened the brown paper bag and rustled around in it, pulling out one of the white bags and handing it to Steven.

Steven opened the bag to find a mix of pink gummi bears, red jelly beans, rose-colored lumps of taffy in wax paper twists, strawberry-shaped gummis, and Tootsie Rolls in red wrappers.

"I will definitely regret it if I eat all of this," Steven said.

John laughed. "Moderation is key." His expression folded, turning serious. "Just keep the bag. Every time you start to worry about the future, about what will happen tomorrow or next month, eat a piece or two and remember that you'll always be rewarded for your hard work. At the end of every day, of every job, there will always be something to look forward to, even if it is only a little sweet."

Overwhelmed, Steven looked into the bag again, avoiding John's eyes.

"It's very pink," He said senselessly.

"Strawberry," John said. *"Juste une fraise pour un petit fraisier."*

Steven picked apart the translation, because he must have misheard. *Strawberry for a strawberry boy* couldn't be right.

"Merci beaucoup. Really. This means a lot." He wanted to tell John how much it meant, this small gift: John wanting him not to worry *was* so much more important than the actual candy.

He caught the flash of John's watch and looked over, realizing this lunch couldn't go on forever.

"Meeting time for me," John said, looking as if he regretted the end as much as Steven did. "I'm going up Stewart Street in hurry. Is that out of your way?"

"I was just going to catch a bus up the hill on Pike Street."

"You'll be in the office tomorrow?"

"I will be."

"Hopefully I'll see you then." John turned to walk away, but stopped and turned back. "Don't forget to brush your teeth."

Steven's brow furrowed, parsing the anomalous statement.

"After the candy," John said, eyes twinkling. "And don't call in sick tomorrow because you ate all of it."

Steven watched John walk away, the world spinning one hundred eighty degrees from when he'd watched John last September. Adrian had no say in either of their lives or happiness now. John walked uphill, not down. And where there had once been devastating misery over the thought that he might never see John again, Steven was now filled with a glowing satisfaction, a sense of being carefully looked after.

◊

The next two weeks dragged by. Steven got the workstations set up and created a utilitarian file system. He unscrambled the tangle of bookkeeping records stored in the same folder as business letters on the office's original computer. He'd spent a week walking through everything with Shirlene, documenting what they did and what she asked, so he could create the manual.

As much as he longed to be around John, Steven was glad it was his last week here. Steven couldn't let go of the two-weeks-old memory of John standing so close to him. He thought he remembered John staring at his mouth, John's hand gripping Steven's for an extra second before he let go, as if he didn't want to release Steven. Was John's voice deepened by lust?

By that last Thursday afternoon, Steven had organized everything as much as he could. He'd had the manual copied and bound at Kinko's. Lisa was out for the rest of the day. John hadn't been in all day. And tomorrow was the dreaded end; Steven wasn't sure he was ready for it. He stood in front of the office-supply armoire, a beautiful Art Deco piece that deserved to be filled with silk and cashmere in a gorgeous house. But John said it was a fine place to store printer cartridges and paper. Steven went through the supply pages in his manual to ensure everyone would understand the instructions he'd left.

John came in just as Steven was thinking he couldn't come up with any more reasons to dawdle in the office. Sweat trickled down Steven's spine. It was now or never.

"John, hey, I was hoping I'd see you before I left."

"What can I do for you?" John stepped in, as close as he'd been that day after lunch. Steven had to tip up a bit to make eye contact though John was only slightly taller than him.

"Do you—would you like to go out with me? Tomorrow night. We could get dinner?"

John's face was impassive, though Steven imagined he saw calculation there as well. "No."

"No?" Steven's stomach dropped. He'd known it was a possible answer, but he hadn't truly prepared for anything less than friendly acquiescence.

"No, I can't do tomorrow night, I'm sorry. I have a business event I can't miss. But Sunday would be good if you'd like to join me. I'm meeting some friends for dinner, but I'd love to have you along, if you're free." John's smooth blank face cracked into a warm smile. He reached and curled his hand around Steven's upper arm, which Steven grateful for. He hadn't breathed since John said "no," and he felt so faint now he wasn't sure if he was imagining this new invitation.

"I'm free. I'm free for you for whatever," Steven stumbled over the words trying to get them out before John changed his mind.

"Nothing fancy, just dinner with some friends, who are also clients that you should meet, people who can help you in the future."

"That sounds good." Steven watched John looking for some clue about what this invitation meant to John. He flashed on John fixing his tie, a clear memory of how John had looked at him. Like puzzle pieces sliding into place, or like wiping fog off a window and instantly seeing clearly everything he wanted laid out in front of him.

"And of course after tomorrow, I won't be your boss any-more." Did John sound disappointed at the prospect? "I'd like you to go as my date."

"Oh. That sounds good." Steven did his best to sound casual. On the threshold of his endless fantasies coming true, Steven worried he might throw up on his shoes. His fantasies hadn't prepared him for how his throat tightened with surging excitement and his stomach churned in giddy anxiety.

John smiled, stepping toward Steven. "Sometimes I've caught you looking at me admiringly. But then you're looking away, busily occupied, and I can't be sure of how serious your interest is."

"Very interested. Since I first saw you." It felt amazing to admit it.

"Then you only have to get through tomorrow, and I'll see you on Sunday night. You can show me how interested."

Lisa clattered into the office, her hands full of shopping bags. "What's interesting about Sunday?"

John smiled at her. "Steven is coming to dinner with me," he said, matter-of-factly.

Lisa raised an eyebrow. Steven stepped back and grinned crazily at her over John's shoulder.

"I knew it wasn't safe to leave you two alone," Lisa said, laughing. "When did this happen?"

"Just now," Steven said, "Like, literally, just now."

"Then don't let me interrupt." She whisked her bags to her office at the back of the room.

"Sunday?" John asked, catching Steven's eye.

"Do I need to dress up?"

"It's casual. Whatever you're most comfortable in. I'll pick you up at seven o'clock."

Later that evening, Steven couldn't remember how he got home from work. Yes, it was just a group dinner for making connections, but he was going as John's date. And John had been clear that he was interested in Steven. Making it through the next three days would be a Herculean task. This was how heroes in ancient myths felt when commanded to do the impossible.

34.
Out in the Open

SATURDAY STRETCHED AHEAD, FULL OF hours to fret about his date with John. Steven lay in bed, staring at the ceiling, mentally arranging the possibilities to fill his time, perhaps by calling everyone he ever met and joyfully exclaiming that he had a date with the most amazing man he'd ever met.

The more practical options included: call his mother, do his laundry, think about job hunting, plan interview outfits, clean his apartment, buy groceries. Be responsible, get on with his life. But how could he focus on any of that when John would here in less than thirty-six hours? And yet, how could he bear the time in between if he didn't fill it with as many distractions as he could think of? Steven tossed the covers off and sat on the side of the bed, determined to get on with the day.

The phone rang. He lunged for it, grateful for the distraction. "Hello?"

"Good morning, Steven. Did I wake you?" The deep rumble of John's voice was so surprising that Steven barely stifled his gasp.

"No, John, hello. I'm awake, just planning the day. How are you?"

Every possibility of why John would be calling cascaded through Steven's mind. Was he going to cancel, had some-thing important come up, did he need to secure some details for tomorrow, did he just miss Steven? Steven thrilled at the possibility of the last one. It wasn't too much to hope for.

"Good. How busy are you today?" John sounded as unflappable as always, business-ready. Steven hoped it wasn't work that John needed him for today.

He said, "I'm pretty flexible. Why, what's up?"

"Let's go for a walk."

Steven fell back on to the bed, clutching the phone to his ear. There was little better he could think of to distract from fretting about seeing John than actually seeing John. He worked to keep his voice calm. "Sure, yes, when?"

"I'll pick you up in an hour, unless you have any objections."

"Yes. Great. Totally. Do you remember where it is?"

"I do. Tenth and Republican. I'll see you outside in an hour."

Steven's heart hammered as he got up to shower. By the time he pulled on his hooded sweatshirt to go wait for John on the corner, Steven had thought of six hundred increasingly insane reasons why John wanted to see him in person today. Surprisingly few were negative, but the possibility that John might still cancel tomorrow's date dominated Steven's mind.

Every possibility washed away when John pulled up in his black Lexus, looking amazing in a deep blue pullover and jeans, his hair still damp from the shower. He smelled of cedar wood and the green lushness of fresh leaves. Steven resisted the urge to press his face into John's neck.

"You look great," John said. When he smiled, Steven felt warm all the way through. "Foster Island sound good?"

"Sure." *Anywhere, everywhere, with you*, Steven thought, certain his eagerness was written all over his face.

John put the car in gear and turned left to take them up and over the hill.

"So what's up?" Steven asked, anxious and eager. "Just couldn't wait to see me?" he joked.

"Actually," John's voice deepened, "yes." His hand brushed Steven's knee, lingering a second before John pulled it back to the gearshift. Steven could feel the warm shape of John's fingers on his knee. He wasn't sure how to make it through a whole walk.

"Well, that's—" Steven's voice creaked; he cleared his throat, "good. That's good. Because I wasn't sure if I could stand waiting until tomorrow to see you again."

At the next stop sign, when John turned to him and smiled, Steven felt as if he was shifting out of his body, his joy too vast to be contained within his skin. They went up Aloha Street and then down Twenty-fourth Avenue, cutting over to the parking lot at the trailhead before the traffic waiting at the University Bridge caught them.

A sunny spring Saturday, and the whole city was out. They set out over the interconnecting series of paths, bridges, and docks that made up the Foster Island trail. Chatting meaninglessly about the weather and sunny days in Seattle, Steven felt happier than he had in years. Ten minutes down the trail, they stopped to lean on a railing and watch the parade of boats go by, big and small, moving through the Montlake Cut between Lake Union and Lake Washington.

"It's so beautiful out here," Steven said, not for the first time that day. He felt John's eyes on him. Their shoulders touched where they leaned with their elbows on the railing. John was close enough to kiss if he turned toward Steven.

"How's your weekend so far?" John asked, his eyes back on the passing stream of boats.

"Being young and unencumbered by responsibility, I think I've made the most of it. I went dancing last night, stayed up late, slept late, ate a healthy breakfast, and now I'm out with a handsome man. I'm not sure anyone could ask for much more." Steven looked out at the boats, grinning.

"Dancing with your friends? At Neighbours?"

"Dancing, yes—friends, not really. I saw some people, but I just went by myself to dance. Helps relieve tension."

"What are you tense about?"

He met John's eyes, checking to see how seriously he should take the question. John's gaze was warm and open with genuine curiosity. Steven looked away again as he spoke.

"There's this guy that I've been kind of into for a while. Like a year. And I think I might have a chance with him. I think we're friends." Steven caught John's agreeing nod out of the corner of his eye and shifted so he could look sidelong at John as he spoke. "But I've already thought a lot about it, and I'm not interested in being his friend."

"Oh?"

"Nope. He's the most handsome man I've ever seen. I'm not sure how much more time I can stand to be in his presence as just his friend." Steven's heart hammered like it might burst from his chest. If John decided now to reject him, at least Steven would know he'd been entirely honest first.

"And being in his presence is making you tense?" John asked.

"No, I'm tense because I'm not sure I've always shown him my best side. I'm still embarrassed by some of our meetings, and I'm not totally sure what he thinks of me." Steven faced John, prepared for any response.

John's face remained neutral. "Ah. That morning was an unfortunate meeting. And certainly your friend—" he paused.

"Adrian," Steven supplied.

"—succeeded in embarrassing you, which he was obviously trying to do. But I don't yet know you well enough to guess what the situation was. Jealous ex-lover? New jealousy spun from inside a crumbling relationship?" John met Steven's eyes, only curious.

"No, we were never together. He—I don't know—makes himself hard to love. Like, he trusts you more if you stick by him when he's utterly awful? Or maybe he was jealous in a way he couldn't express. It ended our friendship. Or it was the beginning of the end anyway."

John shifted so their arms touched again, his fingers curling over Steven's on the railing. The touch emboldened Steven to go on.

"I'm tense because I'm worried that you think I'm some scene queen club kid, all screaming fights and drugs and partying." He was almost there, everything would finally be on the table for both of them to examine.

John's fingers closed over Steven's. "You think that's how I see you?"

"You never called me after that night in Fremont. I was already unsure how you saw me, then the Adrian thing happened, sealing it. I assumed." Steven awaited judgment.

"That night we had dinner in Fremont, when I drove you home, I wanted to walk you to the door and kiss you until you begged me to come inside." John's eyes were soft, regretful.

"But you didn't." Steven remembered how much he'd wanted John that night, sure John had been flirting with him, leading him on. And then he never called.

"I didn't. I saw the way Gabriel looked at you that night, like he was ready for good gossip to tell. It wasn't hard to convince myself that our age difference was too great to overcome." John squeezed Steven's hand on the railing and then stroked his fingers across Steven's wrist, gentling him like a wild horse.

"You dated younger before. Tom."

"Yes, but Tom was a mistake. We both paid heavily for that relationship."

Steven studied the tiny care lines at the corners of John's eyes, which were highlighted in the bright sun. The remembered hurt shining in those blue eyes. "I don't know the story, but that was a long time ago. And I'm not Tom. You can't judge the possibility of us on that."

"You're right, but the reasons it didn't work out between Tom and me could still apply. Sometimes people just aren't compatible, no matter how much they love each other. I don't know if I could stand to go through that again. And you're still becoming who you are. The rate at which you change as person in your twenties is exponentially larger than later in life. I thought it was best to put some distance between you and me. Remove the temptation. So I didn't call you, even though I wanted to."

"And then Adrian came along."

John nodded. "Adrian was justification for sure, but he wasn't the reason." Steven wasn't sure he knew John well enough yet to read it correctly, but John's face was a mix of tenderness and regret as he added, "I'm sorry." John's fingers caressed Steven's wrist, causing an echoing flutter low in Steven's belly.

"But you changed your mind. Or we wouldn't be here."

"I couldn't stop thinking about you." A smile broke through gloom on John's face. He squeezed Steven's hand again and Steven squeezed back. "For months I asked Lisa about you. Wondering how you were, what you were doing. Christmas seemed like a safe way to see you again, in a room full of people. But after that it just got worse. I was determined to avoid you after that."

"What changed your mind?"

"Sitting in that movie theatre with you, watching a foolish man on screen decide that the best thing for both of them would be to suffer apart, that he should leave because they wouldn't work, never telling her why. I realized that's what I was doing. I'm not superstitious, but what are the chances I'd run into you again at that movie? More than that, though, I can't resist your smile. I want to be responsible for it. I want, sometimes, to be the one that makes that beautiful smile happen."

The boats continued by in their endless progression through the ship canal. Steven let out his breath slowly, listening to the boats, the distant talk of the canoers paddling near the docks, gulls calling above. This was everything he wanted. Standing close on perfect spring day, with a man, whose eyes were as blue as the sky confessing his desire for Steven alone.

John's fingers traced over Steven's palm, his thumb rubbing small circles on the back of Steven's hand. Steven looked to find John watching him again.

"Should we keep walking?" John asked.

"Sure."

John didn't release Steven's hand as they set off down the trail, stepping into the shady brush of one of the marsh islands. Steven shifted so their fingers entwined evenly and John squeezed, acknowledging the change. They remained quiet as they stepped carefully along the muddy trail. Steven loved coming here as a child, imagining every small path into the brush held new magic, dragons or unicorns waiting to be discovered. Childhood memories were a nice distraction from the intensity still lingering from their conversation.

They came out of the trees and bamboo onto the next series of docks, where John stopped them on a small bridge, barely high enough for canoe traffic to pass under. His grip on Steven's hand tugged when John stopped moving and Steven kept walking.

"I never answered your question: I'm not sure what I think of you yet, Steven. Not entirely. But I'd like the time to decide. To see as much of you as possible so I can make up my mind about you." Steven felt a blush crawling up his neck as John went on. "Of course, I'm a bit tense too."

"Why?" Steven asked. That he could disturb John's eternal calm seemed impossible. "I'm definitely not someone you have to be worried about."

John faced him, his expression serious. "I am much older than you, Steven. People, your friends and mine, will wonder at my motives, even if you don't. It also means that perhaps in the end we won't ever quite understand each other. It feels important to get this out in the open now. If we date, it comes with more problems at the outset than other relationships. And people will say disparaging things. Unexpected people, people you thought you could trust."

Steven understood, though there was so much to take in. The underlying pain in John's casual comment about friends turning on you. His acknowledgment of how his previous relationship ended. Yet the fact that John was saying any of this meant he was willing to try with Steven.

Steven took a second to make sure he said what he really meant. "For a year, I've wanted you. I don't care how young and stupid this sounds: fuck the consequences and what people think. When I'm with you, it feels like everything inside me clicks together and I'm instantly better than I was alone. I don't care. About age, or what people say. I think we need time to get to know each other. We can't say it won't work until we try, and I want..."

"Tell me what you want."

"I want you to kiss me."

John cupped Steven's jaw in both hands and gently drew Steven toward him. His lips barely brushed Steven's before they came fully together, warm and soft. Steven opened into the kiss, letting John lead, though he reached for John's hips, holding them together.

The kiss had enough heat to breathe life into Steven's whole body, enough connection that he could feel how well their bodies fit together. It was perfect, soft and dreamy like water lilies blooming in warm sunlight, floating and calm.

It ended far too soon. John pulled back, his hands still on Steven's face as he looked into Steven's eyes.

"Is that what you wanted?" John asked, a tiny smile at the corners of his lips and eyes.

The dreamy peace of the kiss cracked as Steven fought the grin trying to split his face. "But now I want so much more. In private would be a good place to start." A canoe full of college students paddled beneath the arching bridge where they stood.

John laughed. "I don't think we're quite ready for privacy yet, but I am looking forward to it." He kissed Steven again, more chastely this time, and then let his hands slide down Steven's arms, catching his hand and turning to lead them down the trail. "Let's be less heavy for the rest of today."

It was hard to think about anything but sex, now that he knew how perfectly John's body fit against his. John asked leading questions, distracting Steven, getting him to talk about his family, where he grew up. Their easy conversation covered everything from childhood to safe sex and recent testing as they made their way off the tiny connected island trail and into the main park. The trail was busy with Pacific Northwest sun worshippers, so Steven gave up his secret hope of finding somewhere private today.

The kiss had been unlike any Steven had ever shared with anyone. The charge of his own passion made the day brighter with the lingering possibility—that seemed like surety now— that soon John would do more than kiss him.

John kissed him again in the car when he dropped Steven off. He lingered in it this time, his thumb lazily tracing the edge of Steven's ear, his other hand firmly on Steven's thigh. Steven wasn't sure if he'd be able to get out of the car without exposing his erection, though he didn't think it mattered at this point.

"Tomorrow," John whispered, his forehead against Steven's.

"Yes. Not soon enough."

John chuckled. "I'll pick you up at six?" he asked. "Which apartment? You shouldn't have to wait outside."

"C. Apartment C. Third on the right in the courtyard." Steven was definitely going to have to clean his apartment. "I'll see you then." He didn't want to get out of the car, didn't want to break the spell of today.

"I'm looking forward to it." John pushed a stray lock off Steven's forehead, his fingers tracing down Steven's jaw as he pulled back. "I hope the rest of your day is good."

"I'm not sure anything could compare to this morning."

35.
The Absence of Suffering

SUNDAY MORNING, RYAN HAD ALREADY secured a table for them when Steven arrived at Eggs Cetera.

Steven had found every possible distraction after John drove away on Saturday. He channeled all his pent-up desire into cleaning and organizing his house. He called his mom and then one of his aunts at his mom's insistence. He did all his laundry and walked up to Safeway to get groceries and the early Sunday paper. He called Lisa, who wasn't home. Finally he called Ryan and made plans for breakfast Sunday morning.

"Look at you, man. You're a jittery ball of nervous energy," Ryan observed, kissing Steven's cheek before he sat down. "What's up?"

"I have an actual date with him. With John."

Ryan's eyebrows shot up. "When? Are you still working for him?"

"Tonight. And no, Friday was my last day."

"Nice. Very respectable that he waited to ask you. But, damn, man, I told you. I told you he liked you." Ryan looked positively gleeful. Steven wasn't sure if it was about being right or about John. Ryan went on. "It wasn't just the way he looked at you, but his friends knew who you were. He'd clearly been talking about you, thinking about you, since before Christmas."

"I see it now, but it was like everything suddenly snapped into place. My shitty insecurities made me blind."

"Or you were busy trying to make sure he didn't notice you checking him out and daydreaming about him and that distracted you from seeing the signs," Ryan said kindly, then wrinkled his nose and finished, "Or maybe you're oblivious, insecure, and don't listen to your friends."

"Thanks, jerk." Steven looked away in mock offense but couldn't maintain it. There was too much good to talk about. He sighed. "You're not wrong though. As soon as it happened, it was like suddenly I really saw him. He'd been looking at me all along, and I *didn't* notice. Ugh, I feel like my life is this bizarre thing that everyone else sees and understands from the outside, but I never know what's going on until after the fact."

"Always easier to see things from the outside."

"Yeah, I guess. Anyway, how are you? Did you order yet?"

"No, I was waiting for you," Ryan said. "Although I hope they at least bring coffee soon. I barely slept last night."

"Good not sleeping, or the bad kind?"

"Bad. I don't know if I want to talk about how I am without drinks. Fuck it, this is brunch, right?"

"Yes, and brunch exists for morning drinking," Steven said.

"Good. We'll say we're celebrating your date, or maybe to calm your nerves. Have you talked to him since Friday?"

"Oh god. He called yesterday and we went for a walk."

"What? You already went out with him?"

"Yes. He said he couldn't wait to see me, which was amazing because I was not going to be able to stand waiting either. We walked in the Arboretum and had this intense talk where I sort of spilled my guts, and he told me he was anxious about the age thing. Then we had this incredible kiss and we talked about, I don't know, everything and I pretty much haven't been able to think about anything except his mouth since then."

"Are you kidding me? Are your feet even touching the ground right now? You must be floating high on this. This is like some movie shit, totally a meet-cute story from *When Harry Met Sally* or something. Jesus, fuck, I'm jealous. Where are you going tonight?"

"I don't even know. He said dinner with some friends he thought I should meet. About work prospects for me."

"Oh fuck, this is too good. He's in enough for you to meet his friends, and he's worried about your future. The deal is sealed already. I hope he's good in bed, because that could be a deal breaker. How was the kiss?"

"Perfect, like the one you hope for every time."

The server arrived to take their orders and fill their coffee cups, which was for the best, because otherwise Steven would spend the day talking Ryan's ear off about John.

"So, really how are you?" Steven asked again, wanting the distraction as much as he wanted to know.

"Dude, I'm fine. I don't want to bring you down with my bullshit in this amazing weekend you're having."

"Now you have to tell me, because I'll worry and also, fuck, man, we're friends. Never worry about bringing me down. I'll always listen."

"Thanks. It's stupid. I've been going back and forth all weekend, trying to figure out how I feel."

"What's going on?" Steven asked.

"Hector, my ex, is getting married."

Steven set down the creamer pitcher a little too hard on the table and some splashed out. "To a woman?"

"Yeah, his parents arranged it. I think that's still kind of common in Filipino families? I don't know."

"Okay, well, I feel sorry for her." Along with his pity for a girl he'd probably never meet, guilt crept in too. How careless to have let his mouth run about John when Ryan was clearly not okay. "Shit, I can't believe you let me ramble about my stuff. Are you okay?"

"Yes. No? Part of me feels like, fine, this settles it. It would never work out between us anyway. And knowing this is why he broke up with me is kind of okay, because it wasn't about me. But then when I think about it, it's still totally about me— he didn't love me enough to say no, to come out and be himself for me." Ryan fidgeted with a sugar packet while he talked, finally pouring it into his cup.

Ryan not having his usual surety made Steven want to reach over hold him close, restaurant or not, but he didn't think Ryan would appreciate it, so he did the best he could with words. "I feel sorry for her. You are worth so much more. You know there's someone out there who will love you like that, right?"

The server brought well-timed Bloody Marys.

"I know, I do know. It feels shitty, like I put up with his closeted bullshit and hiding for two years. What did I think was going to happen?"

"I think you always knew it wasn't right. Remember when I was moving out, and I asked where you spent your time? You told me you were out making your own bad decisions."

Ryan looked up, his forehead creased with curiosity and surprise. "I said that?"

"Yeah."

"It was a messed up situation from the beginning." He nodded, confirming that truth. "My dad knows his dad. We met at a church event, where I only went for my family. I knew from the beginning Hector was struggling. And now, I don't know if I can get past it. Like, I can live with a broken heart, but I don't feel like I was even true to myself through all of this. How do I get over that?" Ryan's disappointment was clear on his face as he sat back in his chair.

"I wish I had an easy answer. You just decide who you need to be, I think, and you keep trying. One foot in front of the other, going on, always trying to be better. I feel like that's all I'm ever doing."

"That seems to be working out for you," Ryan said without malice. He sipped his Bloody Mary. "You're seriously glowing right now, and I know you aren't high."

"We'll see what happens. I have to get through the first date still. Are you really okay? This is pretty heavy." Steven felt divided. The urge to ramble on about John bubbled up in him again, but he was genuinely hurting for Ryan and didn't want the attention back on him if Ryan still needed it.

"Yeah. I'm sorry I brought it up. Can we talk about something else? Japanese upbringing means I hate fucking examining feelings in the light of day." He gestured out the wide window. "It's best done drunk, late at night when you can pretend in the morning it never happened."

"Okay, then another day I'm going to have to take you out, get you drunk and make you spill."

"Yeah, maybe. You're a good friend. I'm sorry we weren't closer when we lived together." Ryan finished his drink and glanced around for the waitress.

Steven drank the rest of his in solidarity and caught all the pepper in the last sip. "No regrets." He coughed, pulling it together. "Seriously, don't dwell on what we can't change."

"You're like a fucking fount of Buddhist wisdom today." Ryan grinned and put his chin in his hand, elbow on the table. "Tell me about the absence of suffering," he said with an artificially serious expression.

"You have it backwards. The absence of desire is the end of suffering," Steven said imperiously, then smiled and picked up his coffee, hoping it was cool enough to drink. He still had pepper in his throat.

Ryan rolled his eyes. "Forget what I said about you being someone I'd ever consider dating. You're insufferable, and you've ended my desire."

"Funny."

"I try." Ryan smiled. It looked genuine this time. Maybe, Steven realized, for the first time all morning.

Steven said, "Usually you succeed too. Usually."

Ryan scowled, but Steven could see he felt lighter.

"Yeah. I can't take anymore heavy conversation. So what are you wearing tonight? Have you already tried it on three times to see how your ass looks in it?"

Steven laughed. "Oh god, no. I have, like, three choices, but I don't know. He said casual, but I don't know if it's casual-straight-people casual, or gay-people casual, because that's different."

"I wish I knew where you were going to eat. Jeans, your best ass jeans. No underwear. Hmm, I'd say t-shirt, but that's what I'd be comfortable in, so whatever shirt makes you feel the best but the most like yourself."

"That's actually good advice. But no underwear?"

"You want to get some, don't you?" Ryan nodded, as if Steven agreed with him, "Show him you mean business."

"How will he know I'm not wearing underwear until we're actually down to business?"

"He'll know. He'll be looking at your ass in your good jeans and he'll be able to tell. I always can. And he so likes you. I can't believe he called you for a pre-date yesterday. Yeah, whatever you wear will be good enough. He wants you."

"You think so?" Steven flushed at his childish need for validation. John had been clear about his intentions. Still it felt so good to have it confirmed.

"Shut up, you know he does."

Ryan's gloom was lifting as they got a second round of drinks and ate slowly, neither of them having anywhere to be. It was comfortable to talk. Steven remembered Christmas, and his determination about having friends and lovers and keeping them separate. He was glad he'd found Ryan. By the time they finished, Steven was full of gratitude at the universe, for his friends, for his life, for whatever else it was going the throw at him.

"Hey," Steven said as they stood on the corner of Broadway and Mercer, about to head their separate ways. "Call me whenever—late, drunk, whatever—whenever you need to talk. I'm sorry I made today all about me."

"It was your day, Steven. I needed your goodness and your happiness. It helped. I feel less grim than I did this morning. We'll totally hang, and I promise I won't even be a bummer."

"Be whatever you want, just call me, okay?"

They hugged and Steven watched as Ryan took off, his lanky form graceful in retreat.

◊

At the last minute, Steven rejected all the outfits he'd laid out. Instead he chose a floral print button-up shirt, all shades of green and grey. He put it on with grey jeans and his Doc Martens, wanting to feel like his everyday self, not dressed to please, when he wasn't even sure what exactly would please John. He was buttoning the last button when John knocked.

Steven froze for second, with his hand on the door knob, took a deep, centering breath, and opened the door.

"Hi." Giddiness rose like champagne bubbles in his chest. He smiled goofily as he let John into the apartment.

"Hello, Steven. I'm happy to see you. You look gorgeous." John stepped forward and caught Steven's chin, kissing him lightly on the mouth before he pulled back.

"Oh, thanks." Steven felt his cheeks pinking, a happy flush at John's compliment, at his kiss. "You look amazing. I'm not underdressed, am I?" John was wearing black jeans and black loafers with a soft-looking pale blue t-shirt and a grey blazer. Strikingly handsome, like he belonged on TV. Steven bit his lip to keep from saying his ridiculous thoughts.

"No, you look perfect. It's Seattle, can you ever be underdressed for anything here?"

Steven smiled, hoping the question was rhetorical, since John ran in different circles than he did. "Do I need anything?"

"No, not even a jacket, if you're feeling brave. It's unseasonably warm out."

His wallet and keys were on the kitchen counter. Steven grabbed them. "Ready?"

John nodded and followed Steven out, his fingers brushing lightly over the nape of Steven's neck as Steven locked the door.

"I am pleased to see you," John said, standing close as Steven turned around.

"Yes, me too," Steven fumbled out. He couldn't remember the last time a guy made him feel this giddy, joyous anxiety. Maybe not since his junior year in high school when he and his first boyfriend had finally confessed their feelings to each other. "Where are we going?"

"The Dahlia Lounge. Have you been?"

"No, but I've heard good things." Steven followed John to the black Lexus. John opened the door for him. "Thank you," Steven said, moving toward the car, but John caught him and kissed him again. Just a brush of his lips, but Steven could feel heat in it, intention. He wanted to push against John right there and beg John to touch him. His dick twitched with interest at the idea, but John was getting into the car.

They talked easily on the drive downtown about the friends they were meeting and how John knew them. John drove with his right hand mostly on the gear shift, but at every stop light he rested it on Steven's knee. That gentle pressure was making it tough for Steven to pay attention to anything else. It was such a casual gesture, and yet it felt both possessive and like a question or an invitation. A sure sign that John was interested in being more than Steven's friend, though their conversation the day before had already confirmed that.

The restaurant was dark, with lanterns strung everywhere and lots of shiny wood. It was much nicer than the places Steven usually went, but most everyone was dressed in jeans. Typical Seattle, like John said.

John's friends were already seated in a large booth toward the back. James was John's age, maybe older, with a grey beard and tweed blazer like a professor; his partner Ken was perhaps slightly younger—his Korean features made it hard to tell. He shared a strange similarity with James, the way couples do when they'd been together so long that they'd taken on each other's mannerisms and speech patterns. Nick was younger, in his late twenties or early thirties. Steven thought maybe he'd seen him before, probably at Neighbours or some club. He wore a white t-shirt and black leather blazer, his black hair stylishly spikey.

"This is so exciting," Nick said, as he pulled out the chair next to his for Steven. "John's birthday and we're the ones getting a treat."

Steven raised an eyebrow John, who was settling in across the table. "It's your birthday?"

"Oh, it's surprises all around tonight, is it? I'm just glad you finally had time to see us," Nick teased.

John smiled, his eyes glittering, like Nick was a child he indulged. "Well, perhaps if you don't embarrass me, I'll come more often."

"I'm certain one of us will find a way to embarrass you. What's the fun of meeting your friend if we don't?" Ken winked at Steven, letting him in on a joke. "John and James went to college together. We've heard all the stories—" Ken nodded to include Nick "—but new blood is an open invitation for James to tell them all over again."

"Telling me stories about John is an excellent idea," Steven said.

"Good. We'll need drinks first. Liquor makes him more likely to spill the good parts." Ken gently elbowed James as he said it, and James laughed.

The menu was overwhelming. When Nick suggested ordering a bottle of wine for the table, Steven agreed, glad to have that decision taken away from him.

The conversation was friendly and easy. Nick grilled him about school, and talked at length about the company he worked for, doing database programming for another company that made computer encyclopedias. James came through with stories while they ate amazing food, much more elaborately plated than anything Steven had seen before, leaving him a bit out of his depth.

Whenever Steven looked, John was watching him, offering a suggestion, a smile, a compliment, redirecting conversations and generally making Steven feel at ease in the unfamiliar surroundings. Their feet bumped beneath the table. Steven stretched, hoping for more. When dessert was served, an amazing coconut cream pie, he was rewarded with John's ankle pressed against his. The connection was electric, simmering in Steven as he hoped it was a promise of more touches later.

Steven was warm with laughter and wine by the time they stood on the street saying their goodbyes.

"So please call me this week, Steven, and I'll have some leads for you," Nick said, wrapping both hands around Steven's as they shook. "Maybe you'll get lucky and you can come work with me. As far as I can tell, we'd be lucky to have you."

"You haven't seen my work yet, but I'm grateful for the leads. Any help I can get at this point."

"Then make sure you call me first," Ken put in, "I'll help you get that resume whipped into shape. There's a few secrets I know." Ken patted him on the shoulder. "Get my number from John. Really, call tomorrow if you like. I'm glad to help."

"Thank you, I really appreciate it."

James took Steven's hand in a warm, friendly shake. With a fatherly hand on Steven's should, he leaned in close and said quietly into Steven's ear, "John looks happier than I've seen him in a decade. I hope you're the cause of that." He stepped back. "Looking forward to seeing you again, Steven," he added more loudly.

36.
Discovery

ON THE DRIVE HOME, JOHN'S hand only left Steven's knee when he had to shift gears. The drive back up the hill was too quick in the light Sunday traffic.

"Can I walk you to your door?" John asked as he found an astonishingly good parking place in front of Steven's building.

"Yes, please."

Steven, aware of the neighbors' lighted windows as they walked quietly across the courtyard, spoke softly, "You can, um, you're welcome to come in."

He fumbled for his keys as they got to his door. He focused on getting it unlocked while he waited for John to answer. John's hand closed over his as Steven turned the knob. John stood close enough that Steven could feel the heat of his skin.

"Are you asking me in to be polite, or because you'd really like me to come in?"

"I'd very much like you to come in," Steven said, leaning in so that his lips brushed John's. Their hands still entwined on the knob, John pushed the door open, backing Steven into the apartment as he covered Steven's mouth in a deep kiss.

Steven sank into the sensation of the kiss, John's hot and soft mouth, forgetting everything else. His head spun, pleasant dizziness tipping his balance until he wasn't clear which way was up, but John's hands held him as they fumbled into the apartment, the door closing behind them.

Steven pushed his body into John's heat, offering his body up, finally finding his back against a wall with John pressing closely against him as the kiss deepened. Steven ground against John's hip, hard already. He whimpered when John broke the kiss and pressed his face into Steven's neck, breathing heavily.

"It was a terrible idea to take you out with friends," John said, pulling back to look at Steven.

"Oh?"

"I didn't get to talk to you enough. Your attention was always elsewhere."

"You have my attention now."

Neither moved or spoke for a second. Desire hung between them, pulsing with the sound of their breathing. Steven boldly thrust his hips forward again, into the firm muscle of John's thigh and shivered at the pressure on his dick.

John threaded his fingers through Steven's hair, turning him until their eyes met. "You have to tell me, Steven, what you want tonight."

Steven grinned, feeling a little urgent mania in it. "It's your birthday. What do you want?"

"My birthday isn't actually until tomorrow, but my wish is for you to tell me what you need, what I can give you."

"Fuck, I want you so badly. I need you to touch me." Steven's breath sped up, dizzy at the idea of John giving him whatever he needed.

"How far do you want this to go? This is only our first date."

Steven laughed, the sound coming out strangled and desperate. "This is a year's worth of pent-up longing. I don't care what date it is. I just need you to touch me. I want to please you." Steven put it out there, how he'd do anything for John, to please him.

John's answering laugh was smooth and warm, his hand sliding to cup the back of Steven's head. He tipped Steven back, looming with his slight height advantage. John captured Steven's mouth again, his tongue pressing for entry. Steven eagerly surrendered to it, opening his mouth and letting John lead. He slipped his hand into John's jacket.

John's heat under his soft t-shirt pulled another desperate sound from Steven's lips. Steven tugged at the shirt, wanting more contact. John stepped back to give him room, though he brought his other hand to Steven's jaw, keeping them close even as the kiss slowed.

John licked lightly over Steven's lips. Steven opened his eye, still dizzy, as if he hung between awake and asleep, between his year of fantasies and his new reality. His heart was pounding so hard that he felt sure this must be real.

John's skin was warm under his hands, and Steven skated his palms over all he could reach: the smooth muscles of John's back, the faint ridges of his sides, down his waist, trying to memorize it all before John's kiss made him forget where he was again.

They moved together easily. Steven arched into the touch as John's fingers stroked Steven's neck. Deeper longing bloomed in his chest when John nipped at Steven's lower lip. When Steven rubbed against John's thigh, the sensation contrasted sharply with the rolling waves of pleasure, making Steven very aware of how he wanted to be *taken* rather than just fucking. Steven's hand drifted to John's hips and pulled their bodies tighter together, discovering John's need was as pressing as Steven's.

"Oh god," he whispered into John's mouth, "You're hard for me." Steven wiggled, wedging his thigh between John's. John thrust slowly back against him. Steven, high with the pleasure of it, licked a line up John's neck, needing to engage all his senses.

"You're incredibly sexy, Steven. It's been torture all night, watching you put things into your gorgeous mouth, watching you pay attention to everyone else at the table." John's words, hot in Steven's ear, motivated him to get them quickly to more comfort, less clothing.

"We should be not standing here. Bed," Steven insisted, pushing with his hips to bring them closer to his bedroom door.

John released him, but kept a hand on the small of Steven's back as they entered the room. Steven flicked on the lights and sat down on his bed to untie his Doc Marten's with clumsy fingers. John got down on one knee in front of him and made quick work of the laces on the other boot, pulling it off and setting both boots to the side. He kissed Steven, then stood and toed off his own loafers, putting them next to Steven's boots.

John towered over him, his dick nearly at face level. Steven watched as John adjusted himself, his fingers trailing briefly over his own hard length in his jeans. He licked his lips and looked up further to find John's hot gaze on him as John slipped off his jacket and laid it over the back of a chair. Eyes full of dirty promise locked on Steven, breaking his scrutiny only to pull off his t-shirt and set it with the jacket.

Steven admired the fine tangle of dark and light hair on John's chest, his stomach tight and flat, the vee of his pelvic bones visible where his jeans rode low. John stepped in close, looking almost straight down at Steven now. Steven wanted to mouth the erection in John's jeans. Feel the heat of it under the denim, leave a sloppy wet spot to show he'd been there. His breath hitched as he thought of his mouth on John's cock.

Steven reached for the top button on his shirt and started to undo it, but John pushed his hands away.

"No, you're mine to unwrap," John said, his voice thick and deep. He stepped in closer, bending down to reach Steven's buttons. Steven tipped forward and opened his mouth against John's denim-covered bulge.

"Fuck," John gasped, pushing against the contact, his fingers still awkwardly opening Steven's shirt. Steven let his saliva soak through John's jeans, working his mouth up and down the length, feeling it get harder for him. When he undid the last button, John rested his hands on Steven's shoulders. Encouraged, Steven pulled his mouth off John and reached for the button on his jeans. He paused, looking up, needing to see John's desire.

"Can I?" He asked, feeling shy. The urge to ask for permission was unexpected, but felt right with John's earlier question about what Steven wanted.

John skimmed his hand up Steven's neck and cupped his jaw. "How far do you want this to go, Steven? Are you just going to suck my cock? Tell me what you want." John's voice rasped deeper, his obvious need scraping the words down. Steven wanted to learn how to bring that sound forward as often as he could.

Steven licked his lips. "I need your dick. I want to taste it." He watched intently for John's reaction, pleased with

John's acknowledging nod, his slightly parted lips, red from the crush of their kisses.

John asked, "And then?"

"I want you to fuck me." Steven shivered, surprised at his forwardness. He'd never been this direct with his desires. *I want you to fuck me* asked for so much more than *let's fuck.* Steven knew that John wanted him to be explicit about his desire. Exposed already, there was a raw freedom in being so plain-spoken that gave Steven the power to ask, for the first time, for what he really wanted. Still the words came out low and broken. "Hard so I know how much you want me. Please tell me what to do, show me how to please you. Hold me down and make me feel you."

John traced his thumb over Steven's mouth, his expression a heady mix of fondness and pure lust. He knelt down in front of Steven, Steven's thighs bracketing John's hips, their faces even.

"Oh god, I want you," John whispered and kissed Steven softly. "I want you," he said, louder, more firmly, as he pulled back to see Steven's face, "to be a desperate, needy mess who can't think of anything but me and how good I make you feel."

Steven let out a choked whimper. He cleared his throat and bravely held John's eyes with his own. "That's me already, every time I see you. You don't even have to touch me to make me feel like that."

"Good." John smiled, tracing Steven's mouth again. He stood up and undid his jeans, pushing them down until his cock was free and hanging in front of Steven's face. Steven licked the head, craning to look up at John, to know he was watched.

John's expression, a mix of awe and satisfaction, made Steven quiver, acutely aware of his own cock trapped in his jeans. Steven licked wetly over his own palm and wrapped it around the base of John's dick, closing his lips over the head. Steven sucked slowly, feeling the silken skin of John's dick and savoring the salty taste that was just John.

Steven pushed down as far as he could, taking John into his throat and pulling back, doing it over again. Gripping the base as he pulled back, Steven eagerly stroked his tongue down John's length.

John rested his hand on Steven's head while Steven worked. His fingers tangled in Steven's hair, he stroked over the back of his skull. Steven's dick throbbed at the contact, at the control. Trying to be as careful of his teeth as possible, Steven's arousal surged higher as John took charge, leisurely fucking Steven's mouth. He reached under Steven's chin, pressing his thumb and middle finger gently into the hinges of Steven's jaw, opening his mouth so he could push his cock deeper in.

"God, you're beautiful," John said, letting go of Steven's hair and tracing his fingers over Steven's lips as they stretched over his cock. He pumped in a couple more times and then pulled all the way out, releasing Steven's jaw, leaving him moaning and straining forward for more.

John tipped Steven's face up, watching him as he pushed his thumb into Steven's mouth. Steven bit it gently, then sucked it in, working it wetly like he had John's cock.

"I want you to say 'stop' if I do anything you don't want. I don't want to push you too far. So you have to tell me when something is too much, okay?"

Steven nodded against John's grip on his chin.

"Tell me what you're going to do if you're uncomfortable." He pulled his thumb out of Steven's mouth and looked at him expectantly.

"I'll tell you to stop if I don't like something." Steven replied. Though he could not imagine a single thing John could do to him that he wouldn't like, anxiety crept in under his arousal. Mixed together with his excitement at how dominant John appeared to be, Steven's stomach fluttered. Every word from John was a step into a world Steven was anxious to get to the center of, so he could find the secret to pleasing John and find a place where he'd be brave enough to give his pleasure over completely to another person.

"Good. Take off your shirt and get on your knees," John instructed.

Steven complied as gracefully as he could, feeling the blood rush down as he stood up and pulled off his open shirt, tossing it behind him. He knelt as directed, reaching for John's cock again, but John pushed his hand away.

"Just your mouth. Open your jeans and stroke your dick while you suck me."

Steven sighed in pleasure at the command. He carefully slid his mouth around the head of John's cock while he unzipped his jeans and pushed them down his hips. A closed circuit of pleasure rippled through him, connecting his hand on his own dick to his mouth on John's.

Steven was going to come too quickly, he knew, but he didn't care. He felt charmed, protected, like anything that happened now was right, whatever it was. He was in John's hands, and that was all he needed.

John was vocal as Steven sucked him, moaning and sighing. He stroked Steven's hair and cupped his face, directing him as he chose. Steven relaxed into it, following the pace that John set.

Time stretched and bent as Steven's focus narrowed to only John's cock. Disoriented, Steven acted slowly when John asked him to stand up. John kissed him fiercely, backing him up until the edge of the bed hit Steven's calves and John tumbled them both down on to it.

John's weight on him as they kissed was both comforting and sexy. Steven whimpered softly at the loss of it as John moved down his body to kneel at the edge of the bed and strip off Steven's jeans.

"You aren't wearing any underwear," John observed, sounding both pleased and scolding. "Is that for me, or is that your normal state?"

"For you."

"So you expected this tonight?"

"No, I hoped."

Happy at having given the right answer, Steven smiled back at John and watched him stand up to shuck his own jeans off before crawling back over Steven, straddling his waist this time.

"Do you trust me, Steven?" John asked from above him.

Steven trembled faintly, the mixed anxiety and eagerness rolling forward again with another opportunity to give up control. Pinned to the bed, John's hot bare skin against his, Steven took a breath, keeping his eyes on John's, and feeling relieved and ready, gave up a little more.

"Yes."

John rewarded him with a kiss, pulling back when Steven arched up for more. His mouth close by Steven's ear, John asked, "Do you like to play rough? Or keep it sweet? Are you a top or a bottom?" He sat back after he asked, his eyes on Steven, his weight balanced back on his legs so he wasn't crushing Steven as he straddled his hips.

"Bottom." Steven licked his lips nervously. He'd never said it out loud before, hadn't known for sure until this minute. Before he'd gone along with his partners, whatever they wanted most, but was always vaguely disappointed when they asked to be fucked. Topping felt amazing to do, but opening for and taking in another person made Steven hot in a way that he couldn't explain, that he'd never examined closely.

John nodded at Steven's answer, like he'd expected as much, but didn't say anything, just waited for the rest of Steven's answer.

"And, I like sweet, but..." Steven trailed off, uncertainty twisting in his chest.

"But what?"

"I think I like rough, too."

John's patient expression cracked into a smile. "Then we'll have to try everything and see what you like most."

"Yes, please."

John scooted up, his knees coming down to press Steven's upper arms against the bed, pinning him in place, his weight settling over Steven's upper chest. "Lick my balls and my cock," John said. "I already think you like that, but let's be sure."

His arms trapped, Steven had little leverage but he did his best, laving his tongue over John's balls, carefully taking each one into his mouth and sucking it. John shifted his hips gracefully, giving Steven more access as he bent his neck to reach as much of John's dick as he could, licking and kissing it open-mouthed until his chin was as wet as John's cock.

Steven focused on doing the best job he could. John assisted, directing his dick down so Steven could suck the head, thrusting when he wanted more, pulling back occasionally and making Steven work for it.

Steven reveled in John's scent, his weight, his power. Steven's own erection was hard, flat against his belly, throbbing with his pulse as Steven tried his best to relax his throat so John could fuck his mouth deeper. He felt super-attuned to John's breath, hearing him speed up when he did a good job. He was elated when John let out a series of staccato moans in time with his thrusts into Steven's mouth. It was bewildering when John finally freed Steven's mouth and lifted off him. He felt unmoored as if John's weight had been anchoring him to reality.

"Let's see what else you like, beautiful boy," John said, stretching his length over Steven, anchoring him again with rough kisses. Steven responded eagerly, letting John plunder his mouth. "Your lips are so red," John said pulling back. "You look amazing like this."

Then John's weight was gone again, taking the gentle feeling of security with it. Fretful, Steven lifted his head and watched John settle on his knees at the bottom edge of the bed. He put his hands behind Steven's knees and pressed back, forcing Steven's legs up, thighs pressing onto his chest, knees at his shoulders. Steven felt spread, exposed. John's securing, firm grip behind Steven's knees made his cock throb more, pre-come leaking onto his abdomen. Though he wanted to be touched so desperately, Steven reveled in the depth of his own need. He wanted to stretch it, make it last.

"Please," he whispered, not sure if John could even hear him. John ducked down. Steven let his head fall back against the pillow, sure that John was finally going to touch his neglected dick.

Steven bucked up in surprise when John's tongue ran over his hole, all wet heat and amazing sweet slickness.

"Oh, you like that." John's voice held a smile as his hot breath tickled Steven's tender skin. John tightened his grip on Steven's thighs, pressing him back into the bed.

"No one's ever—I haven't done this before."

A pleased hum vibrated over Steven's exposed ass, making him shudder. "No one?" John asked. "Well, lucky me. Lucky you." And then his tongue was back on the incredibly sensitive skin around Steven's hole. He lapped, teased, and tickled until Steven was trying desperately to buck up for more, as John held him down.

Steven cried out, gripping John's head as John pushed the tip of his tongue into Steven's entrance. John worried at the tight muscle until Steven relaxed, opening for him as much as he could, marveling at the intimate sensation of being pressed so open.

Lightheaded and feeling so sexy, Steven tried again and again to shift his hips for more contact. When John changed direction, licking Steven's balls and then closing his mouth over the head of Steven's cock, Steven bit his own lip hard, clutching at the sheets, trying not to come right away.

John sucked his dick in deep, pulling up in rapid strokes and going back down in slow, wet ones; every time the rhythm was nearly enough to make Steven come, John would find a new target, driving Steven to edge of tolerance. Crying out in desperate frustration, Steven was tantalizingly dragged along the edge of his orgasm; he could feel it like a weight in his balls, curling in his lower belly.

John released Steven's thighs and his legs fell open, relaxing as John gripped Steven's wet cock tightly and slid his mouth over the head again. The shocking rush of pleasure ripped the last of Steven's control away, like a rug suddenly pulled out from under him.

Steven tumbled into the shifting blue undertow of his orgasm. The wide ocean of it was rushing in his ears, his heart pounding as he thrust into the slick heat of John's mouth. Come pulsed through him, his thoughts a white void, every other need and memory pushed down by the waves of pleasure.

Breathing ragged and loud in his own ears, Steven gradually returned to awareness at the sensation of John's hands caressing him as he crawled up to kiss Steven. Some of his come was still in John's mouth, and Steven lapped at it, swallowing it, surprised at how sexy it was. One more thing he'd never done, his dick twitching too soon at the unexpectedly illicit thrill of it.

"Mmmm, he likes that too," John said, breaking the kiss. *"Une petite salope." Dirty boy.*

Steven felt wild at how pleased John sounded with him. Even after coming so fucking hard, he still wanted to be dirty for John, to please him. The desire for it filled Steven like an ache, an emptiness only John could fill.

"I want you to fuck me, please, John," Steven begged, his arms around John, holding them together.

"Do you have condoms?"

"Under the bed, the left side." Steven released John from his tight hug, so he could reach for them.

"Are you sure?" John asked, coming back to straddle Steven again after he'd retrieved the condoms.

"Yes."

John traced his fingers down Steven's chest, leaning over him as he did, and following with his lips. He planted firm kisses across his lower abdomen. Steven twisted, trying to see as John wet his fingers in his mouth and then slipped them into the crack of Steven's ass, slick with saliva. He pushed one in. Steven inhaled sharply and turned away as John quickly breached the tight ring of muscle.

"All right?" John asked, pausing.

"More," Steven gasped.

John worked slowly, sometimes leaning down to lick and spit around where his finger breached Steven's body. When he finally added a second finger, Steven reached down and clutched at John's wrist, trying to force him faster, deeper.

"Hands behind your head," John commanded. Steven complied, whimpering.

He defiantly bucked his hips up against John's careful strokes, panting and whispering, "Please more," until John added a third finger.

Strung out with need, Steven couldn't have enough of John. John's fingers and tongue felt amazing, but he wanted more. Steven was twisting and trembling, begging without words when John finally sat back and tore open a condom, quickly rolling it on to his dick. Steven was taut with electrical excitement as John tapped his erection against Steven's ass.

"Is this what you want? Are you ready?"

"Yes, please, oh god, please."

"How do you want it? On your side? I think that might be easiest for you."

"No, please, I want to see you. Need you."

John looked at him appraisingly and smiled indulgently, his own need darkening his gaze. "Okay, because you've been so good, keeping your hands where I told you."

Already overwrought, Steven gasped and cried out when John finally pushed inside of him. Steven shoved his hips up hard, trying to take back some control when John slowed, giving Steven time to adjust to the intrusion. John took the hint and worked back to a steady rhythm.

"Please, please, can I touch you?" Steven begged, filled so completely by John, but needing more contact.

"Yes, you've been so good, you can have whatever you want now," John said, breathless, leaning down to lick Steven's nipple.

Steven let his hands roam all over John, tracing the muscles in his back as they bunched and released with John's thrusts, scraping his nails over John's nipples. He ran his hands across the soft curve of John's ass over and over before gripping it and pulling John deeper into him. John's thrusts sped up then, pounding deeper, and Steven could only hold on and keep begging for more.

The sound of his own voice was strange in Steven's ears as he demanded *more, harder, take me, want you, oh god,* over and over. He needed to make John come with his body, to make John lose control too. Pulse pounding in his ears,

Steven lifted his hips, pushing back, forcing John deeper with each hard thrust.

They rocked together, pure need overriding everything. Their skins, slick with sweat, slipped against each other. Steven dug his fingers into John's hips, keeping them together, making as many points of contact as possible. He found John's mouth again and he pushed his tongue out, letting John suck it for a second before their tongues were twisting over each other. Steven panted for air when they came apart, foreheads still touching, both thrumming with the same steady rhythm that John pounded into him.

"You're so fucking tight, I'm gonna come. Can't stop, gonna come."

"Come on me, please, please, John." Something Steven had never asked for, never realized he desired. He wanted to be marked, to see John's release, to know he was responsible for it.

"Fuck fuck fuck." John's face was twisted in a tight grimace as he pulled back and stripped off the condom. He fisted his cock fast between Steven's legs and came hard over his hand, Steven's stomach, and dick. John collapsed down on him, not catching his own weight, but Steven absorbed it, loving how hard John's breath rushed through him, rejoicing in the sweat-slick touch of their hot skin. Steven was hard again now, so turned on by having made John look like that, having seen him come apart.

John lifted his weight off Steven and rolled to his side. Steven followed, keeping their bodies together as he embraced John, thrusting his cock into the sticky mess between them. He found John's mouth and kissed him fiercely, eager with renewed need.

"Ah, the resilience of youth," John laughed, still breathless as he reached between them and gripped Steven's dick. "Are you going to come for me again, you beautiful boy? What do you need, to come for me?"

"Fingers," Steven gritted out, thrusting into John's fist.

John pushed Steven's shoulder, shoving him onto his back again. He spit on his hand and slipped two fingers easily into Steven's ass and thrust them in time with the hard strokes on Steven's cock.

Steven rocked his hips into it, panting, begging wordlessly, just moans now. His orgasm coiled tightly in his spine already. He'd never been this hard, this needy before, not after he'd already come once. John's face was close, watching Steven with awe and determination.

"Your mouth is so red and pretty, I can't wait to have it on my dick again. God, you were so fucking tight and hot, Steven, and such a good boy. Are you going to be good and come for me again, come with my fingers in your ass?"

"Yes, please, oh god, please, want to come." Steven let the tension arch his body up, opening for John and pushing his dick into John's blissfully tight grip.

"So perfect, the way you begged for my cock. You wanted it so bad, didn't you?"

Steven couldn't answer, crying out as his second orgasm of the night tugged at his balls and bloomed up his spine. Pinpoints of light spiked behind his eyes as he shuddered through it, aware only of John's hands, the sound of his voice deeper, gentler; then calming as Steven came out the other side, panting and still feeling desperate.

John slowly pulled his fingers out and tugged Steven close to him, murmuring into Steven's hair as they curled together.

His breathing finally slowed, Steven was nearly asleep when John whispered next to him, asking for a towel.

"Let's get you cleaned up, *chéri*, then you can sleep."

Steven stumbled after John into the bathroom. He leaned one hand on the tub's edge as John wiped over him with a warm wash cloth and then rinsed it and cleaned himself. He kissed Steven gently.

"All done. You need some water too."

"Glass by the bed."

John nodded and followed Steven back to the bedroom. Steven lay down and listened as John filled the glass, drank it, and filled it again. The bed dipped next to him. John's hand was warm on his back.

"Okay, drink this, then you can sleep."

"Are you going to stay?" Steven asked, sitting up and taking the glass.

"Do you want me too?"

"Please, yes."

Their legs twined together as John's chest pressed tightly against Steven's back, his fingers caressing Steven's chest and hips as Steven tried to stay awake so he could keep this feeling. But it was too good, too calming. He was so spent from coming so hard that he drifted off quickly with John's breath against his neck. He tumbled into soft dreams, always aware of the warmth of John's body next to him.

◊

"Hey, mon pt'it rouquin."

Steven felt the warm press of lips by his ear and opened his eyes to find John leaning over him, rather than curled next to him.

"I'm pleased to find enough in your fridge to make omelets. May I?"

"Oh god, you're amazing," Steven answered, fully awake. "Are you even real? Am I dreaming you?"

John kissed him again, on the mouth this time. "Definitely real," he said. "It'll take me a bit, so shower or go back to sleep or whatever. I'll come get you when it's ready."

The shower was hot for once, the old plumbing in Steven's building cooperating. To keep the perfect morning going, when he got out of the shower, he put Madonna's "Into the Groove" on the turntable and was shimmying into a pair of electric blue briefs as the beat kicked in. He danced across to his dresser and pulled out a pair of jeans so worn they'd long since gone a pale shade that was barely recognizable as blue. He danced into them. As he buttoned them, he heard a noise and turned to find John leaning in the doorway, watching him.

"Come dance with me," he said, beckoning with his finger.

John hesitated for a minute then moved toward Steven, fitting his hands on Steven's hips, his thigh between Steven's.

He moved effortlessly with John, grinding them together with the same beautifully synchronized rhythm they'd had in bed last night.

As they danced, Steven sang the lyrics about fantasies softly into John's ear, and John laughed, a deep, scraping chuckle. "No, *fraisier,* you already are all of my fantasies come true. Let me make all yours come true now."

Steven pressed his face into John's neck, seeking reassurance over and over that this was real. "My first fantasy involves having a handsome man cook for me," Steven said.

"Then I hope I prove worthy. It's on the table already."

"I don't know what I did to deserve you exactly, but I hope I keep doing it."

John nuzzled in and kissed behind Steven's ear. "If I make you look this happy, I hope I keep doing it, too," John said softly into Steven's ear. "*You look beautiful like this,*" he continued in French and Steven shivered at the intimacy of it, a secret only they shared.

37.
A Lucky Boy

"So, this is kind of a crazy crowd." Ryan sipped his drink, looking around the room. Steven followed his gaze as Ryan took in all the unlikely conversational pairings around them.

"Yep." Steven considered how much he'd need to drink to feel comfortable in this room and decided that alcohol poisoning probably wasn't worth it. "My mom insisted I invite all my friends, so I did. But she wasn't forthcoming on just how many people she was inviting. I guess I should have figured it out when she wanted to do it graduation weekend, so my grandfather could be here." Steven looked past the crowd of cousins in the dining room to the couch where his *Papi* was deep in conversation with Finney. Steven took a healthy swallow of his drink.

"You are a braver man than I am. I would never agree to this. I would have insisted on separate parties."

"That just shows that you really are smarter." Steven reached around Ryan to the makeshift bar on the kitchen counter and poured another shot of vodka into his glass and squeezed a lime wedge in, not bothering to get the cranberry juice from the fridge. "I think my mom just wanted an excuse to meet John. I'm honestly not sure if this is more or less awkward than just going out to dinner with them."

Ryan hummed noncommittally. He leaned back against the counter and sipped his drink. They watched the weirdness quietly together, the kitchen offering a clear view of everyone in the living room and dining room, until Steven's aunt Lillian approached.

"Steven, oh honey, look at you, so grown up. Graduating from college. We couldn't be more proud!" She squeezed Steven tightly to her chest. Steven held his drink out to the side, hoping not to spill it. "Just look at you!" She exclaimed, releasing him. Her attention turned to Ryan. "So are you the boyfriend we've heard about? The man good enough to finally make our Steven settle?"

"No, ma'am, I'm just a friend. Not good enough for this one—he deserves even better." Ryan winked, then smiled kindly at Lillian. "John is his boyfriend. He's with Mrs. Frazier." Ryan indicated outside, to the deck, visible through the wide dining room windows.

Lillian's eyes followed to where Ryan was pointing with his drink. "Oh. Oh my," she said and turned to Steven smiling. "He's very handsome, isn't he? Aren't you a lucky boy." She swatted Steven's shoulder, a little too hard. Steven clutched tightly to his drink, sure that Lillian was going to send it down the front of his shirt. "And he's a little older, isn't he?" She asked, squinting toward John and Steven's mother. "Yes, a little older. Oh that must so nice for you, Steven. It's always better when they have a little experience, isn't it? Frank is ten years older than me, and I swear I married him because he was the first boy to kiss me without slobbering all over me. And the sex is just so much better when they know what they're doing. You know how it is, of course." She nudged Ryan who nodded, looking slightly terrified.

Stunned, Steven managed to murmur, "Yes, of course."

"You'll excuse me, I need to see this one up close. Find out if he smells as good as he looks." She laughed and hustled off across the room, to the deck doors on the far side of the living room. Steven watched through the windows as Lillian came around the corner to greet his mother and then shook John's hand.

"It could be worse," Ryan said.

"How?" Steven asked.

"You could be high on cocaine. Or, ooh, maybe LSD. That would make this worse."

"I'm not convinced you're right about that. At least then I'd have an excuse for feeling as weird as I do." Steven glanced around again. "This open format remodel my parents did is hell. I might actually feel better about all of this—" Steven gestured with his drink to his *Papi* Jean-Michel and Finney on the couch, Marcus and Steven's father on the chairs across from them, the clusters of his cousins crowding around the dining table stacking snacks on little plates, Rae and his aunts all standing next to the wide windows on the far side of the dining room, the whole morass of weirdness around him. "If I couldn't see them. Or at least I might care less."

"Do you need to rescue John from your aunt and mom?"

Steven bit his lip thoughtfully. "I don't know," he said finally. "But I should probably check." He finished his drink and carefully made a new one, taking the time to get the cranberry from the fridge and giving Ryan a pained look before slowly making his way across the house.

It wasn't just reticence that slowed Steven down. He had to go into the living room, go all the way around the couch to reach the deck door, and walk out to where John stood trapped between the two middle-aged suburban women.

Along the way he stopped to accept congratulations from his uncles and his parent's neighbor, Ron Forssblad. Some of his cousins crowded in, the younger ones bouncing with sugar overindulgence, and the older ones patted him on the back before he moved on.

"Cupcake!' Finney called out, as Steven tried to pass unnoticed behind the chairs where his father and Marcus sat, leaning in as they talked. Both men looked up as Finney spoke. "Come here, kid," she insisted. Steven walked over to where she patted the space on couch between herself and his *Papi*. He stood next to the arm of the couch, unwilling to get stuck in the middle of this group.

"Hey, Finney."

"Hey yourself. Why didn't you tell me your grandfather was a cranky old Canuck? I'd have been fishing for an invitation ages ago if I'd known your family was so much fun."

Jean-Michel laughed and patted Finney on the knee.

"I suspect Steven's sorry by now that he agreed to this," Steven's father said to Marcus.

"He's usually pretty good about thinking things through, but this time I'm sure he's second-guessing his choice," Marcus answered.

"I am standing right here," Steven said.

"And don't you look pretty doing it too," Finney said. "That's a fine tie. Did it come from your shop?" she asked Marcus. "I need a tie like that," she added before Marcus could answer.

"Would look very handsome on you," Jean-Michel said as the doorbell rang.

"I should get that," Steven declared, smiling brightly.

"Just looking for an excuse to get away," his father said.

"Well, it's really fucking weird over here," Steven said as he started to walk toward the door.

Behind him he heard his *Papi* Jean-Michel proudly say, "He doesn't talk in dirty words like that because he's gay. I taught him when he was eight."

"Better you than me," Steven's father said. "You know worse words than I do."

Steven tuned out the rest of the conversation, hoping some sort of salvation was on the other side of the door.

"Oh, thank god," Steven said when he found Lisa. "Please save me from these people. Or kill me. Whatever. Either way is fine."

"Well, now I'm not sure if I want to come in." Lisa peered around the door. "Looks okay to me," she decided. Steven stepped aside so she could enter.

"You can put your jacket and your bag down here," Steven said leading her down the hall, away from the crowd, to where coats where piled on his parents' bed.

"So this isn't anything," Lisa said, as she settled her things on the bed and dug into her purse, pulling out a small box she handed to Steven. "You don't have to open it now."

"What? You didn't have to get me anything, Leese. It's really enough that you came." Steven turned the box in his hands, feeling a rush of love for Lisa so strong he thought he might cry for a second. He probably had been drinking too fast. "Can I open it now?"

"If you want, it's your day."

"Well, not until tomorrow, really," Steven said as he tore open the paper. The box was leather and clearly a far nicer gift than he anticipated when he shredded the wrapping. "What is this?"

"Open it."

Inside the box was a stainless steel watch with a black face, the little red Swiss Army cross where the 12 would be. "This is too much, Lisa. Oh god, I love this watch."

"I know, I remember when we saw it at Nordstrom that day. Turn it over."

Steven pulled the watch from the box and turned it over:

SCF UofW 1992 No time better than now

He clutched the watch to his chest for a moment before putting it on.

"You might need to get the links adjusted. I wasn't totally sure about your wrist size."

Steven turned the watch. It was loose but not too loose to wear. "I love it! Thank you so much." He hugged her hard. "This is amazing, Lisa, you didn't have to do this."

"I know, sweetie, but you deserved something special. You worked so hard and I'm just so happy for you. I mean with everything, finishing school, what you've done with your life. And John. You deserve all good things happening to you, and I wanted to commemorate that for you. Plus you can't wear that ugly pink Swatch forever."

"You're going to make me cry."

"If that's true, then I need a drink to catch up to you."

"Ha, yes, sorry. But I warn you, it's kind of a gauntlet to get to the bar."

"How bad can it be?"

"You'll see," Steven said. They made their way back into the living room.

Stopping at the arm of couch again, Steven let Lisa step closer in. "This is my *Papi*, Jean-Michel Frazier. *Pere*, this is my friend Lisa."

Lisa stepped forward and shook his hand. "Nice to meet you, sir."

"I think you know everyone else."

Finney winked at Lisa. "We go way back," she said.

"Marcus," Lisa said by way of greeting. "Gerald, good to see you again." Lisa shook Steven's father's hand.

"You too. I hope you've been well," Steven's dad said.

"I have, thanks."

"Hey, is Jess coming?" Marcus asked.

"She can't. She has a hospice shift tonight she said she couldn't miss. She said we could all celebrate together later."

Steven frowned wishing Jess were here to further distract the weirdness around him.

"Sounds good," Marcus said.

"What's this hospice?" Jean-Michel asked.

"Our friend Jess does work with AIDS patients who are about to die. She reads to them and helps them out around the house if they're too sick to manage, but not so sick they need the hospital."

"Huh. She sounds like a nice girl." *Papi* Jean-Michel looked at Steven.

"But not for me," Steven said.

"Of course not for you, stupid. And this one," he patted Finney's knee, "already has a pretty girl. But what about you?" He looked expectantly at Lisa.

"What about me?" Lisa asked, looking confused.

"Do you have a pretty girl?"

"No sir, I'm single."

"But you like girls?"

Lisa nodded.

"Have you met this friend of Steven's with the care work?"

"I don't think so." Lisa looked at Steven, her eyebrows raised in question. Steven shook his head. "I haven't met her," Lisa confirmed to Jean-Michel.

"You get him to introduce you. I have feeling about this one."

"*OK, Papi*, let me get her a drink before you start match-making." Steven took Lisa's hand, "C'mon, in the kitchen."

Ryan was still leaning against the kitchen counter, next to the makeshift bar. He was deep in conversation with Steven's uncle Frank when they came in.

"Lisa!" Ryan set down his drink and reached to hug her. "Do you want a drink? I'm playing mixologist."

"And doing a good job," uncle Frank said, raising his glass.

Steven made introductions to the family in the kitchen while Ryan made Lisa's rum and Coke. Outside Steven's mom and aunt Lillian stood on either side of John, each with a hand tucked into the bend of his elbow, as if he was escorting them both somewhere. Lillian leaned in closer as she spoke and John laughed.

"I was just on my way to check on John, when you showed up. He's been stuck with my mom and aunt forever. I think he might need rescuing. Are you okay here for a minute?"

"Of course, go see your man. I'll say hi to your mom in a bit."

"Thanks, Leese."

Steven rushed past the chuckling coterie in the living room, not making eye contact lest they drag him back in.

"Hey," Steven said, smiling as he approached. "How are you guys doing out here?"

"Hey you." John's smile was like a cloud break after heavy rain, warm like unexpected sunshine. "We're having a great time. Maggie and Lillian were just telling me about the time you tried to dig a river in the side yard so that your pet hippopotamus would have a place to live. Your mother says you annexed the land as an independent country."

"He made flags for it and tacked them up all along the fence line. He was a very creative child," Lillian said, smiling at Steven as if she were doing him a kindness.

"I don't remember the flag part," Steven said, feeling the strain in his own smile.

"I think I still have one somewhere," his mother said.

"Excellent. Maybe we can save that level of reminiscing for another day? Mom, does Aunt Lillian need a new drink? Maybe you could help her? And I think Lisa wants to say hi to you."

"Oh silly," Lillian said. "Of course I need a drink, but you stay and talk to your handsome man. We've been keeping him from you long enough."

Steven's mother had the grace to give Steven a sympathetic look as she led Lillian away.

"Are you having fun?" Steven asked.

"Yes, wonderful so far. Your mother is very sweet."

"You don't know her that well yet."

John smiled indulgently. "How are you holding up?"

"Fine. Just coping by drinking too much." Steven raised his glass in a little toast. John looked amazing as always, the blue stripes in his sweater bringing out his eyes, jeans just this side of indecent. "You know when we first met, I had this fantasy—"

"Are you sure this is the place to tell me about it?" John arched an eyebrow but looked amused.

"Not that kind of fantasy, though I had plenty of those too. No, when I discovered you spoke French I thought we'd be at parties and I could slyly tell you it was time to go without other people understanding us, or ask if you need rescuing. You know, whatever the situation called for. But that won't work here, since half the people speak French."

"I'm sure you'll get plenty of chances to use that tactic in the future." John reached to hold Steven's hand and pulled it up to look when he saw the glint on Steven's wrist. "Ah, she gave it to you," he said, running his finger along the band of Steven's new watch. "I went with her to pick it up from engraving. It suits you. Classic with a twist." John looked into Steven's eyes and then kissed his fingers before releasing Steven's hand.

"I don't suppose I could convince you there's a decently private place around the corner that we could go make out?" Steven hopefully suggested.

"How much have you had to drink? And what are you drinking?" John took Steven's glass and had a sip, wincing at how strong it was. "Too many of those, *fraisier*," John said, handing the glass back, "and I won't be able to take advantage of you later."

Steven dumped the rest of his drink over the deck rail, and John laughed.

"I'm ready to go now. We can get this 'taking advantage' thing started sooner that way." Steven moved in closer to John. The sex they'd been having the last few weeks was intense and intimate in ways Steven hadn't known was possible. John set clear boundaries about work and life and the time they spent together, but if Steven had a choice, he'd forgo food, sleep, and his entire social life if it meant more time in bed with John. He imagined the newness of it was some of that. Perhaps over time, he'd have enough of John so he wouldn't always feel so desperate for more. Right now, Steven was always ready to leave whenever he was in favor of being alone with John's hands on him.

"Too early, I think. I haven't yet heard stories about you from all your family members," John said, looking sorry to disappoint Steven and yet also gleeful at the prospect of Steven's humiliating history as told by his family.

Deflated, Steven asked, "Do I even want to know what my mom told you?"

"I know that you did quite an impressive job of peeing on the ceiling regularly during diaper changes, going so far as pull off the extra diaper your mom laid over you. Even her preventative methods didn't stop you. And let's see. You refused to wear pants for several months when you were three, unless your mother sang to you first. Hmmm," John tapped his finger against his lips thoughtfully. "You cried through your second grade class play but wouldn't get off the stage and—"

"You can just stop there. I get the idea. Christ, why did I agree to this party again?" Steven complained.

"Because you love all these people, and they wanted a chance to celebrate you."

"I'm not sure that's working out so well for me."

"I can promise you that your night will end well." Heat flickered in John's eyes, and his gaze moved down to Steven's mouth and back up.

"How well?"

"I want make you come so hard that you can't remember your own name." John's tongue darted out, slightly wetting his lips, like another dirty promise.

Steven groaned. "Are you sure we can't leave now?"

"Not yet. Some things are worth waiting for. What's going on in the living room?" John redirected the conversation, but traced his thumb over Steven's lips before pulling his hand back and putting it in his pocket, as if he needed to stop himself.

Knowing there was no way to convince John once he'd made up his mind, Steven returned to the present. "It's horrible. Like a car crash you can't look away from. I think Finney and *mon Papi* have become best friends."

"Now that I can't miss." John held out his hand. Steven took it, feeling the heat of John's skin and hoping to feel it all over his body later. Their shoulders touched, hands clasped, as they headed into the fray together. Steven was acutely aware of how lucky he was.

In the living room, Lisa sat between Finney and *Papi* Jean-Michel. Ryan perched on the arm of Marcus's chair.

"Hey," Steven's dad said, "you're just in time. Jean-Michel was just telling us about teaching Steven to ride a bike."

"Yes," Jean-Michel said, "John, you should hear. I think the ladies will scoot a little, come sit by me."

"Perfect," John said, "just what I wanted. Do you mind?" John asked Steven softly.

"Of course not," Steven said releasing John's hand.

Steven looked around the room, not paying attention to the story. His mother and Lillian came in and stood near Jean-Michel listening. Even with the indignity of having his childhood publicly rehashed, it was a room full of love. Steven was overwhelmed by his own good fortune again. Not just for finding John, but for everyone, his friends and family. It was incredible to be able to bring John here and share this.

"C'mon, son," his dad said, breaking his reverie. He patted the arm of his chair for Steven to sit on. "Join us, you don't want to miss this."

Steven sat, not completely listening, feeling lucky simply to be present.

38.
Shooting Star

Hᴀɴᴅꜱ ꜱᴛʀᴇᴛᴄʜᴇᴅ ᴀʙᴏᴠᴇ ʜɪꜱ ʜᴇᴀᴅ, knees wide apart, and feet flat on the bed, Steven arched up, trying take to more of John's fingers inside him. He gripped his own wrist, anchoring himself in his body. He was so close to losing control that he truly felt like he might fly apart.

John pumped three fingers into his ass, just deep enough to brush his prostate on every stroke but not enough to bring the relief that Steven's body craved. Steven lifted his hips higher, trying to get enough purchase to thrust back.

"So needy," John murmured, slowing his strokes when Steven tried to get more.

Frustrated, Steven tossed his head on the pillow. "Need more," he gritted out.

John stroked his free hand on Steven's abdomen, tantalizingly close to Steven's rock-hard cock, but not giving any satisfaction. Steven twisted his hips, wanting to force John to touch him, but with his hands still above his head he couldn't get enough traction to be effective.

"Tell me what you want," John demanded. The request added to Steven's frustration. John wouldn't let him get away with an easy answer, Steven would have to have a specific detailed response. Rationally, Steven knew this always made the sex better between them, more perfect, more intimate. But he was so far past rational right now, he wanted to just beg until John let him come, so he tried that.

"Want to come, need you closer." It wasn't enough, Steven knew, but he hoped John would give into him.

"Hmm, that's all?" John asked, the amusement in his voice clear.

"Please," Steven answered, stubbornly hoping for quick release.

Steven whimpered and closed his eyes as John removed his fingers and shifted on the bed. In the dark, his breath loud in his own ears, Steven felt John's weight move over him and settle on him. He opened his eyes to John straddling his thighs. John reached for the lube on the side table and squeezed some into his hand, holding it for a second to warm it before he closed his slippery hand around Steven's dick. Steven cried out at the slick contact, wanting to thrust into John's not-quite-tight-enough grip, to get more friction. But John's weight held him to the bed, and Steven's hands were still above his head. John hadn't given him permission to move them.

"Love to see you like this," John said, his expression softened with fond affection.

"Tell me," Steven answered. Every night with John had eroded his shyness. He could ask for anything now, enjoyed hearing every dirty thought John had about him.

"Stretched out in my bed, so eager to come." John continued his too gentle wet strokes on Steven's cock. "The high flush across your cheekbones and down your chest from exertion and desperation. So responsive to every touch, and still being so good." John reached up with his free hand and ran his fingers over Steven's own hands, held above his head. "Being so careful to do exactly as I say. You've gotten so good at waiting for me to tell you what to do." He traced his fingers down Steven's arm and across his jaw. Steven licked at the pad of John's thumb as it ran over his lips. John settled his palm at the base of Steven's throat, thumb, and forefinger along the bones of Steven's clavicle. No pressure or grip, just weight of his hand resting there as John looked him over intently, taking in the way his ribs flexed with each breath, the tense muscles of his stomach and finally his stiff prick, shiny with lube and half hidden in John's large hand. John's gaze followed the path back until he met Steven's eyes.

"You like being looked at, don't you?" John squeezed Steven's cock too quickly before returning to his slow strokes.

"Yes. Especially when it's just you."

"I don't think I'd want anyone else to see you like this. This is only for me, making you look like you're about come apart." John laughed as if the idea was so ridiculous he couldn't keep it in. "No, don't want to share you at all." He stroked harder, pressing his thumb in the sensitive vee at the head of Steven's dick, then rubbed his thumb over the whole head before repeating the whole delicious action again.

"Don't want anyone else," Steven said, his voice breaking as his breath hitched with John's attentions. "Nobody's ever been as good as you." Steven's voice was clearer but he could still hear the whimper of need in it.

"I could happily spend a whole day learning every freckle, every scar you have, and then do it all over again the next day," John said before coming down, slightly awkwardly, to plunder Steven's mouth with a possessive kiss. Steven melted into it, pleasure from it rushing down his spine to pool low in his belly. John's hand on Steven's dick sped up, the sweet wet grip tightening as it slipped repeatedly over the head. Steven panted when John broke the kiss. Steven's arousal was expanding, racing along his nerves, like the tide rushing in to cover his body.

"You have been so good, so patient," John said, sitting back on his heels again, his weight still holding Steven's thighs to the bed. "Tell me what you want now. Do you want to come?" John jerked him harder, just the tight circle of his thumb and forefinger over and over, barely any distance down the shaft, just tightly teasing the head.

Pleasure spread through Steven's belly, across his lower back. He was so close, the right turn of hand and word from John, maybe a finger in Steven's ass, and he'd be coming. But this felt so good, hanging in the balance of not quite coming and coming.

"Yes," Steven said wanting more of this sensation. "No, no," he protested when John's full hand closed around him again.

"Which is it, *Amour?*" John asked, his hand stilling but not releasing Steven.

"No, don't want to come yet. Not yet. Feels so good."

John stroked over Steven's dick once more, then dropped his hand down to gather Steven's balls. He lifted them up, against Steven's shaft, and circled his thumb and forefinger around the base of both.

"Look how hard you are."

Steven bent his neck and looked down his body. John's grip had Steven's cock jutting straight up, perpendicular to his body. It was wet and red, pulsing gently.

"You say it feels too good to come yet?"

Steven was on fire. He'd been using the word lust wrong all these years; surely that was what was screaming through his veins now as he watched John handle him.

"So good," he affirmed. He dropped his head to the pillow, but kept his gaze down, eyes slit, so he could still see John.

"Then let's play a new game."

Steven's shoulders ached slightly, with the effort of keeping his arms in an unaccustomed position for so long, but he wouldn't let them go until John said. Pleasing John mattered above all else. "Okay," Steven agreed.

"You're not going to ask what, before you agree?"

"I trust you not to hurt me." Steven lifted his head as he spoke, meeting John's eyes. "If I say 'stop,' you'll stop." His was tension easing slightly as they spoke.

John smiled, obviously pleased. "I will stop if you don't like this, but I think you will." He let go of Steven's cock so it slapped back against Steven's belly and reached up to pinch Steven's nipple. The shock sent an electric thrill, connecting Steven's nipple directly to his dick. The jolt barely passed when John pinched the other, triggering a second jolt. Steven sucked in a surprised breath, his whole upper body rising slightly off the bed. His blood was rushing again, Steven could hear it thrum, feel the flutter of his pulse in his neck, his wrist where his hand still clasped it, and low in his belly as it fed his dick, pushing him back into rising lust.

John spread his legs wider and moved up, lining his erection up with Steven's until they lay evenly, their balls hanging together. John's lube-wet hand closed around both of them and stroked them together. The slip of their cocks together was sexy, but not enough friction, not enough contact for Steven. He wanted to complain, to beg for more, but John settled over him and closed his mouth over Steven's nipple, licking and sucking it to a hard nub before turning his attention to the other one.

A thread of pleasure ran through Steven, from his nipple to his cock, pulling tight and making him ache again. His nerves sang with the rush of pleasure, and Steven arched up trying to keep contact with John's mouth when John pulled back. He rested his chin on Steven's upper chest.

"The rules of this game are very easy." His voice vibrated from the base of his throat through Steven's solar plexus, in a new, strange, and exciting connection. "You can't come until I say so."

"That's all?" Steven rasped out.

"If you think you're about to come because of what I'm doing, you tell me. That's all." He sucked Steven's nipple again. The shocks repeated. Steven moaned and twisted for more contact. John released him and moved up, pinning the full length of Steven's body down. One hand came up to cup the back of Steven's head, the other trapped between them, squeezing their cocks together.

The touch of John's lips to Steven's was as electric as John's mouth on Steven's nipple had been. Steven opened, pushing to explore the soft press of John's tongue, to feel the pearl slip of his teeth. A kiss like hot silk, more open, more intimate than any Steven had ever known. John's hand on both of them tightened and sped up.

Steven flashed on the rest of the night, knowing that John would tease him to the edge and hold him there, again and again until Steven couldn't take any more. A powerful surge of emotion crested in Steven, blending with his desire and leaving him exposed. Steven didn't know if this was him falling in love with John, or some high he was rising on, believing that John would take care of him and make this so good. Steven tumbled deeper into John's spell with each long kiss. John's grip was tight around their cocks now, unmoving as John pumped his hips, fucking into the circle of his fist, snug against Steven's dick.

The bright new feeling blooming in in his chest, the wide-open emotions spreading out like ink in water, coloring the longing that throbbed through his veins, left Steven over-wrought. He cried out into John's mouth and turned away, as if he could somehow escape the sensations in his body by moving away from them.

"Please," Steven whispered, "don't let me come yet." He didn't want this to end. It was too much to bear, but Steven wanted to be strong enough for it, to prove that he was good enough, ready for anything John would give him.

John eased off, trailing kisses along Steven's jaw and rolling carefully to the side, keeping his hand gently cupped over Steven's rigid prick.

"So soon? Are you okay?" John asked, his own breathing labored.

"I'm okay." Steven wanted to explain but he didn't have the right words for his emotions. "I just got really over-whelmed for a second."

"Do you want to keep going?"

"Yes. Fuck. Please, yes."

John chuckled. "Okay, *chéri,* be patient. I'll be right back." John got up and walked to the bathroom. Steven heard water running then the toilet flushing, then water again. John came back with a warm wet cloth. He carefully cleaned all the lube off Steven, folding the cloth over and reaching in to wipe away the lube from where he'd fingered Steven earlier. Steven's cock jumped eagerly at the drag of the cloth over his hole.

John returned the cloth the bathroom but didn't come back to the bed. "Turn over," he directed Steven. "You can put your arms down at your sides."

Steven obeyed, the ache of holding his position relieved as he rolled his shoulders and then flipped over on to his stomach. John settled back on to the bed, straddling the back of Steven's thighs this time. Behind him Steven heard a cap snap shut, and then the flats of John's palms slid over Steven's back, greased with oil. He pushed up and kneaded Steven's shoulders, erasing the last of the stiffness and ache before pressing his thumbs into the muscles around Steven's spine.

Moving his whole body down slowly as he rubbed, John worked over Steven's ass, squeezing and releasing, digging his fingers into the muscles there. Steven's rigid cock was trapped between his body and the soft sheets. He tried to grind down, to get some traction as John massaged his ass, but there wasn't enough room to move, the little friction he got just ratcheted up his need.

John pressed open Steven's cheeks with his palms and skimmed a greased thumb over Steven's opening. Steven tried to lift his hips into the touch, bucking back unsuccessfully. The ineffective drag of his dick on the sheets at this motion just pushed his arousal up. No satisfaction, only harder and needier. Steven whimpered as John teased his hole again, just tracing his fingers over it as he held Steven's cheeks open.

"Let's get these hips up," John said, patting Steven's ass.

Steven lifted up on to all fours. John closed an oiled hand around Steven's prick and lightly pressed the tip of a finger against Steven's hole. "Now move those hips, yeah, find what you need, c'mon," John instructed.

Steven rocked his hips evenly between the heat of John's hand on his dick and the teasing touch on his asshole. Rocking harder, Steven moaned in frustration as John held still, just letting Steven try to pleasure himself with John's hands. But it was all a tease. John's finger slipped in a tiny bit deeper with every thrust, but it wasn't enough. The oil-slick hand on his dick just made Steven feel harder and hotter as he slipped through, but he kept trying. The roll of his hips added to the taunt, making him feel sexier, so ready, but bringing no satisfaction.

"More, please, more," Steven begged.

John hummed noncommittally behind him but he pushed deeper into Steven's ass and gripped his dick a little more, working in slow counterpoint to Steven's thrusts.

"Yes, fuck yes," Steven moaned, panting, his upper body trembling.

"Breathe, *chéri,* deep and slow. Like meditation, let's get some air. Deep in and slow out."

Focus was so difficult, John's hands finally doing more than teasing. Steven struggled to take in a full deep breath as John pushed two fingers all the way into him. John jacked Steven through his slow exhale. Warm pleasure lit up Steven's entire body like a sunrise and spread through his chest and out his limbs. On the next breath, it contracted and gathered at the base of his cock, building against the twists and jerks of John's hand job.

"Gonna make me come like this," Steven pleaded.

"Not yet, *fraisier,* not yet. You are doing so good," John said softly as he took his hand off Steven. "On your back, beautiful, I'm not done with you yet." John got up for a wash cloth again and wiped the last bit of oil from Steven's dick. Steven trembled and whimpered at the scratch of the terrycloth. Every part of him felt sensitized, but his cock was like exposed wires.

"Breathe, *mon Amour,* deep and slow."

Steven took a breath, trying to forget his body and just concentrate on letting it out slowly. John's mouth slipped wetly over the head of Steven's cock and he shuddered, the air rushing out of him. Steven tried again, carefully drawing in as much air as he could as John dropped light kisses along Steven's dick and abdomen. John's fingers combed through the curls of Steven's pubic hair and tickled at the crease where his thigh met his pelvis. Endless licks and whisper-soft touches crawled over Steven, making him shiver as he tried to keep his breath slow. The extra oxygen stretched his consciousness. Steven was wide like the summer sky, each touch on his skin exquisite, a flower opening on the field of his body. His chest burned like the sun, lighting him up as he briefly held each breath, then slowly let it flow from his body.

Time and space merged into a boundless moment. Each stroke of John's tongue, each brush of his fingers was a new star in Steven's universe, a pinprick of light flaring brightly. He floated along the crests and surges of every new sensation while John teased him endlessly.

The word *euphoria* tickled at the back of his mind, but that wasn't right, this was ecstasy, real ecstasy. This was where the drug had tried to take him but never succeed. His memories of chemical highs paled and diminished as this new high made Steven's entire body vibrate with the delirious tension of suppressed release.

Unable to distinguish between when John touched his cock and the other parts of his body, Steven whimpered and begged for each delicate touch to stay, to be more. When John pushed hard on the pressure point behind Steven's balls his prostate sparked fireworks of pleasure through his body. It was way too intense but still not enough.

Fuck me, fuck me, fuck me. Steven wasn't sure if he said the words or heard them but he liked the steady rhythm of them. Like an invocation, the way they both promised release and begged for it. He needed John to be here, inside this universe, to share in mapping every star in their sky, tracing lightning between each bright point of John's touch.

The room shifted, and Steven felt the soft sheets below him as John's touches trailed off. He let his own hands fill in, tracing new paths over his electric, sensitive skin. He heard foil crinkle and the bed moved and though he didn't open his eyes, Steven understood that he was getting what he wanted, prayers finally answered.

It was exhilarating, like being a shooting star falling through the heavens, as John entered Steven. His whole body sang at the connection. Steven opened his eyes, back inside the limits of his body, and watched John's slack expression transform into the ecstasy that surged through Steven's veins. Each hard thrust fixed Steven back into his body, but sent firework bursts of pleasure though him until it was too much to contain.

Bringing his knees together and sitting back on his heels, John pulled Steven's hips up higher on his lap to thrust deeper. Each push sparked a new storm in Steven.

"I can't, I can't," Steven cried out, trying to twist away from the intensity rampaging in his body. His delayed orgasm surged up, biting into Steven's resolve to wait, to draw it out more.

"Can't what, *chéri?*" John sounded strained, his voice roughed with exertion and lust.

"Can't hold it, can't wait."

"Just come, *chéri,* come for me." John pumped harder.

Steven reached for his cock and stroked it only once as John pinched his nipple, breaking open the storm. Lighting jagged down Steven's spine, flashing so bright that stars danced in the corners of his vision. His orgasm thumped through his body, a roll of thunder that kept shaking and booming so deeply that Steven felt it in his bones.

"Holy fuck, fuck," Steven cried out, shuddering as John held his hips. He came like the rain rushing in the wind, felt it splatter his face, his chest. He licked it from his lips, catching the sea water taste of it as he shivered through the aftershocks, rumbling in like baby earthquakes with each hard thrust from John.

"Steven, Steven, yes," John cried above him, gripping Steven's hips too tightly as he quaked through his own orgasm, holding Steven to him.

Their heaving breaths filled the room as they collapsed together, rolling until they lay with chests together, hands entwined. Steven kissed John's face, licked at the corners of his mouth, not sure how to say thank you.

"You were amazing," John said when they both finally calmed enough to talk.

"No one's ever made me feel like that." Steven kissed John again. "Getting high has never made me feel like that. I'm not even sure what happened. It was like flying out of my body and yet somehow feeling everything in my body all at once."

"Mmmm, that's what I wanted, to make you come apart, to make you come so hard." John let go of Steven's hand stroked his face. "I just want everything good for you."

"*You're* good for me, *mon loup.*" Steven caught John's hand and kissed it. "Thank you for tonight. For everything. For being you."

John smiled, his pale blue eyes looking deeply into Steven. "You're welcome," he said pulling Steven against him.

"Do you need anything? You should sleep. You have a big day tomorrow."

Graduation. Steven had forgotten in these hours when his whole world had become nothing but John's touches.

"I should clean up," Steven answered.

"We need to clean up more than you," John laughed, looking up and nodding.

Steven bent his neck back to follow John's gaze. There were splashes of come all across the rippled bird's eye veneer of the Art Deco headboard, wet drips across the pillows.

"Holy shit," Steven said, awed that his body had been capable of that. He looked back at John, his eyes wide. "Yeah, wow, I've never done that before."

"I like being part of your good firsts," John said and caught Steven's lower lip lightly with his teeth before kissing him. "Come on, dirty boy, let's clean up your mess."

39.
Graduation Day

STEVEN SAT AT JOHN'S DINING room table slowly turning through the Sunday paper. The sun fell through the broad leaded-glass bay windows behind him and cast diamonds onto the table and the paper he was reading. Roberta Flack played on the stereo in the living room, adding to dreamy, slow quality of the morning. The sun on his bare shoulders made him feel like a sleepy cat: warm and relaxed but not interested in doing much of anything with effort. Steven's warm satisfaction was as much last night's incredible sex as it was this morning's sunshine.

Casting the business section aside, Steven reached for the bright pages of the comics. Since he wasn't really paying enough attention to gain anything from his reading, he might as well not read anything of consequence. He folded the pages open and stretched before he settled in. He turned to grasp the back of his chair and twist his back a bit.

The bow of the window behind him was filled with plants, all kinds, large and small, pots set in old plates covering the top of a cabinet that fit perfectly in the space below the wide windows. Steven glanced around, taking in the room all over again. The wall at his right held high bookcases running its length, books of all kinds stacked haphazardly at the ends of tidy rows. An Art Deco sideboard ran the length of the left wall, with a huge, brightly-colored abstract painting above it. The opposite wall held more bright paintings between the doors at either end, going into the kitchen and the living room.

In his year of fantasizing about being right here, in John's house, reading the paper the morning after a night together,

Steven had never envisioned a room like this one. But it was perfect, lived in, comfortable. Like the rest of the house, it was filled with art and furniture that, after only six weeks together, Steven recognized as being very specifically John.

The sound of water running in the sink abruptly shut off in the next room. There was a clank of metal and plates settling together, and then John came into the room. He was wearing a sleeveless black t-shirt displaying the strong curve of his biceps, and artfully worn jeans that looked like they were made to show John's long legs off to their best advantage.

"Hi," Steven greeted him.

John's smile was tranquil, something Steven only saw when they were alone together, a private smile, just for him. John came behind his chair and kissed his neck before putting his hands on Steven's shoulders and rubbing enough to drain away any motivation Steven might have had to do anything but sit here in the sun and feel good.

"Do you want more to eat?" John asked, his hands slowing as he leaned down to kiss the top of Steven's head.

After waffles with jam, eggs, and cantaloupe, Steven wasn't sure how he could eat anything else. "No, thank you, I think I've had enough." Steven tipped his head back to try to catch John's kiss. He succeeded. John twisted one hand into Steven's hair and laid the other lightly across his neck as they kissed. Steven shifted and pulled back, trying to find a less awkward angle. He could easily be convinced to do something more than sit in the sun, if it involved more kissing.

"Time to start getting ready." John said, breaking into Steven's sunlit kissing haze. "We're meeting your parents there, right?"

"Yeah."

"We don't want to be late. Enough people come to graduation to make traffic terrible. Though I'm sure your mom will have your dad there half an hour early. She's very excited."

"Okay." Steven folded the unread comics back up and set them on the stack of the other sections. "Are you going to come help me in the shower? I'm not sure I can manage by myself."

"We can't be late," John said, looking serious, but Steven could recognize the sparkle of interest in John's eyes, so he pushed it.

"We'll save time by showering together. It's better for the environment, too."

"I don't think it works like that."

"It definitely works like that. C'mon." Steven stood up and reached for John's hand to lead him up stairs.

John gave him a doubtful look but followed Steven up to the bedroom.

Steven stopped and reached for the hem of John's t-shirt. "You can't shower in this. We'll get ready faster if I help you get it off."

"I'm not convinced expediency is your real end goal," John teased, but let Steven strip the shirt off him. "Oh, before I forget, I got you something."

Steven skated his palms over the firm expanse of John's chest. "I don't know if I need something more than this."

John laughed indulgently. "You will, if I can convince you that you need to get ready." He went to his huge dresser, which had a burled-wood waterfall pattern running down the front. He picked up a white box. "I meant to give this to you after the party last night, but I got distracted."

"I could distract you again," Steven said hopefully, though without much conviction. He knew he needed to get dressed for his own graduation. But every moment with John was still so exciting that Steven slightly resented having to put on clothes and see people.

"You are very distracting, *mon fraisier,*" John agreed. He stepped back in and kissed Steven softly, holding the box awkwardly between them. "You'll need this when you're getting dressed, if I can manage to get you in the shower."

"You can get me in the shower if you come with me."

"Even the promise of a present isn't enough to divert you?"

"You're a good present to unwrap," Steven replied, reaching for the buttons on John's jeans instead of the box.

John laughed and pushed the box into Steven's hands. "You can be bad later. It's time for good Steven now."

"If good Steven gets presents, I guess I'll cooperate. But no promises when I get you alone later."

"*Bien, mon petit.*" John kissed him again, quickly. "Open it."

Steven did. Inside the box was a tie, rich purple silk, shot through with gold threads. It took half a second but Steven realized it was his school colors, John's too since they shared an Alma Mater now. The colors together like this were tasteful, not garish like so much of the UW Huskies' purple and gold.

"It's perfect," Steven breathed, pulling it out of the box and running it though his hands. John took the box and set it aside. Steven looped the tie around the back of his bare neck and ran his hand over it, down his chest. "Will you help me tie it?"

John ran his hand over Steven's, then took the end of the tie and pulled it off, folding it neatly. He ran his thumb along Steven's jaw, looking at him with such warmth that Steven, weak-kneed, felt grateful all over again to have found John. "Of course, but you need to get in the shower," John said, reaching to lightly slap Steven's butt to spur him on.

"I think you better come with me, and make sure I stay on track," Steven insisted.

◊

"It's going to be epic. The party to end all parties. You're sure you don't want to come?" Davy asked. His long blond skater bangs were carefully pinned up inside his graduation cap. Jess had to redo it three times, because Davy kept wiggling and insisting she was poking him with the pins.

"Yes, sorry," Steven said, glancing over at John, "I have better plans."

Davy followed Steven's glance. "I can't believe you dragged your heels and didn't try and get with him from day one." Davy shook his head in disbelief. "He's perfect. Hell, I might let him do me if he asked." Steven narrowed his eyes. Davy waved him off. "Don't worry, he's all yours. Besides I think he knows my dads, so that would be weird. But damn, brother, you did some good work finally picking that one up."

Next to him, Jess rolled her eyes. "We should go find your dads," she said to Davy, before turning back to Steven. "I'm going to sit with them, but I'll still be cheering for you." She hugged him and they walked off, Jess chastising Davy not to touch his hat.

John put his hand on Steven's shoulder as he watched his friends walk away.

"I can't believe he's graduating college," John said, watching as Davy pulled his cap off and Jess slapped him in the back of his head.

"Yep, he's an idiot," Steven said grinning, full of warmth for Davy's absurdity.

"No, I mean I can remember when he was actually a kid."

Steven raised his eyebrows in question. "So you do know his dads?"

"Yes, his father's partner is one of my clients. I've worked with them for years."

"Small town," Steven said.

"Smaller every year," John, agreed. "Let's go find your parents, shall we?"

When they reached the appointed meeting place, Steven's mother was looking around anxiously, his father was staring off into space.

"Hey," Steven said, pulling his mom into a one-armed hug, "almost time to find seats. Are you ready?" He kissed her cheek.

"Oh honey, look at you." She reached and adjusted the tassel on his hat.

As Steven's mother fussed over his cap and gown, John caught his eye and nodded to the left. Steven turned to see Adrian standing a little ways away.

"Mom, stop. I have to go talk to someone."

"I can't believe he's here." He heard his mother say to John, while Steven turned and walked calmly across the grass. He knew this was coming eventually, and now was as good as ever.

"Hey, there you are." Adrian's voice was soft, his smile small and tight.

"Hey. I'm surprised to see you here."

Adrian nodded. "Probably not as surprised as I was when Lisa called me." He paused as if he was unsure what say. "She's proud of you. And I am too. You did it."

"Thanks." Steven had been overwhelmed all weekend, with family party, with this new intensity shared with John, the reality of graduating and moving forward. Steven's emotions were close to the surface and all over the place, like tears might spill at any second, and now here was Adrian looking awkward and out of place.

"It's nice to see you," Steven offered, not sure where to start.

"You look good. Success looks good on you. Very grown up." Adrian reached and brushed his fingers over the knot on Steven's purple-and-gold tie, a complicated knot that John had done for him. "So, are you and John together now?" Adrian looked over to where John stood with Steven's parents.

"Yes, we are. It's new."

"He better be good to you. You deserve that." It was, the closest to an apology that he'd ever get out of Adrian, but Steven heard it for what it was.

Steven said, "We're all going to Ray's Boathouse after. If you want to come, I'm sure we can make room."

Adrian grinned, his face suffused with a childish pleasure that Steven hadn't seen in a couple of years. "Hmm, that sounds like a social nightmare for everyone. I think maybe I'll skip family fun time. But it's nice you asked. Really. I'll call you some time? We'll go celebrate some other way?"

"I'd like that." They hugged hard.

Even with as busy as he'd been, even with John and everything good, he'd missed the parts where Adrian was just his friend, without all the drama and everything that had happened between them. He wanted that part back.

"Call me, please?" he asked as they parted. Adrian nodded and walked away. The back of Adrian's nice silk dress shirt was fine fishnet, a grey veil displaying the tattoo over his back. Steven smiled; even in a nice shirt and dress pants, Adrian managed to be completely outrageous.

"Everything okay?" John asked softly when Steven rejoined everyone.

"Yeah, he just wanted to say sorry. To tell me congratulations." Steven felt his face crumple as he tried to hold in the tears.

John tipped up Steven's face, his thumb light under Steven's chin. "Even he can see your worth, don't forget that, *chéri*. You have a light that draws people to you. Just make sure you only let the good and kind ones in. You deserve everything you've worked for, but you deserve kindness too, so demand it from your friends. Even Adrian." Steven nodded, and John kissed him chastely, holding his gaze for a second afterward. "You're amazing," John whispered.

"You're like something I dreamed. How can you be so good?" Steven asked.

John said softly into Steven's ear, "I'll show you how good I am later, and give you the reward you deserve." Steven suddenly was aware of his family pointedly looking the other way. And very glad of the concealment of graduation robes.

"I hope you're not going to surpass last night, because I might need a little more recovery time," Steven whispered, kissing John lightly. They turned together, John reaching for Steven's hand. "Ma," Steven called as they crossed back to his family, "do you know where your seats are? I should get in line."

"I'm sure John can help us find them," his mom answered, smiling, stepping in close. "I like him," she said quietly before turning and fussing at his dad that it was time to sit down and looping her arm through John's extended elbow. John winked at Steven as they walked up into the stadium stands.

Steven felt like everything was starting right now, laid out in front of him, a map he couldn't quite see, but one he knew would take him only to good places. All his ducks were in a row. Whatever that meant.

◊◊◊

PREVIEW:
Bad Reputation

1. A Paler Blue Glow

AT THE END OF COYOTE Run Lane, on the edge of the Olympic forest, miles from Port Angeles, Shane Fontaine visited an intimate world of comfort and pleasure inside Trevor's old Chevy.

The vinyl seat stuck to Shane's bare back. A sliver of starry sky shone through the window. Patsy Cline sang on the radio.

"Listen," Shane said.

"Yeah?" Trevor stretched over him, grinding against Shane's hips, the two of them slick with sweat. "It's an old song."

"Not just 'You Belong to Me,' but also the hum of the heater. The wind in the cedars. The scent of them. We're in a forest palace, the trees protecting us from the world, keeping winter at bay."

"You sound like one of your fantasy novels." Trevor bit Shane's lip, then kissed away the injury. "You're talking too much."

"Maybe you were right earlier. Maybe 1982 will be our year. We could leave. Go to San Francisco. Or Seattle."

"It's going to be my year because—" Trevor kissed him, wet and teasing "—I finally turn twenty-one and get my trust fund. We can leave after that."

"That's a long time." At six-foot-two, Shane was cramped in spite of the Chevy's spacious back seat, but the true source of his discomfort was his fear of a future when Trevor might disappear. "Eight months until we can be together somewhere besides the middle of the woods." Shane wiggled into a better position.

"Mmm, do that again." Trevor's hips pressed on Shane's. "While you're at it, I can think of better uses for your mouth than this pointless talk. You could—"

A tap on the driver's window.

Trevor jerked to attention, knocking heads with Shane, who struggled with his jeans, a door handle digging into his spine. Then the door opened behind him, and Shane sprawled on the cold dirt road.

An unfamiliar face loomed over him. Blue-and-red lights flashed, spoiling the forest palace.

"Exit the car slowly, hands where I can see them." A deputy shone his blinding flashlight at Trevor. "Oh, what's this? I come out here to keep the boys off little girls, not this mess."

"You don't know who you're dealing with, Deputy." Trevor spoke with a haughtiness Shane rarely heard from him. Out of the back seat, Trevor stood face to face with the officer.

"What? The all-American captain of the Port Angeles football team?" The deputy mocked him.

"Yes, as a matter of fact."

"What's a good-looking guy like you doing out here?" The deputy put his hands on his hips, the light from the patrol car flashing over him. Handsome. New. Not from any nearby town. "Rolling around with a dirt-brown Indian?" The deputy did not acknowledge Shane.

"I'm not an Indian." First words out of his mouth. Shane hated that everything always started with that.

"That what your mama told you?" The deputy smirked. "Get up. Put your hands on the hood of the car. Stay there."

The hood was at least warm where Shane leaned with his arms spread, bare-chested, jeans still unbuttoned. He knew this forest. He could run—and wander in the winter woods shirtless. Risk charges for assaulting a cop.

"You don't know who my father is." Trevor's voice promised punishment.

"This buck says his father isn't an Indian. You gonna tell me yours is, blondie?" The deputy unclipped cuffs from his utility belt. "Even if he's a chief, he likely won't be happy with this. Get your shirt on. Then you, too, put your hands against the car."

The deputy reached in and shut off the idling Chevy, pocketing the keys. He crawled over the seat, rifling through the glove box, searching the ashtray and under the floor mats, reaching under the seats.

"Doesn't matter what you find. You're going to be sorry." Trevor slipped into his jacket and put hands on the cruiser's hood without glancing at Shane.

The deputy backed out of the car, holding up the last two cans from a six-pack of Olympia that Shane had bought weeks ago.

"Hope you're both twenty-one. Don't think I'm going to be the sorry one here." He tossed the beers into the trunk of the police car and came back around to the front.

Twisting Shane's right arm, lifting him off the hood of the car, the deputy jerked the left arm back to cuff Shane's hands behind him. Tugging at the cuffs, the deputy shoved Shane into the back of the patrol car, making Shane duck to avoid hitting his own head on the doorframe. While blue-and-red lights still flashed, the deputy handcuffed Trevor's hands in front, opened the far door, and let Trevor step in to sit beside Shane.

"Fuck," Trevor muttered. "Happy Valentine's Day."

Retrieving Shane's shirt and jacket from the Chevy, the deputy tossed the wad of clothes on Shane.

Shane's shoulders burned, hands mashed in fists behind him. But the growing wedge between him and Trevor hurt more. When the deputy put the cruiser in gear, Shane longed for one gesture, one word of comfort from Trevor.

"Guess this is it." Trevor stared out the window, voice pitched low.

Neither spoke during the three-mile ride to the Clallam County Sheriff's office. Whatever they'd been to each other these past six months vanished under the flashing blue-and-red lights. Shane wiggled enough that his old motorcycle jacket partly covered his bare chest, so he could stop shivering.

◊

Does Seattle give a damn about his past reputation?

After being caught in a backseat tryst with the mayor's son, twenty-one-year-old Shane Fontaine is exiled from his small hometown. Now, alone in the city, he seeks solace in punk show mosh pits and bathhouse saunas.

But the music scene and gay community in 1982 recession-era Seattle aren't always safe. Rescued from a brutal beating, Shane forms a friendship with a Russian engineering student that launches a confounding set of traumatic and ecstatic encounters.

Shane's quest for human connection sends him down dark, dangerous streets. To survive, he must become the man who chooses to persist, to do the right thing and stand up for others.

This close-up portrait of pre-AIDS Seattle illuminates dark corners, where homeless kids cluster for safety near the revitalized Pike Place Market. *Bad Reputation* contrasts the deeply personal need for friendship with the universal dilemma: people aren't always what they seem.

Find Bad Reputation
and all Queen City Boys Books:
https://flickerjax.com/books/qcb/

Acknowledgments

For my fantastic editor, Annie Pearson, who made this a real book. Above and beyond her job, she taught me so much about writing. I am forever grateful to her for everything she has done to make this book possible. Leta Blake for unwavering support, for making me laugh even as she tore apart the manuscript and made me do it all over again until it was good. Without Annie and Leta, I'd never have written at all; because of both of them, I am a better writer. Jodie Ralston, for talking me into starting this in the first place and holding my hand all the way through. For my beautiful beta readers who suffered through my poor comma usage and my desperate pleas for feedback when I was still stumbling through the story: Darrah Glass (and her glorious hair), my sister Riri, Mae Sardarsa, Punny McLeod. And Eva Dawson, for finding me David Thepaut, who did exceptional work on my peculiar translation needs. I love you guys. Giant, brimming cups of love.

Love to everyone living on or around, or cruising Broadway from 1987–1992. Even if I don't know your name, surely we nodded in acknowledgment of familiar faces at least once. Thanks for being part of the village that raised me. I love your sparkle and your swagger. I hope you never change.

About the Author

A SEATTLE NATIVE, AJAX BELL likes pretty boys, beautiful women, and good jokes. According to Ajax the best things in life are loud music and bourbon. No matter what the task, Ajax always has the right pair of shoes. Never a sea captain, but a background in library sciences and a lifetime of pencil pushing together left Ajax with a rich fantasy life and a compulsive need to write it down. One day Ajax hopes to own a genetically altered hippopotamus the size of a small dog.

You can find more of Ajax at:

> http://flickerjax.com
> https://twitter.com/flickerjax

By Ajax Bell:

> Queen City Boys Books:
> *Bad Reputation*
> *This Charming Man*
>
> Novellas:
> *Star Quality*

From Jūgum Press

QUEEN CITY BOYS BOOKS by Ajax Bell

Bad Reputation, This Charming Man... and more titles

Spanning four decades in Seattle, Queen City Boys tells the explicit adventures of an eclectic group of gay friends as they find their way through the ends and beginnings of their most important relationships.

RAIN CITY COMEDY OF MANNERS SERIES by Annie Pearson

The Grrrl of Limberlost

A murder in a Seattle coffee house. A murder on a decaying boat dock on Puget Sound. Samsara Byron, the security expert, insists this has nothing to do with her. She's heroically fending off an attack on the world's cyber infrastructure—if she could only get a cell signal.

Nine Volt Heart

He said, "I love you." She said, "You don't even know the real me." He said, "Great title for a song. Key of G? Can we try close harmony?" Jason, the singer-songwriter, and Susi, a music teacher, meet by accident in Seattle. Secrets, songs, and stalkers quickly entwine their lives in unpredictable ways.

ACCIDENTAL HERETICS SERIES by E.A. Stewart

Bone-mend and Salt (Book 1)

Fight or beg for mercy when enemies turn an unjust war against you? Three ruined crusaders battle conspiracy and disaster while trapped in the war against the Cathar heresy.

Trebuchets in the Garden (Book 2)

How do you prepare for the dawn of the Inquisition? Embattled crusaders seek justice and respite amidst terror, siege, and conspiracy—as zealots prepare to ignite the next heretics' pyre.

Find print and ebook editions:
www.jugumpress.com
Sign up to receive email notice of new books by Ajax Bell:
http://eepurl.com/bmlxl1